PENGUIN BOOKS

Tomorrow

'The story of a dog that doesn't die, of the wonders he's seen, and the horrors, who lost his master a hundred years ago and has been searching for him ever since, *Tomorrow* is an epic tale of love, of courage, of hope' *London Evening Standard*

'Original, ambitious, moving' *Stylist*

'A stunning and captivating tale' *Sun*

'Definitely – HIGHLY – worth the read!' Seth Meyers

'A tale of love and unbreakable bonds' *New York Post*

'Dog lovers will want to have this heartbreaking, century-spanning novel for their next discovery' *Entertainment Weekly*

'My heart swelled with FEELINGS!' Sarra Manning, *Red*

'Damian Dibben's novel is guaranteed to make you shed a tear . . . sure to appeal to readers who enjoy fiction embedded in history' *Heart*

'Beautiful. Rich in perseverance, love and the sweetness of life' *Kirkus*

'A lyrical commentary on war, rivalry, sacrifice, and above all else, loyalty' *Publishers Weekly*

'Timeless. Humanity's foibles and failings are on full display. This soulful debut is a charmer' *Booklist*

'It's a rich and complex tale, beautifully told. Historic detail and do . . . the thinki . . . arrying the reader al . . .

'A grand sweep of adventure and travel, war and romance – along with a generous amount of face licking – that will have dog lovers enthralled . . . *Tomorrow* offers a rich exploration of love, life and loyalty, in a world whose sensory atmosphere is irresistible' *NPR*

'With a hint of Mary Shelley's *Frankenstein*, *Tomorrow* confronts big questions about life's purpose and celebrates life's pleasures' *BookPage*

'A rich and complex tale, beautifully told . . . historic detail and dog-like thinking are vividly conveyed, carrying the reader along. It is a joy to read. It raises deep questions about what it means to be human.' *Sussex Life*

Tomorrow

DAMIAN DIBBEN

PENGUIN BOOKS

PENGUIN BOOKS

UK | USA | Canada | Ireland | Australia
India | New Zealand | South Africa

Penguin Books is part of the Penguin Random House group of companies
whose addresses can be found at global.penguinrandomhouse.com.

First published by Michael Joseph 2018
Published in Penguin Books 2019

001

Set in 11.76/14.46 pt Bembo Book MT Std
Typeset by Jouve (UK), Milton Keynes
Printed and bound in Great Britain by Clays Ltd, Elcograf S.p.A.

A CIP catalogue record for this book is available from the British Library

ISBN: 978-1-405-92578-5

www.greenpenguin.co.uk

For Ali,
& Dudley, of course,
my constant companions

After

1603 ~ King James I ascends the English throne.

1606 ~ Shakespeare writes *Antony & Cleopatra* and *Macbeth*.

1608 ~ The London frost fair.

1616 ~ Galileo suggests the Earth is not the centre of our universe.

1618 ~ The Thirty Years War begins in Prague.

1620 ~ Amsterdam's grand expansion heralds its golden age.

1631 ~ The Siege of Magdeburg.

1638 ~ The future Louis XIV, the Sun King, is born in St-Germain-en-Laye.

1642 ~ In England, civil war breaks out and the royal court moves to Oxford.

1649 ~ King Charles I is beheaded outside the Banqueting House in London.

1673 ~ Molière dies on stage during a performance of *La Malade Imaginaire*.

1681 ~ La Salute cathedral in Venice opens after five decades of construction.

1767 ~ At eleven, Mozart tours Italy.

1796 ~ Napoleon's troops occupy Venice, bringing an end to the Republic.

1815 ~ The British and their allies defeat Napoleon at Waterloo.

1837 ~ In London the Reform Bill abolishes slavery.

Before

1337 ~ The Italian scholar Petrarch coins the phrase '*the dark age*' to describe the last 800 years, whilst predicting a new beginning.

1347 ~ The Black Death wipes out almost half the population of Europe.

1418 ~ Filippo Brunelleschi designs the octagonal dome of Florence cathedral.

1426 ~ Masaccio's *Virgin and Child* heralds a new 'realistic' style in painting.

1439 ~ Gutenberg pioneers movable type and the mass production of books.

1453 ~ The Fall of Constantinople leads to the migration of scholars and texts to Italy.

1486 ~ Leonardo da Vinci is commissioned to paint *The Last Supper*.

1492 ~ Christopher Columbus lands in the Americas.

1496 ~ Bellini depicts Venice's Piazza San Marco in *The Procession of the True Cross*.

1504 ~ Michelangelo completes the statue of David.

1543 ~ Nicolaus Copernicus publishes *On the Revolutions of Celestial Spheres*, triggering an upheaval in scientific thinking.

1580 ~ Francis Drake successfully circumnavigates the globe.

1599 ~ William Shakespeare writes *Hamlet*.

1603 ~ James I ascends the English throne . . .

Prologue

Elsinore Palace, Denmark, 1602

It began, this journey of many lifetimes, in an ordinary way: he and I went to pick oysters on the shore. He loved them more than any other food, the ritual of unlocking abrasive shells to discover a treasured interior, smooth alabaster and incorporeal liquor. And when he feasted on them, they had a transformative effect: his shoulders dropped, his brow unknotted and his eyes softened, sometimes to tears.

'We shall have luck this afternoon,' he said, pulling on his boots. 'The tide is low. So low, we could almost walk to Sweden.' He took down his cloak, shook it out and tied it at the neck, throwing the weight over his shoulders. 'And I have a sense –' He unbolted the front door and barged it open. 'Yes, there is still a good light.' When he realized I was not following, he stopped and turned, head tilted to one side, a questioning silhouette in the doorway. 'Where are you, my champion?' Even now the memory of his voice – as deep and gentle as a forest ravine – makes my heart split like a husk.

I hung back in the shadows, half hidden behind the baluster legs of the great hall table. It's easy to believe – now half a continent and centuries away – I had a presentiment of dread, a doomy foreknowledge of what we'd discover on the silt flats below, but I had none. Neither did insolence nor stubbornness keep me there; I had yet to learn those traits. No, my reasons were less remarkable. We'd already been roaming that morning and soon evening would be drawing in. It was the time to build a fire in our oak-panelled parlour, or in the palace library, for me to sit beside it and feel the warmth against my fur, as he pored over the inscriptions in books, chatting along all the while.

He discovered me in the gloom, and the corners of his eyes creased with a smile. 'What a fuss is here?' He came to my side, knelt and ruffled my neck, making me tremble with shame. 'Where will life lead us if we hide behind tables? The world out there is where we will find answers. And joy. And oysters, my champion.' He laughed, turned on his heels, and this time I went with him.

Once outside I revived. A warm wind carried with it scents from inland, sweet pine, woodsia and wild thyme, and I realized, after all, it was far from darkening time: a benign rose-pink sun had only half descended. I stared for a moment, back straight, ears proud, surveying the coast from the castle walls to the open sea. In that time I knew no other place but the little town of Elsinore and its castle. I had no sense I was, in fact, destined to be a wanderer, perpetually travelling from one palace to another, and then from battlefield to battlefield. But that afternoon I remember being thankful for my lot: my home, my companion, my happy life.

He sensed the change in my mood and laughed again. 'So you've come back to me have you, my virtuoso, who has nothing but sensibility?' He picked up a bucket, swilled out the rainwater and we went side by side down the stone staircase to the shore. 'Look, my champion, the ocean has all but deserted us! How kind it is to relinquish its spoils.' Ahead was an endless plane of silver wet sand disappearing towards a dreamy mystery of horizon.

In no time he found a cluster of shells, crouched down, took a knife from his pocket and prized one apart from the rest. He tested its weight, examined it from all sides, his face folding this way and that. 'Perhaps too timid for us? Or we too rough for it.' He held it out for me. I didn't care for oysters then, any more than I do today – their saline stench has always stuck in my nostrils – but out of courtesy I passed my snout around its form, making him chuckle again. 'I agree wholeheartedly. A slip of a thing it is. We'll return it to its family and wish it good luck. Onwards. Let us search for the bolder, brinier ones, the ones I truly love.'

We ventured further from the shore. The sand became stonier, colder and wetter underfoot, like unset cement. And the weather altered too; a chillier breeze crept in from the north. It seemed to wash away the colour from the sun, and from the sky too, turning it as hoary as the silt flats, making everything dimensionless. It was as if we were in one of those opera sets I would see later in my life – dramatic shrinking perspectives, alternate worlds in a box – two characters wandering a boundless landscape.

By the time my master had discovered the larger oysters, started cutting them from their beds and putting them into his bucket, my mood had turned again. I looked back at the palace. It had a grim, inert air. Except for our quarters close to the kitchens, the windows were all dark. Most of the royal party had gone for the winter. Although my master had kept me largely apart from them when they were here, as I was still puppyish on my feet, I had nonetheless relished the sense of a pageant unfolding in the main part of the building, of cooking, children playing, a thrill of stewards and chamberlains, lutes and harpsichords and peals of laughter. Now, other than the old queen – whom my master had stayed to attend to, in case she grew sick — only the dourest of staff remained: unsociable guards, washerwomen forever veiled behind wind-flapped cloths, and night-wardens with heavy sets of keys. I turned back to my master, hoping he would have finished by now, but found him standing bolt upright, arms out, with the bucket dropped on its side.

'Sssh,' he went as I padded towards him, his tone so sharp that my ears folded back and I wondered if I'd done something wrong. But his eyes were fixed on an islet of crooked rock some distance ahead. Usually it dwelt beneath the sea, but the low water had exposed it to its foundations. As a breeze sighed across the plane, one side of it stretched into a crescent before returning to its crooked form. I was startled and looked up at my master but he offered no explanation or reassurance. His eyes remained riveted. The wind whistled and charmed up ghoulish spectres of sand, sending them rolling past us. Once more the side of the rock heaved, but this time I realized that it was a shape behind it that moved: the sail of a boat.

'Who is it? Who goes there?' My master's voice was stern and I barked. He took my head firmly in his hands. 'Not a sound out of you, you hear? Not a sound.' He continued forward, cautiously approaching until we had a view of the wreck: a small craft beached on its side, a navy sail strung between spar and stern, the underbelly holed and gaping open. There was a third weightier blast of air and this time it carried a smell with it, an acrid ammonia stench that stung my nostrils.

A pair of crates lay upturned in the sand, one intact, the other cracked in pieces, a rainbow mess of glass phials spilling from its interior. My master righted the undamaged box, wiped the mud from the escutcheon on the front and jolted in surprise. 'From Opalheim.' He turned to me, a peculiar slant in his eye. 'From Opalheim he comes.' I would hear the name spoken often in years to come and it always carried with it a sense of magnificent doom. The insignia showed three turreted towers below a crescent moon. My master's hand jittered over the flotsam of bottles, but he didn't pick any up. They were exactly the type he kept in his workroom, which contained quantities of powder or metal.

'Who is there I say?' he ventured again in what I came to know as his battle voice, but the only reply that came was the creak of ropes, the flutter of sail, and the irrefutable sharp sodium stink of putrefaction. By then I knew the scent, to a degree, from the odd dead gull or rat, but nowhere near as thick and pungent. My master must have also noticed how strong it was, for his hands shook and a faint adrenal surge lifted off him, the aroma of fear. We circled the ship and saw the body on the other side, legs tangled in rope and hoisted up towards the mast, whilst stomach and head were half sunk in the silt below. And as the boat groaned back and forth, so the corpse was dragged with it. My master smeared his hand up and down his cheek, pulling at the skin. 'My champion, what are we to do?' Then, in a small voice that had, I fancied, an undernote of hope, he asked the corpse a question: 'So now you are dead, are you?'

He pulled himself together, squared his shoulders, marched over to the cadaver and hauled it on to its back. Instantly my master's face uncreased, the fear snapped from his eyes and a gasp came from him that sounded almost like a laugh, though I couldn't tell if it was from relief or disappointment. 'A courier,' he said. 'When I saw the intaglio, three towers, I – just a courier, though. Poor soul. Drowned. A courier returning my chattels that is all. It was so long ago I asked for them. I had all but forgotten.' That same curious laugh. 'The storm, you remember it? When was it? A week ago? Just a messenger returning my old compendium, poor thing.'

Close up, the stench gloved my throat. The body was grotesque, chest and face bulging and bloated, skin unlayered and marbled with veins. Its tongue was a coal pebble sticking out from a bone-white mouth, and its eyes were pale-grey glass.

'What shall we do with him?' my master was saying. He looked up at the waves breaking beyond us. 'If I drag him to sea, the tide will bring him back again. That is no end for a man. Not a good man.' After his fit of terror, he was practical now, as I had always known him to be. 'I shall do as the Romans did.' He cast his eye at the sun, split in half as it sank. 'Quickly, my boy, it shall be dark soon.'

He hurried homewards, but I stayed in front of the cadaver, as fascinated as I was repulsed. It did not *live* in the true sense, did not breathe, but somehow it seemed to exist with greater force than the other humans I had met. Perhaps because decay is the most virulent form of life, or perhaps because nothing speaks more of the phenomenon of *being*, than the absence of it.

'Do not get left behind.' My master's voice twisted away on the wind. He was already halfway home, cloak flapping from side to side as he dodged rock pools. I went after him.

He shouldered open the doors to our quarters and ushered me in first. 'You wait here for me, understand?' I obeyed, reluctantly, stalling in the unlit hall as he hurried off down the passage. I started to sit, but the floor was cold, so I half hovered over it, cocking my ear to clanks of metal and screeches of wood that came from the boot room. He returned with a heavy jar and a tinderbox and, as he rushed past, I caught the scent of lamp oil and tallow. 'You wait. I shall return.' And the door slammed shut.

My stomach turned. His footsteps descended to the beach

again. The hall darkened and I circled, one way then the other, reassuring myself there was nothing to be afraid of, that my master would come home soon and all would be well – but still dread mounted. I cast my eyes to the statue enthroned at the base of the stairs, the sculpture he spoke to sometimes, an ancient, sad-eyed hound carved in marble (extraordinary that hands had fashioned those emaciated bones), its head turned as a man in rags approached from behind. '*Good morrow to you, Argos,*' he would say stroking the dog's skull. '*How patiently you have waited for his return.*'

I had to see what my master was doing, so I slipped through a side door into the principal part of the palace and took the stairs up to the long gallery. I'd visited it once, in summer, when the building was lively. Now it was peopled only by statues. I mounted a chair and leaning on to a sill, I had a view of the ocean. In the distance, my master was a shadow cutting across the mercury stillness of the silt flats. He stopped just beyond the crooked islet, busied himself around the boat, until moments later a golden light flared up. The glass panes of the casement shimmered with it. He was burning the body. I recall – how it seems like yesterday – my guts knotting as the blaze reached its apogee.

My master stayed there, dutifully waiting until the fire had diminished, before he turned and started to lumber back. I slunk down on to the floor and glanced at the congregation of sculptures: a bearded colossus wrestling a sea creature, a young lady reclining on a chaise with a lyre tipped from her hand, an old sage brandishing an open book. The night shadows bending over their contours made them all come to life in a monstrous way. And there were paintings too, even more illusive renditions of people, deceits of canvas and pigments: a gentleman in a fur-collared robe with a kestrel on his forearm, an old crone bodiced into a carmine gown, a young rake dressed in black and clutching a skull. All that time ago I had yet to travel the realms, to know the majesty and horror of cities, to witness war first-hand – its stench of hot metal and coppery blood – or to lose a friend I loved. I'd yet to learn also how centuries would pass for me, that I'd live and live. All that was to come. And yet, in that moment, amongst those ghostly watchers, somehow I felt the presage of those things weighing upon me. Dusk engulfed the room, sending me mad with fear – then at last I heard my master coming back in below. I bolted down the stairs two at a time. He had filled one of the crates with coloured glass, the phials that had previously lain strewn across the sand, and now he set it carefully down in the doorway. I leapt up, welcoming him with ecstatic barks and licks of my tongue.

'What a fuss is here! What a fuss,' he said, even though he too was shaken. I followed him into the boot room and watched him in the gloom as he washed his hands, and then to the parlour where he lit candles and shuttered the windows. Before he closed the last of them, he paused and peered out towards the crooked rock, still frightened it seemed by what he might have discovered.

'Everything shall be well, no?' he said, kneeling down and holding my skull in both hands. 'We are content with our lives, are we not?' His tone, the abrupt intensity of it, unnerved me and at once I thought of the body, of fat catching light and bones turning black as they incinerated. I thought of the statues and paintings in the dark gallery of the palace – the bearded colossus, the reclining lady, the rake with the skull – and they too seemed to belong to the world of the dead. It was only after he'd built a fire in the hearth and we'd sat in the warmth of it – he on an armchair and I at his feet – after the stone had heated beneath me, that my heart began to settle.

'No!' He sat up and looked round. I lifted my head to the door, wondering what he'd heard. 'The oysters.' He sighed. 'Left them on the beach. And our bucket too. The tide will take it.' He shrugged and sank back again. 'No matter. Tomorrow, we'll go once more. Maybe tomorrow we'll find finer ones still.'

I watched him from the tail of my eye as he fell asleep and his hands went limp at his side. Only then did I recall his strange behaviour on the beach. 'So now you are dead, are you?' he'd asked in as curious a voice as I'd ever heard from his lips. I wondered who he'd been expecting.

I would find out soon enough.

ii
Whitehall, England,
five years later

We waited in the cold at the gatehouse until a lady came to meet us.

'Yes?' she asked tersely. She was as thin as a bird, all in black and clenching a fistful of keys.

My master removed his cap and smiled. 'Can it be you do not remember me?'

Her tiny chest jumped. 'Not possible. The vanishing physician.'

My master smiled. 'Forgive me, Margaret, for sending for you, but so much time has passed since I was here and I was unsure who remained from the old days.'

'Indeed. I remain. I shall leave only in a box.' She peered in disbelief. 'How long? Fourteen years?'

'Twenty-two.'

A gasp. 'You lie. You are quite unchanged and yet I am an old maid.'

'Nonsense, nonsense.'

Laughter.

'And you come with a companion this time?' She looked down at me and my tail swayed side to side. I liked her immediately; she had vitality. 'What a handsome fellow. And how he seems to smile.'

'Indeed,' my master bragged, 'he is all smiles, my champion; he has one for everyone.' The compliment set my tail wagging at double speed.

'Two decades, really?' Margaret said. 'How time slips through our fingers. Where on earth have you been gallivanting?'

'I —' His cheeks dimpled as they always did when he was unsure how to answer. 'We arrive from Denmark. Before that Florence. A short stay in Madrid. And more —' He gestured. 'To travel is to live, is it not?'

I'm not sure if Margaret agreed, but her smile did not falter. 'And now?'

'Whitehall? If there is need of my services, lowly as they are. I have thirsted for London, above all places.'

Her delight was clear to see. 'I could play the coquette, but I shall not. I have missed your remedies too greatly and I have more need of them than ever. I will find employment for you. New dynasty or not, you will note I still carry the keys. Come in, come in, you and your gracious companion — this chill is maddening.' She motioned for us to enter, but my master paused.

'Tell me first, did a gentleman come looking for me these last few years?'

'A gentleman?'

'By chance. I do not expect it, but you always followed so carefully the comings and goings —'

'I recall no one. Is there some trouble?'

'No, not at all.' Though my master had brought the subject up, he now seemed to regret it. 'My former associate in business, of years gone by, a chemyst such as I.'

'Another of you, how thrilling. What is his appearance?'

'Truly it is of no matter. He visited me here once, long ago, and I thought you might recall, but — forgive me. The long journey. I am at sixes and sevens. And you are right about the weather – lead the way.'

Margaret steered us round a cloistered quadrangle. The castle at Elsinore had been plain in comparison to Whitehall, which was a pale mountain range of halls, towers and colonnades, windows brilliant with multicolour stained glass, roofs fluted with a thousand brick finials.

'You heard the news of course? The queen. Four years and I still fancy she will barge through the door and rail at me.' She lowered her voice to a whisper. 'Perhaps, if you had been at court, she would live. She would not be counselled on the matter of lead ceruse. They say it all but poisoned her. Her end, needless to say, was like a piece of grim and fantastic theatre. She ordered the removal of every mirror in Richmond Palace, took to the floor on cushions and lay for days, her fingers in her mouth, like an infant, still wearing that cartoon wig of hers. Eventually she pronounced, "I wish not to live any longer, but desire to die." And she kept her word.'

'She will not be easily forgotten.'

'No indeed. And then, of course, last November's episode. Did you hear of that?'

'Varied accounts.'

Margaret halted, threw her eye around the cloister and held his arm. 'Unspeakable, unspeakable.' She had a playful quality that was a refreshing antidote to the long-wintered, wide-sky austerity of Elsinore. She resumed her march through the labyrinth of passages and courtyards, her voice sotto voce. 'A time of horror it was. In the undercroft they found it, three dozen barrels or more. Pure gunpowder. Here, almost beneath our feet. A bedlam of interrogations followed, appalling torture, court writs and trials. The king himself attended, hidden behind a curtain. Can you imagine the scene? This entire court shredded to nerves. Everyone distrusting the other. Then the executions. Dear me. I would not attend. But the crowds that massed, to witness the dismemberments. Gruesome, gruesome. But imagine if they had been triumphant, the plotters? We'd be on another path entirely.' We had come into a room with a fire. 'You left him on bad terms, did you?'

'Who?'

'Your associate? I know how feuds develop. A dispute between two glassmakers in the Strand, over formulas, turned so violent one ended up in Newgate. Were secrets stolen?' she enquired with an air of scandal. My master's brow corrugated. 'You poor creature. I'll not extract it from you. What a gossip I am. Wait here, warm your bones, I shall talk to the powers.' She lingered a moment. 'My vanishing physician and his smiling hound. It is extraordinary how unchanged you are.' And she went.

'Let me see you,' a voice said.

The chamber we'd been shown into was dim and so over-ornamented with gilding and fretwork I hadn't noticed the man seated in the corner. A pale, paunchy face mounted over an elaborate lace ruff, heavy lidded eyes, thin beard. His clothes were fine, a complex symmetry of pleated velvet, but he had the fresh rotten smell of cheese. A wolfhound lay before him. She looked round at me and I bid her good day with a bow of my tail. To which she stared back so disdainfully I was embarrassed by myself, before she lay down again.

My master stepped forward. 'Sire.'

The man, King James, as I would soon learn, studied the vellum parchment that my master had given him. He'd inscribed it, in his steady slanting hand, on our passage over the North Sea.

13

'You were engaged in all of these palaces?' The king spoke with a cumbersome lisp, his tongue too large for his mouth. Dirt had caught in the lines of his hands, so that only his fingertips were flesh-coloured.

'In all the various courts of Europe, sire. And here at Whitehall too: six years at the service of your cousin the queen.'

'Then you know these halls better than I. Chemystry? Is that the magic that witches use? To make storms from the air?'

'That is not chemystry, sire, with all respect. Chemystry is a science. A sound and logical art. I am no magician.'

The king looked back at the paper and his head twitched in surprise. 'And in Persia too? Truly?'

'Indeed, sire. At the palace of Ismail in Tabriz.'

'Persia?' He was stunned. 'It is a world away from us. In that realm, for sure there is magic?'

'Mathematics perhaps. Wisdom resides in the very bones of the Persians, sire. Ancient wisdom. There, far along the silk roads beyond the desert, I learnt the specialties of my craft, more than any other place.' In the years to come I would hear my master talk often of Persia, of Tabriz and mathematics, and he always shone when he did.

'And what age do you have?' The king shook the parchment. 'To be in possession of such a curriculum?'

'Fifty –' my master replied quickly, though it sounded more like a question. 'Or thereabouts.'

The king smiled at this and his teeth were as discoloured as his fingers. He pushed himself up and shuffled over to me. He was not old, but weak on his legs, ordinary-looking, like a street seller in fancy dress. He dropped his hand before my nose to let me sniff it. Out of politeness, I took in a draught, but it tanged of ink phenol and faeces. 'Welcome to Whitehall,' he said to my master, signalling that the interview had been successful. 'You and your hound.'

'The costume box city' my master called London. I have seen so many places since it's easy to forget how struck I was by my first true metropolis. Long squares of gabled houses, each a castle in itself, but joined together in miraculous geometrics of glass. And a new universe of odours. After the dull smokeries and fish hauls of Elsinore, the all-pervading rye-starch smell of painted timber, here the air was spiced with exotics: sugar, cinnamon, nutmeg, coffee and chocolate. The smell, I would come to recognize, of money.

And the humans that clipped on pewter cobbles along her avenues and through her colonnades were grand too, with their knowing confidence and froideur. It was the time of cartwheel ruffs, richly sombre fabrics and tall conical capotain hats. Men were bearded, moustached, with hair swept back from the foreheads, some with lovelocks, many with short cloaks draped from one shoulder. And women, bodiced into gowns with high necklines and wings at the shoulders, were just as self-assured.

As he had been at Elsinore, here my master was always vigilant of new arrivals. In our lodgings, when boats arrived at the palace quay, he'd peer from the edge of the window, studying who came ashore. Or if he heard an unfamiliar voice from the courtyard, or the adjacent suites, he'd cock his ear to the wall. I was certain why: he was anticipating the person that *hadn't* washed up on the silt flats of Elsinore. The eyes of that stranger, the human I hadn't even met, seemed to stalk us wherever we went, even hanging, I fancied, in the darkness as we slept. I knew nothing more about him, other than that his seeming appearance had been heralded by that intaglio of three towers below a crescent moon.

A few years into our time at Whitehall, on a winter's day, we went to visit the frost fair on the Thames with Margaret. In fact, it was her idea to go. She and my master were firm friends, always laughing together and talking over each other, often staying up late, perusing books by candlelight, whilst sharing sweet snacks, marzipan and gingerbreads. I sensed an attraction between them that was distinct from friendship. My master was one of those rare humans who was naturally unmannered around women, innately gracious and thoughtful, yet virile enough to make even sour ones smile. It seemed to me that having Margaret as a companion put a spring in his step. So, at Whitehall, I used to wonder why he didn't allow their friendship to develop: for it was he, without doubt, that held it back. She was the one always coming up with plans, always holding out her hand for his. In a few years I'd understand his behaviour completely.

The Thames had frozen over entirely, enough for horses and carriages to be able to travel along it all the way from London Bridge to Westminster. Here and there, ships had been encased in ice, their masts bare like winter trees. Hordes of people, red-cheeked and wrapped up to the eyes, bustled between the attractions – archery, bull-baiting, skittles and see-saws – whilst children skated about or pulled each other in sleighs. My human companions were thrilled by it all, but I felt uncomfortable on ice, though I tried to keep it a secret. I never liked, not even today, the intense squeeze of cold against my paws, the odour – like sharp peppermint I always thought – and worse than all, the fear it might break at any time.

'Look, let us buy hats,' my master said, alighting on a stall. 'I know this gentleman. *The Masque of Queens*, that was you?' he asked the elderly stallholder, who replied with an ancient crinkle of a smile. 'The man is a genius, Margaret, a milliner. We shall have one each.'

'Not I, not I,' Margaret begged, but in no time he'd paid for two and crowned her with a headpiece of plumes in parrot colours, and himself with a turban studded with a glass ruby.

'You shall be the Queen of Amazons, or some such, and I the Sultan of Arabia.' It was so entertaining I barked, and forgot all about my fear of ice. My master loved putting on costumes. Whenever players came to a palace, he'd follow them round in an almost intoxicated state, only to become tongue-tied if any of them actually spoke to him. Once an earnestly drab playwright came to our rooms in Whitehall and questioned him for hours about his work. During the interview my master was so star-struck, he seemed to forget how to speak, but for months after he boasted to anyone who'd listen: 'Did you know, Mr Jonson is writing a play about me? I shall be famous the world over.' (Unfortunately, when we saw the piece, he was shamed by the portrayal of a con artist masquerading as an alchemyst and slipped out of the theatre before the final song.)

We went on to watch a troupe of dancers. To the fast running of fiddles, they reeled in figures of eight. My master started to tap his feet as he always did when he wanted to join in. He loved dancing as much as dressing up, though in my opinion he was best left out of it, as he was inevitably the clumsiest on the floor. When one man stepped away, leaving a space, I thought he'd join in – but something at the edge of the river had caught his attention. The light dropped from his face, like a block of snow falling from the eaves of a house. His nostrils flared and a keen odour – of hysteria I fancied – lifted off him.

'We should return. This is meagre entertainment.' He set

off hurriedly, not even making sure we followed. I tried to see what had stirred him so, but a group had pressed in behind us. He was so distracted that he slipped and knocked into one of the dancers, sending her off balance. She fell and my master didn't apologize or help her up, as he normally would, but forged on. 'Quickly,' he snapped. He'd dropped his turban and I was about to rescue it when he shouted again for us to 'hurry up'. With the happiness apparently gone from our day, the rabble seemed shrill and disobliging now, with all their clattering patterns, and I began to feel nervous again of the ice breaking, imagining how cold and dark the river would be underneath. We came to a clearing and my master stopped dead and swore under his breath. 'Why do I run? Face him.' Margaret was nonplussed, as grimly he turned his body about. 'How long has he been watching?'

That is when I saw the lone figure standing on the steps of the Embankment, his black cloak picked out against the snowy city. He came down on to the river and advanced towards us at a measured pace. Even at a distance, he was striking: broad-shouldered, confident, gliding swan-like across the ice, at a different speed from the masses swarming about him, with a different quality, in a different universe from them.

'The gentleman you'd been expecting?' Margaret asked, her wits always about her. 'Your once associate? Is there cause for concern?'

My master made no reply, just shoved me behind his legs. The stranger halted some yards short of us and held out his palms.

'So I find you in London?'

His smile was so self-assured I tingled. His face was hidden like treasure beneath a wide-brimmed hat with an ostrich feather plume, and by his hair; ink-black curls that tumbled to his shoulders. His face was not cold or pinched like everyone else's; it shone with a Mediterranean light. He dripped in riches: a doublet of Prussian blue, velvet and satin dropped with pearls; floating collar of Spanish lace (the type that even the most fashionable courtiers were yet to wear); patent shoes that reflected the entire scene; a gold-tipped swagger stick; and an emerald about his neck. Another person may have looked gaudy, or effeminate, but not he. My master, who I'd thought of as handsome, with his large nose, oversized hands and unruly scrub of sandy hair, was diminished in the other's presence. He stepped forward, inclined his head and spoke the stranger's name:

'Vilder.'

The stranger, who was slightly shorter than my master but with a stronger build, stared back, puffs of condensation smoking from his nostrils, apparently relishing the discomfort, before speaking. 'It is good to see you, sir.' Then he glanced down at me, eyes as glittering as coal pits, making me almost light-headed. 'He is yours?' he asked my master, before turning to Margaret with a slight but vanquishing bow. 'My old associate is a fool for the species.' He examined her with a wry twist of the mouth. 'I like your hat.'

Margaret had forgotten she was wearing it. I'm sure she longed to snap it off, but she endured, reddening slightly, and gave a comical shrug. There was an uneasy silence; three humans gathered on the ice.

'Have you travelled far?' Margaret's voice got stuck in her throat and she coughed, whilst rearranging her collar. 'Where is it you have come from, sir?'

'The Hunsrück mountains. Rhineland. The *old* country.' He spoke graciously and smiled often, but his words were gilded with mischief.

'The Rhineland. A place of fairy tales surely?' Margaret rejoined.

I had the sense that Vilder was not one to make small talk, but he answered nonetheless. 'I would travel ten times the distance to hunt down my oldest acquaintance in the world.'

My master seemed to measure Vilder's words, as if they contained hiding meanings.

'An arduous journey from there?' Margaret said. 'And you have a shared fascination with chemystry? With metallurgy and – and such matters? Where does *your* interest stem from, sir?'

Vilder regarded her with sunny disdain, before answering. 'My parents owned mines, long ago. I inherited. A grimy business.' He twisted an immense sapphire on his finger in a dazzle of light.

'That would make sense, mines, and the materials that are found in them, for chemystry I mean. And you speak the language like a native.' She was a magpie for facts but her persistence was making me anxious, and my master too.

'My mother was English. And on her instruction I was tutored at John Balliol's college in Oxford.' He motioned at my master with a flourish. 'He and I studied side by side – though I was far from a model pupil.'

'Ah, all becomes clear: your connection, the university at Oxford –'

Vilder interrupted her with a tap of his swagger stick. 'I so look forward to speaking to you at greater length, but you must excuse us. An age has passed since last we spoke.' He gestured towards my master and Margaret's cheeks turned the colour of boiled ham.

She nodded, mumbling an apology, picked up her skirt, left, realized she'd gone the wrong way, came back and departed in a muddled zigzag, her parrot headpiece going with her.

For some moments a magnetic silence held the men together.

'I am pleased to see you well,' said my master at last. 'When I was in Elsinore I thought –' Whatever he was going to say, he decided against it. 'I was most grateful to you for sending my materials. Though I was sorry to return such a grim report. You received it? Did you know the poor fellow who drowned?'

'Not personally.' Vilder studied my master as a gentleman thief might peer through a jeweller's window. 'Well, as the lady noted, I have travelled far in this bitter cold. Invite me to your rooms?' He nodded towards Whitehall, smirking. 'The court of the Scottish king.'

'May I offer you some refreshment?' my master asked him as we entered our parlour. Vilder glanced about, noting the shelves of little glass bottles and phials that my master always assembled in his place of work.

'Yes,' he said. 'Mix me one of your reviving tonics. I have missed them.' Vilder kept his cloak on but removed his hat. I tried to see his face properly, make sense of the fragments I'd glimpsed beneath its brim – squared jaw, broad nose, heavy brow – but the room was too dark.

'A tonic?' my master asked.

'Yes, with a dash of –' Vilder shrugged – 'some opiate or other. Laudanum if you have some?'

My master seemed unsure. 'Are you ill?'

'Do I need to be?' My master lit the candles on the stand by the door and I crept forward to see the visitor closer, but he went to the window and became a silhouette. 'Come now, don't look at me like that,' he said to my master. 'A tonic would make me happy. Is that not reason enough?'

My master set about concocting a brew, first stoking the furnace, before collecting phials from his shelves and measuring out ingredients. Though he seemed reluctant to be doing it, he kept his tone friendly. 'London, you will see, is greatly altered. It is as Florence once was. There is zest here, inquiry, and such thrilling science that sometimes I cannot sleep with sheer excitement.'

'Scientists?' Vilder laughed. 'We are the most ill-gotten creatures of them all. The fool kings.' He nodded at my master's preparation. 'Why not put some hemlock in too?'

'What?'

'I'm joking with you, dear fellow.' Vilder chuckled again and turned to look out from the window. A pale winter sun slipped behind the forest of ship masts on the Thames. With the visitor's back turned my master quickly hid his red velvet wallet under the worktable pans. It was his only truly precious possession, containing two objects: a hexagonal glass phial with a dash of grey liquid in the bottom and a tortoise-shell case, the size of a snuff box, containing a quantity of grey powder with no odour at all, like dry dirt. I'd only seen him *look* at the things, checking they were there, but never once using them. I would learn later that this substance, in raw and liquid form, *jyhr* as it was called, would play a profound part in my life.

'Do you know how those people became rich?' Vilder said, tapping the top of his swagger stick on the window pane. 'The sea traders and the sugar hagglers there, where their wealth came from?'

'From foreign lands?'

'From death. It came from death.' He half turned his head to my master, and back again. 'The great plague of two centuries past, and all those since. The ruination of the species.

The world diminished of people, but still bursting with treasure: iron, copper, gold. A void left *just* at the moment of new invention. And who better to fill it, to capitalize, than merchants and spice men?'

'A sombre subject, no? After all this time.'

'And the plague not only made people rich, it made them clever.' He deepened his voice ' "If I – *everyman* – am to suffer an horrendous end, to be eaten alive by buboes in my groin and armpits, whilst my skin turns as black as tar, if my life will end *that* way, I must surely make something of it first. What if there is no paradise? What if this frail body is all I have?" Would Michelangelo have picked up his chisel otherwise? Would Euripides or Plato have recorded their thoughts? Or Spenser or Donne put ink to paper? Their endeavour to cheat mortality.'

'Have you come all this way to talk of the plague?' There was a coolness in my master's tone that made the visitor turn back.

'You are right. I have a purpose here and I shall be direct. Return with me to Opalheim. I have a commission for you there.'

'Opalheim?'

'You recall the place?'

'Yes, I recall it.'

Vilder chuckled quietly to himself. 'How bad tempered you've grown.'

'I will not go to Opalheim. I will not set foot in that place. It is your home and I do not wish to speak ill of it –'

'You *are* speaking ill of it.'

An electric silence. The palace bells rang out. My master shook some powder from a bottle, sprinkled it into the pot and stirred. 'What commission?'

Light from the furnace flickered against Vilder's tourmaline pupils, otherwise he was a magnificent shadow. 'I wish you to perform a conversion.'

'No.'

'I would not trust myself with the procedure, otherwise –'

'Nor should you.'

'Otherwise I would not be seeking your help.'

'I say no.'

'And that is that?'

'You are as qualified as I. You know how to do it. Do it. I will have no part of it.'

Vilder looked towards me, smiling subtly, and whispered, 'It seems we're no longer on good terms, my friend and I. I suppose time does that.'

'Who is it you wish to convert, huh? A lover? Some caprice of yours? You joke of hemlock. It is no joke. And you wish me to put a curse on them, whoever they are? I'll not. It would be unconscionable in the extreme, immoral, to burden another living thing with – to find later you've tired of them, as you tire of all your caprices. No, I will not do it. You are irresponsible and you give our craft a bad name.'

'He is no caprice.'

'Well, I am no fool king.' The fur lifted from my back: I had never heard my master shout before. He wiped beads of perspiration from his brow and stirred the pan. His hands were shaking. 'All good, my champion, all good,' he whispered to me. He presumed I was frightened by the visitor, but I was more intrigued than anything. He was like a character from a play or an opera come to life. From a piece that was full of tension and drama, where murder was in the air, and powerful women and flawed heroes whispered in dark palace rooms. Vilder possessed a quality, in his demeanour, in how he spoke and moved, in the indefinable odours that sung from him, that I'd never encountered before and rarely since. I had no notion if he was brave and honourable – or a villain who took pleasure in enchanting others. The only other human I would meet, decades later, with such a quality of grave extravagance, was Louis, 'the Sun King' of Versailles.

It was some time before my master spoke again to him. 'I wish I could help you. Truly.' His tone was at once conciliatory. 'You know I would assist you in any other matter, in profound matters if you asked me, but I *cannot* in that way. You know why. It is the only rule of my life.' He cleared his throat and funnelled the contents of the pan into a cup and set it on the table.

Vilder heaved a sigh. 'You're right. I should not have made the suggestion. The idea took hold of me and –' Now I know Vilder to be a dissembler, a double-dealer, who'll say one thing and mean another, but at the time I was amazed by how quickly his irascibility drained away, a seeming penitence in its place. 'I will think on it no more.' He took off his cloak and laid it carefully on the back of a chair. 'I have a better proposal: that we revive our old association. Too many years have passed for resentment.'

Vilder was so gracious, my master dropped his guard. 'Nothing would make me happier.' They embraced, only with a little awkwardness, before Vilder sat down and picked up the cup of liquid.

'Whether you approve of such tonics or not,' he said, 'you are the best of all at making them. Perhaps it is a deceit of the brain, but my own medicines never seem to work as well.' He studied it with his nose and used the tip of his finger to touch a single drop on to his tongue. Immediately his jaw loosened, his shoulders dropped. After it had cooled a little, he drank the rest and sank like warm wax. My master watched him, with distaste I fancied, but when he poured two beakers of wine and they both toasted, their animosity was put away. They talked, more like friends: Chemystry, silver mines, Florence, Rome, the dead queen.

Past midnight, both on the cusp of falling asleep in their armchairs, Vilder said: 'His name is Aramis, my caprice. He is a soldier. And a fine man.'

I was woken by a tap of metal and a feather of golden light on my eyes. Vilder was retrieving his swagger stick. It dazzled against the dawn light through the window. He swept back his cushion of hair, put on his hat, curled his fingers through the feather. He looked down at the place where my master had hidden the wallet, a sliver of red beneath pans. He smiled, I think, but didn't touch it. When he noticed I was awake, he bowed at me, then slipped from the room. My master was still asleep and I wondered if I should rouse him, but I had a more mischievous urge: to follow him on my own. I crept out of the door as it was closing. The shadow of the ostrich feather stole down the stairs and I went after it.

I trailed him out of the palace on to the Thames. Snow was falling and I couldn't even see the south bank of the river, just an otherworldly swirl of blizzard, of shape-shifting silhouettes of lumbering morning people. Vilder strode across the ice, neither slipping nor skidding. There was a moan of wind along the river and the tendrils of his ostrich feather shook against it and would have flown free had the unyielding shaft not kept them in check.

I went in his wake almost to the other side of the Thames, longing for him to turn and see I was there, regarding me in that dark, extravagant way of his, that I might feel his grandeur one last time. In the end, I stopped. Vilder did not turn, nor break his stride, and it was almost painful watching him vanish into the white.

For a moment I was lost in a trance, then the sky must have darkened a shade, as I realized how cold it was, and that I was standing on the ice, almost alone on the river. I turned and found Whitehall vanished, consumed by white, and all of a sudden I felt a keen shame that I had somehow betrayed my master, allowing myself to be charmed by a man who clearly distressed him. I began to return, but the streak of superstition in me – that I always had and still do – made me think, for my disloyalty, there'd be a break in the ice, that a fissure would open and I'd fall through. I imagined the current taking me, and my body tumbling along beneath the bumpy ceiling of ice as I was carried away seawards.

I longed to get back to our room, to my master's bed, so he knew I hadn't left him, so I could show I'd never leave him, but it took me ages to cross back to the north bank. I kept having to stop, to summon my courage, shivering on the ice, appalled by how London had been stolen away from me, before marshalling myself to continue. At last the towers of Whitehall began to refigure, and I sped up and kept going.

I tore across the courtyard, up the steps, then drove through the door into our room – and relief. A shape still lay beneath the blanket, and that smell that was vital to me – like midnight in a tall forest, stiff parchment paper and a whisper of pine sap. My master.

I jumped up and he, half dozing, lifted the cover.

'All good, my champion?' He smiled, then added, 'How cold you are,' before he nodded off once more.

I burrowed down to his feet and lay there, in warmth, wild in my heart.

My home.

How many years ago was it now, that morning on the river? More than two hundred. In another age, at the beginning of my life. More than two hundred winters have come and gone since then, more than two hundred times the November winds have arrived from the north and humans have put on their furs and hats and lit fires in the streets. I have counted all the winters and always say the new number to myself when the day of the new year comes around. That's how I know my age – two hundred and seventeen.

The visitor, Vilder, would of course return to our lives, casting a shadow over everything, the man responsible – I have no doubt – for taking my master from me.

I often think of Elsinore and Whitehall and the other courts in which my master worked. I think too of our later years – those after the dreadful events in Amsterdam – trailing armies, the battlefield, the red-mist bone-smash horror of war. The memory of those decades spent together pulse through me perpetually. I dream of them every night, fantasies so vivid and intense, I struggle to believe they're not real.

As to why I, a mere dog, have lived for more than two centuries, that is a question to which I only have vague answers.

Of course, if I could find *him*, my master, who was no dissembler, or enchanter, or mystery-man like Vilder. Who was honourable and constant and loyal to his core, a softly spoken angel too modest to ever tell the world how great he was. If I could find him, my beloved, if he is still living, somewhere – I might understand everything.

Tomorrow

1. Lost Soul

*Venice, May 1815, a hundred and twenty-seven
years since I lost him*

What a ravishing morning!

For two weeks I've been cooped up in my den, watching
from the entrance, as it's rained and rained, and cheerless
huddles have sloshed back and forth, all wet hemlines and
squeaking soles. But today, the air is newly spun from the
Adriatic, and clean again.

'*Buongiorno!*' comes a voice and a pair of boots approach,
the porter from the customs house. 'A surprise for you.' He
crouches and slaps down a pie on the cobbles before me. '*Torta
di fagioli!*' he boasts with a kiss to his fingertips. I pass my nostrils over it. Spinach and beans cased in pastry, only a few
mouthfuls missing. The porter, who's as straightforward as
the barrels he unloads all day from the merchant ships, often
comes to chat, and sometimes brings me treats, but rarely
anything this enticing.

For me? I ask with a studied lift of my brow.

He laughs, scruffing my neck in his giant palms. '*Si, mio
signore*, who never leaves his post, who sits all day watching the
ships arrive. To your feast.' He does a comical curtsy and goes.

I press my snout over the *torta* and inhale. I've barely eaten
in days and I could wolf it straight down – but I'll ration
myself: a quarter tonight, a quarter tomorrow, enough for a

week if I'm disciplined. I come out into the sunshine and cast my eye along the quay: a ship setting sail, another docking, half a dozen crewmen winching crates down to the quay. *He* is not amongst them. I inspect the cathedral steps: a young priest ascends and slips through the double doors.

There comes a playful bark and a familiar dog trots across the port. I nudge my treat out of sight. Sporco, as I call him, 'the messy one', a local stray who often hangs about the customs house, bothering for scraps. He's the sort of creature I might have avoided in that splendid time of my former life, when I was a courtier hound, when I might have found him a little too much of an animal, a slave to mechanical urges, the permanent want of food. But nowadays, I am equal with them all, except in one way of course. In any case, Sporco had a dreadful beginning, which I myself witnessed.

'Muggy today,' he says. 'We're still in spring, but it's muggy, no?'

I don't reply, for it's not muggy in the slightest. He snouts the air, but doesn't realize there's a *torta di fagioli* sitting right behind me. I observe him down the length of my snout. When he was a puppy, his fur was golden, but years on the street have matted it into dirty clumps. He's half my size, but has uncommonly large ears that point up quizzically, with tufts sprouting from inside them. He's scruffy and smells of canals, but fine dark lines around his eyes give him a touch of Arabian mystery. And he smiles, always, like I once did.

'Ah,' he gasps. I presume he's finally detected the *torta* and brace myself for an argument. From sheer persistence he usually wears me down until I give him half of what I have, or all of it. But something else has caught his attention – the appearance of another dog on the quay, a Dalmatian who passes from time to time with her master, each as sleek and self-regarding as the other. 'She is dizzying, isn't she? You see how she wants me?' Sporco boasts, pushing his chest in her direction and swinging his tail in virile strokes. 'She's crying out for me that one.'

He couldn't be further from the truth; the Dalmatian avoids him pointedly, often sailing past with a quip, 'What a sad little dreamer,' or 'I thought it was August again and the canals were stinking.'

'You know where to find me. Don't be shy,' Sporco tells her, undeterred, as he is with every lady dog he badgers – and I've no idea if he has luck with any of them. He turns back to me. 'That reminds me. What of La Perla? She hasn't been by this morning, has she?'

'No?'

'Usually she's been and gone by now, hasn't she, her and Beatricia? But you haven't seen her?'

'No.' I make a point of not meeting his gaze, to avoid one of his long-winded musings about the comings and goings of dogs in the morning. Though he is right: she hasn't been. She and her mistress, Beatricia, almost always take their walk very early. La Perla is a nervy lapdog that has never once left her small city quarter, but who carries herself with such resolute primness, I can't help but be a little fascinated by her.

'Is that meat?' Sporco says, finally spying my *torta*.

He tries to slip round me, but I block his way. 'I've told you many times, my friend: I don't eat meat.'

'Right you are, right you are,' he says, understanding nothing. He scratches his ear and I scratch mine.

'How would you like it if someone chopped you up and cooked you?'

At that moment, there comes a soft groaning of metal. The weathervane on the tip of the customs house, a sea-goddess holding out a golden sail, is turning. With it, a curious pang shivers through me, the tiniest twitch of some bygone rapture, intangible and elusive. The sounds of the city seem to fade away, and I stare at the vane, unsure what is so strange; I've seen her pivot round a thousand times. Then I realize: she's not turning with the wind, she's shouldering against it, as if she had a will of her own. For a while, she holds firm, before there's a crank and she rights herself once more.

'Just a morsel,' Sporco's saying. 'I'm half-starved I am. In three days nothing but fish bones. A couple of brutes have been stalking the wharves at night. Surly hounds from the coal yard.' He impersonates them by pushing out his shoulders and baring his teeth. It's almost impossible not to find him entertaining. 'Those wharves are ours by right. There's a pecking order. It is meat, isn't it? Can you spare a morsel?'

'No.' I nudge my treat to the back corner of my den and set off.

'Where are you going? Off on your travels?'

'The *torta* is mine, you understand?'

'Off on your travels, are you? Shall I come?'

'No.'

He asks me every day and the answer is always the same.

'Let's play,' he barks, blocking my path, ducking down and rolling his tufty brows. 'Play! Come on!' He thumps me on the snout, wheedling me with tricksy growls, before taking off around the quay in a figure of eight, and back to me. 'Play! Huh?'

Part of me would like to. It seems decades have passed since I scrapped for no reason, for the thrill of bashing against another. But I'm too old for games and, besides, it's better not to set a precedent. 'Look, she returns, *tuo amata*. Now's your chance.' Sporco, flummoxed, glances from me to the

Dalmatian and back again, his outsize ears pivoting in tandem. 'Go on, before she gets away.' He flies from the bridge in one leap and I escape across it and into the heart of the city.

I've lived so long in Venice, and seen it from the tops of so many bell towers – most particularly the Campanile in St Mark's Square, the highest – I have a precise sense of its shape. In a lagoon of many far-reaching islands, Venice is the largest, a dreamy sliver of a city, a mirage, where land becomes sea and sea becomes land, as mysterious as the glass that's furnaced in nearby Murano.

Venice itself is a fish-shaped island, marbled with canals and with a serpentine grand waterway bisecting it. The two halves are joined in only one place, almost in the centre of the mass, at the Rialto Bridge, a confection of white marble arches ascending and descending, on which there are shops, and almost always a heaving mass of activity.

Due south of it, at the edge of the water, are the principal institutions and buildings of the city, the doge's palace – the giant cube of pink sugar – the old, Byzantine cathedral, the Campanile and the prison, all around St Mark's Square. Whilst the *new* cathedral, *my* cathedral, lies opposite, on the southernmost slip of land.

Far east of the Rialto is the *Arsenale*, where the navy is stationed – whatever navy that may be, as there have been, in just fifteen years, variously a Venetian, French and Austrian one. North and west of the Rialto are the commercial areas, and the docks where most the ships come in from the mainland. It is to those that I head.

Though I live and spend most of my time in my den – the stone hollow in the side of the customs house, where rope used to be stored long ago – from it I have a view of the steps of the cathedral. *If* he comes, he will come searching for me there. It is where he told me to wait. But the northern port is the place where he and I first docked in Venice, and I've always thought that it would be miraculous if I could surprise him as he alighted from a ship. So I go to it every morning. I thread a time-honoured course around the maze of alleys and canal-ways to the fish market, turning north through the streets of Santa Croce and on to the port. The routine is sacrosanct. I've followed it day after day, week after week, year after year, decade after decade.

Occasionally I'm gripped by a need to visit *other* places, perhaps the *Arsenale*, or maybe one of the outer islands. But in general I'm too anxious to stray more than a few hours from my home.

I arrive at the harbour and head, as always, to a little terrace by a tumbledown church at the edge of the water. I'm about to sit when I remember the weathervane and, as I do, the euphoric throb comes again, like a door coming ajar, letting in a murmur of heat and light, before quickly pressing shut again. I stare fixedly across the lagoon towards the distant smudge of the mainland, alert, the fur on my back lifted, antenna-like. Along with these shivers of elation, the change in the weather, the guarantee of summer, I have a sense of optimism, of good things about to happen.

Unlike the quays close to my den, the western *fondamenta*, with its big skies and giant cranes, has more in keeping with the brash ports of northern Europe. Cologne perhaps, or Amsterdam. I stay much longer than I usually would, and even when I have the notion to leave, I find myself wandering along the quay instead, the image of the turning weathervane coming back to me time and time again. I watch a barge dock, its crew jumping ashore to hurriedly unload its cargo of boxes, whilst a supervisor in a top hat takes stock. The insatiable merry-go-round of trade and money. The boxes contain glass – I can hear it shiver as they're set down.

Five times I pad back and forth, for what reason I have no real sense. The city chatters and sings behind me. Its perpetual out-of-kilter peal of bells swells and wanes. Occasionally funeral gondolas, with their mournful awnings and flying-eagle figureheads, set off from the pier heading for the 'island of the dead'. Sailors and harbourmen, finished for the morning, gather in clusters: bottles of ale are uncorked, china pipes are lit, trails of tobacco smoke curl up to the sky. Grey clouds roll in and it starts to get cooler, no longer spring-like. I feel idiotic for staying so long, thinking that something miraculous might come across the sea. Why, after all this time, would he come today? I'm hungry and I decide to return home to my *torta di fagioli*.

As I reach the little bridge that crosses to the city's final promontory of land where I live, Sporco comes bounding towards me.

'Quickly, quickly, something terrible has happened.'

Having just watched funeral gondolas processing across the lagoon, I get a shock to see one docked in front of a tenement that overlooks the side of the cathedral. An insistent barking comes from a top-floor apartment. It's a voice I recognize: La Perla.

'Beatricia, Beatricia, Beatricia,' she's crying.

On the pavement a body has been covered with a blanket. An undertaker is in conversation with two people I recognize: the hard-drinking son of La Perla's owner and his efficiently unsociable wife. I don't know the son's name, but he's one of those humans, cheeks permanently livid with irritation, who seem like they'll hit you as good as look at you. Their presence there, the son already driving a hard bargain with the undertaker, along with La Perla's desperate bays, can surely mean only one thing, that Beatricia is dead. Approaching and peering under the cover, my fear is confirmed: a polite sack of bones in a lace-fringed dress, a cobwebbed profusion of grey hair, all colour eviscerated from her face, even from her lips.

'Is she?' Sporco enquires, staying well back.

'Yes. Gone.'

Sporco makes a pantomime expression of disbelief. 'And what'll happen to La Perla?'

I glance round at the son and his wife. '*Si vuoi una buona sepoltura*. If you want a good burial,' the undertaker is explaining to them, 'a plot on San Daniele –'

The son cuts him off. 'Give me none of your sales talk. A hole in the ground is a hole in the ground.' He bends down and reaches under the cover to unclasp a string of pearls from Beatricia's neck, but his fingers are too thick for the job, and he has to tug it over the corpse's head, leaving its hair sticking up.

I cock my ear to La Perla's howling and take a deep breath, before passing on into the courtyard of her building. 'What are you going to tell her?' says Sporco, shadowing behind. I don't know, but keep going. We go up three flights of stairs. At the top, hearing paws clip back and forth along the tiles inside the apartment, La Perla's voice hoarse from constant wailing, my stomach gives a little lurch. She and her Beatricia have never left each other's side. I know those first hours are the most unnatural, the overturning of everything, the absurd reality – unthinkable even a day ago – that you'll never see your beloved again. I stand on my hind legs, push my paw against the handle.

'*Mamma!*' La Perla thrills as the door opens, skittering towards us. She halts when she sees it's me. She peers over my head – but her mistress isn't there either, just Sporco. Her eyes founder. I'm so used to La Perla being young, looking like a cotton ball, I often forget she's past ten now, her tight white curls gone sepia with age.

'How are you, Perlita?' I ask softly, slipping in. A thousand knick-knacks crowd the little place, amidst the smell of urine and lavender.

'How am I?' she trills. 'A fine question, I should say. Sick to my stomach I am. Have you seen my mamma, my Beatricia? They carried her away. Why?' She could be one of those melodramatic actresses that so amused my master, only her tragedy is all too real. 'Have you seen her?' She returns her gaze to Sporco in the porch. 'Who is that? He smells.' She's not so distracted that she can't serve up an insult.

'You know Sporco. My –' for lack of a better word – 'my neighbour.'

'No,' she replies grandly. 'I don't believe we've been acquainted.'

This isn't true. She's clapped eyes on him every day since he washed up in our corner of town three years ago.

'Hello, La Perla,' Sporco chances, entering gingerly. 'What a beautiful place!' Sporco has never lived in a house and rarely gets invited into them. 'You have a fireplace!' He dashes towards it, before remembering why we're here and stops. 'Are you bearing up all right?'

She pinches her nostrils, pads round him on the balls of her paws and sniffs, just very lightly, at his behind. When Sporco tries to sniff back, she scuttles away. 'I'm fine, just fine. But you shouldn't be here. My Beatricia will be back soon and she doesn't like *wild* animals in the house.' She jumps up on to a little pink armchair and nestles into it, old and frail.

For a while it has concerned me about what would happen

if Beatricia dies. Her ageing had seemed to accelerate in the last year: she'd grown paler, unsteadier on her feet, almost unrecognizable from the vigorous talkative being that used to dart about the city. But I thought, I hoped, she had plenty of years left. Even so, I'd formulated a plan, as I often find myself doing, for the inevitable day. I'd decided, even if the son and his wife deigned to keep La Perla, which was unlikely in the extreme, that it would be too cruel to allow it. Sharing my den was out of the question: not for the inconvenience to me – though that would be considerable – but because it's just a plain hollowed-out cavity, an utterly inauspicious place that smells of damp and rope – a residence that La Perla would deem far beneath her. Other options were limited. Despite her high regard for herself, La Perla's never been particularly pretty to humans, is no longer young, and is as obstinate as she's bad-tempered. In the end, I settled on the plan of taking her to the palazzo in San Polo, where an elderly foreign couple had accumulated a menagerie of abandoned animals.

'La Perla, your mamma's not coming back.' The phrase drops out of me before I can stop it. Sporco freezes, mouth gaping. He stares at La Perla, waiting for her reaction. 'There is no easy way to tell you, so I will just say it plainly,' I continue, 'Your Beatricia is dead.' Her eyes muddle and darken. Sporco looks from me to her and droops his ears out of respect. 'We need to – to come up with a plan for what we're going to do now.'

She blinks but says nothing.

'La Perla, do you understand what I am saying? Your mamma –'

She sits up, stiffens her tail, bares her teeth – little nuggets of off-white – before leaping from the chair and nipping me hard. 'Kindly leave. Nobody invited you in.'

Footsteps come up the stairs, the door swings wide and La

Perla lets out a squeak as she's thrust aside. The son and his wife stalk in. 'The state of it,' the husband puffs and his wife shakes her head in accord. 'And that silly creature of hers too.' The son scowls at La Perla, but gasps when he realizes there are two other dogs. '*Fuori di qui!*' He swats Sporco towards the door and kicks him in the backside. '*Pulcioso! Parassiti.*'

La Perla runs one way and then the other, before scuttling under the pink armchair. When the son tries to pull her out, La Perla bites his hand. Furious, he turns the chair over, grabs her and throws her out of the door. She cartwheels down the stairs, bumping against the landing banister. I rear up and bare my teeth at the brute – but stop myself. A hundred years or more have passed since I've drawn blood. The son actually looks contrite, but hides it with a laugh. I leave and he slams the door behind me.

Sporco is helping La Perla to her feet. 'I'm quite all right, thank you,' she asserts. 'No need to trouble yourself.' She gazes at the door, the entrance to her home, just a plain timber slab, but one that has been essential to her entire life – and she's still expecting a miracle, the poor soul.

'Come on,' I say and eventually she turns her back on it and we descend.

Going back to the quay, there's no way of avoiding Beatricia. But better La Perla sees her, and understands her mistress is not returning. She stops in front of the body and pauses, before pawing the blanket from Beatricia's face and revealing it to the midday glare. I brace myself for a scene. So does Sporco, his outsize ears doing a fretful caper. But La Perla just lifts her foot and prods the old woman's cheek. Solid. I wonder how long she's already sat with the body, and how much she comprehends the situation.

The undertaker and his assistant push through, load the

body on to a stretcher and carry it off to their boat. Now La Perla will shriek, I assume, but she remains mute, watching Beatricia being loaded up as if she were some piece of furniture. I say very softly, 'Perlita, do you understand what has happened?' I press against her, so she can feel the warmth of my body, and her chest makes tiny kicks up and down. 'You're being very brave, but you don't have to be, if you don't want.' After we've watched the black-sailed ship set off and turn out of sight, and still she's made no response, I say, 'Well, as it happens, I have a plan.'

Before leaving, I say to Sporco, 'You go back home.' His tail halts mid-air and begins to droop, until I add. 'You can look after my *torta* until I return. Make sure it's safe.'

'Yes, yes,' Sporco agrees enthusiastically, the hair about his shoulders puffing up with the pride. He goes, but comes back. 'Goodbye, La Perla. See you again soon.' He hazards one last attempt at smelling her behind.

'Goodbye, sir,' she says emphatically, avoiding him.

Crossing the city, La Perla trails a few steps behind me, head low, but otherwise continuing to show no emotion. I try to cheer her up, nodding at passing sights. 'Look at that cat watching the singing gondolier.' 'You see that funny lady with a ship-shape hat?' 'What a family, marching to lunch in identical outfits.' She doesn't involve herself in my conversation. And for my part, I grow more anxious than usual at being away so long away from my den, and wonder again if the creaking weathervane and my curious pangs had any meaning.

The Mulhernes, the people I'm taking her to, are a wealthy couple that settled in the city in their middle age 'for its art, its weather and its distance from the gossipers of County

42

Cork,' I heard the wife comment once. She's tiny, always beautifully dressed in layers of silk and batiste, and as energetic as a clock spring, whilst her husband, a rangy, jovial mischief-maker, is blind. She acts as his eyes to the city. It's been at least a decade since they discovered me, at the entrance to my alcove. 'Poor creature, all on his own. What's he waiting for?' she said. 'Someone coming on a ship? It breaks my heart.' Her husband got down on to the filthy flagstones to cuddle me. 'He's ever so noble,' he said. 'Let's take him home, my darling. Would you like to come home with us? You're quite enchanting.'

It was tempting – they were clearly kind-hearted and the golden barge they arrived to church in, with its crew of smartly dressed attendants, suggested a luxurious home – but I didn't go. Not then, nor on any of the subsequent occasions they tried to cajole me. They lived in the north of the city, too far from the cathedral to be practical for me. I did, however, occasionally take 'lost causes' to their door. Not dogs like Sporco, who are more or less happy on the streets, but ones like La Perla, who wouldn't stand a chance anywhere else.

'Isn't it a paradise, Perlita?' I say, once we arrive at the gates of the palazzo. 'You don't often find gardens like this in the city, do you?' No reply. 'And the Mulhernes, you couldn't have kinder people. They'll spoil you rotten. Dogs are their family. They adore them. Did I tell you about the food here? They have, I don't know, three chefs? *Tortine*, ah, like you've never had. Rich pies with ricotta and mushrooms and all sorts. That's right, you'll have to watch it, Perlita, or you'll get dumpy. You don't want to lose that figure of yours.'

She pivots one eye towards me and holds it there. 'If they're so kind, why don't *you* live with them? You don't have a master or a mistress either. You don't have a *real* home.'

Her barb catches me by surprise. I open my mouth to reply, but nothing comes out, so I push open the gate and motion for her to enter.

The gardens have got overgrown and I realize it must have been a few years since I was here. Then, it was an organized riot of colour, now lanky weeds and nettles have sprung up between the terraces, and long fingers of ivy have entrapped the company of statues. For a moment I fear the couple may have moved on – or worse – when, amidst an excitement of barks, a pack of dogs emerge from the house and straight away engulf us. La Perla makes a display of distress as two terriers and old Spinone take the measure of her.

'That will do! Quiet, you rabble.' An old man chuckles, shuffling forth, feeling his way down the steps. 'Enough of your histrionics.' I don't recognize him for a moment. His hair has thinned to nothing, his ruddy cheeks hollowed and I'm reminded, as I so often am, how quickly time does its work, on humans and dogs and all. That is their curse, the opposite of my own: the never-ending ache of long life.

'What is it?' says his wife, bustling out, a vision of tuille in peacock colours. She takes her husband by the arm to guide him down.

'Something has caught the attention of these monsters.'

'Good grief,' she says, spotting me. 'He's returned.'

The husband stops dead. 'Who? Not our friend from the cathedral?'

'The very same. How old must he be now?'

Being blind, her husband looks to where he thinks I am and holds out his arms. 'Welcome, friend. Our valiant Robin Hood. Have you brought us something, as you used to, years ago?'

'He has,' his wife says, her face muddling at the sight of my companion. I fear she may reject La Perla, who's hunched up like an old cat, with an expression that is more spiteful than frightened. I have in mind to tell her to stand straight and look more desirable, when the old man drops to his knees and, by luck, catches her in his arms.

'She's gorgeous, just gorgeous,' he says as she tries to free herself. 'We've room for one more, haven't we, my darling?'

His wife gives a long-suffering laugh and rests her hand on the top of my head. 'I'd prefer it was this one. Come inside all and let's eat.'

I'm desperate to get back, but I go with La Perla into the palazzo to make sure she settles. Within, I find the same sumptuous pigsty I remember, a palace for animals, the entire piano nobile given over to their welfare, every priceless chaise and settee flattened, discoloured and furred by dogs and an assortment of other animals – cats, two rabbits in a birdcage and a parrot sitting on a perch by the window. (When I first came to the place, I was put in mind of Queen Henrietta Maria's eccentric, unruly menagerie at Somerset House in old London.) The animals' food is served up in grand, eccentric style in a string of mismatching china bowls in front of the fireplace.

'I don't like these people,' La Perla asides to me, making a point of refusing her meal.

'That's not fair, Perlita, they're very kind.'

'So you keep saying. But I shan't stay here. It doesn't suit me.'

'It will have to.' The sharpness of my tone surprises her. I soften. 'La Perla, this is a good place.' I want to tell her that she won't do better, that she's old and difficult, too cowardly to scavenge for fish bones in the wharves and too fussy to eat them. I want to tell her how lucky she has been to have had

Beatricia in the first place, when dogs like Sporco were tied to a pontoon post as a puppy and left for dead. 'You'll have a chance here,' I say. 'You'll make new friends.'

She shows her teeth and before I know it, she's bitten me on the ear, sharply, drawing blood. She runs to a corner to sulk. My heart could break for her, the smallness of her indignation, the tininess of her existence. Poor soul. I go to her and sit with her a while longer. The lady of the house is watching us, brows bunched together as she tries to fathom who or what I am.

'Now, where's the new arrival?' her husband is saying, holding up a treat as he feels along the litter. I kiss La Perla on the nose. 'You're a good sort, La Perla,' I say and leave the room.

Hurrying home for the second time in a day, I'm so preoccupied by visions of her in her new home, keeping her distance from everyone, being brittle if they try to be friendly, even as she is breaking to pieces inside, that I make a wrong turn and find myself in the street where half a dozen butcher's shops are bunched together. I always avoid this loathsome thoroughfare, revolted by the stench of meat, by the blood-sloshed, offal-coated cobbles, but now I must pass along it or retrace my steps entirely. It's more frenetic than anywhere. Humans, with almost savage end-of-day urgency, thumb coins into butchers' palms and take hold of packets of flesh, as packs of wide-eyed dogs linger about, spellbound by the trophies that hang in every window. 'Some of that would go down nicely,' or 'What I'd give for a piece of it,' they murmur to one another, eyeing up headless rabbits and bolts of fatty entrails stockinged in red string. I double my speed.

By the time I get back to Dorsoduro and crown the bridge before the cathedral, I'm morose to my bones. So often, even after all these years, the phenomenon of the view thrills me – two great churches separated by the mouth of the grand canal, the forest of masts and rigging in between, the ever-changing miasma of odours that sweeten the air, the galleons gliding away, the sheer possibility of it all – but not tonight. I'm beset with indefinable anger. I study the front of my cathedral, scowling at the pale flight of steps, the bronze doors shut for the evening, and it could be yesterday that my master and I stood in front of them, when the building was brand new, he chatting along to me. *'And the stone is Istrian, no? You see how the marble dust glitters in the light?'*

Sporco is waiting at the entrance to my den, lying with his head angled towards the place I stowed my *torta*. I know he won't have touched it, in that way he can be trusted, but all the same I'm in no mood to be sociable. When he notices me approaching, he gets to his feet, tail spinning. 'I kept an eye, just as you asked – all is safe.' He licks his lips.

I push past him into my den and sink at the sight of it. It's a prison: barely large enough to contain me, three decrepit walls that still smell, even after all this time of wet rope. This is how I live? This is what I have to show for myself? 'Why don't *you* live with them?' La Perla had said before. 'You don't have a master or a mistress either. You don't have a *real* home.' She's right. No matter the wonders I have seen, or the palaces I once lived in, I'm unrooted, a wanderer, a vagrant. *'One day we'll settle down. One day we'll find a home,'* my master always promised. We never did. I have no home. *He* was my home. I paw the *torta* from the corner. This morning it had filled me with delight, but now it smells ordinary and stale. I slip down a mouthful, but all I seem to taste is the bile inching up from my stomach. Sporco's shadow hangs over me and his tail slaps, infuriatingly, against the wall. I catch up another piece and swallow. What does my master look like now? Is he changed? Is his aroma the same? Midnight in a tall forest, stiff parchment paper and a whisper of pine sap.

'It is meat, isn't it? You can't fool me.'

'Get out! Out!'

Sporco skitters away.

'A hole in the ground is a hole in the ground,' Beatricia's son had said earlier, pocketing his mother's pearls. If he had love for her once, it was gone. I bite into a piece of pastry, chomping joylessly, before I remember, as I always try to, the phrase my master always used when things didn't go our way.

'*Tomorrow we begin again*,' he'd say, sometimes over a trivial thing, a burnt dinner, or our coach getting stuck in mud, but other times, uttered in defiance, a call to hope, when something had shaken us to our cores.

I calm down, gradually, and a while later I look round for Sporco. He sits at a remove, hunched, ears wilted, eyes scooped together – no longer smiling. I should be kinder to him, for he is a lost soul too. 'I am sorry, friend.' I nudge the pieces of *torta* out into the open. 'Here.' At first he hangs back, but eventually his tail reanimates to a half-speed loop and he returns. 'Eat,' I say, stepping back. 'Finish it.' No sooner have I spoken, than a chunk has vanished down his throat, and another and another until it's all gone and he's lashing the cobbles clean.

Tomorrow we begin again.

A thought strikes me: that tonight, for once, I should treat myself. I should give myself a dose of splendour, of magnificence, to remember the old days. That's what my master would do.

'I shall sleep somewhere else this evening,' I say to Sporco, hesitating before adding, 'come with me, if you like?' Sporco's ears stick up.

We go to the opera house on the other side of the Rialto. I know it's closed today, a Sunday, and also how to break in. Like La Perla, Sporco has barely ventured beyond the spit of land he inhabits, its little grid of streets and canals, and I have the sense, though he tries to hide it, he's spooked to venture so far from home, halting whenever he hears footsteps approach and backing into the shadows, until they've passed.

We steal along a ledge beside a back canal and under a gate into a vaulted space at the rear of the theatre where the scenery is kept. I come to the opera from time to time, mostly lingering in the piazza at the front, craning my ear to the thrum of music inside, but sometimes I enter when everyone has gone for the night.

The scene dock is perky with aromas of flax, cedar oil and varnish. A silvery gleam filters through skylight. Painted flats, as high as the room, lean against the wall, cycloramas of faraway places, mysterious in the half-light. There's one of a turreted castle, nestled amongst white-tipped mountains; another of a terracotta palace rising up from an emerald jungle; a third of silver halls with onion-shaped roofs against an icy shoreline.

'What *are* those?' Sporco asks, tilting his head at them.

'Those? Those are the realms,' I say with pride. 'All the places you can voyage to. Though some of them have been lost in time.'

'The realms?' he says, enjoying the sound of it in his mouth, and repeating it. 'I like them, I do.'

'The world beyond our sea is a more surprising place than you could ever imagine.'

Sporco's gaze lingers on a backdrop of a pine forest in winter, a winding path disappearing into the snow. 'This is where we're sleeping?'

I lead the way along a passage into the auditorium. Half a dozen theatre chandeliers hang at head height, extinguished for the night, groaning under their weight, brass branches and festoons of crystal drops, fantastical jellyfish in a dark sea. We jump down into the stalls and pass up the aisle, Sporco ogling the stage set, an audacious vignette of ancient times, columns receding in a false perspective.

I will never forget my first time in an opera house, in Mantua, how my fur tingled at the sight of a thousand golden stalls honeycombed to the ceiling, every box a secret in itself: a conjuration, two, three or four humans in their own little plays; candlelight catching the glint of enrapt eyes and tremors of gilt thread, the thrill of scandal whispered behind hands. When the curtains opened and the music began – when I first felt the soar of bow on strings in that room – my insides ached with joy. The piece we saw that night was as strange and beguiling as a dream. A young shepherd, a lyrist, takes a ferry to a treacherous underworld in search of his bride. He meets a god king there who has a face of shadow and a crown of fire and plays a melody for him – to win back his beloved. When I was very young, I hadn't understood music, it was just an incoherent babble, but that night in Mantua I grasped the advantage that humans had over our species, to create such marvels from contraptions of wood and metal, from mere thin air.

We go upstairs and nudge through a door into the royal box with its scent of beeswax polish, velvet, shellac. 'Here we shall sleep,' I say, nodding at the four silked armchairs. 'Kings and emperors have put their backsides on those seats.'

Sporco giggles and in a flash he's jumped up on one. He circles three times and drops down in a ball. He'll be dirtying the fabric – artisans would have spent weeks working on the silk of that chair – but let him enjoy it. I mount the adjacent throne and survey the empty stage. The silence is surprising, the absence of water lapping against pier stones, a ringing, cushioned hush in its place. 'We should stay every night,' Sporco says and within moments his eyes are closed.

Yes, he is a lost soul like I.

I witnessed his abandonment. I woke at dawn, three years ago, at the entrance to my hideaway and noticed a young man waiting on a pontoon on the other side of the water. He was twitchy, kept looking at his pocket watch, a holdall slung from one shoulder and a bundle of books tied with rope from the other. A girl hurried on to the pontoon, excited and apologetic. She too had a travelling case, which he tossed into a boat, along with his own luggage. She was no more than fifteen, neat and timid, whilst he was older by a number of years, and had a kind of dishevelled self-importance.

I hadn't seen the puppy – it had been enfolded under her cloak – but it yapped when she set it down, a bundle of gold wool skittering against its leash, a pup of five weeks. But the man refused to let him come. There was an argument, angry whispers echoing across the water. The scoundrel fastened the dog to a post and hastened the girl into the boat. It devastated her to have to leave her pet, but she was too in awe of the rake. My breath quickened as he jumped aboard and cast off towards the sea, pushing hard down on the oars.

'No! Come back!' I barked and the girl, eyes stung with tears, looked round to see where the noise came from. The poor puppy pulled against its leash, whining as his mistress vanished round the curve of the water.

I set off immediately for the abandoned puppy through the city, over the Rialto, double backing, all to arrive at a short distance from where I started. I untied his leash and asked if he'd like to come with me, but he just sat, confused, his eyes on the horizon. Eventually, I returned to my own lookout. He stayed for days, on the opposite side of the canal. After a while I found it too heartbreaking to watch and found myself looking in the opposite direction. The next time I dared peek, he was gone.

Two months passed before I chanced on him again. He had filled out into a dog, caked in dirt and reeking of the street. And, though he was surly and streetwise to begin with, I made a point of watching out for him. I never once mentioned the pontoon to him and, though I always hoped he had somehow blotted the memory from his mind, I knew it certainly must lurk there. Worse: it probably shaped everything in his life.

Indeed, we are *all* lost souls. He, I, La Perla. And it gives me no solace that I have been lost longer than any, a hundred and twenty-seven years since my master vanished on our trip to the cathedral.

At once I recall the golden weathervane and the abrupt twitches of joy I had this morning, and fear wildfires through me: what if he comes tonight? Of all nights, when I'm sleeping in another place. I sit bolt upright, resolved to return, then dismiss the idea, calling to mind the damp walls of my alcove. I'm being superstitious, that's all. I sit back down and curl up to sleep.

'Why, after a hundred and twenty-seven years, would he come tonight?'

2. The Slayed Giant

Venice, August 1688

It was nearly eighty years after the frost fair in Whitehall, that we went to visit Venice, my first time there. I'd never seen a city floating in the sea. As we'd approached the Embankment, my master grew more and more excited. 'This is the place,' he said. 'Great, great city, audacious republic, tiny but colossal. *La Serenissima*. Vain perhaps, self-regarding, but splendid, splendid. And enlightened too. Such artistry is here. You think I'm mad, don't you?' He laughed, stroking the top of my head. 'But prepare for rare treasures, my champion.' I straightened my spine and lifted my ears to the wind. It seemed like decades since I'd heard him talk in that way, or seen his eyes spark, a charge of energy about him, bright and vital as he used to be.

His life, and thus mine, could be divided into two parts. The first thirty years, from when I was a puppy, travelling between the various courts of Europe – first at Elsinore, then London, Prague, Paris, Madrid and so on – he in employ of the palace, chiefly as a doctor, but often more than that, as he had numerous talents and interests, from astronomy to engineering and the science of plants. We lived those years in comfort at the very least, and often in luxury.

The second phase of our lives had started in Amsterdam, on a dreadful August night that I try to think about as little as possible. After it, my master had embarked on his *'new beginning'*, his mission to be a doctor on the battlefield. To atone. For decades we trailed armies, sought out war – of which there seemed an endless supply in those years – and attended the injured, in body and mind. It was gruelling work and it took its toll. My master's character, and no doubt mine, gradually transfigured, as we became entirely practical creatures and a good deal of joy was washed from our lives.

Of course, it was not total hardship. Apart from the fact that years could pass between one battle and the next, there were periods when my master would enforce a break and we'd leave the trail of armies for a while. Usually we'd return to one of the courts we'd lived in before and my master would seek a spell of employment, partly for money, partly to replenish our supplies, but also to bask a little in the splendour of the old days. But sometimes he would take time off from even that and we would make an excursion that involved no work at all. 'Just you and I,' as he said. Our trip to Venice was such an interlude. So we were tired, dirty, our heads still full with the racket of armies, but in those two days we found our spirits again. Who knew they would be our last together.

We took private lodgings in a tumbledown palazzo near the Rialto, an inscrutable landlady showing us to a suite on the first floor. '*È perfetto,*' my master smiled, as he pushed open a pair of shutters, so light streamed in from the Grand Canal. I did not find the room as inviting as he, with its mismatch of furniture, bare walls and peeling plasterwork. In particular, the bed, raised from the floor like a sepulchre, with a pair of mahogany bears cresting the headboard, had a maudlin feel, but I was so accustomed to the filth of army camps by then, to sodden ground and leaking bivouacs, it was a relief to be there.

'My companion and I have come especially to see the new cathedral,' my master told the landlady. '*La nuova cattedrale. Abbiamo sentito è magnifico.*' He hoped for a reaction, but received none. 'What goes on in the *piazzale* there?' he asked instead.

She whisked her hand and shrugged. '*Festa di San Rocco.*'

My master became even more excited. 'The feast of St Roch, do you hear, my champion? The patron saint of dogs himself. Ha. Of course! Where are we? August. How auspicious to arrive today. There will be dancing for sure, at the *Festa di San Rocco. La danza?*' He nodded at the lady before setting off in a jig across the room.

He washed, changed, unpacked his things, stowing them in tidy piles. (I had always loved his neatness, it calmed me.) 'We shall view the cathedral first at a distance, from the Piazzetta at San Marco. Then we shall visit in person tomorrow. Much better to tease ourselves a little; we've waited so long. What say you, my champion? In any case, we need to go in the early morning: it will seem as if created for us.'

We set off into the boisterous throng of streets. I don't know how many times he'd visited in the past – before I came into the world – but he knew his way around like a local. We came from an alley, through an arch into a shock of space and sunlight and he laughed. '*The greatest rectangle in all civilization.* That's what I used to call it. I still do. Does it not make your hairs stand on end? Even you, my virtuoso, who has so many.'

Of all the places in the world I've known, the Piazza San Marco is the most unaltered by the years. I suspect it will be so until the very end of time. Now it is just another reminder of my loss, but then I was surely thrilled by it, the bravura of its colonnades, the startling red immensity of the campanile, the fairy-tale church and the sugar-pink palace. We weaved through the crowds, beneath the winged lion that looks out to sea, to the edge of the quay. 'Look!' My master gasped, pointing across the water. 'There! Where once was just a bog of land. Look, my champion.'

And so I saw it for the first time: the cathedral, *my* cathedral. A domed mountain of white marble so luminous that it seemed to charge the city with light. It was brand new, still scaffolded in places, with artisans at work, clipping and sanding.

'The new world, you see?' My master's hand was hot on the back of my neck and tears shone in his eyes. 'How marvellous to live in such a time of revelation. And what joy to discover it together, you and I, side by side.' He knelt and stroked me beneath the chin. 'How patient you've been. What troubles I've put you through. But here we are, safe and quiet for a spell and the world offers up its treasures.' There was a scent of cloves from a nearby skiff, the sky was clear lapis, the air still and warm – and I remember how content I was.

'My companion can be a fussy eater,' my master confided in the proprietor of the trattoria, a portly, giant smile of a man. We'd come to an exuberant locale close to the fish market, and my master had insisted I sit up at the table next to him, *for a better view*. 'He'll not eat meat, nor fish, but has a passion for beans, *fagioli*, in whatever style suits your kitchen.'

The proprietor grinned and pinched my cheek between his thumb and forefinger. '*Capisco*. An animal of distinction for sure. And for you?' he asked my master.

'Oysters. And many of them!'

After dinner, we went to the square close to our quarters where the festivity was already in full swing.

'Will it shame you greatly if I partake?' Before he'd even finished the sentence, my master was whisked into the maelstrom by a lady reveller. *That* night, I was not embarrassed by it. The opposite: it cheered me to my core to watch him sail by on his clumsy feet, forever going off in the wrong direction, apologizing and laughing all the while.

Then, a shadow seemed to fall on the square, not literally – it was night by then – but a feeling of it, an invisible pall of unease, or danger. I stood up, tense, lifting my snout and cocking my ears. Whatever it was, only *I* had sensed it, for everyone else carried on the same. For me, and only me, the music went quiet and I had the sense of a cold hand touching my heart. Through the spiral of dancers I saw a figure hurry away, a broad-shouldered man. He moved differently from everyone else, like a thief hurrying off. I went after him, but by the time I'd got through the crowd, his cloak was disappearing round a building. Cautiously, I padded to the corner and peered round, but found just an empty canal-way and a pair of vacant bridges. The cold hand inside released itself slowly – but the fear remained. There had barely been a time in my life when Vilder had not seemed to stalk us. The stranger that had once dazzled me, gliding over the frozen river in London. *'My parents owned mines, long ago. I inherited,'* he'd purred, twisting the sapphire on his finger. Although I only met him once more after Whitehall, in Amsterdam, twenty years later, he ruled our lives. Every street we turned down, we would check he did not follow. Every room we went into, we'd make sure he was not there. Every passer-by we'd scrutinize, every soldier on the battlefield, every man we ever met.

There was panic in the voice that came from behind me – 'Where are you? Where are you, my champion?' – and my master tore up the street, the lights from the dance making his shadow as high as the buildings. He found me and breathed a sigh of relief. 'You frightened me.' He grinned, hugging me, and I wondered if I should warn him in some way. But I thought I was just being superstitious. 'Enough dancing for one evening,' he said. 'Let's go home. We have much to do tomorrow.'

That night, guarded by the mahogany bears, he made a special place for me on the bed with his pillows, so I'd sleep by his head. In truth, I always preferred my own corner – but I stayed close as he wanted.

In the early-morning light, last night's worries seemed absurd, and, as my master had promised, we went to the cathedral. As soon as we crossed to the promontory of land on which it sits, we stopped dead on the arch of the bridge. Close up, it was even more magnificent. We circled it, gazing at the domes and towers, the congregation of statues staring down at us, haughty immortals dismissive of us living things. It smelt of fresh plaster, lime and furnaced iron, vital scents that have long since been overthrown and turned bland by age.

We ascended the white staircase and my master chattered, excited as a boy. 'Octagonal, you see its eight sides, ingenious, Byzantine almost. It has borrowed that from its rival church. But only that, for this building has its own rules. And the stone is Istrian, no? You see how the marble dust catches the light? They say they sank a million poles into the ground to bear this marvel. I know my boy, I am quite mad, a fool for beauty.' The doors at the top were towering, *new* bronze, not a touch of the muddled, zincy green they are now. They were open and we were about to step inside when he stopped and scanned the *fondamenta*, regarding each person in turn, before shaking his head and smiling. 'Just superstition. In Venice, of all places, I – we –' He didn't finish his sentence, just straightened his tunic. He was about to go in, but halted again. 'If we lose one another inside –' He motioned towards the multitude ascending behind us. 'If we lose one another, my champion, wait for me on the steps. Just here, by the door. Yes?' I understood precisely.

Inside, there was a sweet smoke – a sickly incense of camphor, sandalwood, myrrh and gum Arabic – that shrouded the murmuring clusters of churchgoers and tourists, turning them to dreamy shadows. At the altar, a priest swung a silver thurible and smoke arced in its wake, like a comet's tail, back and forth, accompanied by the tinkle of chains. Here and there bowls of the same incense smouldered, adding to the fog. Even then, before my master's disappearance, I hated the smell; it crept, teasingly, into my lungs and left a bitter aftertaste in my mouth. My master stopped and stared, a shaft of light from one of the high windows catching on his face. I did as he did, surprised to find a new sky, high above us, a giant cupola, a false world hiding the real one.

'Like a great crown upon our heads, is it not?' he said. 'We all become kings.' He turned on the spot. 'Eight chapels, three altars. We shall *all* be forgiven.' A chuckle. 'And look, the fresco in there. Is it Titian?' The sunlight through the window must have been hot on his face, as I remember him slipping his scarf from his neck and winding it round his wrist. It was a cherished piece, bought in a market in Florence, woven silk in a puzzle of geometric patterns.

He stepped over to the side chapel, his eye upon the ceiling. 'Titian indeed,' he thrilled. 'You see? A rare find. David and Goliath. Such ecstasy and turmoil. I met him once, here in Venice, in his studio by the Arsenale. He had a canvas, half painted, of Theseus on which I complimented him. But he did not care for me.' Another chuckle. 'Let us look closer.' He ruffled the fur on my head, before entering the annex to examine the fresco. If I'd known it would be the last time he would touch me, I would have welded myself to his side like molten metal, but I did not go with him. The chapel was busy enough, so I stood guard at the gate instead, glancing up at the picture. A muscular warrior lay upside down on a rock, slain, dead, colour drained from his body, head twisted at an angle, arm outstretched in startling perspective and a vivid splash of carmine red spilt from it on to the stone. Behind, a slight boy jutted his arms up to the heavens. The sky, otherwise a mass of brooding clouds, was ripped open in the centre and a stabbing yellow light pierced through.

Wondering why my master was so entranced by such a grim tableau, I turned the other way, facing the main chamber. More and more silhouettes were pouring through the entrance in exaggerated wigs and giant cuffs. They clutched at their companions' sleeves and muttered proclamations. As I had been at the dance, I was beset with worries once more: my master stopping at the top of the stairs had given new weight to them. Chatter whispered around the walls, bouncing off the marble floor and dancing high in the dome. Then – and again I will never know if it is a real memory, or if time has made me imagine it – but the invisible hand of yesterday, colder than the tiles beneath my paws, gently gripped my heart. My haunches went up. One man moved more quickly than the others, a shadow in the gloom. He slipped behind the columns and disappeared. The icy fingers seemed to tighten their hold and I was overpowered by dread. In an instant, fragments of memories rushed into my mind – of the night in Amsterdam when Vilder turned so violently against me, of my head striking hot brick and the smell of my fur catching light.

Light-headed, I turned back to the side chapel but my master wasn't there. I swung round, scanned the central chamber, nose and eyes. I saw him, I thought, under an arch, lighting a votive candle. Relief. I bounded over, pressed my nose to his boot, only to find it was someone else. I ran back to the chapel with the fresco, but there were three new pairs of feet, sightseers babbling reverentially, as they admired the gruesome painting. But I could still smell *him*, my master, clearly. I had an absurd thought that he had become invisible before I found his scarf on the floor. A little heap of silk where once he'd been.

My dread thickened. I circled the interior, nose to the ground. For the third time I returned to the side chapel, but it was empty now. Just the scarf coiled there. It taunted me. I went back to the votive candle. I let out a bark, calling his name. He had never left me before. My hollers were loud and coarse. 'I'm here. I'm here. Where are you?'

A warden with the build of a bargeman approached, his hard soles pounding the tiles. 'Silence in church,' he whispered angrily. '*Uscire, cane, uscire!*'

I kept on barking: 'Are you lost? I'm here.' The warden tried to seize me, but I got away, made another lap of the church in ever more desperate zigzags. Shoe to shoe. Nothing but strangers' feet. Widening horror. Then I remembered his instruction before we entered. '*If we lose one another, my champion, wait for me on the steps. Just here, by the door.*' My fear melted. I pushed through the crowd and out of the main door. He was not there. I circled on the spot, whining. I snapped back and forth down the stairs, up again, down once more, across the quay, left, right, clockwise, anti-clockwise. 'Where are you?

61

Are you lost? I'm here.' I scouted about the quays of the customs house and the passages at the back of the church. 'I'm here. I'm here. Where are you? Are you lost?' I barked until I had no voice left.

I resolved to try to find my way back to our lodgings. I tried to retrace the path we'd taken. Now I'm familiar with every alley and passage of the city and could walk them blind, but then I was baffled, exasperated and finally infuriated by the maze of seemingly identical streets. Countless times I made wrong turns, halted by a cul-de-sac or a canal. Eventually I reached the bridge of white arches, put my head down, and shouldered over it through the heaving crowds: buckled shoes, brocade heels, petticoats, overskirts, coloured ribbons and bows. I remember thinking how ridiculous humans could be, making such shows of themselves with clothes, with frills, trinkets and trimmings.

I came out, head spinning, into the great square. The Campanile stood guard, the city's sentry, colossal and plain, careless of my plight, its bells silent. I doubled back once more into the snaggle of streets until at last I found our palazzo. I had to bark and bark until the landlady let me in. I raced past her up to our rooms. There was no sign he'd returned, no new smells of him, no candles lit. His things were left exactly as he'd laid them out that morning. Neat piles. The room, with its bare walls and peeling plasterwork, its miscellany of mismatched furniture, its bed guarded by mahogany bears, was sinister now.

I was half aware of the landlady hovering in the doorway. '*Sei solo?* Are you alone?' she said in her high, prim voice. 'Where is the gentleman?'

In the early hours, when the streets were empty, I returned to the cathedral, mounted the pale flight of steps, but found the bronze doors closed. As soon as they opened in the morning, I slipped in without the wardens seeing me and tiptoed to the side chapel where I had last seen my master. On the ceiling, the warrior lay slain on the rock, upside down, with blood drizzled from his skull. Below it, the room was empty.

Even my master's scarf was gone.

3. The Vigil

*Venice, 1688–1815, the hundred and twenty-seven
years I have spent waiting*

It's extraordinary how whole decades can pass as if in a dream,
how one hour can turn like a hundred years and a hundred
years like one hour. To begin with, I never strayed from the
steps. Not having my alcove then, I camped wherever I could
find shelter, butted against the walls of the customs house,
beneath the window ledges of the church or ensconced on
nearby skiffs and gondolas – anywhere as long as I had a view
of the front of the church. '*If we lose one another, my champion,
wait for me on the steps. Just here, by the door.*' I turned my nose to
every shoe and boot that passed, thousands upon thousands of
them, the dull and banal odours of *other* humans, not my
master's vital scent: midnight in a tall forest, stiff parchment
paper, a whisper of pine sap.

In those first years, I dreaded, above all else, the onslaught
of winter, weeks of grey drizzle smudging the city, the first
chimneys lit, before the chill set in, making the canals smoke
and cobblestones sweat with frost. And then, in the bitterest
weeks, in the darkest vale of the season, humans would put on
masks, grotesque versions of their real faces and flap through
the city like giant insects, congregating behind quickly closing doors, as orchestras struck up in unseen halls. In those
weeks, however tightly I curled up to sleep, the flagstones

stayed cold beneath me, the chill would insinuate my bones and the same twitchy nightmare would haunt my slumber: a babble of sightseers, silhouettes and periwigs, sweet smoke and swinging thurible. And always, when I woke, teeth chattering and eyes sore, a fresh charge would fire through me, and I'd stand, fur prickling hot and cold.

No, he never came. I never saw him, smelt him. I never felt him.

Eventually, I had the idea to leave the island and search elsewhere. I'd learnt from my master how to travel, how to navigate by the sun, who instinctively to trust and who to be wary of. I did not have gold to pay my way, but I could charm a wagoner. Humans possess a fascination for our species, and an innate kindness that they do not always have for each other. I thought of all the places my master and I had been long ago, but being perpetual wanderers, there was nowhere I could call home, no particular place to begin my search. My master never spoke, as all other people did at some point, of the place he grew up, or his 'family'. Only once, in all our time together, when we went into hiding in the Carpathian Mountains after fleeing Holland, did I hear him mention the words 'mother' and 'father'. There was never mention of 'sisters' or 'brothers'. He had that self-contained quality that only children have. But neither were there 'aunts', 'uncles' or 'cousins', no 'relations', or 'ancestral seat', or 'birthplace'.

And he hadn't married either. Despite the fact he'd fallen in love, I was sure, more than once. Despite the fact he was always more comfortable with women than with men, that he appreciated them on a profound level, talked more to them, shared confidences and fears that he'd never admit to his own sex. But of course it didn't give him, or me, any comfort at all that he would need to end any liaison before it had fully come to life – and I knew why: his sense of right and wrong demanded it. So, there was no specific place to go, which he and I had made our home. And besides –

'If we lose one another, my champion, wait for me on the steps. Just here, by the door.'

I delayed time and time again, but one morning when the agony of inaction, of not knowing, became too fierce, I crept on to a ship unnoticed. My heart banged as the last of the cargo was loaded and the boat readied to set sail. 'Tomorrow we begin again,' I reassured myself. For a moment I was emboldened, then straight away terrified. I jumped ashore as the gangplank was being raised, hurried back to the church, thrilled with relief for not having left. For once, the sweet smoke inside gave me a punch of hope, a connection with him, but on visiting the side chapel, with its painting of the slayed giant, now with its colours slightly faded, and finding the room bare, the taste grew acrid again. For hours, even into the night, I snouted the front steps, up and down, up and down, checking and double checking until I thought I would lose my mind. There was not so much as an atom of him. But I never let it enter my mind that he wouldn't come back, that he might be dead, that he might not exist any more.

One day, a young man passed that I recognized, the musketeer son of a duke with whom my master had been friends in the decade before we came to Venice. I'd almost forgotten the idyllic summer we'd spent, between our campaigns, in their palazzo at Lake Garda for the young man's marriage. The whole family had so doted on me, they'd joked of kidnapping. And there he was in Venice, with his father still, both unchanged. I followed them barking, until the old duke stopped, peered round and I realized my mistake. *He* was the son, the once musketeer, his visage sunken and shrivelled with age, its vigour gone and a muddle of irritation in its place. His moustache, once acrobatic with expression, the badge of an intrepid adventurer, was painted on now, and not well, one side shorter than the other. He stared at me, baffled, before the young man, who I'd never met, put his hand to his father's shoulder to ease him on his way.

No one noticed me. Why should they? I was just a dog like any other. Only I knew the obscure secret of my age. I often passed by the little palazzo where we'd taken lodgings. '*My companion and I have come especially to see the new cathedral.*' One day I found the doors open and voices coming from the upstairs windows where our room had been. It was ludicrous in the extreme to think my master might have been there, just a short journey from the place we'd been separated, but I was too muddled by loss to be logical. I ran up the stairs and nudged through the door. I found an office, a pawnbroker's den, with shelves of random chattels where the great mahogany bed had been. How it saddened me to find the pair of bears gone. A brash young broker, his feet on the desk, was shaking his head as an old man offered desperate pleas.

'See it from my point of view,' the pawnbroker bragged, 'if I help you, I have to help everyone.' He noticed me and cursed, half getting to his feet. 'Out of here! Get out.'

By then, bitter cold had taken hold again and turned the sky to iron. In the streets, the people lucky enough to have cloaks or furs had buttoned them tight against the north wind. As a crowd of children herded past me, I saw him, my master, his back to me, waiting on the steps of an alleyway church, curled sandy hair, a grey cloak thrown over his shoulder. *He has gone mad*, I thought, *he's waiting at the wrong doors. That is not our cathedral.* I hollered at him and when he moved off, I chased him down the street, surprised by his cologne – bergamot and bitter orange – wondering if it was a new habit of his to wear it.

Finally I overtook him. He was not my master. This man had a small nose, thin lips and an ineffectual air, the opposite of my master. He'd done me no harm, but I glowered at him nonetheless.

Over the years I have made many human friends, all gone now, bones cold under the ground or dissolved beneath the sea, but my first true companion in Venice was Angelique. I came upon her outside Florian's in San Marco, secreted beneath the arcade, sun slanting against her face, a book open in front of her. I was intrigued that she sat alone, before I realized I knew her already. She lived in an apricot palazzo close to my cathedral and passed me sometimes, head down, trailing a scent of alkanet and belladonna. She was about thirty I guessed, and had a shy beauty, somehow enhanced by the porcelain-thin cleft that ran from her nose to her mouth, slightly buckling her upper lip.

She noticed me. *'Je pense que nous nous connaissons?'* she said, her voice as warm as the sunlight on the pages of her book. I was drawn to her side, where I found her odour was more mysterious than I'd realized: like a souk at night, or an untamed tropical garden. She took off her glove, lay her hand on my neck and the heat of it sent a tremor down my spine. 'You're a gentleman, no? A softly spoken knight?' After coffee, she stood up. 'I have to go. *Enchanté, mon seigneur,'* she said, curtsying. I followed at a distance. 'You're coming?' she said.

I had never intended to take another master or a mistress, it was unthinkable, and I certainly would not have accepted her offer to stay in her house had she not lived in plain sight of the cathedral – but when she opened her door and beckoned me with a smile, I caught once more her scent of alkanet and belladonna – I could not resist.

Her situation at home was unhappy. Her brooding husband, a fur merchant, lived separately on the palazzo's piano nobile – the first floor, as the Italians call it – and only ever spoke to her to scold or criticize. He had many personal callers, courtesans who would trail mockingly up and down past Angelique's rooms at the back of the building, but even then he would often come in the dead of night, pull down his breeches and rut her from behind.

Despite this, and the fact, I sensed, she'd lost a child, as she often talked to a picture of a dreamy-eyed girl that hung over the fireplace, she was contagious with unexpected joy. She, like my master, took interest in things and people that others of her rank would ignore. We were forever going on mischievous trips, to spice bazaars or silk markets or gem emporiums. I recall her closing her eyes as she touched the faces of statues, or stifling giggles at a recital of harpsichords, or insisting we slip, uninvited, into a gondoliers' dance.

In time she grew sick, turning first hot, then so cold that her skin coarsened like rock. All her enticing aromas deserted her, the whites of her eyes browned, her kidneys and liver stank of abscesses and diarrhoea slipped down her legs, browning her petticoats. I watched, ears folded back, as she vomited thick nubs of blood, and I longed for my master, that he might help her with one of his medicines. She shivered for days beneath a blanket and her husband never came. One night, she pushed open her windows to find the sky awash with stars. She sat, out of breath, peering up at them, then turned to me, and her smile became a question mark.

After they'd put her body into a crate, rolled it down the stairs and taken it away, her husband chained me up in the cellar like a rat-catcher, until I found a chance to escape and return to the cathedral steps. It was some months later when it struck me, quite plainly, that the picture of the girl that she spoke to had a cleft above her lip too and was not her daughter, but her younger self.

Some years later, I met Jerome, a fast-talking, always-laughing bachelor, who rented rooms behind the cathedral. In his younger days, I was certain, he'd had a daring life at sea, and though his work was no longer intrepid, filling ledgers with information about ships, he kept his sense of adventure. His rooms were alive with fascinating comings and goings, all-night card games, musicians and artists. The various ladies in his life were so charmed by him, and so like-able and fascinating themselves, there was never any rancour. He had a manservant, Benjamin, who bore the scars of slave ships, and was a lion of a human: unprejudiced, intelligent and almost heartbreakingly faithful. Jerome returned one night drenched in blood, a gash in his abdomen, his fingers bare where he'd been robbed of his jewels, and died in Benjamin's arms. The poor man cried for days on end, and when Jerome's plain sister arrived with her ungracious children, she gave Benjamin short shrift, refusing even his request for a keep-sake of his master's hair. After the funeral, I went with him, saw him off on a ship for the mainland – to what I have no idea – and he was crying still.

I returned to Jerome's freshly filled grave and lurked into the night, growing furious with the world: the trickery of it, the pointlessness, humans and animals born simply to suffer, for the pain to invariably worsen with age, for anguish to thicken and veins clog, until they were skidding down to death, to one of the cold-hearted graves that lay about me. Why? Even the fortunate people, those whose special lives began in cosy wood-panelled nurseries, a trill of softly spoken humans leaning over the cot, even *they* were doomed, before long, to disease or madness, and certainly death. And for dogs, meaner still, more than a decade of existence was miraculous before limbs stiffened, backs ached, tumours grew from ravages of matter, memory broke up and dissolved, breath rattled, and then . . .

I had never felt as lonely as I did in that churchyard. In the morning I went to the cathedral and looked at the painting of the slayed giant. I'd always focused on the dead giant, but it was the boy who gave me hope that day. That and my master's words:

'Tomorrow we begin again.'

Times changed, over the passage of drizzled autumns, long winters and stenching summers, and fashions too: the age of powder and panniers, of elaborate headdresses and white wigs. Sometimes I'd wake up, in the strange half-light of early morning, or puzzled and headachy from a daytime nap, and forget which era I was in. In my mind, I'd slipped back to a past time, half a century ago or more, when smells were different, softer, harsher, coarser, gentler, an age when men wore wide ruffs or short boots or lace collars, and drank mead, eau-de-vie, juniper gin, corn brandy, Armagnac. Sometimes I'd even return to the time when we were still together, my master and I. I'd wake, puffed up and proud, my fur like velvet. For minutes, hours sometimes, I felt so content, so warmed through, so excited by possibilities, that I didn't care that it had only been a fantasy.

Awake, I thought of him ceaselessly. I checked every shoe and boot that passed. Even when I was occupied with other thoughts or people, he reappeared in an endless loop, with every tenth beat of my heart. And lurking beyond him, always, in the dark architecture of my mind, was Vilder, the man who had tried to kill me. The monster – I was sure – who had taken my beloved.

Such was my vigil. Over the decades I would make new companions: soldiers, dukes, gondoliers, marble-cutters. But they would die, all of them, from disease, or old age. And I'd become friends with dogs – street dogs, house dogs, palazzo dogs – and they'd perish too. A person who keeps dogs will lose many in their lifetime. I was a dog who lost people. Time took from me everyone and everything I'd fallen in love with.

But I was sure, in the very core of me, that one day my true master would return. For if I was still alive, surely so was he.

4. The Deluge

Venice, May 1815

In my dream, the weathervane, the golden goddess astride the
customs house, comes to life at dawn. The boatmen and customs counters, still sleepy as they arrive for work, don't notice
the miniature spirit spring from her perch and take to the
amethyst sky, little wings carrying her across the city, over the
canals and bell towers to the opera house. She finds the front
doors barred, but slips through the glass, then the walls, and
into the auditorium. She circles once, her shadow flying fast
across the painted dome of heavens, before coming to land on
the balustrade of the royal box. Two dogs are fast asleep there,
I one of them. She whispers in my ear, telling of good news . . .

In the opera house, I wake and stand straight up, listening.
There is an unusual clarity in my head and all around me. It's
morning and several theatre chandeliers, now lit, are being
raised. The jingle of glass is both ethereal and lucid. Light
inches up the wall of the stall, making the crimson silk throb.
My fur tingles, inexplicably so. I steal from my chair and peer
over the parapet. A lady is pacing the stage, half in costume.
A pair of set decorators are at work, whilst a handful of other
men lounge about the stalls. Everything is sharp and clear,
but has a peculiar otherworldliness too. A pianist strikes up
and the costumed lady begins to sing musical scales, notes rising to a falsetto, descending, then rising again.

'What's happening?' Sporco says.

'Sssh!' I tell him, not because I'm frightened of being discovered – what can they do but throw us out? – but so I can understand the sensations that are assailing me.

Doors below swing open and a man strides in, velvet jacket, grey ponytail, self-important, the director, with a trail of assistants in his wake. He claps. '*Buongiorno, tutti. Tancredi* by Gioachino Rossini,' he declares. 'Act One, Argino's palace in Syracuse.'

'Let's go,' I say.

Leaving the compartment and retracing our steps down to the front hall, I feel dizzy, the stairs seem alive and unanchored to the press of my paws. At the bottom, the front doors are still locked, but a barred window, close to the ground, is open. Drawn to it, I put my snout through and take a draught of the air outside – and at once a heady charge shakes through me as I realize.

He is here. My master has returned to the city.

For an insane moment, I believe it, but almost immediately I discount the notion as fantasy. It's impossible I could smell him even if he was. But it's not a smell; it's a *sense*. That special awareness I always had for my master, which I believe all dogs possess for the ones they love. In the decades we were together, there were a handful of times he had to hurry off and leave me with a friend. He might be gone for days, but I knew precisely when he would return, when I'd hear his carriage approach. I put my face to the window again, but this time I listen rather than smell, closing my eyes to the infinite sounds of the city, and suddenly I can see him, in my mind's eye. I can see my master ascend the steps of the cathedral and halt before the front door, looking for me.

He is here.

74

My heart races. I try, idiotically, to push through the bars of the window, but they're too close together.

'What's happened?' says Sporco.

I turn from the window and rush past him – no time for his clowning now – and dive through the doors into the auditorium. 'I'm coming! I'm coming!' I bark to my master. It's lunacy: he can't hear me inside the building. I pound down the aisle through the theatre. Its thousand honeycomb stalls are the colour of galaxies. A new stage flat is coming to land: pretend castle, flying buttresses and dark orange sky. 'I'm here!'

'*Che cos' è?*' says the director, appalled. 'Dogs? Who brought dogs in here?'

I bound on to the stage and the opera singer gasps and gallops to the wings, half her costume coming off in a cloud behind her. Sporco scampers after us, thinking it's a game. 'Whose dogs are these?' bawls the director, as everyone in the stalls gets to their feet.

I race behind the stage, to the scene dock where we entered, but the way to it is locked. I double back, avoiding the gang of theatre people pursuing us, into a corridor where the dressing rooms are, flying in and out of each, searching for an escape, Sporco scampering at my heels, laughing. 'Fun, eh? Chases. Adventures. Hurrah!' Going into the last of the rooms, the door slams shut behind us.

'They can stay there until someone comes for them,' says the director behind it, and a lock turns.

I try to push the door open, bashing at the handle. 'Let me out! Let me out!' But all the footsteps retreat and there comes the sound of another door slamming shut at the end of the passage, blocking all sound completely. 'Let me out!' The room doesn't even have a window. 'Let me out!' I circle the walls, bashing through the congregation of mannequins that are pinned with costumes. I go round and round, every time returning to the door, hammering my shoulder against it, dragging my claws up and down against the lock. 'Let me go!' I've become one of those halfwit dogs that whines for things it'll never receive. Sporco watches me, no longer having fun, his ears stuck out in bewilderment.

Calm, I eventually tell myself. *He is here, that is all that matters.* I have waited and he has come. I am sure of it. To escape I must be methodical and calm. My chest heaves. Methodical. No sooner does my panic melt, it comes again, for I can't sense him any more. I snout the air for that special odour – midnight in the tall forest, stiff parchment paper, a whisper of pine sap – but there's nothing. I close my eyes, try to imagine him on the steps of the cathedral, but in my panic I can't remember what he looks like. I bark and bark until I have no voice left.

Finally, in the afternoon, footsteps return, the door is unlocked and opened. 'I must go,' I pant to Sporco, tearing out before anyone can stop me, through a jumble of legs, dressers with armfuls of clothes, singers readying for the show. This time, the scene dock is open, I charge across it and exit back on to the canal-way. Perhaps it's just the excitement of escape, but I'm sure I sense him again, a scintilla of him.

On I gallop, to Dorsoduro, back to my alcove, on fire inside – passages, canal-ways, bridges, until at last the cathedral rises from the sea, the sun behind it, like a giant with its back turned. I have looked on that building a thousand times, but never has my heart raced so fast.

I go to the steps, trance-like, on air it seems, burning all over, the colours and smells of the city so intense I could throw my head back and howl. A mob of choristers – boys in white surplices, boisterous and noisy – are on the threshold of the church, waiting to be issued in for evensong. '*Buonasera, cane,*' they say as I barge through.

I press my nose to the stones. At once a shock: he was here! Yes. But no sooner have I caught the scent it eludes me. '*Buonasera, Signor Cane.*' Two children stroke me and I snap them away and they laugh. I zigzag down, probing each step. Dizzying shreds of him. Midnight in a tall forest, stiff parchment paper, a whisper of pine sap. The choir master gives an order, choristers file in, and I go with them.

The church is like a dusky jewel-box inside. Statues watch me and sweet smoke hangs in the air: camphor, sandalwood, myrrh, gum Arabic. No blend on earth is more thrilling or appalling. For a century congregations have poured in and out, but the incense survives. I inch forward, peering up at the cupola.

'*Like a great crown upon our heads, is it not?*'

He turned on the spot and a shaft of light from a high window slanted on his face. The organ starts up, a morose end-of-the-world dirge that plunges right through me. I pad round, behind the altar, to the side chapel.

'*And the fresco there. Is it Titian?*'

The slayed giant, colours muted now. The warrior upside down, head twisted, spilt blood. The spot where his scarf fell still empty. I paste my nostrils to the tiles, inhaling over and over.

I return to the front steps and survey the port, back straight, ears alert. The city is not as it was yesterday, not as it has been for a hundred and twenty-seven years. It rings with a new possibility. A troop ship is docking, soldiers coming ashore. He's not amongst them. I snout along the quay, this way and that, like one of those lunatic spaniels maddened by a scent it can't trace.

There's no proof of my master, no certainty, but still I'm teased by the sense of him.

I wait, sitting precisely halfway up the steps, in the perfect place, darting my head to every passing human. Minutes pass, then hours, and I begin to wonder if my mind is playing tricks, after the upset of La Perla yesterday. I look up at the golden weathervane, but she is still and rooted to her perch. Gradually, my conviction begins to fall away. I fret about whether I should go and search other places, the northern harbour perhaps, or even to the Arsenale in the east, but I'm too frightened to move: '*If we lose one another, my champion, wait for me on the steps. Just here, by the door.*'

At sunset, clouds start to mass, and the sky turns the colour of gunmetal. For a while, there comes a taut silence over the lagoon, before the sea whips into rolling waves and the boats along the quay bounce furiously to the incessant strum of rope on mast. Knowing a storm is coming, people begin to hurry, all wind-blown hair, tailcoats and skirt hems, dancing bonnet ribbons and laughter – the adventure of weather. On the other side of the Grand Canal, a hotel awning flaps and a wall of scaffolding that fronts a building groans.

At once there's a collective gasp and Venetians take off as a wave licks up and crashes across the pavement, almost to the cathedral steps. There's a beat of thunder, lightning zigzags the sky and for a split second it's coruscating white. Rain starts to fall, first in a thick, gouty patter, then lashing curtains that set the weathervane spinning. My master loved storms and I wonder if that's a sign. In the distance, over the sea on the Giudecca, cypress trees sway crazily and a slash of phosphorescence rends the sky. I retreat to the shelter of my den, eyes fixed on the steps as the downpour bombards the city. Soon I seem to be the only creature left in it.

Later that night, when the tempest has finally passed, the church has closed and the quayside is a battleground of puddles, Sporco returns. 'The rain, huh?' He see-saws his head and saucers his eyes. 'Catastrophe, isn't it?' His preposterous ears split in different directions as he waits for a reply. He hovers by my den, but I don't speak, don't even ask him how he found his way back from the opera house. A dark thought is stumbling around in my head: what if my master has another dog at his side? Perhaps they came to the cathedral early this morning and sat on the steps. This other dog may have wondered what they were doing there. It would be a younger animal, compact, one of those little hunting terriers he was always petting in the street, a dog full of tricks, not shy or sullen, like I became sometimes – when once I had been the dog that always smiled. Maybe he just happened to be passing through Venice and thought he might as well see the old church. I lost a dog here once, he might have thought, a good animal, but untraceable now. He'd remember me for a few moments before departing with his new partner. I stay up all night, my eyes riveted to the spot where he told me to wait.

Five days after I thought he'd returned, I enter the church and go back to the side chapel. Within it, on a bench, a man is slumped, comatose, a reek of brandy and sweet tobacco about him. He wears an old-fashioned frock coat, the type of gilded, over-embroidered garment that dandies sported decades ago, but never seen any more. He looks old from behind, but his hair is thick and dark. Usually I have nothing but compassion for the dispossessed, but I resent him being there, sleeping off drunkenness in this hallowed place. I have half a mind to nudge him awake to send him on his way, when I notice some valuables have fallen from his pocket on to the floor: a silver timepiece, a handkerchief and a miniature portrait, the type that humans carry sometimes. It's half hidden under the handkerchief, but the watch looks fine and I wonder if it truly belongs to him or if he's stolen it. Then I notice the insignia in the centre of the dial – and my breath catches in my throat.

Three towers beneath a crescent moon.

The inside of the cathedral spins in silence and bile inches up my throat. I examine the man afresh: clothes that belong to another era, which no one wears any more, the kind I've not seen in a half a century, soiled by journeying certainly, but of a high quality. I paw the handkerchief to one side and a fresh shock jolts me. It's a miniature portrait of my master, younger than as I remember him, elegant and rested. After more than a century, after all the excitement of today, he comes back as a picture! In token form. His eyes stare up from the floor, vivid nuggets of cobalt blue, unaware that I, his champion, his beloved, his partner in all things, stand before them. There's a rasp of phlegm, the sleeping man wakes, sits up and I dart behind a pillar. Blood bangs around my brain as I try to comprehend.

It is the fiend. Our nemesis. The man who surely took my master from me. He has lasted as I have.

Vilder.

5. The Man From the Past

Venice, May 1815

He's altered beyond recognition. His face, which once seemed bathed in a Mediterranean glow, is a pale outcrop of quartz, a face on which sunlight, or any light, has not shone in generations. His eyes, treasures of tourmaline before, are rounds of discontent, sinkholes into the unknown. His legs are skinny, his upper body stout, all his athleticism gone. Only his ringlets of inky black have vigour still. A lunatic thought occurs to me: that it was he, not my master, who I sensed all along, that I detected his presence in the city and it was so startling that it played a trick on my mind.

He reaches inside his pocket, retrieves a little bottle, and half turning his back, takes a swig, before pocketing it again. His shoulders loosen and his pupils swim and I recall how he acted in Whitehall, when he drank the 'tonic' my master made for him. Then I knew little of the world, and had no sense of what it meant to be so charmed by opiates as to be addicted to them. Particularly during the last hundred years I've witnessed them ravage lives first-hand.

Vilder realizes his things have dropped to the floor and scoops them up, mumbling. He puts the watch, coins and handkerchief into his coat pocket, but keeps hold of the portrait. He pushes himself to his feet, using the wall to balance and – the once legend that glided over the frozen Thames – shambles over to the side chapel and stares up at the painting of the slayed giant. When a priest comes, Vilder collars him and shows him the miniature.

'*Conosci quest'uomo?* Do you know this man?' His voice is gravelled, like the low notes of a church organ. 'Have you seen him?'

The priest glances primly at Vilder, who impatiently taps his finger against the frame. The priest shrugs. 'No.'

'Idiot,' Vilder growls at the priest as trots away. 'You think all this will bring you an afterlife? It will not.' He spies a trio of young choristers and intercepts them, this time forcing a friendlier tone. '*Mi scusi, ragazzi*, do you recognize this gentlemen in the picture? Have you seen him about the cathedral?' He takes a gold coin from his pocket and holds it to the light. 'For whoever can help me.' This captures the boys' attention and they study the painting keenly.

'*Un Veneziano?*' asks one.

'*Quando era qui?*' another.

'*Credo che lo conosco. Lui è un avvocato,*' says a third.

'Never mind.' Vilder tuts, indicating with a sweep of his hand that the negotiation is over. He crosses the transept and they follow until he turns and hisses them away. He halts a few more people, showing them the portrait, but receiving no information, he makes for the door.

Just as I come from my hiding place he turns and is about to see me when a beam of sunlight – surely the same shaft, through the same window, that blinded my master on the day he disappeared – falls upon his face. He tosses his head as if to shake the light off, before continuing, lurching out of the church. My heart pulses in slow, palpable bangs.

From the top of the steps I watch him weave through the crowds: sailors embarking, cabals of fast-talking merchants, customs men, porters with barrows. Occupying the whole south section of the harbour, platoons of infantrymen perch on kits, playing cards and dice, waiting to board the troop ship that docked the morning I came from the opera house. Vilder passes amongst them, eyeing up every face before alighting on a sergeant, showing him the miniature and starting up a conversation. The sergeant studies it distractedly, before shaking his head. Vilder shuffles on, showing the picture to anyone who has time to look. I shadow at a distance, not wanting to lose sight of him, but wary of getting too close and being recognized.

Some time later, when he's all but given up and slumped on a window ledge of the customs house, a young soldier goes up to him and asks to see the likeness. '*Ja*,' the man says with a certainty that makes Vilder get to his feet. 'I've seen him.'

'Really? When? Where?'

'Five or six days ago.' The soldier points across the sea. 'In Mestre.'

'Are you sure?'

'Yes. He came to the field hospital and asked if he could help. I remember because it was strange. He was good for nothing this man.'

'Good for nothing?' says Vilder and the soldier does a mime drawing in his cheeks and showing the whites of his eyes.

'In no state to help.'

Vilder bristles at this. 'What happened to him?'

The man shrugs. 'We came here. I didn't see him again.'

Vilder pushes some money into his palms, and sets off. He's so distracted, he forgets his hat and comes back for it. There comes a twang of rope from the ship in front of me, followed by a chorus of cries. A crate unravels from its fastening, drops and shatters. A cloud of vivid lemon-yellow powder mushrooms up, followed by billows of lapis blue. The crowd freezes in unison, dazzled, some clapping. 'It'll be taken from your salary,' a man calls out, making his fellow workers laugh. I half think the city's dissolving, like a painting dropped in water – before realizing that the smashed crate contains pigments. Clouds of colour drift out to sea, a rainbow mist, before the whole place becomes frenetic again, as boats begin to depart in rapid succession. For a moment, I lose Vilder in the chaos, before spotting him on the troop ship, slipping some money to the sergeant.

Without thinking, I make a dash for the gangplank, but stop, terrified. '*If we lose one another, my champion, wait for me on the steps. Just here, by the door.*' I have not left Venice in a hundred and twenty-seven years. But the soldier pointed across the sea. 'He came to the field hospital,' he said. I wonder if it's safe to board a ship with Vilder, or if I should take another. No, I don't wish to lose sight of him. He is all I have of my master.

I wait for the way to clear, before darting up the gangplank, leaping aboard, skirting the rim of the bulwark and hiding under a tarpaulin at the prow. I inch my head up over the parapet. The deck keels. Vilder skulks like a giant crow amongst the troops and once more smuggles his bottle of tonic from his pocket, takes a sip and puts it back. Behind him the cathedral dome looms. My cathedral. Every part of me, every muscle, tendon and hair, tingles with uncertainty, but I stay my ground. I'm aware of a sashay of hair sweeping up the ramp, and there comes a roguish bark.

'Where are you?' Sporco has followed me on board, the oaf. They'll find me out straight away. 'Where are you?' he

84

calls again. I put my head up, furious. He races over. 'Hiding, huh?' He spins round idiotically, trying to catch his tail.

'Get off.' I punch his snout with my paw. 'Off with you. Now.'

'I like boats I do. I slept in one once. Cosy, cosy.'

'Off with you.' Vilder has turned his ear, hearing dogs. If it weren't for the pair of infantrymen standing in his way, he'd see us. Sporco burrows under the tarpaulin, snaking round until only his head sticks out, like the cartoon of a dog in a bonnet. 'Off with you!'

It's too late: the boatswain calls out and the ship lurches from the quay and banks of oars start cutting through the water.

Sporco rolls out his tongue. 'Setting sail, huh? Where we going? Adventures, huh?'

I push my weight against him to make him keep quiet, and the boat picks up speed. As soon as we arrive at a port, I shall put him on the first transport back. Dozens of them ferry back and forth daily. The water is choppy and Vilder keeps losing his balance. 'You can sit?' a soldier says to him, motioning towards a space on a bench at the side of the deckhouse.

'I am fine,' Vilder replies. He teeters towards us and I duck, before he turns the other way and goes to the prow instead, where he holds on to the rail, looking towards the mainland. I do not take my eyes off him for one moment.

'Who is he?' Sporco asks, before he realizes something and gasps. 'It's not, is it? Is it him?' He pivots his head from Vilder to me, to Vilder and back to me again. 'Your master?' he barks.

'Sssh!' I bash him. 'Stay down.' It was not long after Sporco came to live in my quarter and noticed how closely I watched men disembarking from ships that I told him I was waiting for someone. *'He's coming back, but I don't know when,'* I said then, and many times since, and he's always nodded knowingly. *'Your master, that's right,'* he'd say, as if, in fact, I was deluded.

'No,' I tell him now. *'He* is not my master. But he was a companion of his.'

'Really?' Sporco studies Vilder with exaggerated interest, which makes me wonder if he still thinks I'm imagining things. 'He must be important for you to get on a ship and go.'

I don't reply, just peer back at Venice, at the shrinking lineaments of her domes and bell towers and a primal panic prickles all over me: I have left my city.

Little more than an hour later, we approach the mainland, the cream-coloured port of Mestre. A melody comes from the harbour, not the music I admire, but banal army jingles, marching pipes and bugles. The sergeant gives an order and the troops assemble at the bow, blank faces and rounded shoulders, like sacks waiting to be unloaded. Even in his decrepit state, Vilder is an exotic amongst them, a haughty parrot to their drab pigeons. The frigate bumps the sea wall, everyone jolts forward and the gangplank is lowered. Vilder goes first.

'Let's go,' I say, vaulting the balustrade on to dry land, Sporco coming after me. When we see what's there, we freeze, our tails disappearing under our bellies in unison. The harbour teems with soldiers, thousands of them. The world of men – the lowly, the lofty, nervy cadets, seasoned professionals, swaggerers and drunkards – and their smells too: tobacco, gin, flax, saltpetre, steel and sweat. Everywhere the hubbub that came to background my life: the click and rattle of muskets, shearing of metal, buckle of armour and the low burr of camaraderie and exhaustion. I follow Vilder with my eyes as he pushes through the battalions, studying faces.

Sporco's hackles go up as a brace of horses clip by. He's never seen such creatures before, for there are none in our city. The odd cart mule maybe, but not beasts this size with colossal skulls and oiled flanks. He barks at a passing coach, having lived only in a toy world of gondolas and rowing boats. In truth, though I once spent my life jostling up and down on hard carriage floors, I'm taken aback too. For more than a century I've not heard the din of traffic or the grind of wheels on cobbles, and never so much of it then as now.

Vilder has gone over to a group of cavalry officers lunching at a table and is showing them the picture. Most of them ignore him, whilst others reply with shrugs. When he shambles on, in his outmoded frock coat, grimacing and talking to himself, they snigger at his expense. Despite everything, I can't help but feel indignation on his behalf. I've always found cavalry the vainest soldiers. They'd have no notion of the immensity of Vilder's life, the voyages he must have taken, as I have, from the Atlantic to the Pontic Seas, and the great men and women he would doubtless have known. No, if these cavalry officers with their boastful lives knew even half of what Vilder and I have had to necessarily learn, they'd surely be kinder human beings.

There's a blare of pipes, a cumulative shouting of orders and all the soldiers littering the quays press on to troop carts and the vehicles muster into lines. They begin filing out of the square, and Vilder speeds up his search for a while before giving in. He comes back towards us at the edge of the water, moving with such purpose I fear he's spotted me, but he alights instead upon a carriage waiting at a nearby jetty. I'd been so engrossed with his movements, I hadn't noticed it. And even then, it takes me some moments to recognize.

Vilder's old carriage.

I have not seen it in almost two centuries, not since Amsterdam, when he arrived in it with his dreadful cargo. Then it had been so glorious – like a vast precious stone of dark brown magicked from the night, the colour and lustre of smoky quartz – it had made me bashful. Now, like its owner, it's worn and unloved. Its wheels, which were elegantly high and as fine as spider's legs, have been replaced by the fatter, more modern variety, which don't suit it. Its mud-splattered hull is scratched all over and its windows spored with mould and clouded with age as to be virtually opaque. One of the doors is open and legs stick out.

Vilder kicks them. 'Wake up, you oaf.' Another kick. 'Braune.' The man gets to his feet, straightening his driver's livery, putting on his cap. 'Is this what I pay you for? Have you seen him?'

'No, sire.'

'Well, you wouldn't when you're sleeping.' Vilder smacks him across the cheek, undaunted by the fact Braune is at least a head taller than he, and built well.

'Forgive me, sire.'

' "Forgive me, sire." Imbecile. Fetch me a drink.'

The lad takes a flagon from the perch, uncorks it and passes it to him. After one sip, Vilder spits it out. 'Not water. A drink! Never mind.' He reaches into the carriage and snatches a decanter from a shelf – those clever ledges held up with little silver hands – and slugs it down. Neat brandy. 'Follow the army.'

'Where do they go, sire?'

'Does it matter where they go? Follow them.' He gets into the compartment and slams the door, before falling back out of sight.

Braune mounts his perch, takes up his whip and sets off, joining the stream of vehicles draining from the harbour front. Now I must deal with Sporco.

'No time to lose,' I say, motioning him over to where some civilian ships are moored. There's a barge with its sails strung up on the point of departure. It's Venetian; I can tell from the escutcheon of a winged lion on its prow. 'This ship will take you home. Stay down and you'll not be discovered.' Pause, deep breath, a scintilla of remorse. 'Goodbye then.' Sporco's outsize ears shift in a curious ballet as he tries to grasp my meaning. 'I have a long journey. So I say goodbye, my friend.'

'Huh? Where are you –?'

'I? The opposite way.' I nudge him on to the bulwark of the ship. 'Keep down and you'll be in the city in no time.' Vilder's carriage has already overtaken a portion of the army.

'And you –?'

I make sure there is cool formality to my tone. 'Goodbye now.'

'I'm coming with you!' he barks, jumping back ashore, see-sawing from his front legs to his back. 'Adventures, huh? Off to the realms, are we?'

'No!' My growl is sharp and this time I bear my teeth.

His eyes fill with surprise and at once I recall the beginning of his life, his abandonment on the pontoon. 'But – are we not a pack?'

My ears stick up in surprise. I've given him no reason to think that. It's ludicrous. We're strays from the same corner of a city, that's all. I want to tell him that I've had hundreds of friends, thousands perhaps, all gone now, and I'm not looking for more.

'*Vai!* Out of the way!' comes a voice and men heave a giant

89

clock to the edge of the water to be loaded on to the ship. It's as tall as a man, and its gold columns and finials support not one but three clock faces in an intricacy of machinery, dials and symbols. It's the sort of piece that would have fascinated my master. 'What a miraculous thing,' he'd say. 'You see, my champion, the ingenuity of men.' When we were together, clocks used to be inelegant and ungainly, even those owned by kings, but this is an object that seems to come from a halcyon future, and it reminds me – with a shock – how plain I've become in the last decade, not caring, as I used to – as my master always did – about invention and beauty.

The battalion drums are calling me. I hover as Sporco still white-eyes me. *Damn him, let him come. I'll find him a place to stay once we're away.* 'The journey may be long, you understand? You can't nag me. If you do, I will leave you without a thought. You understand all this?'

'Yes, understood, sir. The pack, eh? Off to the realms!'

I spot, near the back of the cavalcade, a pontonier's wagon, lengths of wood sticking out the rear. 'Up there, quickly!' I nudge Sporco. He jumps, surprisingly agile, and disappears under the awning. I leap after him, feeling my way. Much better to travel in a cosy pontonier's wagon, with the smell of sweet pine, than one full of gunpowder, terrified of every bump in the road. I nudge aside the awning to see the view. We crank through the scruffy outskirts of the town, crest an escarpment and roll into open countryside. It's been overcast all day, but the murk dissolves and needles of spring sunshine peek through. I've been so used to the stink of canals, of damp stone and salt-sea, that the freshness of the air enlivens me.

Vilder's carriage is tucked behind the cavalry, unable to overtake and has fallen into the same rhythm. We wheel through a wood, crown another peak and striking views open before us: a broad valley misted with wild flowers, cloaked here and there with dark emerald forests, a sinuous river twitches through it and a range of purple mountains in the distance. The sky is clear azurite overhead. After so many years of flat land and plain sky, the sight is riveting and I turn to Sporco – but he's already sitting up speckled in sunlight. A creature that shambles through life, noisy with everything and nothing, is at once curious and admiring, silent even. I'm almost envious of him, of his chance to uncover the world's surprises for the first time. I've all but forgotten the sensation.

'Who is that man?' he asks with a nod to the smoky-quartz carriage.

How can I explain Vilder? The decades we spent on edge, my master and I, never able to feel calm, dining in the corners of inns, eyes always on the door, on who came in – and how we might escape. For fear he might have found us.

'He is evil,' is all I say. 'He will kill you as good as look on you.'

6. Amsterdam

August 1627

We were woken by pounding on the front door of our quarters.

'Doctor, are you there?' came the voice of our footman. My master shot up, hurried down to the hall and unbolted the door. 'I've been told to fetch you,' the footman panted. 'A gentleman awaits you at Dam Square.'

'Who?'

'I was given no name. His driver couldn't get through by road, so came on foot and asked for you to come urgently.'

My master pulled on his boots and threw a coat over his nightshirt. 'Wait here,' he started to say to me, but I was already outside.

The three of us hurried along the Herengracht. It was the dead of night, not a soul on the streets, hot still and the moon so large and bright it cast gigantic shadows of the cranes battalioned about the city. We'd been in the region for a number of years, first at the Dutch court in The Hague and latterly in Amsterdam itself, on the staff of a merchant's family, traders in iron ore and weaponry. I wondered at first why my master had chosen to work for such a clan – they were not of royal stock, and the head of the household was a brute – and in a city that was, in that era at least, scant of charm, being little more than an immense building site. But soon I saw what drew him: the fantastic wealth of the place opened all the doors that interested him. 'Here are great minds,' he proclaimed once, leafing through sketches in the studio of a young artist. They were grisly beyond belief, illustrating an anatomy class: a coterie of gentleman watching as a cadaver was cut up to its very sinews and bowels. 'Science and art – you see, my champion, how they become one?'

We came into Dam Square and my master stopped dead, eyes snapping to the carriage in the centre. There were dozens of other vehicles scattered around for the night, but it had a quality unlike them, drawn from another realm, from another age, it seemed, one of dark and glittering make-believe. On high, slim wheels sat a titanic, spellbinding jewel of smoky-brown quartz. It seemed to capture all the moonlight in the square, only to vainly repel it back. Four black mares, as immodest as the coach, panted from a journey, whilst a man stalked back and forth in the arcade beneath the weighing house.

'We are here,' my master called to him.

The man stopped and swung round, peering about the square, before seeing us.

I tingled hot and cold as he advanced. Broad-chested, the moonlight clamouring to his face, heavy brow, broad nose, a mouth that was cruel and fascinating. Vilder. A man who I'd met only once, but never forgotten.

'A curse on this city,' he said, flicking his gloves at a half-constructed street going off from the square. 'What is the point of roads that you cannot travel along? An hour we've circled these damned canals in search of your residence only to arrive where we started.'

'There is a back way. If I had known –'

'Give me no back ways! We risked our lives to get here. Amsterdam is enemy territory for us.'

'Enemy territory?' said my master, baffled.

'Protestants,' Vilder snapped by way of explanation, though it bemused my master even more. 'Only a fool like you would bury yourself in a hole such as this, this ill conceit of land dredged from the bog, this swamp peopled solely by parvenus, by glorified sellers of tar and hemp. A curse on it!' As his words echoed around the houses of Dam Square, a window opened and a voice called for quiet. *'Arrivistes. Nouveau riche!'* Vilder swore back at it, before going over to a fountain to drink.

His clothes were streaked with dirt, yet they dazzled all the same: pearl-grey doublet slashed to silken jasper at the sleeves, wide-brimmed hat pinned on one side, as it had been in London, with an ostrich feather, and his magnificent hair spilling to his shoulders like poured ink. He had a dagger sheathed against his hip, its hilt studded with jewels. I was struck, as I had been twenty years before, by how masculine he appeared despite the finery. His sense of style, laboured in others, was effortless and unstudied. In Whitehall he'd so intrigued me that when he'd stolen away at dawn, I'd followed across the frozen Thames, in spite of my fear of breaking ice. His presence had made my blood purr under my fur. In Amsterdam, almost instantly, I felt differently: he seemed to me bad-tempered, unpleasantly arrogant – and quite possibly dangerous. As he turned to the light, I noticed the stains on his tunic were not dirt, but blood, smeared across his side pocket. My master saw it too.

'I need your help,' Vilder said, before pointing his index fingers skywards to re-emphasize. 'I *need* your help.'

'Are you hurt?'

Vilder's eyes seemed to warm with loathing, before he said: 'Not I.' He nodded at the carriage. 'Aramis.' Then: 'My *caprice.*' He dropped the phrase pointedly.

My master had been steady until then, but at once atoms of anxiety sweated from the backs of his hands. 'Of course I shall help. Let me see him.'

Vilder caught him by the arm. 'Be quiet, won't you? He is sleeping at last. Three days from Grol –'

'Grol?'

'The war. Have you heard of it?' he asked like a sarcastic school teacher. 'The Protestants against the Catholics. We've had an inexorable journey. As if the siege was not punishing enough, the wretch must be shaken from his skin by these Dutch roads. Explain to me, will you, how these people who are richer than the gods, these conquering accountants who've plundered the treasures of the world, who possess nothing but flat terrain, are incapable of building a level road?' Vilder clung on to my master's sleeve, a manic kick in his eye, and dropped his voice to a whisper. 'Blood rot. It ravages him. Sepsis. I know it. From a bullet, here.' He fingered his thigh with his free hand, whilst clenching my master tighter with the other. 'He should not have it. He is – the operation succeeded. Five years of infernal injections, one every week as we did – which he bore like a saint, a braver man than either of us – and it succeeded. The azoth, as healthy as mine. He has not aged since, younger if anything. See it in his face. And yet blood rot. Make him well, do you hear? You owe it to me. Make him well.'

Vilder let go at last. He sleeved the sweat from his brow and my master quietly clicked open the door. I should have hung back, but my curiosity was too great. The compartment seemed larger on the inside than the out, even with a curtain half drawn across the rear. With its little lanterns and velvet walls of dark chartreuse, it had the feel of a private chapel, the type an overly devout king might hide behind the panels of his bedroom wall for his private salvation. It was lavish – there were even shelves of crystal bottles and porcelain phials held up by little silver hands – but the smell was revolting: lemon cologne gone rotten, ambergris, and the tang of faeces, blood and infection. A sigh rustled against the curtain and fingers dropped into view: pale, waxy and bloated.

'*Ich bin hier*,' came a tired voice.

Unsure what to do, my master looked round at Vilder, who motioned impatiently until my master pulled back the shade. He was met with a stare that was at once timid and imperious. A young officer, a boy it seemed, of almost picture-book beauty – fine-boned, blond-haired, coral lips, powder-blue eyes – lay shivering. I could smell his illness from the street, the necrotic, yeasty, sweet-beer scent of blight besieging his insides. His cheeks were as livid as rain-lashed stone and he was furnace hot.

'Good day to you, Aramis,' my master said. 'If I may call you that?'

'*Der berühmte Arzt.*' His voice was slight, reedy and edged with insolence. 'At last I meet *the great chemyst.*'

'You were shot?'

Aramis passed his hands down the length of his uniform, a splendid road-soiled heap of Prussian-blue silk, towards the bandage knotted round his thigh. Drenched in gore, it was the place from where most of the stench emanated.

'How is it that you feel?' my master asked.

Vilder glowered from behind. 'He feels like death.'

Aramis grimaced, noticing me with a worry of a smile before telling my master, 'I am burning in ice. But I shall survive, shall I not? Videy tells me so. And you will tell too, the architect of our – of our fortune?' He frowned pointedly.

'Of course you shall survive,' my master promised. 'We will take you to our lodgings. We're sorry you couldn't find them the first time. No more roads. We will make you better.'

My master seemed determined to keep me separated from Vilder. Leading the way from Dam Square to our house on Herengracht, he twice pushed me back and told me to follow behind. I obeyed, but I had only been staying close out of protection, not because I wished to see more of Vilder. In any case, Vilder had no interest in me. He was one of those humans that would not be charmed by my species, who made me feel inferior for being born so.

The moment we arrived back at our rooms, my master put me in the bedroom. 'You wait in there.' I tried to follow him out again. 'Get in,' he said sharply and closed the door behind him. But the latch did not turn and I had a view of the work-room. He hurriedly cleared a table, threw a blanket across it and lit the lanterns.

There came a shuffle of feet from the hall and the footman and two of his cohorts entered with Aramis and laid him out on the table. I tried to see the invalid in the light, but my master stood in the way and began to undo the bandage. Vilder came in last, taking a measure of the room, just as he had in Whitehall.

'Bring me brandy,' he said to one of the men. 'French if you have it. Cognac ideally. Calvados if you must. Anything but Dutch.' He dismissed him and the others with a flourish and turned to my master. 'For decades you refuse to come to Opalheim, as if it were somehow beneath you, and yet here you take a commission with the Van den Heuvals of all people. The villains of Europe. Arms dealers. The bullet I fished from that boy's leg would have come from one of his factories.'

97

'Sssh, Videy, why must you talk all the time?' Aramis squeezed his eyes against the pain.

'I will have to cut away your breeches,' my master said to him. 'I am sorry; they look fine.' He went to his chest where he kept his tools. Vilder scowled.

Now I could see Aramis clearly, he must have been more than thirty, and a soldier of rank, and yet he still had the quality of a boy. I felt pity for him. He was fair and athletic, but there was fear in his eyes, made all the more heartbreaking by the impudent face he put on to hide it. He reminded me of one of those princes I sometimes met, steely little souls, miniature versions of their fathers, who could command falcons, hunt deer, joust, even go to war, but were boys nonetheless, with boys' apprehensions and fears.

My master cut down the length of his breeches and carefully peeled the material away, having to tug where blood had glued it to the skin. Underneath the flesh was bloated. My master was taken aback by the rotting-meat stink, but showed no panic in his voice. 'To be so young and a brigadier already, you must be a fine soldier.'

'He is exceptional,' Vilder put in. 'He was born on the battlefield. At fourteen, he already commanded a cavalry. At fourteen, mark you. Impeccable shot, rides like Apollo, but above all he thinks.' He tapped his fingers against his skull.

Aramis's entire leg was discoloured by rot. His thigh, ankle and foot were tar-black, whilst the rest was marbled in dark puce and bronze. Here and there, gas had bubbled up under the skin in blisters.

'And the badge there –' my master chatted on, pointing to a gold medallion that hung from a chain on his breast – 'some honour bestowed on you?'

Once more, Vilder answered on the other's behalf. 'White

Mountain. He won the battle single-handedly, as good as. A wunderkind. The Catholic League, Tilly, the emperor himself, they owe everything to him.'

My master smiled. 'I can believe it,' he said, 'I have nothing but admiration. I could not summon the courage to go to war.'

'It is civil of you,' Aramis panted, 'to keep my attention, but I am no fool. Gangrene. I see it. My leg, it must come off, no?'

Vilder slapped his palm against the wall. 'Off? Nonsense.'

My master drew in a breath, as he often did when he knew the answer to something but was unsure how to broach it. 'Well – in truth – there is every chance the rot will spread if we do not –'

'Take off his leg? Never. He is a soldier. How is he to survive with one leg?'

'Videy, please, don't shout.'

'No, no, no,' Vilder said to my master. 'Do you have any jyhr? Use that.'

'It will not help his leg.'

'You have it, though? Liquid jyhr? No matter how dissolved it is. It is that we have come for. Do not play with me!'

My master was cautious in his reply. 'I have a dose or two, and that, as you say, of a weak grade. I have not used it in years and it has likely lost its strength. But the leg first. I am sorry to be blunt, for both of you, truly. It lives no more and we will do greater harm if –'

'Of course it lives, you devil. A curse on you. He is converted. Give him the jyhr. That will revive him. Give it to him.' He yanked back his coat and thuggishly rested his fist against the hilt of his dagger. Gone was the languid mischief-maker of London.

There was a knock on the door and the footman entered with a tray. Vilder snatched it and dismissed him. He poured a large measure of brandy, drank it down and poured another, whilst my master came into the bedroom where I was waiting, went to the casket where he kept his money and valuables and unlocked a drawer. I followed him with my eyes, hoping to catch his attention, to be reassured, but he paid no heed to me. He retrieved his red velvet wallet in which were wrapped the tortoiseshell box and hexagonal vial, still his two most treasured possessions, though neither of which I'd seen him use. He left the little box in the red wallet, which he tucked into his inside pocket and went out with the bottle.

'Pull up his shirt and clean his skin,' he said to Vilder before going in search of something else.

They carried on talking, but their voices became a blur, as I'd seen the scar on the side of Aramis's abdomen. It was in the same place as my master's and mine, in the hollow above the hip bone, but where ours were neat and crescent shaped, his was a misshapen knot of bruised and livid skin.

My master returned with a plate of instruments. He inserted a quill tip into the hub of a syringe, before siphoning droplets into the chamber. He heated a blade in the yellow part of a candle flame, before saying to Aramis, 'I suppose you shall be used to this by now. Be brave.' He incised the scar with the blade and drove the nib of the syringe into the cut, squeezing the piston. Aramis squealed. An uncomfortable pang heated me from inside, an obscure memory turned over to the light: being taken from a burrow, from the pockets of warmth nestled around me, carried through the air, wild wind, arriving at the castle by the sea, then upstairs to the workroom, fog pressing to the windows as my master held me fast against the sharp pricks in my side. Of course I understand it all now:

taken from my litter, still with my eyes closed, to Elsinore, my first home, the gruelling medications administered over and over again.

Aramis seemed to calm, and soon drifted into sleep. They waited. The sun rose and gradually a bank of light crept up the far wall. Vilder leant against the wall behind his lover, swigging brandy. He was not tactile with Aramis, but rather offered virile encouragement, as a coach might a prize sportsman. 'Come, come, you shall be well.' Or, 'You shall improve, I guarantee.' But Aramis worsened. He grew hotter than ever, trembling so his knuckles drummed against the table, chest wheezing up and down in ragged crackles. When he spotted me in my hiding place behind the door, he blinked, half smiled and his breathing calmed for a moment, only for him to drift off once more. The day ticked by; hammers pounded from the construction sites of the city, and heat boiled up from the canals, seeming to press all the air out of the room.

'All will be well, all will be well.' Vilder tapped his knuckle against the patient. 'Soon we shall be back in Opalheim. Think of the lake there. You are always nagging me about taking a picnic beside it. We shall do it. No, better, we shall hold a ball. Yes. In my father's stateroom. Ha, that would be revenge on the miser. In his stateroom where he liked to play king, the glorified coal miner he was. Richer than Croesus, but what a miser my father was – with his heart as with his money. A curse on the old devil. We shall dance in his hallowed stateroom. Us and all the reprobates of Europe. We'll open the shutters, clean the murals and dance. Enough of this now, Aramis. You must get better.'

I grew almost insanely agitated by his bullish behaviour. Hours later, when Aramis had grown so delirious with pain that his mouth had set into a rictus box, did Vilder hang his head and say to my master, 'Take off the cursed thing. Take off his leg.'

My master prepared the operation, choosing instruments, setting them out, before touching more drops of jyhr into Aramis's mouth. When the soldier looked to me, my master noticed the door ajar. I thought finally he would give me a pat of comfort, but he just shut me in, and this time the latch drove home. I was glad for it. If I had been able to watch, I would have done, but from the moment I heard the first shriek I nudged open the windows so the noise of the hammers would drown it out. They must have put a leather in Aramis's mouth, for the screams became whistles. I climbed on to the bed, pushed my head beneath the blankets and pressed my front legs hard against my ears. I tried to concentrate on the sound of my breath, on the warmth of it in my cocoon, and ignore the crack of metal against bone.

I was half aware of shouts getting louder, of someone knocking from the hall, and my master sending them away. More screams and banging, more people coming and going. In the end there was silence. I came out from my hiding place and cocked my ears to the room, but there was no sound at all. I waited by the door until it opened and my master came in to fetch the coverlet from the bed. Aramis's face was pivoted towards me, no longer frantic but unanimated, with round blanks of glass where his eyes had shone. He was dead.

Vilder sat in a chair, legs crossed, blankly watching my master arrange the coverlet over Aramis's body. 'Leave the face,' he said plainly.

Instead, my master set about mopping up the dark slick on the floor below the table.

'Shall we take a walk?' Vilder asked when he was finished. 'It is a feast day, is it not? I am sure it is.'

My master was perplexed. 'Walking? Now?'

Yes. Get out of this sickroom. I can't bear to look at all your *apparatus* a minute longer. I need air.'

'But – where do you wish to go?'

'To the street. Anywhere.'

'And what about –' My master motioned towards the table.

'Aramis?' Vilder said. 'I don't think he's up for walking.' He stood up malevolently, once more brandishing the hilt of his dagger.

'Of course, as you wish.'

My master was about to lock me in again when Vilder said, 'You can't keep him shut in all day. Bring him. I know how you like a creature at your side.' It was the first time he had properly looked at me, and I could tell he did not realize it was I he had met before.

We trailed through the afternoon crowds up the side of the Amstel. It was impossible not to recall the frost fair in London, for, as well as the three of us, it seemed the same cast of jugglers and entertainers peopled this alternate version, though now there was heat in place of the cold. Vilder was apparently fascinated by it all and kept pointing things out to my master. 'Here come the guildsmen. How proud they are. And these creatures here with wings.' My master, unsure how else to reply, smiled and nodded where it was due, every now and then shifting a glance towards me. We were both thinking the same thing: that a corpse lay in our darkening workroom, its leg half hacked off – the old part of its body dead, and the new part, the army of black, marching on to victory.

On we went into the brand-new part of the city. Beyond

the old perimeter wall, where marshes and slums of timber shacks had become stately crescents of canals and double-fronted mansions, vast buildings waited to be filled with the self-regarding families of merchants and bankers – those black-clad, God-fearing humans who must surely have been secretly bursting with joy at their good fortune. Lamplighters appeared with their ladders and began illuminating the new bridges until the whole quarter sparkled. I had been, at best, unsure of Amsterdam, but on that peculiar evening, as we toured those unoccupied streets, the toy houses waiting to be filled, I, my master and the man who would soon become my enemy, I began to see the city in a different light. It had changed. Without my noticing it had alchemized from a base thing to something valuable.

We doubled back towards the festivities, until we found ourselves in Dam Square, in precisely the spot we had met Vilder the night before.

'I shall take him to Opalheim,' he said.

'Of course. Shall I – should I accompany you? To assist?'

'No. You are not welcome. Our association is over. I regret searching you out in the first place.' He spat on the street. 'Is there an ice house in the city?'

Whilst he thought about how he should reply, my master studied his fingertips. 'Yes, there is a place.'

'Arrange for ice to be brought. And a crate of some description. Not a coffin, they're abominable, as pretentious as the merchant classes that like to be put into them. This city is peopled by coffins, walking ones. A plain crate will do. I will pack him in it, take him to Opalheim, and entomb him in the family crypt.'

'Vilder –'

'Do not speak as if we are friends. Take your hand off me.

We are not friends.' He took a pause before speaking again. 'Do you think what you do is important?'

'What I do?'

'This part you play around the grand houses of Europe. The sage. Progressing from one gilded cocoon to another.' Vilder's tone had a newly malign and sarcastic edge. 'For what? Potions for lovesick princesses and incontinent dukes, back salves and gout treatment for minor royalty? Good fortune for the already fortunate. And I can't guess what you might prescribe for the Van Heuvals. Are there cures for bad taste? Do you consider it a good use of your time, of the endowment you bestowed on us, the gift of long life? Well, has it been important, what you've done?'

My master did his best to keep his tone friendly. 'All great houses have their share of the ridiculous, granted, but they are also centres of learning. They are magnets for the enlightened.'

'Yes, yes, you "learn" of course. You gather information. You enlighten yourself. And then what? Who do you help with all this intelligence? Huh? Whilst the world tears itself apart beyond the walls of your sanctuaries? Whilst men die on battlefields?' He jabbed my master's shoulder, once, then again harder.

On the third push, my master said, 'What is it you are trying to say, Vilder? That you're heroic now, because you had a lover that was a soldier?'

In a flash Vilder drew his dagger. I barked and would have snatched it in my teeth, but my master motioned me back with a snap of his fingers. He seemed to know exactly how to behave, that this was not the first time he'd faced his companion's anger.

'I never sought to be heroic,' Vilder shouted. 'That was

your game. Well, once upon a time, anyway. I have always had the courage to own up to my shortcomings.'

'Come now, put your dagger away.'

'You took me down this road remember? You are the reason I am here.'

'No. Absolutely not. We were equal in that matter. We decided together.'

'You took me down the road and left me stranded.' Vilder clenched the dagger tighter, but kept it at his side.

My master nodded, and his tone was entirely placatory. 'My friend, we are both overwrought. Let us leave this for now, I beg you.'

A guard at the doors to the town hall, having heard raised voices and seen a drawn dagger, came over. Vilder sheathed his blade and said to him, 'Don't worry, I'm leaving this swamp.'

From that moment, barely a word was exchanged between the two men. My master made the necessary arrangements, and by the following morning Aramis had been packaged up and loaded into the carriage. They couldn't fit the box lying down and had to sit it up against the seat, which made for a surreal sight. When my master saw the coach was about to leave, he went out to say goodbye, but Vilder still refused to talk to him. Rather he gave word to his driver and they set off through the gates.

I had never seen my master so distracted as he was that day, sitting down only to sigh and stand again, endlessly tugging his hand through his hair. I trailed him as he worried back and forth about our rooms, groaning, mumbling to himself, occasionally halting to regard the scrubbed-down table where Aramis had lain. At one point, he picked up the bottle of jyhr and warily studied it, before putting it in his trouser pocket.

'What have we done? We have not done well. What have we done?' In the evening he called for wine and drank cheerlessly, until his pupils desiccated and he fell asleep in his chair.

Past midnight, I heard a carriage creep along the lane behind the house and stop. It was not unusual for vehicles to come so late, but I had an uneasy presentiment. It was too dark to see anything from the window, but I heard the coach door thump and low voices. My master's eyes flicked open and he tilted his head to the sound.

'Who is that?' I was so frightened I barked. 'Sssh.' He craned his ears, but there was silence now. He went into the workroom. The moon cast an extravagant shadow across it. Just as he turned back to the parlour, a knock came on the door and the fur on my neck lifted.

'Yes?' said my master.

Our footman put his head round, and we were relieved until he said, 'The gentleman. He returns.' He was bewildered and shaken. 'Upstairs.' He indicated the principal part of the house where our employers lived.

'Thank you.' My master went up the little flight of steps and along the passageway into the great hall. I followed on his heels, certain that he would send me back, but he didn't. I had always found the mansion forbidding, all dark, creaking mahogany and austere dressers of blue and white china that was never used – but that evening it was more uninviting than ever. A staircase, raked at an unkindly steep angle, led to a landing of many identical doors. Our patrons were fastidious at keeping them closed, but one of them was ajar, the library, and flickers of firelight came from within. A fire, on such a hot night. We ascended and entered the mausoleum of a room that looked on to the Herengracht. Shelves of fanatically organized books towered to the ceiling. Whoever had

lit the fire had apparently gone, as the room was empty. My
master turned, and I must have made a sound, when I saw the
figure sitting at a table in the corner, for he stopped, and saw
it too.

Vilder was turning the pages of a book. For a moment a
charged stillness shook between us.

'What are you doing here?' my master ventured, glancing
at the hearth.

'I had travelled some miles before something grave occurred
to me. I have a question, a pressing one.'

'That is all very well, but return to my rooms at least?'

'No. I like it here. Amongst all this clever writing, which
nobody reads, all this enlightenment.' He held up the book. 'I
found this, or it found me. *Ajax*, Sophocles. I was looking for
a particular passage –'

'Vilder, let us take our conversation elsewhere. We will be
discovered here at any moment.'

'Really? By the Van den Heuvals? All the better. I long to
be acquainted. We have so much in common. I could discuss
mines and metallurgy with them, talk about our dynasties,
being born into obscene wealth, the benefits and disadvan-
tages thereof, compare the modern magnate –' he indicated
the room, before turning his hand to himself – 'with the medieval variety. It would be fascinating. But sadly I have already
understood from your footman that the Van Heuvals are gone
for August. We have the mansion for ourselves.' He shook the
book. 'Have you read it? This short jolt of a tragedy?'

'Vilder, I implore you.'

'You know the myth in any case? The soldier Ajax should
be awarded for his bravery, but is passed over in favour of the
lesser Odysseus. He becomes so obsessed with revenge, he

goes mad and hacks to pieces a herd of swine believing *they* are his enemies and at once his shame is tenfold. I over-complicate – it is about suicide.'

'Let this alone now.'

Vilder reads. ' "*Come bright daylight and look on me, for this last time, and then no more. O sacred land that was my home, ye springs and streams and Trojan plains, to you that fed my life, I bid farewell. This last, last word do I, Ajax, speak, and all else I say will be in Hades.* And he drives down on to his sword." '

'Vilder, believe me, I too am heartbroken about Aramis –'

Vilder laughed. 'Heartbroken, really? With a caprice you've barely met?' He got up and threw another log on to the fire, and stoked it with a poker. 'My question. You said something to me in London, something very curious. You said, when I asked for help with Aramis's conversion, it would be unconscionable in the extreme, immoral, you said, to burden another living thing with a life with no plausible end. It would be a curse, you told me. That is the reason you refused the request. Am I correct?'

'I do not remember the conversation well, or the words I might have used, but that is my belief.'

'*Unconscionable in the extreme to burden another living thing with a life with no plausible end.* I suppose you must have thought, from time to time, how marvellous it might have been, if you could convert one of those sparky women you used to like, to keep as a mate, one of those intelligent, often unattractive ladies you were drawn to, the ones always trying to prove themselves, fighting for their place at court, good marks-women, fast-talkers and even quicker thinkers. Thin little creatures with brave hearts. Who was that one in Rome you fell for? The would-be architect, who was she?'

'Stop this.'

'She'd come from the slums of Malta, hadn't she? To try her hand at the game of society, to make her way in a man's world. What was her name? Ariadne? She was pretty that one, but for her moustache. No, Adriana, that was it, that's what she called herself. What rhapsodies you made over her "architectural diagrams", her "vision". She'd designed "a hospital for the poor". What a saviour. You showered her with encouragement, before you broke her heart. Do you think she ended up back in Malta, in a slum? No doubt. You could have had such a prize for all time. But of course you were too honourable for that. "What if it should go wrong?" you always whimpered, if I even began to bring the subject up. Or worse still: "We cannot play god with other people."' His voice had been low since we came in, but suddenly he shouted. 'Why not?!' The fire took a breath before blazing on. 'Why should we not play god when he plays us?'

'Isn't your behaviour now the reason why?' my master replied. 'Is it not proof of how things can go wrong?'

'My behaviour?' Vilder advanced towards my master very slowly, and I stood at his side, chest out, to show my courage, even though I was terrified. 'What do you mean by my behaviour? That I suffer, sometimes? That I find it interminable, sometimes? That I wish to burn to death – sometimes?' He shot a glance at the fire and as it reflected against his face he could have been a demon. 'Well, have you considered the favour I sought from you would have helped me? But you turned me down, *you* played god. And in doing so, you have made my situation infinitely worse. You have compassion for the rest of humanity, why not for me? Deny it all you wish, but you brought me to this pass. You are responsible, not I. You owe me.' He was so close to my master by then, their faces almost touched. 'In any case, I veer from the point. My question. This grave principle of yours, to never afflict *another living thing*? Have you stuck to it?'

'You know I have.'

'Really? You have stuck to it?'

'Yes, Vilder.'

'And do you not count your dog a living thing?'

Vilder looked at me directly and there was murder in his eyes.

'What?' My master floundered, shifting his weight to shield me behind his legs.

'You heard me. Your dog. It is the same one I met twenty years ago.'

'No.'

'Lie. I thought you never lied? Let me see if he has a scar as we do.'

'Stop this.'

Vilder side-stepped him. 'Here,' he purred, beckoning me with little jerks of his fingers. I panted from heat and fear. 'Come now, let me see. Show me if you have the same mark, your own cursed cicatrix. I bet you have, you sly creature.'

'Run!' my master shouted at me, motioning for the open door, whilst blocking Vilder's way, but the fiend snatched up the book and punched the spine of it into my master's neck. He gave out a rasp, teetered across the room and fell, the bottle of liquid jyhr tumbling from his pocket. Vilder grabbed me by the skin of my neck and pulled me over the boards, thumping my head against furniture, towards the fire. I flailed, squealing, trying to get away, but his strength was unnatural.

'There it is, you devil,' he said, stretching my leg so he

could see the mark at the side of my abdomen. He drew his dagger and held it to my throat.

'Please, please,' my master begged. 'Let him go. Hurt me, not him.'

'No. One life for another. That is fair, is it not? More than fair, for I lost a man, and you a mere dog.'

'Please, let him go, I beg of you.'

'One request I made of you. One chance I had, and you denied me.' Vilder seized me by my front legs and hurled me into the hearth. My head struck the red-hot bricks at the back of it and my master screamed. I gasped, but the air was liquid heat. There was a reek of sulphur as my hair went up in crackles. It seemed the shrieks that echoed up the chimney belonged to someone else, but they were mine. My master came for me, horror on his face, but Vilder fought him back. I tried to crawl free, but the room was turning round, my blood in revolt, and it was hot enough to melt my bones. My master must have broken free, as I saw him seize the poker and strike Vilder in the jaw. There was a crack of bone, the monster collapsed and my master pulled me from the fire.

'My champion, my champion, do not die,' he wailed, ripping off his jacket and patting embers from me. I coughed and coughed, but couldn't get air into my lungs. Vilder was on the floor, motionless, blood lapping from a deep cut behind his ear and I thought his head had come apart, opened like a box at the forehead, before I realized it was his hair that had dislodged. He wore a wig. He had always worn a wig.

I jumped from my master's arms and ran from the room. The pain of my burns would come later, the blisters beneath my coat and tar in my lungs, but in that moment I was too shocked to feel any of it. My master came after me and I saw him turn the key of the library door, to lock Vilder inside. We ran down the stairs, out of the front door and into fresher air.

'My champion, my poor champion,' my master knelt down and hugged me.

Above him, at the first-floor window, I saw that Vilder had clambered to his feet. He unlatched one of the window casements and pushed it open. 'You run from me, do you?' With his wig lopsided and one side of his face darkened with blood he looked gruesome, but his voice was precise and carried on the hot night. My master was transfixed and for a moment I thought he might even return to the house, but he pushed me on and we went quickly up the street. As we turned the corner I heard Vilder say, 'Run then. But I'll find you – and play god with you yet.'

The sun was coming up and the deserted canals were turning crisp orange against it. Eventually we reached the street where carriages could be hired. My master alighted on one and snapped instructions at the driver, who looked down at me. I'm sure it was not the case, but I've always imagined I was still smoking. Realizing he had no money, my master tugged a ring from his finger – a gold band that he had always worn – pressed it into the driver's hand, and we were motioned aboard. My master very carefully laid me out on the seat, before checking one last time that no one was behind. He slammed the door and closed the curtains. As we left town, heading south, he kept fussing over me and though I was grateful, the pain had begun to set in and I would rather have been left alone.

He took the red velvet wallet from his inside pocket and retrieved the tortoiseshell box and the remains of the powdered jyhr. 'We have this at least.' He'd lost the hexagonal bottle, the distilled jyhr, a large batch that would have taken years to create. 'But we will survive, my champion, you and I. You and I,' he said over and over, but all I could think of was Vilder in the window, his wig half off and his sotto voce curse as we had turned the corner – 'Run then. But I'll find you – and play god with you yet.'

7. Sporco at the Ball

Padua, May 1815

Sporco nudges me. 'We're arriving somewhere.'

It's almost dusk and the cavalcade, along with Vilder's carriage, is climbing a hill towards the walls of a city. The red brick and broad Moorish crenellations are obscurely familiar: a long stowed-away memory of my master and I spending the night here in Padua. We pass through a gatehouse, along winding streets, over campiellos – the little squares that litter all Italian towns – until we arrive at an elliptical piazza and the convoy bunches to a halt, Vilder's carriage stationing ahead of the rest in the forecourt of a coaching stable.

'Do you know what?' Sporco raises his brow, apparently gripped by some mischief. 'There is another dog in this outfit. A *lady* dog. I caught a scent of her in a wagon ahead. She's special this one. I've thought of nothing else.'

'Well, try,' I reply coolly. 'We keep ourselves to ourselves.'

'Ha, you wait until you catch her scent. She wants sex that one. Well, I don't mind if she does. I will help her, I swear I will.'

'You're not helping any lady dogs. Understand?'

My eyes are fixed on Vilder. He dismounts, stretches and casts his eye about the piazza. From behind us, a carriage sweeps in through the arch. The window is open and, as it passes, a cloud of vetiver rises from inside. I catch a glimpse of a pink gilt interior, two ladies in evening dresses and a gentleman lounging, his hair as slick and black as the vehicle. He peers out quizzically at the soldiers, and the coach sails on, out the other side of the square, towards music nearby. Another carriage speeds through. And a third and fourth. All elegant. A few of the officers – some of the ones that had ridiculed Vilder in Mestre – gather for a discussion, before going off in the direction of the music. Vilder watches them. A song ends and another begins. He says something to Braune and follows the soldiers.

'Quickly,' I say, jumping from our hiding place.

'There she is!'

A Rottweiler shambles down from the back of a gunner's wagon, in heat, musk and yeast pealing off her. She stops in front of us, crouches and shits.

'Did you ever come across anything so beautiful?' Sporco drops to the ground in front of her and writhes on his back in a preposterous mating dance.

'No ladies tonight.'

'Can't I just –'

'No.'

'You're ravishing,' Sporco proclaims, puffing up his chest.

The Rottweiler shows its teeth. 'I'll take you apart limb by limb,' she pronounces in a low growl.

'Just ravishing!' Sporco declares. She growls again and I shoulder him on.

Following the music, we come into another square dominated by a single palazzo, all columns and pediments, antiquity reimagined for the modern world, like a stage set, the type of building that my master would have found enthralling, even as his peers would have found it too modern to be tasteful. There is a ball. At the gates, carriages are disgorging their cargoes of sleek humans, who drift up a torchlit avenue to the house. I spot Vilder straightening his necktie and dusting down his tunic before entering. Music from inside teases through me, the melody of bows on strings, violins and cellos, the royalty of musical instruments. It's a balmy evening and flowers in the front garden are in evening bloom, sweet alyssum, gardenia and honeysuckle. Sporco's tail does a swish-swish and I'm overtaken with an uncommon pang of melancholy, of long-lost glories, of my vanished past, of the decades eaten up by waiting, the search and living alone.

At first I think I'll wait outside, but I would rather have Vilder in my sights. And besides, I want to witness a ball again after all these years, and for Sporco to see it too – for the first of one's life is the most magical. Mine was long ago at Whitehall, on a summer evening such as this. Courtiers came to pavilions on the banks of the Thames in fancy dress, as medieval knights and Indian goddesses, as woodland fairies and the royalty of ancient England. No, indeed, this warm night is for the sharing of good spirits.

I lead him to the fountain on the near side of the square. 'We must wash if we wish to enter.' For my part, I keep myself clean, so I deviously pretend to pass under the spray, so he'll do the same. I brace myself for an argument, as dogs in general, even if they love water, can't abide an actual bath, to be denuded of their scents – but Sporco proves an exception. He's delighted by the procedure. As I paw him clean, washing three years of Venetian grime from his fur, he can't stop giggling. When he's shaken himself dry, and passed in and out of a hedge until the smell of wet fur has evaporated, we're ready. We slip through the gates and pad into the shadows of the garden.

'The pack, huh?' he says, and I pretend not to hear him.

The front portico has two principal arches, through which the humans go, and smaller ones on each side, one of which we pass through. The fragrance of flowers in the hall is almost shocking: peonies, lisianthus and delphiniums in a thousand garlands. Summer capes are dropped in the hands of baby-faced chambermaids, to be carried *backstage*. There's a chatter of champagne glasses, and light from countless chandeliers shines off canteens of silver and bees-waxed tabletops. A staircase sweeps up from the middle of the room and where it divides I can see the entrance to the ballroom. Vilder is mounting the stairs, studying the faces of guests coming and going, before disappearing inside. I look round at Sporco, but there's another dog there, or so it seems. For my friend has transformed; he's two shades lighter, golden blond, as he was as a puppy. And he's grown handsome too. With the mask of dirt removed, there's nobility in the arrangement of his features that I had never guessed was there.

'*Chi sono? Cani!*' calls a lady, coming from a side door and spotting us. She is the mistress here, I can tell from her bearing, and she will have us thrown out. A pity. I'd hoped to see just a little of the dance. Sporco goes to meet her, tail dancing in a circle. I mean to nudge him out of the way, but she scoops down and throws her arms round him. '*Quanto è bello!* Like a baby lion.' She's a beauty, with a swan's neck and golden ringlets falling to her slim wide shoulders. Her voice is deep, like a man's. '*Come sei bello!* This one reminds me of my darling Alfonso,' she says of Sporco. 'Look, everyone, these handsome fellows have come to join our dance. You are welcome. I am Claudina. *Incantata.*' She curtsies and laughs, looking round to an assortment of courteous smiles. '*Adesso*, I must play the hostess.' She collars a footman, entrapping him with her smile. 'Bring these two water, with ice.'

She leaves us, sailing queen-like up the stairs, a nod here, a smile there, her hand raised to receive a gentleman's kiss and, with a final trumpet of laughter, she's gone into the ballroom. My friend watches her, panting in admiration. When the footman returns with a golden bowl and sets it down before us, I could be back at the French court at Saint-Germain-en-Laye, where, to the amusement of my master, cream-gloved butlers would bring me my meals on platters of bone china.

Entering the grand ballroom, we find it thronged with guests, abuzz with chatter, and sparkling like a pharaoh's treasure. The elite of Hapsburg society, wilful, vain and proud. Satined debutantes, boastful army officers, impatient counts and crookbacked dowagers. Deals are struck and little wars waged to the scent of money – kid leather, starched linen, perfumed silk, sable, amber and spikenard. Vilder sifts through them, searching faces. Now that men's fashions are all efficient lines and muted colours, browns and greys, his clothes, of a more flamboyant age, set him apart. But that aside, in this milieu of society, he no longer seems hollowed out, but returns in part to his bygone incarnation, his back straighter and head higher, his demeanour pronouncing him a man of means and judgement. He does a loop of the chamber, before settling by the door. He takes out his little flask and doses himself, but this time – close up and in the light – I realize I know the bottle, though I have not seen it in almost two centuries: the hexagon of thick glass in which my master kept his liquid jyhr that he dropped in Amsterdam when Vilder attacked us. What a crafty collector he is, to have taken and held on to it all these years. Now the bottle contains a pale yellow liquid, which – as I surmised in Venice yesterday – must be some variety of easing potion, for Vilder's shoulders drop and his pupils seem to shiver when he takes a sip of it.

As he stows it once more in his pocket, an old chap next to him says, 'I admire your coat.' The man wears a colourful scarf on top of an otherwise plain countryman outfit. 'Are you an artist?'

'A what?' The look on Vilder's face is pure contempt, but the man doesn't seem to notice.

'An artist, I thought, in your fairy-tale coat. Us aesthetes must stick together.' He waves his hands at the crowd. 'Money, money, money. It's all they think of.' A pause. 'That and its ugly cousin, war.'

A waiter passes with a tray of champagne glasses and Vilder takes two. The man, thinking one is for him, smiles and holds out his hand, but Vilder keeps them both, draining the first, depositing it and starting on the second. 'Who is this?' He motions towards the orchestra on a platform at the far end. 'The music, whose is it?'

'Is it not utterly sublime? A young composer, an Austrian. Franz Schubert. Just eighteen. They say he is another Mozart.'

'A who?'

'Mozart.' For a moment, both men look confused. I myself recognize the name, even if Vilder doesn't. 'Wouldn't you agree the comparison is warranted?'

'I'm sure it is.'

'Eighteen, mark you. His whole life ahead of him. To possess such genius. If this is what he can produce as an adolescent, imagine the glories to come. Think of all those as yet unknown worlds he'll bring to life for us, so that *this* world will be brighter and better.'

'Or he may just go mad and poison himself with night-shade. That's what they do, isn't it, artists?' To this, the poor chap has no reply. Vilder retreats to a chair in the corner, collecting a full bottle of champagne on his way.

'Let's go closer,' I say, 'and hear the orchestra play.' We set off round the edges of the room. I'm dark-furred, ordinary, and can come across as solemn – even though once I used to be called the smiling dog – and no one notices me. But Sporco is an innate extrovert, and loves the attention – he gets tickled, ruffled and complimented on his golden coat. When we get to the front, he sits on his haunches, ears stuck up as enraptured as a child in front of a magic display, staring from one musician to another. It gives me pleasure and a peculiar sense of pride to see how awestruck he is, whilst also taking it all in his stride. The musicians are very fine – I could tell they would be from outside – faces plain with concentration, but fingers acrobatic. They notice the golden-haired dog gaping up at them and when he stands on his hind legs and taps the knee of the lead violinist, smiles spread from face to face.

The music makes me feather light, shaking clouds of happy memories from the remote places of my mind. Music has always been a vital part of my life, most particularly when my master and I were together. 'Who plays?' he would always say, hearing it, perhaps from a city street, or the far wing of a palace, or even when we were stationed with an army, and we'd go and investigate. In Venice, I would seek it out wherever I was able, perhaps thinking that the sublime alchemy of instrument and player would somehow draw him back to me. It was an extra boon if one of the masters or mistresses with whom I shared the years of my vigil brought music into the house, like the banker and his philanthropist wife that I lived with for a while – some years after the bachelor Jerome who'd been murdered for his jewels – in the largest palazzo of Dorsoduro.

They lived for music and company, forever holding soirées and spectacles, always helping out some impoverished composer or other. One summer day, a particularly diverse and interesting crowd assembled, a pageant of powdered wigs and mantillas, constantly whirring fans, all craning their necks as an adolescent heeled into the room, cleared his throat, bowed at my hosts and took his place at the front of the orchestra. I wondered who the youngster could be; with his messy profusion of fine flaxen hair and pitted teenage face, he looked as unremarkable as a kitchen skivvy dressed up for the day. How judgemental I was, and in the presence of so great a man. But when Herr Mozart put his violin to his chin and started to play and the chamber orchestra took flight I thought I would melt across the floor.

There's a rattle of metal against glass, and the orchestra pauses, the master of ceremonies makes an announcement and the guests divide, some shrinking back to the walls as the remainder pair up in the centre. There's a rustle of parchment as the musicians set out new sheets. The lead violinist counts in the others, the ladies curtsy, the gentlemen bow, and the waltz begins. With their first sweep, skirts unleash a wave of jasmine and orange flower. The onlookers applaud, eyes devouring the spectacle. The couples spin, polished shoes on the glassy floor, white breeches and gloves, winging tailcoats, silk ribbons catching the light. Within seconds the room is in motion, circles within circles. Sporco gapes at it and I remember that balls are fascinating not just for the joy of them, but for the zeal, ambition and jealousy that surfaces too. The dance is a battle, and not just between the dancers, but between the many parts of each human.

The first waltz complete, there's a trade of claps, and partners are exchanged as onlookers buy and sell gossip behind their hands. Close by me, a young debutante curtsies at a flame-haired lieutenant, only to be passed over by him. Her cheeks burn pink as he selects a prettier version, and swaggers with her to the dance floor. A coven of ladies delight in the girl's shame, fingertips clasped to their pale chests, as she makes hastily for the door. I pity her – she's barely out of childhood – and gently nuzzle her hand as she passes. She's annoyed at finding that only a dog seeks her attention, snaps her hand away and hurries on. Chastened, I drop back into the shadow behind the door.

'In all the animal kingdom,' a man says next to me, 'are not humans the most savage?' He gestures his glass towards the retreating debutante. 'At least *I* noted your kindness, good sir.' Such is his gravitas, his air of shrewd melancholy, it takes a moment for me to notice he's still young. With his athletic physique, thick curls of mahogany hair, handsome square jaw and cleft chin, he reminds me of someone, perhaps a soldier of old Rome captured in one of the statues there. Or maybe even Vilder, the impressive version that I met in London. Looking over to him, he's sunk in the corner, drunk, whilst his lookalike leans rakishly against the wall, one arm bandaged in a coloured sling, a cigar between his teeth and smoke drifting about his face.

'Indeed, if I had my way, this ball would be peopled entirely by your species, and by bears and cats and all the good creatures.' He takes a slug of red wine, before motioning his braced arm and whispering, 'That is why I play the invalid. To save me from their claws.' I like him; he shines in a way that few humans do. He has warmth, a captivating air of unconventionality, and the odour of books and freshly pressed linen. I sense, as with my master, he's intelligent enough to take the world very seriously, but himself very little. All of a sudden he crouches, puts down his glass, takes hold of my jaw and stares into my eyes. 'Who are you?' he says. There's a thrilling note of vetiver about him, a whisper of the east, the signature of an adventurer. 'Do I know you? I feel we are old friends you and I.' He's so direct and earnest. It's as if he were talking to a human, or one at least that had been transfigured into a dog.

'Have you met our famous English baron?'

Two females have come to present themselves like exhibits in a shop window, one in her vigorous middle-age, a forgery of a lady, and her younger companion.

'George Byron,' my companion rejoins with a brief nod. '*Le diable boiteux. Enchanté.*'

The ingénue blushes almost the colour of a bruise.

'Le baron is not just an heroic gallivant,' the older lady purrs, 'but a great poet and intellectual.'

He retrieves his glass and drains the wine from it. 'If you ever have the fortune to wed, mademoiselle, find yourself one such as this.' He clasps his palm to my head. 'I once had the notion to marry with my Newfoundland dog, Boatswain, but feared society would not abide the union of two males.' There is such strength and warmth in his fingers; I feel as bashful as the ingénue. 'Goodbye, friend,' he says to me. 'I have not even half your kindness and must drink away my sorrows. *Mesdames.*' He gives another bow and he limps off.

'The man is a lunatic.' The older lady bristles, before taking her companion in the other direction. 'And rude with it. Why does everyone talk about him? Come, let us find a French poet.'

As the dances gets noisier and more abandoned and sweat begins to mist the air, Sporco becomes intoxicated, no longer sitting, but seeming to bounce to the rhythm. When the tempo of the band quickens for a quadrille, he begins to let out a whine, quiet at first, but climbing up and down with the music. The dance accelerates into its final riotous reel and the audience cheers, whilst the dancers whirlwind to a rush of silk and flickers of gilt from soldiers' uniforms. Sporco charges through them to the middle point, throws his head back, balloons his ribs and howls.

It's an astonishing sound, as unexpected as a whale cry. He holds the note for as long as his breath allows, then fills his lungs and bellows again. Bewildered, several dancers break from the round, and some of the musicians stop playing. Their leader tries to count them back in, but Sporco gives a third magnificent trumpet. No one can compete, the music unravels and the remaining dancers bump to a halt, turning to the golden-haired dog in the centre of the floor. Guests jostle to see over shoulders and crane their necks through doorways. Only *I* know what he is howling –

'The realms! The realms! The realms!'

In the corner, Vilder has fallen asleep.

Claudina pushes through, scoops up Sporco and bombards him with kisses. '*Meraviglioso! Bellissimo!* What a wonderful singer!'

The dance continues, but for the rest of the evening Sporco, like a dashing prince at his first public parade, is the star. He remains in Claudina's white-gloved arms, gracious and serious with success, coat lustrous with pride, as she tours the mansion, from teeming ballroom to riotous drawing room. I watch from my lookout by the orchestra as he's fawned upon and advised by the tycoons of Europe. They're thrilled, for once, to enjoy a thing as simple as a dog – '*Il cane miracolosa*', '*Die wunderbare hund*' – for once no need to brood over gold and stock, to worry their peers don't respect them, or their daughters are ugly or their sons wayward. Sporco is their new mascot, the very talisman of their rare society, for this evening at any rate. Champagne corks pop and pop. Glasses overflow, conversations slur, couples whisper in corners, the dancing grows yet messier and the gentle scents of before mutate into dirty-sweet smells, feral and fleshy. To the late-stayers goulash is served, but their brains have become too addled for food and half-eaten plates are discarded at the edges of tabletops and silk chaises.

Finally, when the band stops and the ballroom starts to empty out, Vilder wakes, a crumpled mess. Though his head must be pounding, he reaches for his bottle – his fourth time by my count – and drains it down, before getting to his feet and swaying across the room. My friend from before, George Byron, is leaning against the fireplace, lighting another cigar and watching the guests depart. Vilder stops dead and gawks at him, with what could be revulsion or fascination, or both. Byron returns the stare so candidly, it takes Vilder by surprise. He blinks and, for a moment, he seems to admire the Englishman, before his shoulders drop and his head lowers. 'A curse on you all,' he mutters to himself and shambles out.

'It's time,' I say to Sporco, but find he's fallen asleep under a chair. 'My friend –' I'm about to nudge him, when a notion strikes me like a shock of ice.

I should leave him. He could not find a better home than this, and Claudina already loves him. He'll live a long life here, never wanting for anything. Claudina is the most ideal of guardians, fascinating and young, the latter vital if Sporco is to grow old with her. There's nothing more heartbreaking than a creature losing its life companion in its frail final years, as La Perla did. No, even though I've grown used to him and will miss his rascally ways, he must stay. I go, but stop in the doorway.

I should bid him farewell at least. Most certainly our paths will never cross again, as his life will pass in moments compared to mine. But if I wake him, he'll want to tag along for sure. '*The pack*,' he'll say. How boyish and innocent he looks curled up under the chair, too polite to sleep anywhere but the floor, unspoilt and used to hardship, poor soul. No. *That* is the reason I must leave him. My master would agree: it would not be fair to take him from such a fortunate place, on a journey with no determinate end. After all, I have no home to give him. No, Claudina will come looking for him soon and carry him to bed. It will be sumptuous and she'll insist he always sleeps on it. He'll dream there, little legs tucked together in pairs, soft and neat on the sheet. And in the morning she'll chat with him as she dresses in her armoire that smells of sweet chamomile. He'll become, as I once was, *a palace hound*, a four-legged courtier, a lover of the orchestra and fine society. He'll be sad for a while, finding me gone, but he'll be thankful in the end. Spotting our hostess again on the landing, still smiling, though she must surely ache from tiredness, I am convinced and go.

At the bottom of the stairs, the musicians are all gathered, cloaks on and instrument cases in their hands. A footman is passing amongst them, offering little glasses of brandy on a tray. One of them accepts and there's a collective laugh, and they all take one. The scene could be unremarkable but fills me with unexpected comfort. It strikes me how gentle the musicians are, and how each one has a history; each one has come to the decision – for some of them, no doubt, at a great cost – to devote their life to music, an art form that is, by definition, utterly impermanent, for it vanishes the moment it appears. And in turn, the people, their hosts and audience, are grateful to them. The glasses of brandy are a token of friendship between humans, a friendship that surely goes back to the beginning of time.

It's the quiet hour before dawn and the square before the house is full of hazy motion, departing guests, carriage wheels on cobbles, yawning drivers. Vilder sways through it and disappears up the street we came down earlier. Tramping after him, past the fountain where I washed Sporco earlier, I can't help remembering the stolid phrase my master used so much in our latter years, 'our duty'. Inside, I sink a little, and the comfort of a moment ago, of the musicians and the brandy, turns against me – when I hear a familiar bark.

'Wait!'

Sporco skitters across the square, frantic and muddled. 'Did you say we were going? I didn't hear you. Did you say? I heard nothing.'

'Sssh, you go back to sleep. I'm leaving, and you – you –'

He blinks at me, batting his oversized brows, as he begins to understand a calamity is afoot. Though even in the face of it, he has time to sniff my backside. For once, out of commiseration, I return the favour – and I'm struck by how robust and healthy his glands are.

'Look,' Sporco says, his tail stiffening.

Vilder has stopped halfway up the street in front of a shop, a pharmacy, I can tell from the carboy in the window – a bulbous glass container filled with unnaturally light blue liquid. He bangs on the door. '*Apririe adesso!* Open up! I need assistance.' He bangs louder, and Sporco creeps to my side. 'Open, goddamn you, I am ill.' On his third rap, an upstairs window opens and a man in a nightcap puts his head out.

'*Siamo chiusi.*'

'It's urgent. I'm ill. I have need of laudanum. By accident I have travelled without it.' He totters drunkenly.

'We open at seven. Goodnight, *Signor*.' The pharmacist shuts the casement emphatically.

'I'm sick, do you hear me?' Vilder persists, rattling the door handle. 'Do you know who I am? You've made an enemy of me.' He slaps his hand across the sign on the front. 'Doctor Luigi Gasparelli. Doctor? Quack. I could buy this town a thousand times over. I could buy Venice. Europe. All those bottles you have back there, all those powders, they're from our mines. My family's mines. We ruled this continent, your pitiable little shop. Open up, goddamn you!' He stumbles back, losing his balance, and his legs go up and he lands, head banging against a porch stone. He doesn't move for a long time, the ringlets of his wig splashed over the step.

Sporco has frozen into a ball. 'Is he dead?'

If only Sporco knew.

'Our mines,' Vilder murmurs pathetically. His chest shivers up and down and it takes me a moment to realize he's crying. The dim, dry odour of loneliness seeps from his pores.

Go to him.

Ludicrous notion.

But my master would. Console him. I pad forward, but stop at the thought of him throwing me in the fire.

My master would forgive. Once, a young courtier in Naples, a troublesome, self-centred hothead, started a fight over a misunderstanding and took a knife to his cheek. My master calmed him, tended to his own wound, and later they became friends. 'You see, how history can be changed?' he said to me. 'It's never too late. Never too late to fashion the world how you dreamt it could be.' When the courtier died decades later, he'd brought so many reforms to Naples, the whole city turned out for his funeral.

I go to Vilder and sit before him. It's shocking, close up, how dishevelled he is, teeth discoloured, puce swags of skin beneath his eyes. He looks at me blankly with no recognition. 'What? You want food? I have none. Go.' I hold my ground. '*Vai! Idiota.*' He gets to his feet. 'Cursed creatures. Dogs.' He spits on the ground. He's halfway up the street when he slows down and his shoulders freeze. He swivels back. A change is coming upon his face, its features shifting, righting themselves. 'Let me see you.'

He comes back and I hold my breath as he turns me about, gently, not like he did in Amsterdam. Seeing the crescent scar on the side of my stomach, he lets out a strangled caw. 'It *was* you? At the cathedral. I saw you. Can I?' he asks, gently feeling along my flank, touching the scar, the stone beneath. His hands shake. He puts them in the air, whisking them round and round, unable to find the words. 'It is lunacy. You waited?!'

I chance a cautious sway of the tail. '*You see, how history can be changed? It's never too late.*' He reaches to stroke me, but pulls back his fist and hammers my skull. Blur of indigo, sludge brown. I fall, half aware of Sporco setting about him. Vilder seizes him by the scruff and throws him aside. He drags me by the tail, and Sporco attacks again. Terrible screams. He's tossed to the wall. Vilder unholsters his pistol, aims and fires at Sporco. Everything slows as I jump. There's a pall of smoke, a bullet driving through it. A steel slice of pain. The whites of

Sporco's eyes slant sideways. I cartwheel. The ground tips upside down. I fall on to it, hard.

'Braune! Braune!' Vilder calls.

The sky shivers, the stars spin and everything goes black.

The carriage starts moving and I slide to the floor. Blur of dirty chartreuse, ripped silk, tiny silver hands, lopsided shelves. Sporco stands over me. I should have left him with Claudina. Opaque silver clouds my vision, then black.

Hours pass, or days, I've no sense at all, and endlessly turning wheels batter the ground. It's a blur of half-sleeping, half-waking, nonsensical dreams – a curly periwig darts through a forest, the king's head tumbles from the scaffold, a cathedral unbuilds itself to its foundations, a pig asks politely how he'll be cut up, ice breaks and dancers fall into the Thames.

Something warm and wet on my face. Sporco licking me. Muddled bovine stare. Above me, an oval of scratched glass, Vilder on the driver's perch, wig like a storm cloud.

Little by little, I become more lucid. I'm inside the smoky-quartz carriage. Grimy windows, seats ripped to their ticking, gilt worn off the door handles, off the intaglio of three towers. I push on the handle with my nose. Both doors are locked tight.

'Do you hurt?' I ask Sporco. '*Come sei bello!*' Claudina had said to him in Padua. He could be in her arms now, sleeping off the party. He squeezes his brows together, and pushes a nub of metal towards me. It's a mangled bullet, the one that struck me – which my flesh has turned away. I've all but forgotten the sensation, but now I remember the price that must be paid: knife shards of unspeakable pain, brain freezing to ice. Delicately Sporco puts his snout to the place where the bullet struck, where my skin even now knots itself back together.

We're ascending a mountain. All night we shunt back and forth. In the morning the carriage stops, and we listen to the sound of Vilder dismounting. There's a babble of voices and the speedy unshackling and rebolting of harnesses.

As we take off again, Vilder shouts:

'To Opalheim, go!'

8. Christmas Eve

The Carpathian Mountains, December 1627

We fled Amsterdam with nothing the night that Vilder attacked me. As soon as my master deemed it was safe to stop – his paranoia about being followed had no limits, not then, nor for decades after – he searched out an apothecary, brought medicines and attended to my burns, having to bandage me at the shoulder where I'd been scorched through fur and flesh. In truth, I'd not been severely hurt and I healed quickly enough, but my master was so distressed on my behalf, so penitent, as if it had been his fault, I pretended early on there was little pain at all.

My master had used a gold ring to pay for our passage from Amsterdam and, apart from the clothes he was wearing, all he had left was the tortoiseshell box of powdered jyhr and a second ring, one studded with an emerald. He'd cherished it even more than the other, but had to sell it, a week or so into our journey, in order to survive.

We travelled south and east deeper and deeper into the continent, only ever stopping between changes of horses. As we journeyed, for days and then weeks, he never stopped checking behind us. It was natural, I suppose, given how Vilder had turned on us and swore he 'would play god with us yet'. And there was more in my master's mind than Vilder's threat. I could tell by the tempests that came and went across his face, which altered his posture and took speech from him, that deep emotions had been dredged up in Amsterdam.

Finally, after a voyage of a month, we came upon a little village in the Carpathian hills hidden amongst the mountains and forests, as remote an outpost as could be found – and we let a cottage opposite the church. My burns had all but healed, and I could breathe as normal again.

Unlocking the front door to a little cloud of dust and finding a small plain parlour, he said, 'We shall make this home.' Even though he'd promised it before and not meant it, I took him at his word and my tail swayed from side to side. This cheered him up and he sat down in the porch and put his arm round me. 'My beloved boy, my champion, who always thinks the best of everything. This house is not as grand as usual, but we'll find peace in this valley, shall we not?'

Such instances of warmth were rare at this time. There was too much of a jumble in his head. He didn't make the house comfortable, or *homely*, as he usually would, with ingenious personal touches, rather he shoved an armchair to the fire and sat in it from morning until night, gazing morosely ahead, hardly summoning the energy to eat or light up the room after sunset or take walks with me.

Nothing was worse for my master than isolation. He was an inherently social creature, an observer, a conversationalist, a learner who thrived on the trade of ideas. And he liked all culture, the low and high, as happy at a country dance as at the opera.

The village priest, who lived in the rectory opposite us, was a young man called Frantz. My master spoke to him occasionally and they seemed to have interests in common – I'd spied through Frantz's windows shelves crammed with books and pamphlets – but they'd had only short passing conversations until the morning of Christmas Eve, when my master collared the young man as he left his house.

'I would like to talk,' my master said, 'with some urgency.'

'Of course, tonight?' Frantz replied. He was lanky and inelegant, legs too long for him, cumbersome hips and a large nose – even larger than my master's – that went at an angle. 'After mass?' It seemed my master would rather not have waited, but the priest's horse had already been saddled for a journey.

Later that evening, we watched from our parlour window as the last of the villagers pressed into the little church. They'd come from all around, lanterns winking down from the hills, sleighs jangling, and cheery yuletide babble. There was only the barest of crescent moons, but the sky was so alive with stars, with washes of indigo and violet and the earth so luminous with snow it made a halo of that quiet corner of the world.

Once everyone was tucked inside the church and its windows had begun to cloud with breath, the organ struck up and the carols commenced. My master went back to his chair by the fire. 'How long shall they be? An hour?' He sighed and picked up a book, but barely turned a page of it before putting it down, rising once more and lighting candles. He'd been fidgety all day, more so now than ever, but I welcomed the change in his mood. Better he was restless than melancholic.

We went back to the window when we heard the villagers leaving the church. They poured down to the lake, where festivities were due to take place. My master grew more jittery as Frantz chatted, interminably it seemed, to a young couple. Eventually the pair departed and Frantz came over. Even though he'd seen him approach, my master jumped in surprise when there was a knock on the door.

'Yes, come in,' he said abruptly.

'Forgive me. Do I arrive too late?'

'No, no,' my master said, a higher than usual register in his voice. 'Pardon me, I have been engrossed in study.'

I'd learnt over the years to not bombard visitors with showy greetings, but I was so happy to have another human in the room at last that I barked and stood up on my hind legs to paw his chest.

'Down,' my master commanded. 'What has got into you?'

'It is quite all right.' Frantz smiled, offering the back of his hand to my snout. He must have washed after communion for his skin was as clean as fresh linen. I took a position in the centre of the room, where I'd be able to gauge the conversation best. I had the sense that my master was going to discuss something important.

'A drink?' my master asked. 'I have a fine Rhenish here.' He already had the bottle prepared, along with two goblets that didn't match. 'From the county of Katzenelnbogen. 1610. A good year they say. Or perhaps you – does your religion permit?'

I think Frantz found the question bizarre, but did not show it in his voice. 'A glass of Rhenish would be fine.'

My master poured the wine, as music started up from the water's edge, fiddles and lutes. 'Will it go on late? The dance?'

'Ah. It is usually a riotous affair. You shall come of course?'

'No, no, no.' He nodded at the book he'd picked up. 'My studies, you understand?'

'Well, I pray we shall not disturb you too greatly.'

There was silence and my master stood with two full glasses.

'Is it yours?' Frantz asked, motioning at a half-painted canvas. My master had begun it weeks ago, during one of his less morose stretches. (He had always been a fine artist, but gave himself no credit for it, and consequently practised very little.)

'A nonsense of a thing. But it will burn well when the firewood is gone.'

Frantz clearly believed him. 'You must do no such thing. It is exceptional. Here, our little town so faithfully rendered, and the mountain just as it is at dawn. And your dog there in the foreground. It is a masterpiece.'

My master laughed. 'I have seen masterpieces.'

More silence, until eventually Frantz relieved him of one of the glasses. 'Season's greetings,' he toasted and they both drank. 'So, what is it you wish to discuss?'

I looked up at my master expectantly. He didn't notice and just gave out a nervous laugh. 'Tell me of London. That's where you were, no? You told me when we first talked. How long is it you spent there? I mistook you for an Englishman. Three years, was it?'

'Five.'

'Wonderful. The city is enchanting, no? What took you there? Was it vocational?'

Frantz blushed and took a sip. 'Perhaps I am sentimental, but I had wanted to visit since, as a young man, I read the words of a play by your William Shakespeare. I believe he's dead now, but perhaps you know it? *This happy breed of men* – he talks of the English – *This precious stone set in a silver sea, Which* – some business of a wall, or a moat – *against the envy of less happier lands.* That phrase struck me: *less happier lands.* The non-stop war, you understand, in this region of the world. So many dead – but England, a precious stone. A picture I saw once of Elizabeth, the former queen. Spellmaking, is that the word? A sense of fairness, of loyalty, the English, pioneers – anyway, I always dreamt to go there. Most people in this valley, if they ever could leave it, even in a dream, would choose Vienna, but London is the city that called to me.'

'And did you prosper? Did you find the happy breed?'

Frantz took in a breath and let it out again. 'London is – for strangers, it can be harsh. I had little money, days as a building labourer, nights working at a tannery – but the saviour of all was the theatre. For one penny. The wonders put on there. The places to be taken to. I saw, what was it? *The Tragedie of King Lear.* A sublime piece. The frailty of kingship, family, madness. A storm upon a heath, and you're transported entirely with the very smell of the rain and the wind. *It is the stars, the stars above us, govern our conditions.* So says the Duke of Gloucester, wondering how one sister can be good whilst her kin so evil.'

'Kent,' my master murmured, and Frantz did not understand at first. 'The Duke of Kent speaks the line – in the war encampment.'

'You are right, I am sure. Kent. In any case, I would go every week: to Egypt, to Verona, to Athens. Astonishing. Pardon me, how I prattle on. Pray, tell me what troubles you so?'

My master rose and paced the room, then poured more wine and stood by the fire. I went and sat next to Frantz as a kind of encouragement for him to stay, and an apology for my master's long-windedness. An age seemed to pass before he put his hands together and stretched them until his fingers clicked. 'I am not a religious man. I do not go to mass. Or confession. Or – well, I have beliefs – I try to be good.'

'Yes, I understand –'

'I want to say, though not religious, I need to –' he had trouble speaking the phrase – 'make a confession of sorts. I need to unburden myself. I have kept a secret so long it hurts.' He touched his head. 'Here it hurts.'

Now he was beginning to talk of 'secrets', I cocked my ears.

'What is it?' asked Frantz.

My master did not reply at first. He turned a log with his boot so the bark caught the flame.

'This room is our confessional,' persisted Frantz. 'Your confidences are safe with me.'

'What ails me is – I do not die.'

'You – you do not die?'

'That is my principal grievance. Though there are others related to it. You are the only soul on this earth I have told. I should say, you and one other.'

'I misunderstand, you do not –?'

'Die. I *cannot* die. I mean to say, there are ways to do it, by drowning or hanging or removing my head, but I will never take such a course. Not because suicide is a sin, but because – well, perhaps it is a sin.' In the pause that followed the corners of my master's eyes reddened.

'Tell me what troubles you. I listen well. I have had my share of ill fortune, so I shall sympathize. Have you suffered some loss or other?'

'I. Do. Not. Die. That is that.' He got up, took the little tortoiseshell box from a drawer and emptied the contents on the table. 'This powder is called jyhr. It comes from Persia, from a mine in the Kalankash mountains west of Tabriz. A special knowledge of mines, of treasures below the earth and where to find them, had come my way you see? In Kalankash, deep in the earth there's a labyrinth of caves, and there lies a seam of this. As far as we know, it's found in no other place. Listen to it.'

'Listen?' The first time I'd witnessed him opening the box, decades ago, I'd noticed that the powdered jyhr emitted a curious faint hum. 'It sings. All the energy trapped within its prisms, fighting with itself.' Whether Frantz heard it or not, he nodded anyway. 'It takes years to distil a liquid from it. *Years*, mark you. And with a single miscalculation, one ill-judged measurement, the whole thing —' He mimed an explosion. 'And all for half a thimble of serum, which may or may not do its job.'

'Indeed.'

'Dropped in the mouth, in minute quantity, it can take away pain. Like so.' He snapped his fingers. 'Or to a wound, repaired almost instantly, but it can do more. Much more.' He picked up an instrument from the table, a type of syringe that he nearly always carried with his other instruments. 'Have you ever seen one of these? I do not expect it. A Roman invention, improved on by the Egyptians. A glass tube and a piston like so. Originally it was to draw cataracts from the eyeball. But if you fit a quill, here at the nib, and reverse the process, you can feed liquid into the very stream of your blood. Now I frighten you. I see it on your face. Goodness knows what compels me to talk so.'

'Not at all. I am fascinated.' Frantz lowered his voice and cast his eye to the shut door. 'I have read Vesalius and Servetus, the anatomy of organs, the circulation of blood from the heart, and do not consider those works to be anti-theological. Quite the reverse: they illustrate the miracle of man's splendour the more.'

'Well, no doubt.' My master had little patience for a certain type of preachiness. 'I shall not burden you with all the particulars, but the jyhr in its liquid form, when driven into the bloodstream here —' he indicated the point on the side of his abdomen where he, I, Aramis – and no doubt Vilder too – had crescent-shaped scars – 'and injected over and over and over again, little by little – and I am simplifying greatly – a stone is formed inside, a *living* stone, a multiplying one, a crystal, if you like. And that jewel, that azoth, which grows inside, imbues its host with, with . . .' My master gave a half-cocked smile. 'It imbues its host with . . .'

'Everlasting life?'

My master let out a little laugh. 'Well, if not everlasting – long certainly.' Another laugh. 'There it is. Surely you do not believe me?'

'Why should I not?

'Because you cannot give credence to such –'

'The real world is strange.'

'But still –'

'When my father was born, did the sun and all the stars not travel around the earth? And yet now –' Frantz finished his sentence by changing the direction of his forefinger.

A peculiar alteration came over my master. His forehead wrinkled. 'You believe me? Truly?' He laughed. 'What a relief to pronounce it at last. The endurance of holding my tongue –' Then he halted, struck by a new thought. 'But wait.' He shook his head. 'This is not all my confession. You see another person came with me down the road I took. And –' He was lost in thought for a while.

'What happened?'

'He believes, this other man, that *I* forced him. I remember it differently, that it was his notion more than mine, but perhaps – it is so long ago you see.'

'Is he –?'

'Yes, still alive. Yes. Undoubtedly. But what I am trying to say is I have the temperament for this existence. I find a way to survive it; I tangle through. But he is not as resilient and sometimes, right or wrong, I feel culpable.' He trails off again, his eye following the line of the floorboards, before stopping at me. 'And there is more still. Later, a third creature came down that road with us. My champion here.' He knelt and very softly stroked my head. 'But he, categorically, had no choice in the matter, of joining our circle, our society of long life.' Frantz regarded me keenly now, though I couldn't tell if he was intrigued or disturbed. 'It was not fair of me, was it? To take him on the path that has no end, unless by self-destruction, by drowning or fire or hanging? Indeed, no, I see you judge me now.'

'I am not in that business. Your companion is content, no? You are kind to each other, yes? What more is there?' To this day I cannot tell if Frantz truly believed my master's story or not. Perhaps, like a doctor to a madman, he was simply allowing him to act out his passion aloud. 'And that is your confession?'

My master filled up the glasses, and after a pause Frantz asked, 'Why would you want it?'

'What?'

'Why would you *want* long life in the first place? If it is not too dull-witted a question.'

For a moment my master looked like he'd been ambushed. I looked from him to Frantz and back again. 'You have to understand the time we found ourselves in,' he said, 'my associate and I. The time, *the age*, was extraordinary. It was as ancient Greece must have been, better. The previous centuries, if the "art" they produced was anything to go by, were surely small-minded and superstitious by comparison. Perhaps I remember it too passionately, but the quest for knowledge, the zeal to break boundaries, to investigate, deeper and deeper, to understand this world we've been born upon – "*world*", even the word was new in a way, for no one had thought before of the land beyond their borders. The infinitely tiny and the unimaginably huge, to understand even what it means "to understand".' He laughed. 'Pardon me, you probably have these feelings daily, in your profession, but enlightenment was new to me, and took me by surprise. How lucky I felt, even as an adolescent, to have been born in that age. If history is a labyrinth of dark roads through a city, *that* time was its most beguiling piazza, its most victorious square yet, though of course the city of history will be built and built for all eternity, and I hope there are plenty more squares to come. So I had vigour here –' he touches his chest '– as everyone seemed to, because we were on the cusp of things.'

'I met Brunelleschi, you know?' my master went on. 'Have you heard of him?'

I think Frantz wished he did, but said, 'The name is familiar.'

'The man who built the dome of Florence's cathedral.'

'Yes, yes, of course.'

'He was the first I met. In Florence, I had the good fortune to visit the city as a young man and I saw a drawing of that dome – a decade before it was built – and I *had* to meet its creator. I was quite precocious. I camped outside his house, for days and days, until he granted me an audience. I held his hand in my own. This hand I shook with yours, I shook with his. The human who came up with the idea of perspective. What mind could stand outside itself like that? He was not particularly amiable, but no matter. He opened a window to undreamed-of realms. After him, meeting the great minds of the age became our passion, my companion and I. We had money between us, some connections and we were not without charm, but it was our enthusiasm that opened doors. That and a little flattery. There is no man or woman so great that they do not enjoy being told so sometimes. And we had time on our side, ages of it. We could learn and learn. In due course we became patrons of sorts, and by some miraculous sleight of hand some of the thinkers and artists and makers started to come to *our* doors. I'm not sure they even knew why. Just that there was a touch of magic about us. Which was true in a way.

'We met them all: Machiavelli, Lippi, Raphael, Vespucci the explorer, Cardano the mathematician, the Bellini brothers. Some were engaging, others plain in the flesh. I took wine with Michelangelo. He had a reputation for rudeness, but was very agreeable to me. I could go on, but you'll think me very boastful. So, we had this powder, the stones from Tabriz. I'd been told of their – their possibilities, but was sceptical naturally. Arabian tales. To shorten the long story, there began our experiments. Do you understand now? How we were swept up in the age?'

'Yes, but – why that? Why a cure for death? Why dedicate yourself to precisely that? It might sound obtuse to ask –'

'No, it is not. It is the wisest question.' His mouth set into a kind of grimace. 'It is hot in here, no?' He strode over to the window, barged it open and took in a lungful of air, as he wondered how to reply. It had begun to snow and flakes wandered into the room. He laughed nervously, and carried on talking with his back to our visitor.

'The Black Death, I suppose. The Black Death heralded everything I've talked about, that age I'm so bewitched by. In any case, first my father, and then my mother –'

I must have sat bolt upright and made a noise, for my

master turned round, and the priest too. My ears were sticking up on hearing 'father' and 'mother'.

'All good, my boy?' my master asked. I knew, if he was to keep talking of his family, I'd have to not draw attention, so I lay back down, rested my head on my front paws, whilst keeping my ears roundly open. My master carried on observing me until Frantz nodded.

'Your mother and your father?'

'Yes. I was – thirteen? Where we lived, the door of her bedroom was thick oak. There was a key as long as my hand, and she locked herself in with it, so I wouldn't – so no one could – she would not have us even approach along the corridor. She wrote me notes and dropped them from the windows. Before she died, obviously.' When Frantz went to my master, he jutted up his hand. 'No, no, do not comfort me. There was nothing special in my loss. Everyone lost everyone. Besides it is so long ago now, when the world was younger.'

He shut the window and went to stoke the fire, secretly dashing the wetness from his eyes.

'So, you were frightened of dying?' asked Frantz. 'That was your motivation.'

'No, it was the science principally. Always science. I wanted to put my mark on that age, as all the others did. I wanted to be great too – but, yes, I had a fear. It was not small. But it wasn't of dying myself, but of the pain I'd cause to those I'd leave?' He had not meant the sentence to be a question. 'Doubtless, it makes no sense, but I must have thought that when *I* have a family, my own kin – which I had longed for even as a young boy, for children are the heart of the world – I cannot leave them as my parents left me. I cannot die.'

Frantz looked into his empty glass and I sensed he was

troubled by my master's logic. In the silence came the sound of the dance at the lake. 'And do you have your family?' the priest said at last. 'Your children?'

'No,' my master said in as grim a voice as he'd ever used. 'That is the paradox. None. How could I have had children? When either I would have had to outlive them, or convert them too? The first unthinkable, the second fraught with danger and risk – what happened to my former companion, to the state of his mind, is proof of that. And the same would have applied to their mother, whoever she may have been. No, indeed, I had not thought it through properly.' He took a deep breath and closed his eyes. 'No children. No wife.' He had such a look of desolation about him, his eyes so tightly squeezed together, I went over and sat by him, pressed against his leg.

'Well, you have your four-legged companion at least.'

My master chuckled. 'He is not my family.' Frantz was about to apologize when my master said, 'He is my soul. What am I without my champion? Just a box of notions and logics. You should get to your party.'

Frantz observed my master closely before replying. 'Why is it you wished to speak to me tonight? I understand you needed to unburden secrets from your head, but did you have another purpose?'

My master gave it some thought, before shrugging. 'If I did, I do not know what.' The priest raised his brow and seemed to expect a weightier answer, but my master said, 'Tell me something of your own relations. I have talked too much.'

'Oh.' The priest looked at the backs of his hands. 'My mother still lives, as you know, in the rectory with me. But my brothers – more sad stories, what a pair we make on

Christmas Eve – they were killed in the wars. Sebastien at Dirschau, Little Rudolfo at Grol. He was sixteen.'

'Grol? I – Grol, really? You were the oldest?'

A nod. 'Not fit for the army. My legs. So the future rests with me now.'

'Grol, you say? This August past?'

'Did you lose someone there yourself?'

My master shot me a look, thinking of Aramis no doubt, before saying. 'Yes. I didn't know him well. Your brother fought for the republic, the Protestants? On that side?'

'He did, though they are all one to me. Do you understand better than I? For to me it seems we fight over nothing more than the details of how we should worship. It is wretched.' He grew more passionate. 'You must excuse me, but there can be no more desperate place to be cut from life, far from the fires of your home, in the mud and blood and din. Sixteen he was.'

My master threw his arms round Frantz and held on for such a long time, I thought Frantz might be embarrassed, but our companion seemed moved by it, and held on with equal tenderness.

'May we come to the dance with you then?' my master asked, finally letting go. 'I shall not study after all, and a reel or two will shake away the melancholy.' He laughed and clapped his new friend on the back.

The Christmas revels took place on a granite promontory at the edge of the water. The villagers, sphered in lantern light, danced and caroused. The silvered aurora stretched across the valley. The snow fell so delicately it looked as if the stars themselves were dropping from their places to our Earth, and the lake was a frozen serpentine of glass winding to a raven-blackness of mountains.

From the moment we arrived my master joined the dance, and as usual danced badly, forever tearing off in the wrong direction, bumping into everyone and apologizing. For some hours, in our cocoon in the hills, amidst the laughter and overlapping conversation, the play of fiddles and clack of bottles, all the sadness of the past months was put aside, and I felt newly invigorated – when all of a sudden my master stopped dancing.

He had such a surprised look on his face, my first thought was that Vilder had followed us after all, and that my master had spied him. He began pushing through people, just as he had at the frost fair in London. But this time, he was looking for someone, rather than running away from one. It was Frantz.

'May I say something more, father?' my master panted, taking him to one side.

Frantz nodded, but had the slightly ruffled air of someone who'd been disturbed in their leisure 'What is it?'

'You asked me what was my purpose, for speaking to you. *Purpose*, that is the issue. The young man who camped outside Brunelleschi's door – I no longer recognize him in myself. I've slipped somehow into an ordinary state, into automatic ways, the very thing I fought so hard to avoid. I've been going about everything wrong. I have skill, you see? As a physician, a chemyst and what you will. Great skill. My many years upon this earth has provided that.'

'I believe you.'

'Purpose is the thing.' My master laughed, like a lunatic I fancied. I would have thought he was drunk, but I'd watched him and all he'd had was the two cups of Rhenish at home. 'There was purpose *once*, in my work, long ago, when we were – when I was creating and experimenting. But not for decades. Monster or not, my old associate told me as much, but only now do I realize it is true. It is your brothers and their like I should be helping.'

He noticed that Frantz's smile had curdled a little and tried to bring his thoughts to a conclusion. 'I just wanted to tell you: I shall give up my former existence and start anew. I shall do my duty. To the battlefield I shall go.'

Some of the townspeople came to lure him back to the revels – his energetic capering had brought him some celebrity. 'I'm sorry, I should not have talked so long. You've been so kind to listen,' he said to Frantz, patting my head as he went. I watched him start up a reel once more with new vigour. I had no real notion of what he intended to do, what he meant by 'my duty', I was just content that he was happy again. He carried on dancing with the others until dawn.

Little did I know our new life had already been set in motion. That soon the bones of our former existence would be broken by war. And they'd heal, only to be broken again.

9. Opalheim

Westphalia, May 1815

A week passes, or more, and Sporco and I are locked inside Vilder's carriage. For the first few days the vehicle climbs vertiginously, dropping at intervals, only to ascend again, higher and higher. The altitude, and the speed at which Braune tears round every bend is sickening enough, but with my wound, and the process of mending, I sink into a state of near hallucination. I've been struck by a bullet a handful of times in my life, all long ago, during the years my master and I trailed armies. I'd garner my strength to limp to a safe place, where I'd collapse, the battle a whirring dream around me. And afterwards, I woke, not happy to be alive – but almost the opposite: terrified of eternity.

Once we peak the mountains, we shoot down at nerve-shredding speed, Braune whipping the horses to the bone. We travel northwards still; I can tell by how light slithers across the floor. Maybe once or twice a day we'll stop briefly. There are shouts to farriers, hurried rehorsing. Braune unlocks one of the doors, pistol in hand, checks we're alive, slops down a bowl of water and a handful of scraps, before locking up and setting off again.

As we pass from the mountains on to the lowlands, the realm of Saxony I presume, the smells of the countryside change: alpine scents giving way to beech, privet, primrose and forest lichens. Many times, heralded by distant ditties of bugles and pipes, we pass tramping battalions, an army marching north. Through the scratched glass, we pass flickers of uniforms, muddy faces and blank eyes, until we speed away from the thump of feet.

I expect Sporco to be disturbed, at the least, by our change in circumstance, but he adapts to it well. Such is the nature of dogs, to trust. I wonder if he's forgotten I told him Vilder was evil, or careless of it. In either case, I'm glad of it: whatever Vilder has in store, there's no point in Sporco suffering fear until it happens. And besides, he's fed well, kept comfortable and he's aware of a purpose to what's happening. He has no inherent need to understand it. And I'm at his side. We are 'the pack', as he insists on calling us.

At dusk, after two weeks of travelling, we peel off the road and halt.

'What's happening?' Sporco says, putting his paws on the ledge of the window.

Looking out, I can see a mansion, a medieval edifice perched on the crest of a hill. Above a portcullised arch, there's a stone escutcheon emblazoned with the all too familiar insignia: three towers below a crescent moon. I had expected a larger building. Only when Braune dismounts and shoulders open the iron barriers, do I realize it's a gatehouse. From either side of it, boundary walls snake into the distance. It's bleak terrain, crags and tors, thorny shrubs and wind-slanted firs.

We crunch through the arch and set off up the drive, almost immediately entering a wood: a crowded gloom of oak and elm, of squat trees and deformed shrubs. The path is over-grown and low-hanging boughs whip against the side of the coach. The woods go on and on, wheels jerking against ruts in the road. We leave the deciduous trees behind, the path straightens and we accelerate into a matrix of conifers, to an echo of hooves and flickering pins of evening light. We travel through it – for miles it seems – until the echo suddenly stops. Sporco's ears lift.

We've come out into an expansive plain, as barren as the woods had been choked, a droughted prairie, vacuum-quiet, dusty earth, balding patches of heather and bull grass. An immense dried-up lake snakes to a palace in the distance. Even in the vanishing light, I can see it's immense, its front an infinite blockade of brick stretched between three towers. On one side, the building sags, making the central tower lean in at an angle.

Braune unlocks our compartment and wrestles chains round our necks.

'Here,' says Vilder, snatching them from him and yanking us from the coach. He loops the tethers tight and crouches to study me, feeling my side where the flesh has all but mended. Sporco watches him, with a hopeful sway of the tail, before Vilder pulls us up the front steps into the hall. My heart races: there's a trace of something clear, of my master, the barest atom of him, so elusive, it's gone immediately. 'De la Mare,' Vilder shouts and his voice takes time to echo back to us. A life-sized portrait of Aramis looks down on us, more war-like than I remember him, on horseback and silver breast-plated. Sporco takes in the space, ears out and eyebrows lifted, excited by its dimensions, by the sheer height of the many columns of red marble and jasper. He's tiny against them, and I recall that it was just a few weeks ago that he gingerly entered La Perla's apartment and thought *that* was amazing.

'De la Mare!' Vilder calls again. When no one comes, he

sets off, dragging us behind. Dust is thick on the ground and it's whipped up into little clouds, making Sporco sneeze. We pass room after room of faded grandeur, uncared-for statues and paintings layered in dust. Hearing someone, Vilder stops at an open door. 'De la Mare?'

'*Monsieur?*' comes a voice from within.

'In God's name! Have I not told you that this room is to be kept closed?' He pauses on the threshold, hesitant about entering. It's a chapel of the type that are common in palaces of this size. In a murk of stained glass, there are tombs, a pair of them, railed in on pedestals, life-size effigies of a man and a woman, palms pressed together, humans from faraway times, the medieval epoch.

A gaunt man patters from the gloom. '*Désolé, monsieur.* They've made a nest in the ceiling –' He does a double take when he notices Sporco and I, but says nothing.

'Did he come?' Vilder asks.

'You haven't found him?'

'If I had, would I be asking you?'

'No one's called, *monsieur.*'

Vilder hawks up a gobbet of phlegm and spits it on the floor. De la Mare, his retainer I presume, wears a crimson gabardine like a cardinal's. 'What's made a nest?' Vilder asks of him.

'Bats. A thousand of them. They must have broken in there.' He nods to an opening at the base of the far wall where a panel of stained glass has fallen out.

'Deal with it as you must, but keep this door shut. Understand?'

'*Bien sûr.*'

There are no niceties between these men. If anything, the servant – pallid, gaunt and unearthly – is even more unapproachable than the master. 'Soldiers all the way here,' says Vilder, 'the roads choked with them. Why?'

'You have not heard the news?'

'What news?'

'He has fled Elba. Bonaparte. He's returned to Paris. Pronounced emperor, and so and so on.' He holds his palms heavenwards. '*La guerre recommence.* The British come, the Austrians, all. A battle is imminent; in Belgium they say.'

'I want you to write.'

'*Monsieur?*'

'To every king in Europe, every duke, every count, every last pox-ridden baronet, all. One of them will know where he hides. They must return him. To every general too, write. Tell them it is I, Vilder, from Opalheim. Offer them money, gold, whatever they ask for. Every general, mark you. Write to Napoleon too.'

'Napoleon?'

'He has fled from Elba, has he not?' he says in sarcastic imitation.

'Indeed but – I would not expect him to –'

'Write! Tell them, to tell *him*, I have his dog. How absurd the phrase sounds, coming from my own mouth. Curse him.' De la Mare is entirely bewildered. He puzzles a glance at us. 'Dog, dog, dog,' Vilder hisses, raising his palm to strike, but stopping short. 'Have you never seen dogs before? Go, write, and show me a draft before you send it.'

De la Mare remains. 'Sire, perhaps you must –?'

'What?'

There's a pause. De la Mare is almost too scared to speak. 'Face the possibility that –'

'That what?' Vilder grimaces. I know they're talking of my master, speaking of him as if he's alive and I listen intently.

'How far could he go –' De la Mare shrugs – 'when he can barely put one leg before the other? Or speak, or hear? He has no sense who he is. So you must face the possibility –'

Vilder's fists are pure knuckle against our chains. 'That he's dead? That is your suggestion? You know nothing about it.' Before the other can reply Vilder slaps him across the ear. 'If you had not let him roam free in the house, we would face nothing. I told you –' He stops himself from hitting De la Mare a second time, instead saying, 'He's as cunning as he's dangerous. Well, if he returns, you shall learn your lesson. If he hunts you down and cuts your throat, you shall learn your lesson. The letters. Now!'

This time De la Mare goes. Vilder peers into the darkness of the chapel, pivoting his ear to the wet slap of bats, then turns on his heels. I'm newly agitated and confused as he drags us on through anterooms to a set of double doors, which he shoulders open. A little vestibule leads immediately to another pair in cast iron. He pushes us through them, into darkness, slams the doors behind us and bolts them three times.

The shock of my master's smell is so overwhelming that my mind seems to curve and warp, like I've slipped through time.

I've found him, I think in that nonsensical moment, despite everything I've just heard. 'I'm here, I'm here,' I bark, certain they've made a mistake and that really he hasn't left. I set about the place, bouncing my nose along the surfaces: a fireplace with a furnace in it, long tables, countless piles of parchment, an old four-poster bed. I jump on it: straw mattress, hemp sheets, bolster, coverlet – all of them drenched in his smell. I roll on it all. 'Here I am.' I leap down, skirting the walls, nooks and recesses. 'I'm here!'

'We're here!' Sporco proclaims in agreement, following wherever I go.

Behind an arras, we find a tiny side room, a garderobe, with a stone toilet in the corner, but otherwise empty too.

I hurry back to the main room, which is as high as a cathedral. There's a whispering gallery right at the top, but no stairs lead to it. I renew my hunt: furnace, paper piles, tables. I spring up on to one: bottles of ink, quills, brushes, the scent-print of his hand everywhere. Down, back to the bed, skirting the walls, the garderobe. And where I go, Sporco comes too, yapping in delight. 'Is he here? Where is he? I'm sure he's here.'

After two more circuits my joy evaporates and is finally replaced by common sense. Of course he isn't. The fact of my master's smell but the absence of his person is pure physical pain. I'm losing him all over again. I'm back in the cathedral a hundred and twenty-seven years ago, circling the tiles below the fresco in vain, finding his scarf and nothing else.

Many years ago I saw a boy drop from a cliff. He'd been walking with his father when he saw gulls' eggs nestled on an outcrop of rock. He clambered over to look. His father was facing the other way when there was a hollow tear; stone scurried and the ground split and slid under him. He gasped and his father ran to help, throwing out his arms, but the chalk dropped, the boy with it, noiseless except for a gentle crack as he hit the shore below. The father let out no sound; the horror was too unnatural. What had been was gone. The certainty of life had reversed; the change was undoable. For all time he would be cursed to live in that fleeting moment. Now, more than ever, I feel like that man, missing not just a part of myself, but all of it. My master was here, but now he is not. As I sink, so does Sporco, bereft on my behalf. He comes and sits by my side, pressing against me and delivers the last words of his commentary. 'Not here.'

There's a squeal of wood and a door high up in the whispering gallery opens and Vilder comes in to check on us. He moves differently from before, no longer tense but in a drunken roll, and I see why: he has filled up my master's hexagonal bottle with more of the pale yellow easing tonic. When he speaks his voice is blurry. 'Where is he? The creator of our misery. Never mind, he'll return. Now you are here he'll come.' He reels out and locks the door behind him. The last of the evening drips from the high window and all I can hear is Sporco's breathing.

I'm woken by dawn light on my face. Sporco is curled up beside me, snoring, his head half buried under the coverlet, his outsize brows twitching in some fast-moving dream. The room is immense. It could be the Banqueting House at Whitehall, that my master and I visited on its opening. This version is even larger and must have been a stateroom too long ago, where ceremonies would have taken place or ambassadors welcomed – but now, like the rest of the palace, it's an unloved ruin.

Although there are twelve windows, six great arched ones below and six square ones above, they've been long closed up with iron shutters, all except one, unreachable at the top, where the casing has come away. The ceiling frescoes are as bizarre as any I have seen. Usually – like the ones at Banqueting House – they're peopled with far-fetched celestial beings, clouds and chariots, sylphs and immortals. These ones, however, pay homage to a world of industry and metallurgy. A battalion of miners marches through a craggy landscape into a cavern below a mountain, where they dig, unearthing golden light. In others there are molten rivers of silver and mercury, floating ironworkers, furnaces and chimneys, bronze foundries and glassworks.

The principal wall, in which the fireplace is set – which in turn is so colossal it could be the entrance to a cathedral – is patterned with tiers of pale rectangles, where large pictures must once have hung, but which is now marked with thousands of hand-drawn symbols arranged in drifting columns like hieroglyphics.

As I observe it all, looking up from the bed, it strikes me how calm I am. Despite everything, I passed the night soundly. Because my master is alive. He slept in this bed. That is true. He was here. Even now, he is being searched for, waited for, expected. He is somewhere. Alive. After all this time, I am vindicated.

For some moments I cling on to that miraculous fact – before doubts begin to pull me down again. How long was he here? Why did he never come back for me? Determined to stay calm, to remain methodical, I slip down and investigate the room. The furnace within the chimney place is a pitch-black hole where a fire has burnt constantly until recently. My master worked precisely here. His scent flickers off everything like little shocks of static. There's even a halo of smooth stone where he slid back and forth between worktop, fire and shelves.

Smooth stone. It would take years to shine it so flat.

On the worktop there are stacks of jars and bottles, familiar scents – copper, mercury, bugbane, ambergris – and all the various ingredients he used for his distillations. In the past century, if I caught even a hint of one of these odours, I'd feel a pinprick of happiness at the reminder of him.

I study the hieroglyphics, thousands of clusters, each

containing a band of symbols, seven identical ones in each. Seven. Some of the scratched-out symbols have the shape of dogs.

Prickles creep up my spine, from the root of my tail to my neck. My ears stiffen and my throat dries – as I begin to grasp what has happened in this room.

Each mark is a day, each cluster a week, each column a year. My master was counting time. I pad along the wall. Every inch of it, every reachable part, is inscribed with a mark, many in the form of a dog. How many? How many dogs are there? A hundred and twenty-seven years since I set eyes on him.

The gallery door opens, Braune stoops through, throws a bundle over the parapet and goes, leaving a pair of fleshy bones on the floor. Sporco, woken by the noise, unburrows himself, nose twitching. He bounces from the bed and sniffs around until he finds the treat. 'Not to be believed,' he gasps, tail whipping against the floor. He pushes his snout right into them, before taking one in his jaw, shaking it, dropping it, arranging it, tongue unrolling. 'You see this? Not to be believed.'

I'm too distracted to pay attention. My brain is a souring fog, a sickness of shifting shapes, of things just out of reach, of trapdoors down to fiendish places. I can't breathe. I stagger back and knock into one of the towers of papers. It lurches, topples and hundreds of sheets spill across the floor, fanning out, a breeze of dust travelling with them. They are drawings that my master has made, hundreds upon hundreds of them, some so old, they're filament thin.

Heat rises in my throat. The metal door with three bolts, the barred windows.

A prison.

All those years waiting, the mulchy autumns and whet-stone winters, the cathedral steps, wishing on the horizon, all my little spins of hope, dozens of them a day, which were dashed over and over. Yet still I hoped. The cheerless pageant of my time alone, losing friend after friend, whilst all the dis-piriting places of Venice – the inns stuffed with drunks, the slums and plague pits, the charnel houses and burial grounds – somehow all became markers and reminders of my failure. Alone all that time. The burning in my chest is insupportable, like a red-hot morass that will explode. And for what reason this imprisonment? For master to distil for that monster? To be an addict's servant? *You are the best of all at making them,* Vilder had said in Whitehall, having demanded an opiate brew. *Perhaps it is a deceit of the brain, but my own medicines never seem to work as well.*

Then a new fear comes upon me, more dreadful than all that have gone before, a notion that makes me cold to the bone. I look round at the wall. The markings change from one end of the wall to the other. In the first columns, the marks are clear and strong, but grow shakier and fainter the further they go. The last few inscriptions are feeble dashes – then blankness.

I paw apart the drawings that spilled on the floor, vignettes of our life together: one here from Whitehall, another from Elsinore, Amsterdam, Vienna, Prague. The last picture, which had sat at the top of the pile, is a self-portrait. From the faint-ness of it, from the thickness of the dust upon it, it must be twenty years old. My master is almost unrecognizable: a frail old man, bug-eyed and haunted. He's imagined me beside him, straight-backed, ears up, full of life – smiling – even as *he* stares ahead with the look of death.

I rush at the door and cry, 'Give him back to me! Give him

back!' Dizzy, sick, skin crawling, nerves snapping, a bruise-indigo gloom fills my head from the inside, before the floor rolls beneath me and I collapse.

When I come to, Sporco is standing over me. 'What's happened?' he says, ears folded back.

Where do I even start to explain? Just one thought remains in my head: I must escape this place. I must find him before it's too late.

10. War

Vienna, January 1628

The day after my master made his confession to the village priest, we left our home in the Carpathian hills and went to Vienna. The journey was punishing. Not only were we in the bitterest stretch of winter, but we'd barely any money remaining and had to take what meagre transport we could find. My master was undaunted, though.

'The start of a new year, my champion,' he called over the January wind, as we huddled amidst crates on the back perch of a mail wagon. 'What better time to begin again.'

Perhaps it was the weather, but I found Vienna gloomy in that age. There was a long wait at the town gates, as unfriendly guards cross-examined every new arrival. And inside, we found a place so resolutely built to defend itself, with layer after layer of bastions, walls and checkpoints, that civilized life seemed to have been pressed out of it entirely. I expected my master to whisper something amusing to me – 'What an uncongenial locale,' or, 'Where are the dances?' he might usually say – but his mind was on other things. There was a hard glint in his eye and a straightness to his spine that were unfamiliar to me.

We went to the Hofburg palace, to the court of Ferdinand II – both house and household were as plain and unwelcoming as the city, a warren of bureaucrats – and in his single-minded state, my master was faster than ever to persuade the necessary people of their vital need to employ him.

But my master had more in mind than just working as a palace physician. As soon as we were given our quarters, he set about his *project*, his preparations – I would learn soon enough – for joining the war. I remembered his last vow to Frantz on Christmas Eve: *I shall give up my former existence and start anew. I shall do my duty. To the battlefield I shall go.*

The first task, and the most vital – as well as the reason we then spent a full three years at Hofburg, my master playing the role of royal doctor – was the distilling of the powdered jyhr into its liquid form. The tincture would become the central substance of all he would do in the decades that followed, but I had no idea how fiendishly complicated it was to create. The process could not be hurried; it took months and months and was unpredictable at best, and oftentimes dangerous.

Before the jyhr was even added, he had to manufacture a brew of other ingredients, a compendium of chemicals and minerals so diverse we had to go to nearly every pharmacist and apothecary in Vienna, as well as put in special orders for certain materials and wait weeks for them to be sent from some other part of the continent, until he had what he wanted. Back in our rooms, working late every night, he calibrated, mixed and reduced them on the hot plate of the furnace for long and precise periods. It was cooled and warmed and cooled again. When conditions were not exact, if the ratios were out, or the fire not constant enough, the concoction shrivelled into a torpid paste. When eventually he deemed it to be the right consistency, he poured the batch into an iron bowl, went round fastening the doors and windows, before opening the little tortoiseshell box, carefully tweezering up a tiny piece of jyhr powder, just a plain black thing, and dropping it into the brew. He stepped away, shielding me behind his legs.

There followed a chaos of sensations that I would experience a dozen more times, but never understood. The hum the little stone emitted, though still slight, became grandiose, like a choir chanting from beyond the city walls. It seemed as if day became night within the chamber and everything, including my master, appeared to multiply into overlapping versions, as if time itself were stuttering. The stone in the bowl burnt like a little sun before everything returned to normal. The room became completely ordinary again, except for the odour of the newly wrought material: tiny but elemental, with strains of granite, barium and mercury. The liquid was uniquely colourless, monochrome, neither black, white nor grey, but somehow all three at the same time. An abstract.

Of course, the transfiguration was not always successful. More than once, when a stone had been dropped in the mix, an explosion ripped the room apart, upending furniture and throwing phials from shelves. 'No harm done, my boy?' he'd ask, alarmed and pale, coaxing me from my hiding place. We'd sit together on the ground as the light wilted from the windows and the place darkened into shadows. Eventually though, he'd pick himself up and brush dust from his clothes, a multicolour of powders. '*Tomorrow we begin again*?' He'd smile as he'd start to clean up the mess.

He bought a new bottle of clear thick glass similar to the one he'd left behind in Amsterdam, though square rather than hexagonal, and as he began to succeed with his distillations often enough to slowly fill it, drop by precious drop, he went about his other preparations. He cornered anyone at court who seemed to have a military connection and bombarded them with questions.

'I shall make it simple for you,' one of the friendlier palace diplomats whispered at the start. 'The war started when Ferdinand, a catholic as you know, began, in his wisdom, to curtail religious activity, sparking rebellion amongst the Protestant factions. That's why they call it a "religious" war, though of course once Sweden, Austria, Spain and France were drawn in it became less to do with religion and more with rivalry of power. Isn't it always, however they dress it up?'

After every conversation, when my master had found out all about the various armies, how they were divided up, where they were stationed and how great their number, he returned to our room, unrolling newly acquired maps of the continent and scribbling notes and coloured symbols all over them.

He found or produced other more commonplace medicaments and tinctures. He purchased surgical instruments, tourniquets, styptics, forceps and many more, along with all manner of related ephemera from bandages to catgut. He bought a backpack, the type worn by soldiers, and painstakingly adapted it, sewing in pockets and pouches to most efficiently contain the various elements of his kit. He even embroidered on the back of it in yellow cotton a symbol of a serpent entwined about a rod.

'It is the rod of Asclepius,' my master explained to me. 'He being the Greek deity of healing, and we his disciples. Listen how I talk now, my champion, of being disciples? I might have given you a knowing look once, if someone had pronounced that to me. In any case, the emblem is known near and far, and I make it bright, so everyone will know we mean no harm.'

My tail wagged. I was excited by it all, by his cleverness, diligence and how he'd turned his back so completely against his recent misery. No matter that it all turned out to be a precursor to many horrors; it was a lesson to me then of how to survive the traumas that fall in our way.

His mood darkened only when he remembered Vilder and Amsterdam. I knew instantly when he had, for his body sank and flickers of despair scented off him. More than once he sat down and began to write a letter, but would barely get halfway through before he thought better of it, screwed up the paper and threw it in the fire. When it caught light, and he was reminded no doubt of my ordeal, he grew angry. Then anger mutated to fear. He was caught between all these emotions, and whenever he stopped to observe a stranger, in Vienna, or in any of the places we travelled to after, he was frightened, but also peculiarly hopeful, that they might be Vilder. It reminded me of the event at the beginning of my life, of his strange reaction when we had found the corpse on the shore of Elsinore and he'd asked, half dreading, half wishing, 'So now you are dead, are you?'

Once my master was satisfied he had enough liquid jyhr in his bottle, we packed up and left Vienna, seeking out the battlefields most would avoid.

I came across my first army in an encampment a week's journey north-west of the city. I'd seen soldiers before of course; Aramis had been one, and various others at the courts of Europe, but those had been the favoured ones, of higher rank, conspicuously self-important in their battle attire amongst the cosseted civilians. But here was a vast morass, only half uniformed in grubby garb, unkempt, rough-eyed, ale-stained.

'This is a branch of the Catholic League,' my master mumbled like a university novice, broadening his shoulders against trepidation. 'Aramis's army. Wait here,' he said and disappeared into the throng. He started up a conversation with a bearded dragoon who was fixing a leather cuirass to his chest. Being one of those hardened career soldiers who seemed contemptuous of anyone that wasn't a fighter, the man answered with surly shrugs. In this milieu my master's charm, that precious skill he'd honed all his long life, lost its advantage. But he persisted.

I did not like the place, or the men, and the stench had grown quickly nauseating: the grit of male sweat, fermented with fatigue and fear into a sly, cloying odour, like rotting cherries or ripened lilies. An infantryman spotted me and came to say hello. He was young, a teenager, but his face was drawn and his skin puce. As he knelt to stroke me, the reek of gunpowder in the pockets of his bandolier sickened me and I jerked away from him. He tried again to make friends, but I removed myself to a new position and looked in the other direction until he relented. He was the first *ordinary* soldier I'd ever met, and even today, having stood side by side with so many, having felt their sorrows as if they had been my own, I still feel shameful of how discourteous I was. Doubtless the poor soul had been pressed into service by some greedy recruiting sergeant – the type that offers the world to such young innocents in order to secure their cut – and had likely lost his life before it had even begun, struck down in a field somewhere, realms away from his loved ones. I could have offered comfort and I didn't. I would learn to, though, soon enough.

'They march to Magdeburg,' my master said, coming back to me, an out-of-his-depth dither about him. 'There is a siege,' he added, as if it were a question or as if I might understand. 'We must go. Yes?'

That first time, he was too timid to march with the army,

so we followed at a distance, but always with their tail in our sight. When they halted to set up camp, we broke off too, passing the night under whatever shelter we could find. It was late spring and the land was so flat in that corner of the world, so verdant with crops, the days long and rich with genial light, it was impossible to foresee what lay ahead.

I would witness so many battles in the ensuing decades, I forget sometimes what an unnatural jolt the first one gave me, what a violent overturning of my worldview. In truth, it was not so much a battle – as a massacre. Magdeburg was a walled town bastioned on a hill at the edge of the Elbe River. When we arrived and set up shelter, at a slight remove from the main army camp, we could see a siege had been taking place for months. The land all around was gutted with trench-works and the platoons that droned back and forth through them were so filthy and mud-soaked, it appeared as if the earth itself was in constant motion. The bridgeworks across the river had already been taken and every hour more soldiers – in the red uniforms of the Catholic League – poured into the valley. From our vantage point, we could see into the town. Bands of local militia were on guard, but mostly it was strange for not being strange, the inhabitants moving about as on any day.

There came one morning a dream-like rumble and re-inforcements from our side, regiments of them, swept over the mount, until the entire plain was a lake of red, winking with ten thousand iron pikes. For a few moments, I might have thought it looked beautiful, before the first cannon exploded, a missile whistled forth and the town's ramparts shook. Another detonation followed, then dozens more at once, tarry smoke licking through the valley until eventually the walls of the gateway crumbled and the doors gave way.

There was an operatic cheer and the army poured into the town. It was clear straight away its defending army would stand no chance.

'Good grief, good grief,' my master panted, fretting back and forth, dodging imaginary bullets, not knowing whether to go with them or turn on his heels and run away. In the end both of us stood gaping, as we might at an accident on a turnpike, mesmerized by the unfolding horror. The original soldiers, the ones who'd been sieging for months, crazy from drink and mad for blood, were the most savage, rampaging the streets, cutting the throats of burghers even as they held up their arms to surrender. The smashing of glass as cuirassiers plunged lances through shop windows mixed with a bedlam of screams, war cries, muskets popping, cannon discharging – all whilst the childish rhythms of timbales and drums played along. By noon, fires blazed all over the city and the smell of burning flesh bled into the palls of sulphur and grapeshot. Women, their clothes torn from them, were marched out and pushed on to carts like pigs, whilst captured troops of the town's doomed militia were pinned down one at a time and burning pitch poured into their throats. Twice my master turned to a tree and vomited. The looting and the burning went on and on, and by evening Magdeburg was a wasteland. Tons of blistered corpses were brought out and thrown into heaps until they dammed the river.

My master fell down on his knees. I pressed against him, but he could not stop shaking. We watched soldiers carry up crates of loot to their superiors. Those officers, unscathed and dirtless, eating treats and sipping wine from little glasses, heedless of the noise of execution, picked through them like bric-a-brac at a market. When my master's breathing settled, I presumed we'd leave that hellish valley – how I longed to be back in our Carpathian village, or anywhere but there – but to my surprise he straightened his pack and set off.

'No!' I barked, blocking his way, appalled by the notion of him entering the fray.

'You stay out of harm's way,' he replied, pushing me on to my haunches. 'I'll be careful, I promise.'

'No!' I nipped at his ankles.

What was it he said on Christmas Eve? Our young priest? *There can be no more desperate place to be cut from life, far from the fires of your home.* And he went this time, declaring something about duty, down to the river, the yellow emblem of the serpent and the rod on his back.

I followed at a distance, to make sure he was not mistaken for an antagonist and captured – though what I'd have done I had no idea. In any case, he was cautious enough to keep well away from outright danger, going to the place where bodies had been left on the bank. He searched through them until he came across a human that must have been still alive. He took off his pack and talked to him – I heard only a faint murmur – before retrieving the phial of jyhr and applying drops both to his lips and the place he was cut. He waited with him until the man had the strength to half sit up. It was at that moment that my fear waned a touch and a bristle of pride went through my fur. At court he had always been considerate, always hurrying to help people – servants, courtiers, kings, he made no distinction – be it small gestures, like penning a letter for someone who could not write, or acting as a peacemaker between warring factions – or graver issues, such as the time he spent a night on a roof at the Louvre Palace in Paris, persuading the wayward son of a countess not throw himself off. He set an example to me, which I strove to emulate. However, in

Magdeburg his kindness was of a new and entirely special class that made me almost breathless in admiration.

He worked through the night, searching for the living and helping where he could, with whatever medicine he thought best. That first time I wondered what exactly he would be able to achieve. By the time of our third battle, I understood the extent of it: if a wound was clean and not too much blood had been lost, he could mend it, he would use his distilled jyhr if he thought it appropriate, but if the trauma was great, he could only ease the pain before death.

He returned to me just before dawn. 'You see? I am in one piece.' He kneeled to kiss the top of my head. 'And I have these too, though I can't recall if you're keen.' He lay a handful of wild strawberries before me. 'As long as the fruit grows we shall be sane, shall we not?'

With his new resolve and focus he'd already changed since the night of his confession to Frantz, but battle pushed the alteration much further. I had never thought of my master as vain, but in the coming months and years any trace of self-admiration left him. He lost interest in material things too, as well as shedding all excess weight. He became both hard and humble. He became, in short, a crusader, and to an extent I began to understand why the cuirassier we'd met at our first camp had been unsociable. That is what war does after all. But my master was also more tactile. He would hug me as he went to sleep and hold on all night. He was attentive, asking me questions he never usually did: 'How are you faring my boy?' 'Do you need to rest a while?' 'Shall we stop for water? There is a canal there.' 'Is the ground too sharp underfoot?'

Four months after the siege at Magdeburg, we found ourselves carried to Breitenfeld, where the two factions of the war – the *Thirty Years War*, as my master much later referred to it – faced each other either side of a vast plain. Summer was beginning to wane and northerly winds carried with them an unseasonal bite. We were on the other side by then – '*with the Protestants now*,' as he referred to the brown-and-blue-uniformed battalions. I had noted already how armies have distinct personalities. This one was plain and no-nonsense, whilst the Catholic League that faced us were showier, their outfits frilled with ornaments, curling red feathers in their helmets. It made sense that the effete and precocious Aramis had belonged to that side. Seeing them, stretched out from one end of the valley to the other like a giant braid of gold and red, I was struck again by how beautiful armies could be – until the fighting starts.

The beginning of *that* battle was signalled by the sudden whining of artillery shells and eruptions of earth. In no time everything was pandemonium again, though now on an unimaginable scale: the land shook, swathes of horses were cut down, sergeants shouted, cannons jumped back in fugs of black smoke, and there was the sleet of grapeshot, the deafening batter of lances, charges and counter-charges, caracoles, missiles devastating whole squares of soldiers, limbs setting off through the air and pikes falling back to gore their own sides. My master went to a hospital tent, but he'd been so taken by surprise he was tongue-tied and was shouted away by the field doctors. It wasn't until the worst was over, when each side had been decimated, burnt to the earth and battle flags captured by the winning party – ours it turned out, but I wouldn't have known – that he mustered the strength to take out his bottle and go forth with a lantern, his hair flapping in the wind, the yellow symbol on his back, picking through the carnage, the rucked earth and heaped bodies, through the stench of burning hair and salt-meat fetor, to offer aid to those most in need. Men caught up their last scraps of breath and he dosed drops on to their lips or to their wounds, chatting with them all the while: 'What is your name?' 'Do you have a sweetheart?' 'How brave you have been.' 'Calm now, it is over.'

Only when he'd done as much as he could, did he take me behind a barricade to rest. There, where no one could see him but I, his eyes became livid and he cried. Eventually he opened his coat and drew back his shirt to a deep gash in his abdomen and a puzzle of pale entrails. He'd been shot.

'You are a kind soul, you are, my champion,' he said as I whined and panted, whilst gently pawing his side. 'But it is not as serious as it looks.' The lesion hissed as it continued to cauterize itself, and he covered it again and buttoned his coat. It healed quickly, as all his wounds did, and in a couple of days it was the barest filament.

And such was the nature of our crusade, our mission, or what you will. My master and I followed armies, blue, green, red and grey ones, criss-crossing the continent. We took no particular side, but went where we felt the need was greatest. Europe was so fraught with conflict – there were so many battles I was amazed I'd spent the first thirty years of my life ignorant of them. He grew accustomed to the processes of war, soon found his way into hospital tents, first as an orderly, then a surgeon, until he was leading teams of army medics with his expertise and even reimagining the way field hospitals worked. Although the liquid jyhr, which he diluted ten parts to one, was his most precious medicine, he used it prudently and in secret.

I was often frightened, forever dirty and exhausted, but I believed in our purpose too. In time I forgot where it had arisen from – my master's distress over Aramis's death, the conversation on Christmas Eve, the priest's lost brothers and the vows my master had made – and began to believe that war was necessary, important – noble even. Why else would people kill each other with such decency and skill? Why else would soldiers wear uniforms, buttons gleaming, shoes polished like shellac? Battles of course grew jagged and messy, but the lead-up, the deployment, the training, the sacred hierarchy of command was impressive. Only orchestras of musicians, I would discover, had the same admirable ability to tie many humans together in a single purpose.

It wasn't until much later, in the first years of my vigil in Venice, seeing how little time people truly had, that I began to fully realize the absurdity of war, and how unforgiveable it was that the human race – that species of fearless magicians, of enchanters, that creates melodies to break and mend hearts, that builds palaces, cathedrals and cities, that governs even the sky and sea – is bent on war, on brute force and on its own destruction. I realized too, painfully so, in my exile beside the cathedral steps, how futile my master's vocation had really been. He must have known he could only ever be in one place at one time, that he could only ever save a finite number of lives, that so many others would die on battlefields that he would never reach. And yet he carried on.

Every few years, his supply of jyhr would run out. To manufacture more he would seek work at court again, at whatever palace or noble house was close at hand. Of course, as far as his employers were concerned, he was a chemyst, physician, apothecary, astronomer, what you will. But his true rationale was to have all the correct facilities – security, assistance, ingredients – to distil the monochrome tincture and carry it to the battlefield.

After our first seven years of service, and being at that time attached to the French army, we found employment at the

Chateau de Saint-Germain-en-Laye, a day's ride west of Paris. 'The giant French Fancy,' as my master called it. 'They can't quite decide if it's a fortress or a playground.' It was a whimsical construction of medieval towers and bold baroque facades with terraces descending to gardens of almost mathematical strictness. Inside it was monstrously sumptuous – as was the French way at that time – and as busy as an ants' nest – with intrigues and vanities. My master was surprised to find an entire team of doctors already installed. 'The queen has lost four heirs already,' one of them whispered to him by way of explanation. 'Stillborn. They'll take no more chances.'

My master found it hard to settle down. With his appreciation for luxury gone, he seemed bemused by the palace and its occupants. Especially as it was the era of exuberance, of grand hair, heeled shoes, exaggerated cuffs, coloured stockings and everywhere – attached to elbows, knees and ankles – bows and fussy spills of ribbons. He was also much jumpier there, always checking over his shoulder, worried about Vilder turning up. 'Might a man have come looking for me?' I often heard him ask servants and their masters alike. 'He would have been wearing a wig, long like this.'

For my part, though I tried not to show it too much, I was happy to be on solid ground again, warm, well fed and in a suite of rooms that was one of the finest I'd know. I'd developed – not unusually for my species – a sense of beauty, a taste for proportion, quality and colour. As the din and memory of battle ebbed away, I spent hours peering from our windows, entranced by the deer that sometimes would come and press their noses to the glass: gentle, courteous animals. I was fascinated too by the elaborate ceremonies of the household, in particular the *levee*, the rising ritual, when courtiers gravely filled into the royal bedchamber to watch the king throw back his covers, be washed, combed and shaved. Often – and I don't know why, but it always sets my tail wagging with amusement – he would shit in front of everyone, into a gilded china bowl. One of his entourage would then convey it away with haughty solemnity, as if rare jewels had been passed out of his backside.

My master became a hero within the household – reluctantly, for he sought fame even less than luxury – when he helped deliver the queen of her first living child. '*Louis Dieudonné, they call it, the God-given*.' When the infant was barely a week old, he sat for his first portrait, dressed in ermine robes, a miniature sceptre and orb put into its hands. (It's incredible to think I would meet that baby forty years on, in his dream palace at Versailles, a man of such dangerous gravity as to make me freeze.)

It was an incident at the Chateau Saint-Germain, at the christening celebration of the new prince, that had the most brutal effect on me, incredibly so, after all the bloodshed I'd witnessed. The whole court was gathered, a gossipy multitude of chess pieces on the black-and-white marble floor. The double doors stretched open and the excited chattering gave way to a hiss of silk, as everyone bowed, and the king entered with his baby held stiffly out like a sacred relic, the queen a step behind. As they ascended the dais and sat, there came a squeal from outside, a diabolical sound, and something heavy cracked against the window. More squealing, shrill and sharp. A fawn skittered into the room, clods of flesh torn from its flank. Revulsion rumbled through the court, as tipsily the animal tried to breach the wall of dresses. A white mastiff barrelled after, blood moustached, caught it by its leg, pinned it to the floor and set about the flesh once more, tearing off tissue and muscle to the white of its spine. The splitting yelps

of the fawn chorused with human screams. I tried to inter-
cept, but my master held me back.

No one dared exit for the king seemed to want to watch the
massacre – and the infant too. His baby eyes widened with fascination. I thought the fawn would cough up its lungs. I caught
its pleading stare, pupils like little stones of terror. Then the
mastiff must have cut into its neck as a spurt of crimson jave-
lined the air, speckling blood against a lady's skirt. The animal
went limp as blood pumped and pumped into a slick shinier
even than the floor. Perhaps my memory plays tricks, but I'm
sure the infant smiled in appreciation, before the room returned
to the ceremony.

That night, the king, queen and their court dined in splendour. Salvers were put down and domes whipped off to reveal
piles of meat, of venison in particular. I glowered at the
courtiers, furious, unable to put from my mind the pleading
expression of the fawn. I could not comprehend how they
could all have forgotten it so quickly. I slunk into the kitchens
and watched, cold-eyed, as dead pigs were hauled stiff on to
counter tops and their heads sawn off. The flavour of blood
hung in the air like rusted tin. That morning, I'd passed by
the pig-pen behind the kitchen garden. There were eight or
so creatures scoffing from a trough, whilst one slept on its
own, its snout resting contentedly on the gate. Bull grasses
tickled his flank and scents of sweet bay, lovage and sorrel
carried from the walled garden. The gate would be opened in
due course, a swineherd would come in and tattle with his
young, perhaps stroke their ears, even as he decided whose
throat he would cut first. For the first time I wanted to be
back on the battlefield: there at least men died hot-blooded,
for a cause they believed in, the risks mutually agreed. *There*

at least was the possibility of nobility – but the slaying of innocent animals was barbarian.

Soon enough we returned to our crusade, forty more years of it before the afternoon of sweet smoke in Venice, four decades of marches, campaigns and battles – Nördlingen, Breda, Arras, Groningen, Maastricht, Saint-Denis, Vienna – the continent tearing itself apart, fixing and breaking, fixing and breaking. Just one thing was different: after our stay in the court at Saint-Germain, I made a vow that I have kept ever since.

Let humans be savages, if they must, but I'll not kill a creature, not for food, or for any reason. Not ever.

11. False Blood

Opalheim, Westphalia, June 1815

Every waking hour I rack my brain of ways to break out of the chamber, the old ballroom that Vilder has locked us in, but return to the same conclusion: the windows are impenetrable, the gallery too high to reach, and there are no exits other than the door we came through, which is still locked. As for my master, only one thing is sure: he was here, quite possibly for more than a century. The rest is conjecture: it is likely he was in Venice, for I felt him in the city, but how he got there and where he went after I can only guess.

Sporco, mercifully, continues to be untroubled by our imprisonment. In fact, as days pass, he grows even more content. Apart from having shelter, warmth and company – food, a good deal of it meat, is delivered from above morning and night, usually by Braune, but sometimes by Vilder, who'll often linger in the shadows watching us. Sporco has everything he needs, that *any* dog would need. I, though, battle every moment to stay calm. I tell myself that Vilder is bound eventually to unlock the door and set us free – only for fears to come at me, a dread I'll never escape, I'll never find my master, or know what happened to him, that I'll watch Sporco grow old and die. I worry too, conversely, that my master might return, be ambushed by our captor and slain before we even have the chance of reunion.

To keep myself from turning mad, I go through his things, meticulously studying the reams and reams of inscribed papers. Ninety years of our life together. I had always considered him a fine artist who underrated his talents, so it gives me pride (at least I have that) to see how beautifully realized the sketches are, indeed how he has grown in skill as time passed.

There are all manner of familiar vignettes, charting our progress through the courts of Europe, but when I come across illustrations of people and places I do not know, which must have been before my time, a compelling idea strikes me: that they might contain clues of my master's beginning, of his family. I select a number from the pile and study them closely. Almost all are set in a sunny land of rolling valleys, cypress trees and hilltop towns, of bustling cities scattered with ancient ruins, where everyone is outdoors in the warmth. A place that must be Italy.

The clothes are certainly from a century or two prior to my birth, but they are familiar from paintings I've seen: the women with conical silhouettes, wide farthingale skirts and bodices; the men with square padded shoulders, short hose, codpieces and hats with halo brims. There are a number of individual portraits – engineers, sculptors and architects I guess from the emblems around them – but they tell me little more about my master than I already know. I don't have the sense that any are related to him by blood, or that one of the buildings they stand before might be his home.

Gradually I become diverted, focusing instead on the people and places I remember. There is one of us with an old bearded gentleman on the parapet of the campanile in Pisa, Signor Galileo my master called him. He spoke in the singsong way of Venetians, was a professor at the university, and, in common with my master, a fellow disciple of science. I remember clearly the hot summer night when the three of us ascended the spiral stairs of the campanile, the enchanting marble tower that tilted slightly away from the cathedral as if it were trying to set off on its own. At the top, the professor covertly unveiled his 'wonder-instrument', a long cylinder of wood with convexes of glass at each end, pointed it high above the gables and minarets of Pisa, to the moon, and motioned for my master to peer inside the box.

'You'd think it would be as smooth as polished alabaster,' Galileo said in an energetic whisper, 'but look how uneven and rough it is, full of cavities and prominences.'

'I see, I see,' my master thrilled, even picking me up to allow me to observe. I peered through the hole to see into what I thought was another world, a desert sphere of craters and fissures, before realizing it was the moon itself, startlingly magnified. *That* was one such moment when I was in awe of humankind.

There are all manner of other tableaux. Several of us in the bewitching realm of Andalusia, in the Moorish fortress of the Alhambra, with its complex of watchtowers and courtyards, brightly tiled miradors, and a thousand chattering fountains. There's one of my master and me sitting side by side in a box at the Palais-Royal, the theatre in Paris. I remember the night we went to see his favourite actor perform (the same unfortunate man who a year later, during a performance of a play about double-dealing doctors, *La Malade Imaginaire*, coughed up chunks of blood and crumpled to his death on stage). As the curtain came down, the audience, the queen included, stood as one, cheering, buzzing, tapping fans, waving the edges of their clothes until the entire acting troupe was in tears. Reminded of these moments, I feel ashamed that I've chosen to remember so much of our time together as work, a drudge almost, following armies, stalking battlefields, and waiting with scant patience whilst my master worked at the furnace in palace workrooms. There was a whole other universe to our travels. He showed me the realms.

Coming across a group of drawings of a lady my master was close to in our Amsterdam days gives me a particularly keen jolt. The memory of that city, to which I never returned, has been so entwined with my feelings for Vilder, I've all but forgotten the other great event that took place there: of my master falling for a woman in a way that was deeper, and ultimately more painful, than ever before. How shameful of me to not have remembered Jacobina more. She was a rare individual, the type that people call 'a force of nature', vital and kind and brilliant.

'I am from Ghana,' she boasted in her powerful voice when he met her at the entrance to the Amsterdam Stock Exchange. She was even taller than he and had an all-encompassing smile that she wore permanently, with the exception of one time. 'I have come here to pick the brains of you rich merchants, to see all your clever tricks, so one day us Ghanaians can live as you.' My master was almost tongue-tied to begin with, following her as she swept through the prim, self-conscious gatherings of Amsterdam society, a giantess, as dark and rare as obsidian and as assured as the wind.

It was delightful and then unbearable to behold: the harder he tried to stop himself from falling, the greater he fell. Rather than compliment her in person, and show the extent of his adoration, he shared his thoughts with me instead, boasting day after day of 'her outlook', 'her courage' and 'character', 'her exquisite neck', 'the way silk sits about her shoulders', 'her titanic sense of humour', and her 'ears' and 'feet' and 'hands'.

'Tonight, she goes to the ball of the Dutch East India Company, my champion,' my master boasted one day. 'Though not invited, categorically not, she goes anyway, into the very lion's den, to charm the bankers and guildsmen and millionaires, even as their wives twitch in horror beside them, to raise money for her homeland. And she's frightened of doing it, but still she goes. And she'll do it magnificently. And if she fails, she'll do that magnificently too.' Another time, he bragged, 'The risks she has taken, my champion, for the good of others, setting off on her own, crossing seas, escaping the grubby hands of slave-traders, whore-masters and bigots, all of who would do her down.'

After almost a year of keeping the full scope of his infatuation a secret from everyone but me, as we took a boat out of the city one summer's afternoon, along a canal where fields of flowers were grown, he suddenly asked her: 'Would you like to live forever?' I sat up so urgently the boat rocked and almost capsized. He seemed to have taken even himself by surprise: his mouth hung open and he looked terrified to hear her answer.

It was preceded by one of her mighty peals of laughter. 'I could think of nothing worse!'

'Oh.'

She threw her hand around at the expanse of blooms, which seemed to go on forever in that flat land, stocks and peonies, honesty and sweet rocket, and the welcoming sunlit walls of Amsterdam far behind. 'We only enjoy all this because we know it will pass.' She snapped her fingers. 'Like that, it will pass.' My master smiled and squeezed her hand, but inside I knew he was crestfallen, not because she'd said no to him, which she had without realizing it, but because she may have been right.

I think she'd been guarded about giving her heart too, but when she did, with her 'quiet Knight', her 'laughing sage, who travels always with his four-legged soul beside him', she did so with all the strength of her personality, and when he let her go, that same strength destroyed her. And he too.

It's late, the light almost gone from the window and I'm doing my best to tidy the drawings, as my master would have done, when I realize Vilder is watching me from above. I hadn't heard him come in. Even in silhouette, there is something different in his demeanour: he's more composed, steadier on his feet. He studies me very plainly, like a man might watch a caged bear from a place of safety. I stare back and, for a moment, I fancy we exchange the tiniest spark of understanding, of compatriotism even, before he goes for the night, locking the door.

An idea strikes me and by the time he returns to the gallery the following afternoon, I have laid out more than a hundred of my master's best drawings very neatly, edge to edge, making a carpet of them across the floor. Vilder saunters down to the far end of the gallery and back, looking at them with not one iota of surprise or interest, before leaving again. Later, wondering whether I should leave them or neaten them back into a pile, the main door opens, at ground level, and Vilder stands on the threshold, a lantern in his hand. I chill with anticipation. Leaving the door open, he stares at me, stark light on his craggy face (to think how once I longed for him to notice me, that I braved the iced-over Thames alone to catch one last glimpse of him), before walking over to the bed, deliberately treading on the drawings, not looking down even as they tear beneath his feet. Sporco wakes, but I cut round Vilder, broadening my chest.

'You think he's a saint?' Vilder says. 'For this you have made your exhibition? He was no saint. Let me put you right on that.' He picks up a drawing, one of the dozens of his re-imaginations of the battlefield. 'He told me of his "crusade", his would-be atonement for Aramis. He did not atone and it was ill judged in the extreme.' He shakes the drawing at me. 'You think this makes him righteous? Purifies him? Did *he* think that? A soul here and there, the bestowing of a little additional time on this earth? And he lectured me about playing god.'

Sporco sidesteps me, drops on to Vilder's lap and licks his hand. Vilder freezes and I brace myself for an attack, but surprisingly he gives a little chuckle and lets Sporco carry on, even strokes his head. 'What are you?' he says. 'An ordinary thing?' Then a thought strikes him and he turns Sporco on his side to study his abdomen, running his fingers through his fur and making Sporco giggle. 'Yes, an ordinary thing,' Vilder says, finding no scar. 'Good for you. You are a dog I could endure. One who does not take himself too seriously. Good for you.' As Sporco lassoes his tail, I steal a peek at the half-open door. Vilder notices, pushes Sporco away and gets up, stamping back through the drawings and exits. As the bolts hammer home, a new plan, a better one, occurs to me.

'I – I'm not sure I understand, no.' Sporco frets. 'I – I'm not good with schemes and –' He stops and sighs. 'You want that I should –?'

'Sssh. Just howl, loudly. Urgently. That's all you have to do.' It's the middle of the following night and Sporco's walking in circles trying to comprehend.

'And you're going to –'

'I'm going to play dead. Pretend to be dead.'

'Right you are, right you are,' Sporco mumbles, still understanding nothing.

My species is exasperating: the lack of vocabulary, the recall only for food and punishment. 'Look, this is my blood.' I tip over the bottle of cochineal that I found amongst my master's things, and it slicks into a puddle.

'What?' Sporco gasps, his ears pinning back. 'Blood?' He hazards a sniff and I bash his snout.

'False blood. Not real. False. And when he comes – he will come to look, if you howl well – you get out first. Don't wait for me. Run fast. I'll follow. Understood?'

Sporco's brows make a fretful dance before setting in a knot. 'I'm not good with schemes and plans.'

'Just howl. You're maddening. Howl.' I calm myself. 'Just try.'

Sporco takes in a deep breath and lets out a waspish bark. 'A howl is what I need, anguish.' His next attempt is no better. 'Think of a lady dog. You want her attention, badly. Howl.' This time he manages it. I thump him. 'Louder, urgent.' He does as I tell him and this time he succeeds. I wet the side of my head in the dye and take my position, on my side, my legs at unnatural angles. Whenever my master and I watched a man play dead in the theatre, he'd always lean forward to see if they moved, and wink at me knowingly if he caught them. I join in with Sporco for a greater effect, until finally comes the sound of footsteps above, the gallery door opens and lantern light swings across the room. It falls on me, catching the crimson shine of the liquid. Vilder makes a choking sound and hurries away, then there's a pattern of feet descending steps, of them approaching, a bang of bolts and he rushes in. For a few moments there's just the sound of him panting, before he comes in and puts the lantern down.

'What happened here?' he says, inching towards me. His voice could be someone else's: I never thought I'd hear fear in it. His chest draws in and out quickly, and he fidgets his fingers about his mouth. 'What happened here? Dead?' More than fear: abject terror. He takes the hexagonal bottle from his pocket and crouches down to look at me.

'Run,' I shriek, leaping up, pushing Sporco on, before smacking my weight against Vilder, upending him again. He drops the bottle, which skitters towards the door and his head hits the bed leg. 'Run!' I push Sporco through the door, then knock over the lantern so it extinguishes, before seizing my master's glass vial in my teeth and going after him.

'Braune! De la Mare!' comes Vilder's cry, as we sprint on, towards the chapel on the ground floor, where the window was broken. The door to it is shut. I reach up and nudge the handle with my snout. Now two pairs of footsteps are approaching from different directions. 'Braune!'

'They're coming,' Sporco says, and I realize we've left a trail of paw prints in the dust.

I get the handle in my teeth, turn it and finally it gives, the door opens and we race inside the chapel, boots thumping behind us. Vilder stalks in and we hide in the shadows beneath the pulpit stairs. He hates the room and the bronze effigies in their railed-in pen – his parents I presume. The man's stern face has no fat upon it, and his vainglorious wife is crowned with outstretched veils. And there is a third effigy, of Aramis, standing on a newer tomb, a young soldier striking out, one leg off the ground, pointing his swagger stick ahead.

When Braune hurries in with a pistol, we tear from our

hiding place to the hole in the window and I shoulder Sporco through.

'You! Stay!' Vilder snatches the gun, points it to the ceiling and there's a click of metal, a shrill whistle, a flash of phosphorescence and chunks of the wall hail down, setting half the colony of bats about the room. 'You!' He wings across the room and catches me as I try to jam through the opening. Outside Sporco is apoplectic. I drop the bottle outside, dig my claws against the ground, but Vilder's too strong.

'Run,' I bark at Sporco. 'Run!'

Vilder pulls me back, smacks my ear and I could be in Amsterdam again. Braune is reloading the pistol and black powder is tipping from its snout.

At once there's a rush of air and Sporco barrels back through the window, leaping up and butting Vilder aside. There comes a kick of pure heat, a backdraft of sulphur, and Vilder's shoe rips open to a warm spray of blood. He drops the gun and falls against the tomb, gaping his mouth at me, palms out. This time, Sporco and I get away.

Outside, there's a mist of rain, a vacuum stillness teased with hot wind, a storm about to break. 'You're not hurt?'

'I am well,' says Sporco.

'Thank you,' I say, pressing my snout to his. 'For coming back.' I snatch up the bottle in my mouth and we take off across the ruined gardens, towards the wooded hills. I look over my shoulder at the house, tipping from side to side. There come trembles of thunder, rumbles of light, and just as we reach the edge of the trees, the sky chokes, folds back in dark chasms and the deluge comes down, a hiss of water.

There's a cry behind us and Vilder, too far away to catch up, is half running, half limping from the back of the house. 'You should help me . . .' His voice trails off in the wind.

'Help me find him.' He stops and pulls off his wig, to reveal a thin straggle of hair beneath. He stands, solitary on the vast grid of bygone gardens, minute against his doom palace and the great sweep of the prairie. Torrents of water throttle down and smoke rises in fantastical mists.

'You should help me,' Vilder calls as we drive into the woods.

12. The Dance of the Dead

Brussels, June 1815

On we go, Sporco and I, through the trees, through thickets of brambles and gorse, ascending the slope. It's gentle at first, but soon begins to rake steeply, and we have to scramble up rocks and mossy steps, all the while blinking rain from our eyes. When I pause to reposition my master's bottle in my mouth, Sporco takes the lead, swift and uncomplaining. The stray that never left his city quarter has become a pioneer. More than that: my saviour at Opalheim. And, I notice now, his body has changed too from his period of good eating: his once skinny frame has filled out and his fur has become shinier.

Eventually the trees thin out, and there are boulders instead, sharp facets of stone offering little purchase. On we clamber, higher, steeper. The rain stops and layer by layer clouds lift to reveal a coral dawn. I halt to take breath, but slip, and the bottle drops from my teeth, hits the corner of a rock and smashes.

From a dazzle of broken glass, the pale yellow drains on to the rock. I clamber down and paw together the pieces, furious with myself. Not only has the artefact survived centuries, but it is all I have of my master. The tonic is his too – the last drops remain in a little crack of stone. A sudden impulse strikes me: to drink it. I discount it, worried of the effect it might have. But that fluid is more my master than anything. I press out my tongue, but stop when I see the engraving on one of the shattered pieces. I had noticed before that its neck had been inscribed with a faint insignia, but I'd never had the chance to examine it closely. Now I see it, the marks emblazoned by the sun: three towers below a crescent moon. I have been mistaken all along: the bottle was Vilder's in the first place. But not the liquid. Without thinking, I press my tongue down on the residue of it and blot it from the rock. There is more of it than I realized, a good gulp.

The effect is instantaneous and astonishing.

I am composed, fearless, diamond-clear. I have the strength and breadth of armies. Dread, anxiety, disquiet, all gone. I have such lucidity and calmness, such certainty, I can barely recall, or believe, the ages of worry I've endured. There used to be, even a minute ago, a misshapen mess in my mind. Now all things are possible. It is a truth I will find my master. The odours seeping over the lip of the hill – echinacea and foxglove – are heady, as if canteens of royal perfume have been poured into the soil.

'This way,' I tell Sporco, as certain as an emperor, at once finding the precisely correct path to the top of the ravine, fleet-footed. We crest the gorge, coming on to a road and the sun is there to greet us. There's a straw-gold mist over an infinity of hills and fields, rolling jigsaws of greens, ochres and purples. I can smell every inch of it. I could place each tree, shrub and flower. I know where the rivers and streams streak the land. I can smell where the forest beasts are and all the creatures of the underground dominions. Soon my sense of smell has gone beyond the local, beyond this single region of valleys, and I can discern distant towns, churches, hilltop bell towers. And soon, if I follow the snaking man-made arteries that scour the country, the moving clog of carriages and carts, I can detect a city beyond the horizon. *More* – I can scent the coast beyond it, the salt spray of the shore and colossus of water after. And I can, if I try, discern the realms on the far side of those seas, even as far north as the ice lands. I can sense the very curve of the earth.

But something else has arrested me, something infinitesimally small, tiny, tiny, a particular and precise fuse of scent: midnight in a tall forest, stiff parchment paper, a whisper of pine sap.

My master.

He's real and true as a thick gold coin.

He's not close, days away, but I know his exact position on the atom-map in my brain. He's west of us, north-west, on a road, drawing close to the city I noted, a swollen metropolis with its honeycomb of streets that stink even from here. Brussels: he is there.

'We have far to go before nightfall my friend, so not a moment to lose.' Chest out, back straight, tail up, I set off. 'Quickly now.'

'What if he comes after us?' Sporco asks, catching up, ears a-quiver. 'Should we worry?'

'We should not. We should *never* worry. We keep our wits about us, that is all.' On the matter of Vilder, I have iron conviction: he will not stop us. The jyhr has transformed me into a being of pure confidence, of unpolluted reason. Vehicles begin to roll past with frequency. 'We must find our way on to one of those,' I say, nodding at a brace of sleek coaches that must be city-bound. 'The right opportunity will come.'

'Adventures, huh?' Sporco hurries by my side, tail puffed up with purpose. 'Us two, side by side. Voyagers. The pack.'

The pack? I'm so jubilant, I could almost agree with him. 'Look, there is a chance there.'

Ahead, in a copse, a carriage has halted, half off the road, tilted slightly into the gulley. The driver is on his knees, covered in muck, wrenching at the front axle. A woman stands over him, finely dressed, but agitated. The carriage door is wide open, but it would be impossible to sneak inside without them noticing. Close by, children are playing around a little lake. Children are the purest of dog lovers. 'We will make friends with them. They shall be our way on board.' We slip through the trees to find three girls, angels in cotton dresses and blue sashes, teasing and fussing over their little brother. Sporco bounds forward, tail whirling.

'Friends, friends, are we friends?' he barks.

The middle sister – ten or eleven – pounces on him, to the delight of her siblings, whilst the little boy waddles towards me and catches his palm on my head. In his other hand I notice he clutches – as if his life depends on it – a miniature ivory cage containing a single live cricket of startling emerald green.

'*Bonjour, chien,*' he says.

I let out a bark, seeming to greet him, but really to draw the attention of his mother. She must see us together, a happy family. But she doesn't look round, so I perform a series of clownish rolls – it is extraordinary the vitality I possess and I understand why my master loved to dance – until the girls shriek with laughter and at last their mother turns and squints through the trees.

'*Se qui se passé la?*'

As she approaches, the siblings huddle together, conduct a hurried debate, dust the grass from their clothes, straighten their sashes and cajole Sporco and I into position. For my part, I present myself splendidly, my court stance, lengthening my body, turning my jaw and raising my ears into an elegant tilt. The bolder, middle sister duly presents us. '*Nous avons trouvé ces chiens, Maman.* They're lost. Can we keep them? We love them.'

Her mother lets out an impatient torrent of words. '*Absolument pas.* We have enough problems as it is. And they'll belong to someone. They'll have a home.' She claps her hands. 'To the carriage. *Cet instant.*'

'Follow, quickly.' I nudge Sporco on. 'Make a show of how you want to go with them.' When we get to the carriage, we find the wheel has been fixed and the driver installed on his perch. I sit, looking up at the open door, trying to smile, as I used to. Sporco copies me, setting the children off again.

'They have no home, Maman,' one of them says. 'They want to come with us.'

'They're all alone. Can't we keep them?' adds another.

'*Non, non, non.* Enough of this nonsense. Inside now!'

'*Tu es un cruel tyran,*' the middle sister declares, tearing off her sash and pummelling it into the ground.

A whinny of horses echoes through the trees and a vehicle gains quickly. Vilder's carriage. Sporco has seen it too and at once we dive under the family's wagon into darkness. But I am calm, not fearful. I can still smell the land and my master arriving at the city amidst battalions of soldiers. Five pairs of silk-slippered feet collect together, all facing the approaching coach. Everyone falls silent as a shadow falls across them and stops.

'I don't like this man, Maman. He frightens me,' says one of the girls.

Vilder is alone, having driven himself, and fortunately, from what I can see of him, he has a more undesirable aspect than ever. He's thrown on a tatty overcoat, is unshaven, unwashed and certainly drunk, dosed up or both. A dirty, blood-soaked bandage round his foot completes the picture. Though the mother offers him a little bow, she's hesitant.

'I am looking for two dogs,' he drawls, his breath pure brandy. 'Have you seen them?' A pause. The little shoes gather closer. The tendons in the mother's hand tense and she fidgets with her fingers.

'*Non*. We have not,' she answers. '*Désolé*.' Silence. The middle sister edges back, gently lifting her sole, a sign for us to keep still. There comes the sound of galloping horses and a pair of mounted soldiers in red uniforms approach from behind very fast.

'Coming by!' one of them shouts to show they wish to overtake, but Vilder throws out his arms.

'Stop!'

They're travelling at such speed, they can't halt in time, but tear past before looping back. They're worn out, caked in dirt, but have an urgent look about them that marks them out as staff officers, the men that carry messages between the various factions of an army.

'What is it?' the first one asks, catching his breath.

'Did you pass any dogs on the road?' The officers share a look and would laugh if they weren't so aggravated. 'One dark, this high, the other half its size.'

'No,' the officer replies, taking up his rein.

'Wait,' says Vilder. 'You're English? Your uniform is British, is it not?'

'What of it?'

'Is there some matter? Where are you headed in such a hurry?'

'Perhaps you've heard of Napoleon?' the officer comments drolly, about to gallop off, when the mother speaks.

'So there is to be a battle is there?' There's an anxiety in her tone that catches the attention of the officer.

He bows his head, softening. 'Inevitably, madam. You make for Brussels?' The mother nods. 'You'll be safe there, God willing. To Charleroi we go. The Prussians are already on their way, to bolster our forces. Waste no time, but hurry. Good day.' He flicks his reins and this time they tear off, vanishing from sight.

For a moment Vilder stares at the cloud of dust they left behind. 'Charleroi,' he says to himself, before turning to the mother. 'I am sorry to have disturbed you.' He sets off in the same direction as the soldiers and sunlight falls back on the road. Only when he is gone completely, do four faces appear before us, grinning. We burrow out, Sporco and I, and stand to attention before the mother. She studies us, then the open road that Vilder and the soldiers took, and back to us again. She inspects our fur, fingering through it in search of ticks, examines our teeth and pulls down our eyelids. The three sisters wait for judgement. Then Sporco does something that didn't occur to me: gently with his teeth he picks up the girl's blue sash, shakes the dirt from it and presents it to the mother. She takes it from him and, for the first time, her mouth twitches with a smile. 'Let them come.'

We're all together in the compartment: three girls, one boy, their mother, a cricket and a pair of stray dogs. Soon the road widens and we pick up speed, heading north-east. Sporco is thrilled by our change in fortune. The dresses of the girls and their mother merge into an opalescent quicksand in which he drowns again and again, each time resurfacing in a different place, oversized brows raised in triumph like theatre curtains.

Hours pass, games are played, fights erupt, silence is demanded, a sister is pinched, another one cries, threats are made, peace brokered and silence again. On the cycle goes throughout the day. And during it all, I sit, contented. Still I can smell everything, the vales and forests, the city ahead – and my master. He's just a fragment of a fragment of a fragment, but he is there, a beacon to which I am travelling.

'Stop!' I bark, waking from a nightmare: a giant thurible swinging over the blood fields of Breitenfeld, clouds of sickly camphor and gum Arabic sinking on to the dead, the squeal of the fawn at Saint-Germain, flesh eaten off to the spine, crimson slicking the marble floor, the fascinated eyes of the infant king. 'Stop!'

Everyone is dozing except the mother. She stares down at me, the angular line of her jaw catching the last of the afternoon light. She's not one of those humans who seem to be able to see through my eyes into the chasms of my past, into the labyrinthine museum of my life, wings of which even I have forgotten. She sees just a dog, another living thing to fret about. I snap my head away and look from the window.

The carriage lanterns have been lit and the sun is setting, a hoary disc melting into the horizon, hills growing dark, cornfields consumed in sepia twilight. I'm no longer euphoric. The magic of this morning, the all-knowing certainty, the dazzling second-sight, are gone. I shiver with sadness, spores of melancholy gather like mould in dim corners inside me. Foreboding, unnameable anxieties congregate, like dark-clad people clustering around a coffin at an evening funeral. Unease and disquiet. The landscape, the dusk valleys of soft summer, seems a sham.

'Everything well?' Sporco unearths himself from his cocoon, his ears doing a little curtsy.

'Sssh, back to sleep now.' He does as he's told. *Where are you? Master! Where?* I say in my head and I realize I can't smell him any more. The atom-map is all but gone. I search for it, but can barely discern the land before us. In its place: dirty cotton, unwashed travellers, burnt oil and tar smoke from the carriage lanterns. I paste my snout to the glass, inhaling deep breaths. No trace. On we go: endless rocking and prisms of light through the window shiver into shapes, diminishing and growing.

In the dead of night I hear a faraway beating and look out. At first I can't see what it is, but adjusting to the dark I notice a faint band of dark green snaking across the slopes north of us, a shimmering slither so long I can't see where it begins or ends, tens of thousands of soldiers on the move – to the doomy, incessant incantation of boot-steps and drums.

Night passes, day comes around, and by degrees my head begins to ache. I feel nauseous and hot and cold beneath my fur. I've never felt this way, yet it is familiar. *Stay with the plan*, I tell myself. It is more crucial than ever that I find him. The map in my head is gone, but I remember where things lie. He is in Brussels. We are travelling there now. I will find him and he will bow down, beg my pardon and explain everything. I say these things over and over, but they are hollow affirmations.

'We're arriving, Maman, we're home!' one of the sisters bleats on our second afternoon in the carriage, making the others rush for the window and Sporco bark idiotically, squeezing between them and whipping his tail against my face. It's almost sundown again. The turnpike is hectic with traffic and finally we're approaching a hum of light, a walled city rising from the plains like a put-out fire. Still the hot and cold mist sips through me and I realize – of course – my state is the same as Vilder's must be, or any man or woman who's addicted to drink or easing potions. And also, like such a person, I wish I had more of my master's potion, even as it has turned against me and tricked me, giving me fantastical vision, only to take it away again.

At the gatehouse a guard stops us, and the mother fishes around and produces papers, but he just glances through the glass – women, children, dogs – and waves us through. We plough on, juddering on cobbles, the intense evening heat drawing out the filthy smells of the town, making the mother bat her fan at double speed. Throngs of soldiers choke up the streets, the same colour uniform as the officers that passed us: the blood red of the British. They're buzzy, fuelled-up and ready for war. Unable to get through, the mother loses patience. '*Ça suffit*,' she calls to the driver. 'We'll go on foot from here.' She hurries everyone out of the cab. The sun is setting, but the cobbles are still warm. The driver clambers on to the roof, unfastens the luggage and passes it down piece by piece. Everyone takes a case and the mother hurries them through the crowd.

I say, 'I shall not follow. You go though.' Sporco's tail, which had been smiling back and forth, freezes. 'I am settled on the matter. No arguments. You have a fine home with that family. You could wish for no better. Catch them up. We must say goodbye. Really.'

He looks over his shoulder at the white dresses hurrying away. 'Can't we – just –' He sits, stands, sits again. 'But – the pack?'

'*They* are your pack. Not I. Go now, before you lose them.' The look he gives might once have broken my heart — the puppy abandoned on the pontoon — now it's just another slab of misery on top. 'I must stay with the army. To find my master.' The middle sister is looking round, panicked, craning to see between soldiers' backs.

'I'll come with you,' resolves Sporco.

'No!' The crowds, the noise, the evening shadows bending over the buildings, the never-ending trill of pipes and skitter of battle drums are all unendurable. 'Goodbye, my friend.'

As his ears wilt a voice sings from the crowd: '*Chiens, chiens!*' The middle sister dashes back to us. 'Not that way, we live over there, silly. *Venez, venez.*' She cajoles Sporco with friendly nudges, but he shakes her away. When she hovers still, he shows his teeth and growls until she backs away, crushed. Sporco holds out his shoulders against the shame, knowing he's spoiled a measure of her innocence forever — and all for me. He's given me no choice but to keep him with me, for I'll only let him go if there's a real home for him. I'm aggravated by everything: by losing my master's scent, by fears that I imagined it in the first place, by the noise in the street, the multitude of soldiers and the feral look about them. Even the fact that we're at the height of summer and faded daylight is still stubbornly hanging on drives me mad. I want this day over. And I want my master.

'Come then, but do as I tell you,' I say to Sporco, no power left in me to fight.

We turn into the Grand Place, which is full to choking point. Young peacocks in high-collared coats, silky slips of ladies, old dames in bonnets, aristocrats, card-players, mountebanks, delivery boys — and soldiers, soldiers, soldiers. Acres of uniforms, of bottle-swigging, dirty-tunic swagger. I dig my nose to the ground and prowl back and forth in search of my master, careless of who I bump into. After three rounds, I pause for breath and see, through the window of a dressmaker's shop, a lady being fitted into a gown, admiring herself in a wall glass as an assistant praises her. What pointless rituals. Gowns, showing off, hems stitched, lace smoothed, for what? For her later to be struck down by disease? For her skin to blotch, darken and rip into pustules. To die and be nailed into a box and slotted into the dirt? What idiots humans are.

'Sporco? Sporco?!' I've lost him. Damn him. No, he's stopped on a corner to look at something. Four terriers dressed in human clothes parade on their hind legs, as a crookback in a top hat ringmasters them with flicks of his whip. There are three males in toy waistcoats and cravats, and a lady dog in cloak and bonnet.

'Isn't she the most astonishing –' Sporco pants.

'Not now,' I snap, shouldering him on, but he dodges me, goes back to her and introduces himself, not in his usual ham-fisted way – indeed, the realms have changed him – but shyly, treading on the balls of his paws.

'Hello, I am Sporco. That's what they call me.' Very delicately, he takes a sniff of her behind. 'Ravishing,' he whispers, his tail swinging in manly strokes. For once, the object of his attention is not put off.

'You're golden,' she says coyly, shaking in her little costume, her tail setting off in tandem with his. The ringmaster swats him away and when Sporco goes back for more, the audience laugh, but this time the ringmaster kicks him.

'I'll come back to find you,' Sporco says as I pull him on, and the dog in the bonnet watches, as she's cajoled back to work, getting up on her hind legs and parading in her dress and bonnet.

We follow a platoon out of the square, kilted, pasty-skinned and thick-calved brutes. In my state, they seem to sway with the street, the whole city does, buildings like shipwrecked crates rolling in waves. I boil and freeze. Damn my master's potion.

'A ball! Look, a ball,' Sporco yaps, his attention already moved on to a new mischief. The way is choked with carriages and a dance is taking place inside a broad house. A dance as the city sweats with war! Army balls are the maddest and strangest, as everyone knows that dead men turn amongst them, but no one knows who. 'We'll hear music,' Sporco barks, bounding up the steps.

'No!' I pull him back with my teeth and he lets out a yelp. 'Not now. Not tonight. No dancing. I am sick. This way.' I totter up the alley at the side of the building. I need to get away from the noise. 'I am sick in my head.' That is understating it: in all my years I have never felt so wretched. When my master used such tonics, he would barely administer a drop, whilst I must have had a large dose, and now the wearing off of it has acted like an acid, stripping away all the wholesome parts of my mind to reveal a rotten mess beneath, a place where there is only fear, obsession and elemental dread.

There are some steps that lead up to a little landing before a shuttered-off doorway. I go up and sit, pressed in the corner. It could be my alcove in Venice. It's the same size, the size of a tomb, and smells just as damp. I rest, trying to calm the rage inside and Sporco hovers half up the stairs, unsure how to behave, like the dogs you see sometimes with violent, drunken masters, permanently on tiptoes, frightened of doing the wrong thing and being hit.

On the other side of the alley, on the same level as us, at the back of the house where the ball is taking place, a window is open. There's a burst of music as a lady enters the room with three gentlemen. 'Come in, duke, sirs. This is my husband's study.' The alley is so thin and high it amplifies her voice. She could be standing right beside us. 'Please excuse the mess. He shall be with you instantly.' She's stout, jewelled and ball-gowned to the extreme, but her face is coagulated with uncertainty. She's about to exit when she says: 'Should we stop the dance? It would be a great pity of course, but –'

'No,' the duke replies. I can see only his shadow against the wall, but his voice has sardonic bite. 'No need to set tongues wagging. French spies, who knows where they lurk.'

'Spies?'

'They dance too. Like you and I. Carry on as if nothing has happened. Thank you, Lady Richmond.'

He motions her back to the ballroom and when the door closes the music is muffled again. I can see only one of the men clearly, a young officer with a striking face, indigo eyes and dark ginger hair slicked back. He could be a younger incarnation of my old friend from Venice, Jerome, the bach-elor adventurer who ended up being stabbed for his jewels. As the other two talk, he looks from the window, not noticing us, and for a moment he captivates me: the heat of pride within him at being in such company, his certainty that his whole life is before him. In a flash I imagine the swift pageant of it: marriage after the war, a country seat, children with his dark ginger hair, middle age, dotage.

'What is this place,' says the duke.

'A coach builder's house apparently.'

'Really? Are the Richmonds so hard up?'

Laughter. 'They would swear they have chosen Brussels for the unrivalled hunting. The fact you can live here like a sultan for half the price of London has nothing to do with it.'

Another burst of music. 'Richmond, there you are. The map?' The duke takes it and unfolds it on the table. 'You've heard?'

'That the Prussians have retreated from Fleurus?'

'Worse already. Beyond Charleroi now. Napoleon has humbugged me by God, gained twenty-four hours march. I have ordered the army to concentrate on Quatre-Bras. If we can't stop him, we must fright him here.'

Richmond has to put on his glasses to see where the duke is pointing. 'Waterloo?'

'We mobilize at three a.m. Make preparations, quietly. Tell only those who need to know. Why upset your wife more, when she has gone to all this effort?'

'Three? It is evening still. What should we do in the meantime?'

'Dance,' says the duke, exiting, the three men going after him and taking the light with them.

'Can I go back?' Sporco's saying, his voice strange and quiet. 'Can I go back to meet her? The terrier in the bonnet?'

'No, you stay with me. You stay here.' I want to be soft with him, explain he'll only be kicked again if he goes back for the walking dog, tell him he's a good soul – but all my tenderness is stripped away. 'Stay with me. I'm sick in my head.' I sink to the ground. I want the music of the dance to give me solace, but I am inconsolable. Unbearable fever. Now it is I who's a character in an opera, a tragic figure: a dog that has lived two hundred and seventeen years, through wars and revolutions, who lost his master more than a century ago, but still believes they'll be reunited.

'Sleep then, you should sleep,' Sporco is saying, so far away.

Everything slows down. A lady leers from the window of a sedan, a man marches with rabbits swaying from a stick.

Through the ballroom windows the soldiers and ladies reel round and round and round beneath lurching chandeliers. The dance of the dead. This madness will pass, it must.

'You sleep a while,' Sporco is whispering. Poor thing, a good soul, abandoned as a puppy. Tomorrow I will mend everything with him. Tomorrow.

13. The Rod of Asclepius

Brussels, June 1815

Almost always the dreams I have about my master are noisy and frenetic, as crowded as the cathedral was on the day I lost him. I'm always pushing through people as he forges on, just out of sight. I might catch a glimpse of the hem of his jacket, of the heel of his boot, before my way becomes barred. I've dreamt of pursuing him through the banqueting hall at Saint-Germain, through tracts of embroidered silk and stockinged ankles, the chamber growing longer and darker the more panic-stricken I become, until the courtiers turn into windblown trees and the chamber is a forest on a winter's night. I have dreamt of him in London, trying to catch up, as city people pour down to the river, walking on to frozen water to dance quadrilles. Even the dreams that take place in the countryside, shadowing the tail of armies across the land, are inexplicably busy, the sky hectic with dark birds, the route a maze of guarded walls and uncrossable ravines.

But *this* dream – I'm aware, as dreamers sometimes are – is calm and still. The multitude has vanished and Brussels is silent, utterly. Even the birds, the secret armies, have abandoned the horse chestnuts and linden trees of the boulevards. I walk across the city to the building where the dance is taking place. The air is mountain pure, the grime and dirt filtered away, and the light on the buildings has a silver shine. How exquisite to find these frantic roads vacant.

There is no dance. In my dream, the mansion is empty too. I pass up the alleyway and notice that I'm no longer a dog. I walk on two legs, a human, boots on my feet, a staff in my hand, decorated with the figure of a serpent. I find a dog sleeping, curled up in a porch at the top of a little flight of stairs. He's sturdy-looking, inky dark fur on his back turning to light hazel on his stomach, and he has a curling scar on his side. He's shivering in his sleep and I wonder where his master is. I kneel and reach out my hand, my human hand . . .

I wake and sit bolt upright, listening. There is clarity in my head, and all around me. It is still night, I'm in the alley and the ball carries on. The crimson of the men's uniform and the white of the ladies' dresses have a vivid intensity, though their dance is very strange, having lost all its structure, the men moving fast, whilst the women drift at half the speed. My fur tingles, inexplicably so. 'What's happened?' I say to Sporco, but he's not there. The alley is deserted but for me. 'Friend?' My voice has the clarity of a bell.

I realize the dance is strange because, in fact, it has unravelled into chaos. Soldiers are rushing into packs, rallying one another with cries. They've been called to battle. I pass up the alley and on the front steps soldiers are bidding hurried goodbyes. 'Sporco?'

A battalion is driving up the street, on-the-march, in-step, battle-ready, bugles, horns. Then everything goes quiet, as if a cushion has come down over the city, and I notice, further up the road, aboard a troop wagon, a man with sandy-grey hair. The cart is crammed with red-tunic soldiers, but only this man, thin as porcelain, wears just a shirt under his backpack. For certain I'm hallucinating. My heart bumps in time with the drums, but when the carriage turns the corner and I see a flash of yellow on his back, my breath catches in my throat. A serpent entwined about a rod.

'*It is the rod of Asclepius*,' my master said to me in Vienna, sewing on the emblem when he was first preparing for the war. That version had been finely embroidered, whilst this one is painted on, almost childishly.

It is he.

I bark, but there's too much noise. His cart rolls on. Follow it. No, he's an apparition. I'd smell him. Follow him anyway. The serpent and the rod. My dream. The mere action of setting off makes me pulse with the possibility that it *is* my master. I freeze: Sporco. Soldiers bunch into me, push me out the way. I'm split with panic. 'Sporco?' Pointless to shout against this din. What was it he asked last night before I slipped into delirium? 'Can I go back to meet her?' The terrier in the bonnet, he's gone to find her.

I have time, just, to hurry to the square. No, I'll come for him later. Madness, I'll not find him again. But the yellow intaglio. I'll go with the army. I halt a third time: can I be sure it was he? There are scores of doctors in a battalion, and perhaps I read the symbol wrong. Dreams and hallucinations. Go now for Sporco, and catch up with the army afterwards, my final decision. When I get to the corner where the terriers had been, I find it empty – until I notice him waiting in shadow, half leaning against the side of the building, Sporco, looking down the barrel of his nose at me.

'I thought I'd lost you.' I pant. 'You're safe, though.' He stares aloofly. 'We're leaving. The army. Quickly now.' Silence. His tail is a flat coil on the ground. 'Sporco?'

'I shall wait here.' Then, tersely, 'Will you wait too, *friend*?'

'No – I – I must leave. With the army.'

'The army.' He dismisses the notion with a flap of his ears. 'Armies, armies, armies. *Humans.*'

'Sporco, I have seen my master.'

'Well, go to him then. What stops you?'

At once we're characters in one of the mirthless plays my master used to find so ridiculous. I make sure my tone is soft and quiet. 'Please, my friend.'

'So you won't wait with me?'

'Wait? No. What for? For her, you mean? The dog in the dress?'

There's hate in his growl. 'You tell me about the realms, but you don't want me to see them.'

'Sporco –'

'I follow you. I wait with you.'

'Sporco –'

'But you won't wait with me.'

'With females, things *seem* like one thing, but actually –'

'*Fe-males.* Because you know everything. All about the realms. And I know nothing.'

'It's her smell that's all. A trick of smell.' Now he utters a low, threatening snarl. 'Sporco, please –'

The yellow symbol. The wagon is getting away.

'Have you had a girl?'

'What?'

'A lady dog? A girl? Have you *known* one?'

I knew many dogs when I was young, but I remember only Blaise. How do I even begin to tell him of her. 'Yes. One. Properly.'

'Well, I haven't, never.'

'That's not true, Sporco.'

209

'I haven't!' he snaps. '*Trying* is not the same as doing.' His lips curl, showing his teeth, and I'm taken aback. 'I want it. One time. So I'll wait until she returns. Understand, *friend*?'

'Sporco –'

'Fight me.'

'No, Sporco.'

'Fight me!' He throws open his shoulders and punches his chest forward. 'Fight me!' He attacks, biting my neck. I rear up and we lock together, jaws gnashing, claws swiping, a savage scramble, meshed as one, as wheels sheer past behind us, horns blaring. I'm stronger. I push him back to the corner, knock his skull with the fist of my paw and bring him down, pinning him by the neck.

'I'll not fight you, Sporco, I'll not. You're my only friend. Are we not a pack?'

A gulp of amazement passes down his throat and the hate in his eyes vanishes. 'The pack?' It's as if a butcher had invited him in and told him to eat all he can. There's no limit to my shame, telling him anything to make him come. *My only friend?* My only friend is the man I lost a hundred and twenty-seven years ago. But Sporco believes me. The finest quality of our species is its greatest failing: trust, over sense, over logic, trust over everything. 'Of course you and I are tied together. The pack.'

We run until we catch up with the tail of the column.

'The truck there.'

A wagon has halted, the driver tightening the harness, the back open. Sporco doesn't hesitate to spring aboard. I waver, searching for the yellow symbol. I leap up and bundle inside, to a shock of sulphur. It's a munitions cart with dozens of barrels of gunpowder. They always travel at the back of the army line, just in case. There's a thump of boots, hands slam the doors shut, wrangles a chain round the handles and fastens it tight. Moments later, we've set off again, the caskets rumbling against each other as we shake up the road. It's pitch, but for a single slit of light.

'All fine?' I ask Sporco.

He lengthens his neck and glitters his eyes. 'All fine.'

We're locked in a gunpowder wagon, a travelling bomb. As I catch my breath, the same doubts tumble through my mind: did I imagine the man with sandy-grey hair, the yellow symbol of Asclepius on his back? And to where are we travelling?

To battle for sure.

14. Blaise

Oxford, 1643

When England erupted into civil war, my master and I ended up in Oxford, at the bizarre, makeshift court of the Stuarts, in the employment of the queen, Henrietta Maria. She suffered almost constantly from toothaches and colds, according to her imagination at any rate, and liked to have doctors about her. My master was happy to provide, as it gave us the opportunity to replenish our supplies, to continue our crusade. Our *duty*.

The court had taken over a medieval college of cloisters and halls close to the Cherwell River. By then, the city had already turned into a fortress town, the reek of gunpowder everywhere, behind doors, barrelled in the back of trucks, barricaded below traps, but the queen, 'the generalissima', as she, or one of her circle, nicknamed her, did her best to maintain a sense of gracious living, dressing herself morning until night as if for a ball, rather than a time of war.

'She's as mad as a loon,' my master whispered to me at one of her bizarre fancy-dress enactments – a miniature version of the ones she'd once mounted in London, in which she always took the starring role – even as the town shook with cannon fire. 'No wonder the whole realm is in mutiny.'

She'd brought her furniture with her, which didn't quite fit into the cramped rooms of the warden's house, and her entourage too: courtiers, dwarves, hangers-on and a whole menagerie of animals, a monkey, a parrot and half a dozen dogs. Of the dogs, they were mostly spaniels, toyish, with ink-quill tails, and none of them were friendly. One in particular, Mitte, always positioned at the starboard of her mistress's skirts, was spiteful in the extreme. 'The barbarian', she used to call me, or 'the filthy savage'. In fact, she was the unsanitary one, always with a dirty backside, flecks of dried faeces in the wiry hair around it, which she'd stamp, on purpose I was sure, all over the royal furniture.

Sometimes a man came, usually at night, always with a browbeaten face, and though the entourage would drain away, leaving the queen alone with him, I would stay to observe. He smelt of church carpets and stale oil, and I thought nothing of him. They'd have a terse conversation, at the end of which she might unlock a secret drawer in her portable harpsichord, take out jewels and give them to him, reluctantly. It was when he kissed her, lips barely touching her powdered cheek, I realized he was the king, Charles, the son of James, who I'd met at Whitehall forty years before.

It was into that strange milieu, near the end of our six-month sojourn, that Blaise came into my life. Sometimes events occur that are so significant, they act as a fulcrum, against which your life tips from one side to the other – and, without really noticing the change, you become a different creature entirely. It was spring when I was woken by the piercing howl of a female dog, from the direction of the river. I looked up at my master, but the sound hadn't woken him.

I went outside, crossing the gardens to the river. There were steps leading down to a landing pier and a dog, wet through, was worrying back and forth at the water's edge. There had been heavy rains for days and the river was swollen almost to the tops of the banks and moving fast. The distressed animal, a smooth-haired lurcher, had bruises and cuts, as well as heavily drooping teats. She must have given birth only recently, but there was no sign of any puppies. I hurried to her side, seeing what I could do to help.

'I'll drown, I'll drown, I'll drown,' she mewled over and over and kept brushing her paws against the skin of the torrent, until she stepped off the pier and slipped below the surface.

'No!' I barked, jumping straight after, astounded by the speed with which the current took me. Her head came up in the swell; face placid, it turned with the surge and vanished again below the waves. I kicked hard and stretched out my body, gaining on her quickly. I bit into her leg, to pull level, then got her by the neck, turned against the flow until we bashed the river wall, tumbling along it. More steps flew by. They were slippery with algae, but a wave of water spilled on to them and I lunged with it, bunching into the corner where the steps met another pier head.

The poor dog shrieked as I pulled her from the river and dropped her on the steps. She lay there panting and I set about licking her, not just to dry her, but to reassure. She was young, no more than three. Her face was almost shockingly elegant and balanced. Her eyes were the colour of desert sand, striking against the dark, smoky lines of her lids, and when she looked at me I was too shy to hold her gaze.

'Did you? Have you –?' I began, but stopped myself. If she had lost her babies, she wouldn't want reminding of it. She lowered her satin lids to cover her eyes and remained there, lying still, creamy brown against the night. 'Do you – do you have a home?' She made no reply and there was just the sound of the river pouring by. Eventually, she took in a gulp of air, turned and went up the steps. 'Where are you going? Home?'

She flitted across the expanse of garden, which was all orna-mental grids and patterns, avenues of yew and topiary sculptures that looked bizarre in the half-light. 'You'll find it hard to leave that way. There are walls all around,' I said, catching up. Pins were pricking under my fur, just from being close to her. I took secret sniffs of air but couldn't place her aroma; there was so much mystery to it: sandalwood, marula, jackalberry. And more: the shiver of balmy winds, warm-wet, south seas, palm, coconut and sugar cane. She was distant, a stranger, and yet I felt entirely familiar with her, as if in some *other* world that ran secret to my own we had always known each other. 'Where are your babies?' The question came out of me before I could stop it.

At first I thought she hadn't heard me – I was glad of it – as she carried on padding the garden paths with little crunches of gravel. She circled a flower bed and stopped, half shrouded in a thicket of rhubarb. 'Drowned,' she said. I could only see the back of her head. What an exquisite shape it had. 'Thrown from a ship, this morning. All gone.'

This morning! How long had she been haunting the river-banks? They would have drowned almost instantly, tiny packets of fur carried seaward. 'Are you hungry?' I asked.

'Yes.'

Now with a purpose, I steered her to the entrance of our lodgings, keeping my tail erect, so she could see I was strong, whilst inside I spun, my mouth turning dry and my eyeballs ticklish. I found her some scraps from the kitchen, half a pasty of deer and some fish skins, and after she'd eaten them I led her upstairs. She glanced at the statues pedestalled up the staircase, familiar with grandeur it seemed, and I imagined possible histories of her life: aristocratic lineage, reared on a plantation, an island of sugar cane and flowers in a faraway sea, well travelled since. I gave her my basket, plumping up the blanket before nodding for her to get in. 'Will you tell me your name?'

'Blaise,' she whispered, as if it were cursed. When she saw me glance at her chest, at her engorged teats, she said, 'I wanted to go with my babies. They were my home. I'd not expected them.' She shot a glance down between her legs. I was too polite to inspect it, but I sensed, then or later, some long-ago trauma. 'Hadn't yet opened their eyes, poor souls. Better perhaps, to not have seen the cruelty –' Her jaw shook. 'But to kill oneself is –' she couldn't find the phrase '– uncourageous? So I must thank you.' She didn't seem to mean it. Desert-sand eyes stared straight at me, so unflinching; I could have crumbled to dust.

She curled up and slowly lowered her satin lids. For a while I stood, too dumbfounded to move, almost feverish from her perfume. Of course I'd mated in the early years, on our first trip to the realms – brief, friendless trysts with army dogs, farm dogs, the irrefutable draw of glands, a tiny frenzy, uncomfortable for both, then the locking together, sharp and sore, before the relief of freedom again. Better to be *friends* with dogs I would think afterwards, though a month later I could be drawn to the act once more. A mate? A friend? Blaise was neither.

Needless to say, the queen's dogs took exception to her from the outset. 'Where are your children?' asked Mitte on the first morning, censoriously sniffing Blaise's drooping teats, before adding, for her entourage's amusement, 'Unable to care for them, I suppose.'

I was twice the size of any of them and four times as strong, and sent them on their way that day and all that followed, though they carried on their gossiping from a distance.

'Leave them be,' Blaise would say whenever they attempted one of their infantile pranks or stole her food. 'They are the unlucky ones, not us. We are explorers, you and I.'

She was right. The city of Oxford that summer – barricaded from the outside world, and so surreally peopled by the homeless court of England – became our personal realm. We filled our days with adventures. We broke into other colleges, All Souls, Christchurch, Magdalene, each a little walled kingdom in itself and so suddenly deserted that little tokens of life lay everywhere, books open, maps unscrolled, quills in ink, and essays half written. We played games in secret corners of the garden or sat side by side on the pier watching the little ships arriving – miniature versions of the ones in London – and unloading their cargoes. One night, the King's Men stole into town, a theatre troop who'd been forced into exile too, appearing like spies, hooded, cloaked and weighed down with tales of 'the grim theatre the war'. Their arrival threw the court into a collective state of nostalgia. 'They put on *Antony and Cleopatra*,' the queen pronounced to her entourage as dramatically as if the players had brought a cure for death itself.

I took Blaise to see it in the medieval hall of Merton College, finding a spot at the very front of the stage. The candlelit room was hazy with rose incense, and haunting and mysterious music from lyres, tambourines and cymbals played as a prelude to the action. It was a story about an Egyptian queen's doomed love affair with an old soldier. I had no notion how Blaise would react to this odd human invention, ordinary men assuming the mantle of other people, great people inhabiting unexpected realms – but she was bewitched from the outset. There was something in Antony's manner, his shrewdness, his softness and mischievous sense of humour, that reminded me of my master. And the queen – though portrayed by a beardless adolescent boy – was dazzling, even to me, quick-tongued, mercurial, imperious and beautiful. I had the sense that war had sharpened the craft of all the actors, made their performances more urgent and real. When, at the climax, Cleopatra took a snake from a casket and pressed it to her breast, Blaise jumped up upon the stage to stop her and I had to pull her back.

Blaise's sense of humour always took me by surprise. She'd impersonate members of the generalissima's entourage, and not just the dogs, the humans too. (No wonder she enjoyed the King's Men.) She caught brilliantly the obsequious, priggish Denbigh, and the bumptious Davenant, with his syphilis-ruined nose. And she loved practical jokes. I recall a prank she played on the ever-spiteful Mitte. A galleon, bringing more of the queen's possessions, had been too large for the upper Thames and ran aground, drawing the entire household, courtiers and staff, to the banks of the river, some distance from Merton College. Only Mitte had not noticed, as she had been taking her morning 'slumber' on her mistress's pillow.

'Have you heard?' Blaise said, rushing into the bedchamber and waking her. 'The humans are all gone.'

'Gone?' said Mitte.

'They've boarded ships and left the country, to escape the war. They've gone to Egypt.' How I loved her quick wit and sense of the ridiculous.

Mitte screwed up her face. 'That's nonsense.' But she had such an insecure nature, she deemed it might be true and ran about the palace searching for people. Finding none, not even servants, she returned to us.

'They left solemn instructions.' Blaise continued with her mischief so convincingly I could almost have believed her myself. 'We must rule, us dogs, until it's safe for them to return. We shall have a court and a parliament. And, Mitte, this is the part that thrills me most, you shall be queen.'

'I?'

'Who else? You have the finest figure, the silkiest ears and the most bewitching odour in all the court.' This, in particular, set me off, as Mitte smelt as plain as rust. 'Everything pronounces you as regal.' Mitte caught her reflection in the mirror, and her trepidation turned very slowly to pride – until the doors opened downstairs and the humans returned. 'There they are, back from Egypt!' said Blaise, and Mitte bit her and ran off. Blaise looked at me, before doing a little ballet of merriment.

My master was quite as bewitched by her as I was, though I don't think he ever fully understood how diverting and unique she was, as her manner appeared so quiet. Our indivisible bond seemed to make my master proud, as if he had played some part in it. In a way he had. Putting aside the heartbreaking fact that he'd never allowed himself to let love fully bloom, for four decades I'd watched him being enthralled by women. When he fell for a certain lady – such as he had for Jacobina – however much he tried to keep his feelings hidden it was as if he'd discovered a secret that no one else had noticed; like an explorer coming across a lost city. He could have just mated with them, taken 'carnal pleasure' when he wanted it, as so many men do, but the notion was alien to him. In him, physical attraction was rooted in a bedrock of greater things, of respect and kindness. I wondered, given his stance of remaining unmarried, if he would have preferred if I had followed his example with Blaise. But he seemed to encourage me. In any case, it wouldn't have mattered: as not even he could have stopped me from loving Blaise.

Every night we slept bundled up as one, I in the deepest sleep of my life. We talked little, there was no need for it; a universe of things seemed to exist between us already. Very occasionally I had a yearning to know more details of her past: who had been the father of her babies, where her homeland was, and if she'd had a master. But I was also happy not to know these facts, and she, I believed, was relieved not to be reminded of them. And besides, we wanted for nothing, and the world was greater for both of us than the one we'd lived in before.

In the winter, suddenly Oxford fell into chaos. A mob of parliamentarians was spied advancing towards the town's main gates, and our soldiers quickly armed themselves and sprang into action. A battle erupted and the whole night the endless tap, tap, tap of muskets and explosions of fire came and went with the wind, until finally the enemy was repelled. It turned out to be little more than an opportunistic attempt by a few dozen soldiers, but it was enough to frighten the court to action. By morning courtiers were rushing to and fro in urgent conversation and the king appeared in battle garb, his face shot with fear. He and the queen had a raw conversation before he departed, looking back one last time with gull's eyes. For hours after he'd gone, the queen strode back and forth, the hem of her gown hissing against the cobbles, Mitte fretting at her side, until, before dawn, we were all rushed to the courtyard and corralled into waiting carriages. As soon as we'd siphoned through the gates, a crowd engulfed us. A man glowered through the window of our carriage, face like a blood orange, as the carriage was rocked from side to side. Our driver fired a warning shot and we picked up speed and tore out of the city.

'Is there anything more unnatural than civil war?' one of

the queen's courtiers pondered out loud. He was a sly syco-phant who reeked of violet and musk and I'd taken against him from the outset.

My master was not often rude to people, but he replied sternly: '*Every* war is a civil war. Does the fact that armies come from different realms make the fight between them more natural? We all occupy the same realm, sir: it is called humanity.' As soon as the carriage made its first stop to change horses, at an inn south-west of Oxford, my master, Blaise and I got out. 'I'll not travel with those fools. We shall make our own way.'

He waited for the entourage to roll on, the whining of the queen's dogs to fade in the mist, then purchased a horse from the local ostler, a grey mare – not young, but sturdy. He turned his cape inside out, torn lining disguising his court clothes, tied it tight, and the three of us bundled up, Blaise in a saddlebag, I snugged in my master's lap and we headed south. The road, flat when we'd come to Oxford, was beaten by boot-steps, ridged from cannon wheels, and the debris of armies lay everywhere.

Eventually, we came across a regiment billeted on the edge of a town. I was too distracted to notice even which side they were on: the way humans divided into factions made less sense than ever in my life. Muskets were being passed out to a line of troops – that grim, mechanical ceremony – as a ser-geant drilled, breath firing out puffs of frozen air, and I could tell a battle was afoot. I longed for words, to beg my master to resist the call. I could not bear to take Blaise to war. He was lost in thought a while, fidgeting his fingers against the buckle of his holdall, until he unclasped it and took out the vial of liquid jyhr. It was half full.

'No,' I barked. 'No!' Loud enough for some soldiers to turn round.

But my master was not looking their way, he was staring at Blaise.

'My champion, and his paramour,' he said, doffing his hat to us. 'We shall not join this fray. The English choose to tear each other apart. But we have other business.' He placed the vial back in the holdall, took up reins once more, turned the horse about and set off in the other direction, without even a glance back at the army.

We rode into the wintry heart of England, leaving the trails of saltpetre and hot iron, travelling day and night, over hills and through valleys, into a forgotten corner of the land, of hay-rattle moors and wild ponies. Blaise gazed at it in that special way of hers, intrigued by everything, but not surprised. We came across a river that chattered across the country, and we followed it. It took us through copses of beeches, trees that bent towards each other as if secretly conferring. And we found, miraculously, an old cottage, a slate-walled croft, home to someone once, but long abandoned. Tantalizingly the front door hung from a hinge, wide open, a sociable eddy of breeze inviting us in.

My master repaired the ceiling, fixed the chimney, swept out dust, ripped ivy from the window frames, repaired the few broken pieces of furniture and fashioned new ones from odd pieces of wood and plaited stems. When the work was done, he invited us like a grandee at an opening ceremony. 'Let us stay here by the river. Us three, untamed in our hearts.' As he looked at Blaise, a shadow seemed to pass over his face and I wondered what he was thinking.

When summer came he threw open the doors and filled the place with wild flowers: adder's tongue, archangels and honeysuckle. The three of us spent our days foraging mush-rooms and leaves, burdock roots and garlic to roast on the evening fire. In the afternoon, we'd sit by the bank, the sun winking at us from the water, Blaise with her head on my neck. Feeling her warmth, gazing at our secret paradise, a certain peace warmed through me that I'd never known before – or since.

When we'd arrived at the house, my master had stashed his holdall away to make clear he would not carry on his work. One day at the end of the warm season, he fetched it and took out the vial of jyhr. The sight of it sent a shock to my stomach, and to his too I fancied, for at once he was stern. Thinking it signified our return to war, I went to Blaise's side and sat, glowering at him and making a show of how protective I would be. 'It will be uncomfortable for a while,' he said, retrieving his syringe from the bag. 'But the younger she is, the more chance we shall have.' That had been his idea all along: to inject her, make a stone within her flesh and a scar without. To make her endure.

He reached out for Blaise and I growled and stood in his way.

'What's happening?' Blaise said, her tail curling under belly.

I didn't know how to explain, but the notion of what he meant to do seemed as brutal as taking her to battle. 'My poor champion, I do not arrive lightly at this.' In Amsterdam, seeing my master dosing Aramis had unearthed recollections of my beginning – of being taken from my burrow, carted to Elsinore, fog pressing against the workroom window as I was injected – but at once those same memories had sharpened into focus and were monstrous. I felt outrage at being snatched from my family – a sentiment I'd never had before. I felt the cuts of the pin driving into me all over again, the lead weight of the liquid pushing through my veins. Memories I didn't know I had. My master tried again to take hold of her and I bit his hand.

He put the bottle and syringe down. 'Tomorrow then? Or next year. Or whenever you think is right,' he said. 'Or never.'

Over the following weeks, however hard I tried to forget the business, it gnawed at me. Although Blaise was still comparatively young, I found myself worrying about her health. Knowing by then all the signs of impending sickness, I began imagining all sorts of things: that her breathing was becoming shallower, or that she'd lost weight, or was walking slower than usual. It distanced me from her, when it should have had the reverse effect, and she noticed the change.

'What's wrong?' she'd say. 'Something is wrong.'

'No, no,' I lied.

But soon I was unable to sleep either. I'd slip from her side at night and spend the hours padding up and down the river's edge in the dark. I'd return and seeing her again I'd adore her, her jackalberry scent, more than ever. The love I had for her was the sweetest pain I ever had. One day, I searched out the vial amongst my master's things, carried it to him in my mouth and dropped it in his lap. The look he gave me, of admiration, and trepidation, made my stomach swill.

'My love,' I said to Blaise, before my master began the preparations. 'He's going to give something to you. It may hurt a little.' The look of puzzlement on her face was bad enough, no matter what was to come. 'It will keep you from getting ill. From getting old. I was given it, when I was young and – and I have lived a long, long time. Do you understand?' She gave a little nod, but I was unsure if she really did.

'No!' she squealed when he administered the first injection, pulling away so the liquid spilt on the floor and soaked into the stone. A year's work gone in an instant. 'Be brave, my love,' I said as he tried again. And she was, for me, and my master half succeeded, but her scream when the needle drove home, and the fright in her eye, was unendurable. Then she was nauseous for days, couldn't keep food down and was bleary on her feet until the next jab was due. No matter how gentle my master was, how much I comforted her, she could not get used to them, twisting her whole spine in resistance. After just three doses, her character had begun to change, to introvert. One evening, the room was dark and I remember thinking how menacing my master looked in shadow, filling up the syringe, and that I was his accomplice in the act. 'Enough,' I barked. He knew it too. He put his things away and closed the buckle of his holdall.

'Let us light a fire and be calm,' he said.

The three of us sat round it, I not ceasing, not for one second, to catch her scent and wonder, until my head hurt, how to store it inside me. When the fire had burnt down to embers, and my master fallen asleep in front of it, she whispered in my ear. 'You said you want to stop me from being old. Because you are thinking of times to come. But it is here and now I am happy.' The root of my tail shook. I was lost for words and found myself remembering Jacobina on the boat amidst the flower fields. A while later, Blaise asked, very sweetly, 'And what is your age?'

I think I laughed, and certainly my mouth stayed open some time before a sound came into it. 'Almost fifty?'

She kissed my nose with hers and once again she was enthralled but not surprised.

A cycle of summers and winters passed and Blaise got old. Her hair thinned, lost its sheen, her muzzle greyed and her eyes went cloudy. Her mysterious aromas faded away, replaced by the commonplace smells of age: thin blood, hard kidneys, swollen joints, clogged intestines. She liked to walk, but she found it hard. I would pace at her side slowly, reassuring her there was no need to hurry. She became scared of things: noises at night, being left alone by our master, and sometimes she got muddled. But she never, not once, got bad-tempered, like many old dogs do.

I buried my heartache well, in a deep place, but my master knew of it. He eased her discomfort with balms, but he could not stop now what nature had started. She lost her hearing and most of her sight and one autumn day she sat with me by the river, our cheeks touching – hers just bone now – her paw rested over mine. I listened to her deep breathing, a soft rattle that seemed to come from far away. We watched leaves drop from the horse chestnut on the far bank, spiralling down to be carried away by the river.

'You've been my life,' she whispered in my ear, digging her paw tighter into mine, then tighter still. A moment later, it went limp, her breath clattered like metal and stopped. I lay there next to her warm dead body as my insides spasmed with horror.

We buried her in the beech wood, in a place where snow-drops bloomed in the spring. My master and I remained at the croft, but I became listless, always falling asleep, so Blaise might visit me in my dreams. She often appeared as she was in her younger days, idling in the gardens of Oxford, safe in our place. My master never left my side; his warm hand was forever on my back. When he knew I could bear the house no more, he packed up, retrieved his holdall, shook the dust from it, and we left.

I stopped on the riverbank and looked back at the beech wood, now bare of leaves. Blaise would be cold already under the ground, worms would be about her, the soil drinking the last of her smell. An emptiness had been growing inside me, a gigantic space, a gloom that had no end. What would I do with all the years? How could I start the journeys again? *Why*, I raged, *do I live and live?* The years, *how will I last them?*

'My champion, my poor champion.' My master hugged me, and I wished *I* could cry. 'All you can do is put one leg before the other and walk on. All you can do is wake up in the morning and start anew. It will seem as torture at first, but hold fast.' He was right in both ways: it was agony to begin again, begin every day again – but it was all I had left to do.

We journeyed back to the road that we had parted from years earlier and went south-east to London. Remnants of war littered the fields: broken carriages, torn flags, old boots, wheels, horse skeletons chunked with grey flesh, scraps of armour. In everything I saw tokens of worthlessness, tawdry emblems, reminders of the futility of short lives.

It was bitterly cold when we reached the city, the sky iron and the air flecked with tiny stones of ice. The buildings remained as they were, but the streets smelt neglected, stagnant, the colour and pomp washed away. The people were altered too, mechanical, demented almost – or perhaps it was just the Arctic wind that made it seem like that.

At Westminster we found ourselves being carried along by a fast-moving crowd. Bone-chilled, cheeks and knuckles red, they were swarming towards a scaffold put up in front of the great Banqueting House. The scaffold was peopled by half a dozen courtiers, a bishop in a crimson gown amongst them. There came a collective sigh as a man stepped from the window of the hall on to the scaffold and shuffled forward. He was slight but imperious: bearded, cloaked, grey hair curling about his shoulders. I noticed my master's eyes bulge and I peered more carefully – it was the king. He was milk-pale now and the skin drooped under his eyes in swags.

The crowd listened in silence as, chin up, he delivered a speech in a reedy voice. The wind carried it away across London and I heard only the last line of it: '*I am the martyr of the people.*'

He motioned his fingers and the bishop passed him a cap. Another man came forward, the executioner, and politely asked the king to tuck away his hair. It was unruly and the executioner had to help him, the bishop too. Their conversation turned to the block, the king nudged it to see if it was firm and commented on its height. The executioner was good-natured and answered all his queries, but he changed none of the arrangements. They were so casual with one another, they might have been discussing a chest of drawers that the king was thinking of buying.

The king lay down, positioned his neck on the block, trying to get comfortable. The executioner apologized as he tucked a few more stray hairs into the cap, then raised the axe and struck. Blood pumped from the boned neck and a groan went up. I looked up at my master, and though it took a good deal to shock him by then, his face was a cartoon of disbelief.

We went back to our crusade, to the war fields of the continent, forty more years of it before Venice. In time, I told myself, I'd forget the clatter of Blaise's last breath, but I never have. Nor the sight I saw in London that January day: white bone in the thick of the king's neck and his lace collar turning crimson where his head once had been. That vision declared, above any other I'd seen, the irrefutable fact of death.

15. The Pack

Waterloo, June 1815

We travel south from Brussels all day, Sporco and I, locked up in the back of the munitions cart. It is as uncomfortable a vehicle as I've ever known, with its coagulating stench of grapeshot and barrels full of gunpowder forever wobbling towards us, so we have to catch them and shoulder them back. And to make matters worse, the rain began not long after we left town and has fallen in a steady drizzle ever since. It seeps through the cracks, and sloshes around us in brackish puddles, all to the incessant, wet clap of ten thousand marching boots. In time with it, the image of my master aboard the troop wagon in Brussels, jacketless amongst the other soldiers, a scrawled yellow symbol on his backpack, appears to me over and over. Still wondering if truly it was him, I try to hold the vignette in my mind long enough to study it more closely, to see if I missed any clue, but it slips away from me. If I could see out of our cart at least, I could carry on searching for that flash of yellow amongst the lines of troops, but the gaps in the timber are not wide enough. And besides, outside is just grey murk.

I find myself grumbling about everything, even cursing the rain for 'being indifferent and having no guts', and wish – with a total absence of logic – that one of the tiresome powder kegs *would* ignite, so the driver could learn his lesson. Sporco, on the other hand, gives no complaint at all. In fact, he makes a clever improvement. As we descend a slope, the barrels all bunch together and he presses his body against the foremost one, locking the rest into place. He stays there, back straight, proud to be of service – and when a shaft of light catches him across the eyes, he looks at once like a gentleman, a noble Lombardian prince or a dashing captain of the guard. The rough, clownish stray that never once left his quarter of Venice has become a citizen of the world: considerate, resourceful and sophisticated. As for his revelation, that he has never managed to have sex, it makes me fonder of him still. It shouldn't amuse me, but it does, thinking back to his almost non-stop bragging in our old stomping ground in front of the cathedral, him doing little else but swaying his tail at every passing female and pestering them with the most bizarre mating calls I've ever heard: 'You are the sun and I the moon,' 'You smell of donkeys,' 'I am more man than cat'. I certainly saw him try to mount a few of them, and even though some had been apparently halfway obliging, I never watched long enough to realize he'd been wholly unsuccessful.

It's almost dusk by the time the driver snaps the reins and the cart shakes to a halt. The chains are untied, the rear doors shunted open and the driver – short, round, thinning hair rain-pasted to his face – finds us staring back at him. He's stunned for a moment, as if the bad weather had conjured us up. 'Out, out with you!'

We jump down to the relief of fresh air and open space, though a jarring wind brings cold where there should be summer. Immediately I begin searching for the sign of yellow, turning my head from brigade to brigade. When we'd left the city, we'd been at the back of the convoy, but other battalions have joined since and now its tail is a long band of red, snaking back for miles over darkening hills to the dreamy melodies of pipes and chants. Ahead of us, the convoy fans out across fields, trampling crops flat, unleashing the tangy scents of wet corn and maize, and pours over the ridge.

We follow the general movement to the other side of the peak. In all directions, far into the distance, the valley heaves with troops, moving like ants around constellations of bonfires, whilst a million little flecks of metal – of lances, pikes, muskets, sabres – catch the last of the light. On the other side, beyond a thick band of darkness, no man's land, is the mirror image of the spectacle. The sight is both dispiriting – in an instant I travel back almost thirteen decades to my last battle – but also filled with possibility. There are so many souls before us, surely my master must be amongst them, surely we'll find that yellow intaglio? The promise of it gives me a fidgety happiness, a slight quickening of the heart. Sporco's tail has frozen mid-air in surprise, but soon begins to sway in steady beats of curiosity. Of course, I realize, he knows nothing of the meaning of armies and their movements. He probably thinks they're all going to dance.

'Let us look there first,' I say, nodding towards a farm building, lower down, around which hundreds are massed. On a battlefield such places are often used as makeshift hospitals.

We go down, threading through the sea of men, hunting that touch of yellow. The lucky soldiers are crammed under the shelter of flapping bivouacs, but most sit silent in the open air, collectively holding their breath it seems, lines and lines of infantrymen hunched on kits in grim acceptance of the weather and whatever tomorrow may bring. In the four decades I spent trailing armies with my master I've rarely seen fatigue like this, such broken bodies and bloodless faces. I scan every one of them, for him, but strangers stare back, or lift their arms to touch us listlessly as we pass. It doesn't take long for Sporco to realize there'll be no dancing here. His curiosity wanes to uncertainty, his tail stops moving and curls between his legs.

Close up the farm seems bigger. A thick perimeter wall encases a cluster of houses, a stout three-storey chateau and a dozen or so outbuildings. At the front, high gate doors are open and guards are counting in platoons. We sneak in amongst them, coming to a noisy courtyard. It reeks of wet wool, brandy and vinegar-sharp sweat. Soldiers are tending a fire made of furniture looted from the house, but the rain keeps getting the better of it, washing it to smoke, making the fire-builders cough into their sleeves. A cook is gutting rabbits and others are frying the meat in breastplates. Some troops have peeled off their soaking clothes, hung them from lines and stand naked before the fire, skin as pale as pig fat, passing round bottles, cursing and singing. More infantrymen shelter against the walls, fidgeting with their guns, mending buttons with needle and thread or crouching with their arms round their chests. A youngster writes a letter in a doorway, but the ink keeps bleeding across the page. They are all strangers. There is no rod of Asclepius.

I search the various buildings and Sporco trails obediently behind. Room after room is colonized by red-tuniced men, five or ten deep, as someone else's china still sits on shelves, and unknown portraits hang at angles. Shouldering through them all, for hours it seems, and finding no sign of my master, I grow despondent. Sporco has tried not to show his fear, but I can smell it on him. These are such sights as he's never seen. I myself lived thirty years before I encountered war. I lead him out and we slip through the gates, just as they're barricaded shut.

'Where now?' I say. Sporco makes a show of looking around and the rain comes again, ice cold now, in whistling curtains that make the fires hiss. Calls go up and down the length of the valley as troops pack closer together or take shelter in the woods. 'Can you go on?' I could. I could walk and walk all night through the brigades.

'Yes,' he says, water streaming from his snout. 'This way?' I can tell he'd rather be anywhere else but here. His paws sink in the mud and I have the sense once more of his spirit, of his every-day bravery – and that this ordeal would be so much harder without him by my side. I am proud of him, and it strikes me, forcefully so, that he was right: that we *are* a pack after all.

'Let us find somewhere clever to sleep. Tomorrow we can search again. Tomorrow our affairs are always better.' In the distance, away from the battlefield, behind the British lines, I notice a windmill, its sails turning in the gale.

'Make for there,' I nod. 'A safe place.'

We ascend once more the valley ridge. As we reach the summit, there's a clap of thunder, a pince of lightning and in the split second of whiteness the two armies are laid out in all their vastness and I try to catch the flash of yellow, but dark-ness falls again.

The windmill sits on its own bank, edged by a wood on one side and far away from the fray. As we approach it, I notice people – the miller and his family I presume – locking it up, and hurriedly loading their things on to a cart. 'There is a piece of fortune,' I say. 'We may have it to ourselves.' We pause at the foot of the bank, waiting for them to leave, and Sporco inspects a well that is there. 'Careful of that,' I say, as he peers down inside. I'm superstitious of them, of the way they plunge like cliffs into darkness. There comes a whip crack from above and the miller's cart takes off, north.

Going up to the building, we crawl between a gap in the timbers into an octagonal room at the base of the mill. Still warm and homely, the remains of a fire smoulders in the hearth. Many sacks of grain, fresh and pleasant-smelling, are piled about, cushioning the room from the noise of the rain. And high in the eaves, driven by the sails, the machinery creaks and turns.

'*Fagioli!*' Sporco exclaims, his nose disappearing into a pot by the chimney, his tail reanimating. There's not much left, but enough for us.

I use my teeth to drag a new plank of wood on to the fire and once there's a good flame and we've dried off, we eat in front of it, safe from the gale. *Fagioli*, made in the old style with no meat and still warm: surely an auspice of good fortune. Sporco does not hurry his food; he savours every mouthful, and as the firelight catches against his face it picks out threads of gold in his oversize brows – they used to be ridiculous, but now they are wise – and we could be patricians dining in one of those new eating places that had started to appear in Venice, *restaurants* as they're called, where clientele, with a sense almost of scandal, sup on extravagant treats at separate linen-clothed tables.

Our bellies full, I stretch out on the rug and Sporco entertains me by doing tricks with his ears, pointing one up and the other side to side and vice versa, and with his tufty eyebrows rolling them in a wave across his face, then bunching them together to make shapes.

'Do you do impressions?' I ask, remembering how Blaise used to make me laugh.

'Yes.' He sits very straight and very seriously.

'Are you doing it?'

'Yes.' He relaxes, then assumes the position again, this time saying in an earnest tone, '*I wait.*' Still I don't get it. 'It's you.'

I'm not offended. Although I no longer wait, but seek, he's right as far as my past is concerned: once an adventurer, a voyager, a courtier, a soldier, my life boiled down to that one thing only.

From outside there comes music, a guitar accompanying a single voice, a tune so sweet and haunting, I must see who provides it. Getting up and peering from the window, there's a band of soldiers sheltering at the edge of the woods below, close to the well. For a moment, the notion takes me that my master could be amongst them, for he would seek out music such as this on a battlefield. The singer stands in the glow of a bonfire, his face still and concentrated, carolling a lament of love or loss, and his comrades sit around arm in arm. There is no familiar face. Sporco stands by my side and when I notice our tails swaying in concert with the melody, I feel consoled. A new chapter has begun without my noticing it. The travails of our journey have brought us close. I have a friend now. I can teach him, and he I. This scruff who has made me see the world anew. We will search the realms together. And when we find my master – with Sporco by my side, it is surely possible – all the better: for we shall be three.

We curl up to sleep, my heart slowing to the beat of his, to the comforting odour of corn, the fire crackling, the sails creaking against the wind and the calm, assured rumble of cogs and wheels turning through the night.

In the morning, we have a bird's-eye view of the battlefield from the front of the mill on top of our private bank. Surveying it in the crisp June light, the rain of yesterday seems like a distant reverie, the distant tolling of church bells chasing the last of it away. The smudgy vale has alchemized into a velvet of sweeping hills, of silver pools, dark woods and patchworked fields in evergreen, emerald and aubergine.

The massed battalions look tranquil, untroubled, as they assemble into neat squares and columns, every detail of kit and uniform thrilling under the sun: tunics of scarlet faced with cream and imperial blue, white breeches, golden buttons. And the little noises that fill the air – clinking armour, sheaving steel, hammers on horseshoes, squeaking leather – are reassuring and soft, like the hubbub before a dance, the tittle-tattle of guests arriving, the thrips and pops of the orchestra tuning up. The phalanx of mounted officers close by, chatting amiably and peering through their telescopes at their counterparts on the other side, could easily be ball-goers and I wonder if the fantasy will come true after all: that these two armies will meet in no man's land, not to fight but to reel in the sunshine. The sight gives me confidence somehow, and strengthens my sense of purpose. I will find him: if not today, tomorrow. If not tomorrow, the next.

'So you wait for me here,' I say to Sporco. 'You guard our home, whilst I search.' I do for Sporco what my master often did for me at battles, give him a pretend responsibility to keep him safe, whilst I go alone. He assents with an upward tilt of his snout and turns to go back inside. 'And, Sporco –' he halts and looks round '– don't leave this windmill. There'll be a great noise, terrible sounds, louder than thunder, but you stay, understand? You stay in this place. Until I return, understand?' I mean to frighten him. 'Go on.'

Even when he's ensconced inside, I linger, fretting about leaving him alone. I observe him through a crack. He stands, chest broad, tail up and proud with his mission, and once more I remember the puppy abandoned on the pontoon, and my fear for him is crushing. 'Just stay,' I say to myself. 'Just stay.'

Going back into the heart of the army, fleet-footed now I

am alone, gunners everywhere are trying to heave cannon into place. The rain may have stopped, but the ground is thick mud and the cannon wheels, even with horses pulling, have no purchase and keep tipping the guns to one side. I know from past experience any battle is unlikely to begin until the ground has hardened, so I have time on my side.

At last, I find a group of hospital tents and, tail up, as it used to be in my war days, I go from one to the next. Red-eyed doctors are preparing tables and sorting instruments, gorgets, finger-saws, little guillotines and mouth gags. My master would usually be amongst them, calm and steady. And if his compatriots were frightened – for there is just as much dread in these *hacking* tents as on any front line – he'd offer a smile or thoughtful remark. I carry on, weaving through the British lines that seem to go on for miles, regiment after regiment after regiment. Every little while I look round at the windmill in the distance, its sails perfectly still, and I find myself imagining the fine times that Sporco and I might have together, even if we don't find my master. He still has five or six years. I could make them happy ones. A pack is a home after all.

An hour or so passes, burning heat evaporates the pools of rainwater, and though the ground begins to solidify, it's still not firm enough for the cannon. Occasionally, waves of chanting erupt on one side or the other, pumped-up cavalry-men hold their helmets high with the tips of their swords, whilst battalions, sorted into giant rectangles and squares, shimmer restlessly. And still, over and over, I look to the windmill.

When I notice gunners finally readying their cannon, I resolve to make my way back to it. Halfway to the ridge, a peculiar silence falls across the vale, as if the air had been sucked out of it. I hurry on, but pause when I hear a faraway bark. A tiny golden-brown shape flits over the hill between the lines of troops: Sporco.

'Stop, Sporco! Stay!' In the corner of my eye, I see a fuse being lit, a scratch of sparks and a flare of brilliant phosphorous. A blur of soldiers hurry past, levelling muskets, mouths shouting and I don't know if he's seen me.

The boom is so loud and shrieking it shakes the valley. A scorching backdraft boils the air out of shape. Sporco has frozen, clinging on to the ground as if the world were turning over.

16. The Well

Waterloo, June 1815

Another boom comes, then a third, a fourth, and cannons rear up backwards, and my hearing goes with a pop. A soldier next to me, ginger-haired, vomits through his fingers. Suddenly everyone ducks, as a shape tears through the air. The earth explodes, folding into rucks.

'Sporco!' I can't hear myself.

An arm, shot from the body of the ginger boy, somersaults the air, spitting blood into my eye before I'm lapped in black smoke. I stumble on, seizing for breath. A glimpse of Sporco and he's gone. With a snap my hearing comes back to the roar and whistle of mortar, the hammer of muskets, horses neighing, drums beating, men screaming, pipes, bugles, the endless tat-tat-tat of shot hitting metal. A soldier slips in the charge and is trampled by the rest, chest pummelled into red mud. A cavalryman is struck, his head shudders, and pink mist goes up with chunks of brain and bone. He hangs dead from his saddle, half-headed, as his horse, mad with fear, whinnies and races in circles.

Troops line up, aim, fire, retreat, reload, line up again. A lance is driven through the neck of a white mare; it lurches mid-air and falls sideways, hooves up, snapping the pike and burying its rider under its flank. As he fights to free himself, a skirmisher bayonets his chest. I catch his eyes – a sloweddown surprise – before he's shot in the head.

I spot Sporco, in the midst of a marching regiment, bumped and jostled from boot to boot, not knowing where to turn. 'Here!' I dive in to fetch him but he keeps being kicked forward, shrieking as his paws are trodden on, and his ears do a frantic dance. All the while comes the hissing of bullets, the tapping of shot on metal and mists of blood as flesh is struck. I get to him and hold steady against his side, barking loudly for the soldiers to steer clear until finally the flank has passed and we retreat, taking cover behind a tipped-over cannon. He keeps trying to tell me something but I can't hear.

'Him, him, him,' he seems to be saying.

'I told you to wait! Why didn't you wait?'

His face caves in and he trembles all over. 'I'm sorry, so sorry. I was looking out for you through the window, hoping you'd be back soon, and that's when –' There's a scream and an infantryman runs by on fire. A body lands on the wheel of our cannon, legs bent back, stomach ripped open, crinkled white entrails and shiny-jewel organs slipping out. Sporco burrows under my stomach. 'I'm frightened, frightened.'

I peer over our barricade and my stomach turns. The whole valley is eaten up with battle. I can't see where it begins or ends: columns march, mortars rain down, knives of sunshine split through black clouds, corpses burn. A battalion stalks through a field of blood-splattered rye. The walled farm from last night is choked with soldiers. A howitzer hits its roof, cracks through the slates and flames lick out.

'We have to get back behind the ridge, to the windmill. Just stay close to me.' We jump from behind our shelter and shoulder up the hill as a line of drummer boys marches the other way, tartan-clad, chests out, thrump, thrump, thrump. Cresting the peak, I realize in the confusion, we've drifted too far and the mill is behind us, still some distance away.

Between it and us, an ocean of red-coated regiments have sorted into defensive squares, each one made up of hundreds of soldiers, on their knees round the edges, with bayonets out, and in rows behind, all with their musket up, ready to fire.

The earth rumbles beneath our paws, cracks open in the ground and there comes a new cyclone of noise. Glancing back, the valley seems to be folding over itself in a band of blue, as the enemy cavalry charges, whipping up billows of dust, with hooves catching the sunlight like showers of flying coins.

'Make for the first square!' I cry, pushing Sporco on to it, hoping we'll be safer inside it, than exposed in the empty space around. Just in time, we plunge through the crouching soldiers at the front into the heart of the square, as a command goes up and the men discharge as one, to a skull-shattering din. We burrow deeper, choking on smoke, as bodies drop at random, to the reek of burnt hair and hot metal. Sporco keeps turning on the spot, spine arched and his face a picture of horror. Near the back of the square, there's some space to move and a suite of officers are monitoring the attack, blackened brows furrowed with concentration. A sergeant is shouting; I can't hear what he says, only see his spittled mouth open and close.

We push further on, bursting from the rear of the first square, over shrub land, and spinning into the next. And on we go, from one scorching throng to the next, from light to dark to light again – until finally we get away from the worst of the fighting, to the edge of the wood that curves round towards the mill.

'There!' Sporco cries, halting suddenly. 'Him.'

I see it, the silhouette against the sky, the only motionless figure on the battlefield, his insolent face crowned with that diabolical wig: Vilder. Then he's lost in the vale of chaos.

'This way, quickly!' I cry, diving into the wood.

A bullet crackles through the air. There's a thud, Sporco falters and falls. He picks himself up, but drops again. Blood decants from a dark hole in his rump. 'Are you hurt?' Idiotic question. I look around for Vilder, in case he's coming for us, but he's vanished. Sporco stands unsteadily, shambles forward, lopsided, eyes blinking, and falls. I dig my head under his body, lift him over my shoulders and drive into the wood, away from the din of battle until we get to the other side, close to the windmill, where the soldiers made a fire last night near the well.

I lay him down carefully, appalled with myself for dragging him here, for not leaving him in Brussels, or Padua, or Venice, or anywhere but here. He could be asleep on Claudina's bed, legs tucked together, in a room scented with French talc and chamomile. I lick the blood from the wound, but no sooner have I cleaned it, it seeps out again. His flesh is too mangled to see if the bullet's lodged inside or gone straight through him. He doesn't make a sound, just stares at me, a wavering light in his eye. 'You'll be all right,' I tell him, even as my insides flip. 'We'll fix you.' *Where is my master*, I rage inside, *now when I need him more than ever?*

'Something happened a long time ago,' Sporco says weakly. 'And I always recall it.'

'Recall what?' I press my paw against the wound and it heats beneath it.

'When I was a puppy, I was tied to a pontoon and my mistress left me.'

'You remember that?' I can't hide the shake in my voice. 'You remember when you were young?'

'Is it getting dark?'

242

'A little,' I reassure him. I take a blanket that the soldiers have left behind and push the material against his wound. It stains red immediately. Little films of blood are bubbling in the corner of his mouth.

Sporco's sounds are slow and steady. 'When I was left by my mistress, I didn't know what to do. The way she left – with her suitcase packed, sailing away with her cruel lover – told me she wasn't coming back, but I waited anyway.' He closes his eyes and his chin trembles. 'Then I heard someone come on to the pontoon. It was her, I thought, she's come back for me after all. She hadn't. A dog had come instead, with a black back and a brown stomach, twice my size. Kind. He sat with me all night, even as I turned my back on him, not wanting his help, wanting only my mistress.' His eyes grow cloudier. 'It's cold, terribly cold.' I put the blanket over his body, tucking it in at the sides. 'Some weeks later, that same dog found me and tried to help again, and I pretended not to know him, snapped him away.'

'You remember all this?'

'I was angry you see, I wanted *her* to return.' Sporco fixes me in his glare as he lays out his secret. 'But she didn't. And that dog became my friend. My best friend. And that is why I would follow that dog throughout the realms, to any place on earth. Into a furnace I would follow him. The only one that came to help me that day I was left tied to a post by my mistress.' He holds out his paw and the root of his tail twitches where he wants to wag. I try to nod, but something is smashing inside me, ripping to the surface. I go to kiss him, but his eyes have turned to glass. I lick him and his head rocks to one side. I bark, but he doesn't wake.

'Sporco, Sporco.' I lash my tongue over his face, paw at his eyelids, but his pupils have frozen still. I snatch the blanket off him, ease his body on its side, but it lollops over, legs stiff, spilt blood in a slick beneath him.

I lie down and stare at his inert face, the face that laughed, that wanted to play, that wanted a mate, that never had a mate, that said *I* was his best friend. I paw the blond tufts over his eyes, neatening them. I lick the bubbles of blood from the corner of his mouth. The afternoon passes, the muffled scream of battle rising and falling. How dismissive I was to him, how boastful and self-important. Who am I to say how he should have behaved? I try to wake him, nonsensically, but he's stiffening now.

To fight the pain I dig a hole to bury him, taking my revenge on the ground, frantically pulling up the earth between roots until I've made a space that's roomy enough for him. But I can't bear to put him in it and cover him with soil. Not yet. A putrid breeze rolls from the battlefield, licking past us, up the slope to the windmill, making its sails creak and begin to turn again. And the rain returns too, the dismal autumnal drizzle that has stolen into summer. I neaten the blanket over his body, as humans do, and huddle closer as he chills.

In the evening, there comes a punch of hooves and shapes configure from the gloom: a man leading a coal-black carthorse and a wagon of dead animals. He, a furrier, stocky and shoulderless, sees me and halts, before taking the measure of Sporco. He means to pick him up and throw him in his cart.

'Be gone,' I growl. He pulls a knife from his belt and makes a move for my friend. 'Be gone!' I snap, vicious enough for him to waver and then drive on past us.

I shoulder Sporco's body into the hole, prodding and teasing until he's laid out faultlessly on his side, his legs together in neat pairs, just as he used to lie when he was content and full of food. I fill the grave with the excess of soil, pushing it in with my nose, covering his fur and leaving the head until last. 'Goodbye, my friend.' I take a moment staring at his face, trying to remember him as if he's asleep, not dead. I kiss the end of his nose, nuzzle his forehead and fill the last of the grave. The pack. A single grey eye stares back at me. I steady myself with deep breaths and cover it with soil.

In the silence that follows a clear thought occurs to me: *Let me die tonight*. Let tomorrow not be another day. I turn and stare at the wellhead, at the bucket tipped on the ground and the coil of rope connecting the two.

I get up and look down into the hollow. It's so dark I cannot tell if it is yards deep or miles. I push a rock over the side and after a pause a splash echoes back. There is room enough. Of the hangings I have seen, those with a long stretch of rope have been so quick to appear almost painless, a fall, a jerk, a twitch and then unconsciousness.

With my teeth I try to undo the knot round the handle of the bucket, but it's too tight. No matter, let it come with me. I loop the rope round my neck, once, twice, several times, until it's tight, making sure the slack is not so long that I'll hit the bottom. I climb on to the edge. I just have to fall forward and my weight will do the rest. One step is all.

I remember the time at the beginning of my life, in Elsinore – before we discovered the body on the shore – my master had wanted to go out and pick oysters and I hid from him. He smiled, finding me under the hall table. *'Where will life lead us if we hide in corners . . .?'*

I tip forward and fall. With sickening speed I go, into the dark, into the blur of tunnelled rock, the bucket coming after, striking my head on its way down, before the rope snaps tight about my neck.

'No!' comes a cry from above.

The effect – the rushing sensation in my head as my body turns numb – is instantaneous, but seems elongated, as if normal time had slowed.

'No,' comes the call again and I notice, though everything is hazy, a human head framed in the round opening. I'm so dizzy as to be almost content, were it not for the rope slicing my neck.

'Hold fast,' a familiar voice cries and I'm half aware of rope creaking, and I ascending. 'Hold fast!' *His* voice for sure, my master's, the depth and timbre of it. My act of desperation has called him here. 'Hold fast.' I turn my body as he pulls me up and free, taking me in his hands and putting me down as if I were made of china. When I see him, Vilder, I curl back my lips, growl deepening.

'The English camp,' he says, pointing over the valley. 'Follow me.'

I charge, leap from my hind legs and ram the flat of my skull against his middle. As he falters, I take his leg between my teeth and bite hard, pressing my jaw through flesh to muscle. He makes no sound, does not kick or hit me, but prizes my mouth apart and lays me aside. I attack again, his arm now, tearing off a strip of skin. Still he does not cry, just prises open my jaw with effortless strength, grapples me by the chest and eases me down.

'I know where he is, you devil.' He jabs his fingers in the air. 'That way. In Waterloo. There's no time to lose.' When still I hold my ground, he shouts, 'Your master. Will you not come to meet him?'

17. The Church at Waterloo

Waterloo village, June 1815

It seems lunacy, that when I first met Vilder, and followed him across the icy Thames, I longed for his attention. Now, though in just as unearthly a place, I shadow him with contempt, at a distance, not caring if he looks round, or what he thinks of me.

Reaching the peak of the ridge I halt a moment. A burnt sun is setting, casting a tobacco-stained light against the myriad estuaries of flat dark red. In all directions acres of corpses are tide-marked against the valley, tangled up with smashed artillery, cannon wheels, upturned carts and acres of felled horses, some still twitching. Everywhere chimneys of smoke, like hot springs, lift from the cratered ground. Woods are charred skeletons and every farm building in sight is broken in pieces and blackened by fire. The wind is sharp, slanting waves of drizzle against my fur.

Vilder pauses to make sure I'm still behind him and when I press on, he does too. After everything, there's still something magnetic about him: the haughtiness that is both self-regarding and self-loathing, his density, the vanity that is so inwrought it will decay after his bones. Even the soiled splendour of his clothes pronounces him as something *other*, a being beyond or above our world.

We go down into the basin of the valley. Some of the

soldiers who I thought dead are sleeping, propped up by kit or by corpses, or lying motionless, white eyes in smoke-black faces, gabbling to themselves. Crafty looters are already picking through the bodies, pocketing watches, spectacles, purses, tugging rings from fingers. And there are real vultures too, congregations of them massing on branches, waiting their turn.

I pass an infantryman jabbing his dagger into the knee of a dead horse, pulling hard until the cartilage rips, throwing the joint on to fire; his companions are already eating, tearing flesh from long bones and washing it down with water sucked from helmets. The meat tastes bitter, I can see from their faces, and they slit their eyes at me, wondering if I would make a tastier meal. But something in my gaze makes them turn away.

I pass the farm we visited last night. The wall of the main building has collapsed, and in the sooty cavities of the rooms inside bodies are piled three high and burnt together like molasses, reeking of ammonia, petrified mouths frozen in a yell. A man is twisted in the rubble of the blown-out courtyard: white breeches, dark red tunic with golden epaulettes. He has a hole in his chest that has snapped through his ribs, but his hair, though powdered with pieces of bone, is slick dark ginger. I've seen him before, in Brussels. He is the young officer, the duke's companion, who stared from the window as I took shelter in the alley. For a moment I'd been entranced by him and the confidence he possessed that his life would be successful. Now his indigo eyes are as plain as puddle water.

And Sporco. With every step I take, his single grey eye pursues me.

There's a final wink of gold and the sun slips from view. In its place a luminous, stenching fog cloaks the land from the outer reaches in. Vilder checks on me, and carries on. I have nothing else to do but shadow him.

Once, during a campaign in Saxony, my master took me down into a coal mine. We threaded through a hole in the mountain and descended into a labyrinth of passages and caves where teams of mute workers pickaxed the shining coalface and carried away the treasure. The village we come to, in the darkness before dawn, Waterloo, reminds me of that place. Black-faced servicemen swarm in silent packs, to the endless flitting of lanterns, as cannon, and carts – of the captured and the dead – roll in and out, bottlenecking the high street. The walking wounded hobble through in a dream state, and dogs, with the pattern of their day turned upside down, watch from doorways with slow sways of their tails. 'Is it over now, is it?' they murmur. 'Or shall it start again?' Here and there, in pools of lamplight, baggy-eyed orderlies scratch reports and tally numbers.

'They found his carriage in Genappe,' an old man, a town resident, asides to another. 'Napoleon's. He'd escaped somehow, but inside was his hat, telescope and a pouch of diamonds worth a million francs. Now there's a piece of magic.'

Vilder is waiting on the front porch of the town church. It seems, in my hallucinatory state, an absurd parody of the dream I've held for more than a century, of finding my master waiting for me at the doors of the cathedral in Venice. This church, with its domed roof and pale flight of steps up to its large front door, could be a miniature version of it. Vilder motions for me to enter, and I am too drained to do anything but comply. I bristle when I brush by him, not looking at his face, and he does not follow me in.

Inside is a hellish scene, a makeshift hospital, or mortuary, the injured and the dead thrown in rows in the stony gloom, moaning for help, but receiving none, whilst a mugworty sweet smoke, another muddling parallel to my dream, melds with the whiff of infected flesh and surgical preparations.

Yet I feel a clarity inside, a tingle at the root of my tail. I'm drawn towards the altar and the first tentative rays of dawn sift through the stained-glass window and jewels of colour – sapphire, lemon, violet and rose – illuminate a golden sculpture. An ancient man clutches a staff, his gaze fixed on some wonder above, a dog at his side. Every forward step, every pad of my paw is thrilling. The legs of a soldier stick out from behind the altar, muddied boots, torn breeches. Tremors, deep and unnatural, earthquake through me. I edge closer and find him asleep, his chest slowly rising and falling and a sack next to him, daubed with a yellow symbol of a snake and staff. My heartbeat quickens, doubles, then triples in speed.

For a moment I hold my breath. I wait, teasing myself with delicious pain. At last, I lower my head and inhale a minute draught of him.

I am made of light.

It is he.

I dig my nose all over his cloak, extraordinary mewls, whines and squeaks tumbling out of me, sounds I haven't made since I was tiny, if ever. Rearing from his collar, the back of his head, the truth of his hair: tight hazel curls dusted with grey. The sight makes my jaw shiver. Then I glimpse his face, shadowed in the folds of the cloak and I am home. My limbs give way, I drop, but bounce straight up again. His face. A gaunter, sallower version, but his face – his crinkled eyes closed in sleep. I lean down and whisper. How I have longed to make this sound –

'Valentyne. It is me.'

Silence. His eyes stay shut.

'Valentyne.'

Suddenly there's a stab of panic: he's dead. No, I'm not thinking, his chest is moving. I lick his cheek and I'm shocked by the coldness of it. I put my muzzle to his mouth, his lips are bloodless, but breath passes between them. I nudge back the collar of his cloak, shocked at how emaciated he is: where his chest used to bulge from his neck, his collarbones now jut out in shiny ridges. And an unpleasant, rusty smell, foreign to him, lifts from his skin.

'Valentyne.'

This time his eyes open.

He looks at me and my heart stops. He looks, but doesn't see me. I lick his face, wetting the spine of his nose. He just stares as if I were any dog in the world. He sits up then, wheezing with pain, carefully leaning his back against the wall, the sheer exertion making him grimace until his chest settles. 'Valentyne?' There is worry in my tone. I put my paw on his lap, gaping up at him, waiting for the great tide of his reaction. He pads me absent-mindedly, barely touching, like a human who doesn't care for animals.

'Valentyne!' Now my bark is snappish and it makes him wince. 'Valentyne! Valentyne! Valentyne!'

Someone calls for quiet and a soldier laughs like a mad-man. My master does not know me. His pupils swivel up to white, his head lolls forward, mouth dripping slobber and his body slides back to the floor. I paw him, lick him, nudge him with my nose, half-choked yowls whistling out of me. I look round, meaning to catch the attention of a doctor, but find Vilder instead.

'Now that you have been reacquainted, let us leave this hellhole.' He makes a move for my master, but I block his way. Vilder returns my gaze squarely. 'He will have no help here, I assure you. He will die.' He reaches out again, but I let out a growl. 'I did not bring you here to fight. You have already ripped my arm to the bone. I have helped you. Now help me. We must take him from here.' His manner is forthright and blunt and his eyes seem to ask me to trust him. They are deep wells, but still I don't know what lies at the bottom of them, if there are entrances to other worlds, better places. Gently he moves me aside, digs his arms under my master's body and lifts him as if he was no heavier than a bundle of brushwood. 'Follow,' he says, returning down the aisle.

What other choice do I have?

18. Vilder

Antwerp, June 1815

Once again I find myself in the compartment of Vilder's carriage, in its shabby interior of ripped chartreuse silk and scratched glass, but this time beside my incognizant master, who's laid out across the floor, joggling side to side. Vilder drives unassisted, as he had on the road from Opalheim, and I deduce he's not returned there since, but followed in the wake of the army, as we did. He goes in impatient stops and starts, often standing on the perch and bellowing until he gets through the clog of traffic. Over and over, he finds the way barred by immovable brigades or barricades of tipped-up carriages and artillery pieces, and must double back and find another route. When at last we escape the war zone and reach an open road, he whips hard and we course north-west at speed. It's dusk by the time we hurtle from the countryside into the rubbled slums of a port, passing through the outskirts of the city until we finally skid to a halt at the harbour. There are thickets of masts, seagulls wheeling over the estuary to the flat lands beyond, and the air is spiced with sugar cane and pepper. I know the place, the city, the docks – Antwerp – I passed through it with my master many times.

'Not where I would have chosen to end up,' Vilder growls, opening the cab door, 'but we may find some semblance of civilization.' He retrieves my master and folds him over his shoulder. 'Out,' he says, clicking his fingers at me. We go to one of the buildings that face the harbour: sturdy grey stone with diamond-pane windows. A sign hangs from the front pronouncing it as an inn. A youth stirs from the porch. 'My carriage, see to it.' The porter ogles the comatose body across his shoulder, as Vilder furrows his brow, lost in thought for a moment, before saying, 'is there a doctor hereabouts?' The boy nods. 'Call on him. Tell him it is urgent. And buy me brandy, two bottles. Here.' He produces a coin from his coat and gives it to him. 'Go!'

We enter the building and traipse into a gloomy parlour. There's an empty hearth, tiled floors that are cold to the touch and a single candle stands with one miserly smoking tallow and a plain crucifix beside it. Vilder inspects it all with distaste and in the silence my master's boots creak together. It's still incomprehensible that he's here with me, and that Vilder and I have been thrown together as companions. 'Anyone?' Vilder says in the direction of the kitchen.

A man dressed in puritan black sails through the door, the vapour of overcooked cabbage with him. '*Ja?*' He tuts unsociably. He sees my poor master hanging over Vilder's shoulder but makes no enquiry.

'A room,' Vilder deadtones and for once I'm grateful for his plainness. The innkeeper pauses, hooding his eyes at the invalid. I feel a rush of impatience, to get my master comfortable and be by his side. 'We have come from the battleground. My friend is not wounded, but he is – he is beyond exhaustion. We have called a doctor.' He takes a handful of coins from his pocket and leaves them on the dresser. 'For several days in advance.'

The innkeeper hesitates before unlatching a key from his belt. 'The door at the top. The dog can stay outside.'

'He stays with me,' Vilder asserts, ushering me up the stairs before the man has a chance to stop us. On the first floor he shoulders my master into the room, lays him out on the bed and studies him for a moment, pulling up his eyelids and peering inside. He's afraid, I can smell it on him. He inspects the room, frowning at the drab walls, peeling plaster and damp patches. Apart from the old bed, there's a lopsided table, a pair of incommodious-looking chairs and a nightstand by the door. 'So much for civilization.' Grimy casement windows look out on to the darkening harbour. He goes to one of them, unlatches it and, after a struggle, cracks it open.

There's a knock on the door and the youth enters with a pair of bottles and ushers in a slim gentleman in a stovepipe hat. 'Leave them there,' Vilder says to the boy, before turning to the doctor. 'He is in a state of unconsciousness, my companion. I used to have some knowledge of medicine long ago, but it is all in fragments, and I cannot think clearly. Why do you stare at me as if I am some circus monstrosity? Come forward, damn you, or do you mean to escape? Good grief, this is the most inhospitable town on earth.'

I sit where the man can see me, ears up and back straight, to present a friendlier aspect. If he has come to help my master, I cannot risk losing him. A little gulp of uncertainty passes down his throat, before he takes off his hat and sets it down with his case on the trunk at the end of the bed.

'I am Vilder. It was kind of you to come,' my companion says in a more conciliatory tone, offering his palm.

'Fabrègues.' He gives Vilder a weak handshake, before putting on his spectacles and beginning his examination. He repeats everything that Vilder has already done: checking my master's pulse, his temperature, feeling the back of his skull, beneath his jaw and round his groin, looking into his mouth, eyes and so on.

'What precipitated this –?'

'What?'

'How long has he –'

'Oh . . .' He wipes sweat from his brow before uncorking one of the bottles with his teeth. 'Some time I suppose. He suffered a loss –' a shooting glance at me '– stopped eating and –' a swig from the bottle '– exhaustion?'

'A loss?'

'Does it matter what happened in the past? It is *now* he is ill.'

A little battle of wills plays out between them, before Fabrègues opens up his case and takes out a box. 'His humours are – *je dois laisser ses veines respirer*. How do you say, let his veins breathe?'

'Blood let, you mean?'

'To force an awakening. Look at his eyes, there's nothing there, nothing at all. *Les mécanismes de son cerveau, ils sont morts.* He breathes, but in a way he is dead.'

'He is not dead. Feel him.' Vilder puts the back of his hand on Valentyne's forehead. 'He is tired, supremely so. He has crossed the continent, been at war.' Pause. 'He is supremely tired, you understand, and – and –' He drinks. 'Truly, is blood letting all you have? It's medieval.'

'No, no, no,' Fabrègues assures him. 'The procedure is well proven to –'

'Get out,' Vilder says. The doctor doesn't seem to understand, so Vilder goes to the door and opens it. 'Get out I say. It is 1815; have you no sense of enquiry? Learn something new, you parrot.'

'*Excusez moi?*'

256

'Out, I say, before I open *your* veins.'

The doctor holds up his palms, as if to say he has done all he can, before taking his case. 'The gentleman is extremely ill. He will die,' he pronounces and leaves.

Vilder slams the door behind him and returns to Valentyne. 'Wake up. Do you hear me?' He whispers, prodding him, with the same distaste as he had with Aramis. I'm not a cowardly creature, but Vilder intimidates me like no other human ever has. I have seen barbarians and murderers, particularly on the battlefield, where men lose their inhibitions for cruelty, but Vilder is distinct from the species: there are seams within him of such deranged unpredictability that even he seems powerless to temper. I wait until Vilder falls asleep before stealing up and curling tightly up at my master's side. I have longed for a hundred and twenty-seven years to be back in this sacred place, adjoined to his skull; it is beyond belief that he hovers at the very the edge of death. So dreadful is it, I recant entirely my desire yesterday to die, hoping if I grab hold of the matter of life again, my master may somehow follow my example.

Vilder becomes my master's doctor and for the next two days he follows a mechanical regimen of activities. Once in the morning and once at night he turns Valentyne from one side to the other. He attempts to spoon-feed him tepid broth brought up from the kitchen, tipping it into his mouth and holding his head up so gravity will take it down, though most of it ends up on the bedclothes. I look at my master a hundred times an hour, as if by vigilance alone, I'll prevent him becoming sicker. He's so emaciated I can see the grilles of his ribs. In Genoa once, he and I witnessed a band of slaves being given their freedom: helped out from a cotton ship, a chain of skeletal humans were hauled like a grotesque fishing line from the hull, flesh eviscerated from their bones, memories from their brains, without speech, or hearing, or sense of any kind. Whatever Vilder had intended by imprisoning him at Opalheim, it had broken my master utterly. He must have remembered me, for he went to Venice first, after escaping. Not finding me, and being in such a dream state, he must have been drawn back, without even realizing, to his old routine of following armies.

One night talking wakes me and I find Vilder hunched over the bed, gabbling to my master, as if he were some relic in a cathedral. 'I am talking to you, Valentyne. And if you do not seem to hear, then I speak to the part of you beneath the conscious, the place where dreams unfold. Or nightmares.' He swigs his bottle. 'I suffered more than you. My conversion was dreadful, dreadful. Five years, was it? Six? Injections every other day. How did I imagine it would feel? A serene baptism? That vile, unnatural broth we slicked into our arteries. The abominable nights, the constant cold crawling under the skin. It lived, that liquid. You remember all this? You did not suffer like I. You withstood the torture. Without complaint. Such golden patience you had. Wake up, Valentyne. Do not answer with silence. Wake up.'

An hour later, drunker and his voice ground to a slur, he's still talking. 'Is it not curious that as I unravelled, seventy, eighty years later, as I unravelled, so the work of artists grew obscene? Is that not peculiar?' It's the dead of night and in the pauses between his ramblings, a taut silence rings from the city. 'Did I imagine it? The hurricane of ideas, the hurtling decades of genius, the sublime epoch – da Vinci, Michelangelo, Raphael – halted, dropped from a precipice, the lights extinguished, the world turned to a madhouse. Did you feel it like I did? It was there plainly. Look at Bosch, that satanic owl watching over paradise. Paradise? He knew there was no such place. That owl was the harbinger of the mutilation that would follow. Do not tell me I imagined it. I was there on the day of Saint-Barthélemy in Paris. I saw with my own eyes heaps of hacked corpses at the gates of the Louvre. The world was unravelling and I with it. Look, Valentyne, at Palissy, Romano, El Greco, if you will, they saw it too. Apocalypse, deluge, trumpets of the final judgement, horsemen drowning, giants felled, mountains smashed, the countryside overrun with serpents, those deranged colours, everything contorted and unwholesome. I did not imagine it, Valentyne. What happened in the world – also happened inside my head. Wake, goddamn you.' He shakes my master: a compliant sack of bones. 'You shall not do this to me.' I stand upright, giving him a firm look, to show I am ready to attack him if he becomes more aggressive. Vilder shrugs, lets go, and soon falls asleep, slumped across the bed.

Over the next few days, he descends ever more into a state of derangement. First, he comes back from one of his outings with armfuls of flowers – jasmine, honeysuckle and tuberose – but rather than put them in vases, he throws them about the room, crushing them with his feet, until the air is violent with sweetness. Later, he returns with a tapestry. The bemused porter helps him hang it, though it's larger than the room itself, Vilder bashes nails through the fabric – a landscape of peacocks trailing through a verdant forest – cursing all the while, twice deciding it's not straight with the ceiling, ripping it down and starting again.

The following day a harpsichord is delivered after many attempts to get it up the narrow stairs. There's a scuffling, a bumping and a pinging of keys until two men finally turn it through the door. 'Put it there,' Vilder says and they place it between the windows, both stealing a glance around the room, their gaze resting on my master. 'One of you can tune, I presume?' The younger of the two nods, an earnest stripling with neat thinning hair and a coat too large for him. 'And play it too?' Another nod. 'All the better. Get to it then.'

His companion leaves and the stripling opens up the instrument. He tunes it, key by key, plodding each one whilst tightening the string until the note becomes lucid. The monotony of it grows exasperating and I worry, nonsensically, it will disturb my master.

Whilst it continues, there comes a knock, and – in what has begun to seem like one of the surreal enactments Queen Henrietta Maria put on in Oxford during the civil war – a cardinal is shown into the room. Up until now the innkeeper had been at best vexed by the goings-on in our room, but now he gapes from the landing as if a statue had come to life and walked up the stairs. Vilder shuts the door on him.

'Good day, sir. You received the money? The *contribution*, I should call it, the correct church vernacular for those unholy notes. Will it be enough to rebuild your transept? I hope so. I should imagine you could build a whole new cathedral for it. Please sit.' The cardinal is tall and broad, out of scale with the room, and his crimson robe has the effect of making him more so – and he seems entirely perplexed to have found himself here. A glance at Valentyne, at me, at the harpsichord tuner, gives him no more clarity.

'It was beyond generous of you,' the cardinal says, '*Monsieur* –?'

'Carry on,' Vilder asides to the musician, before turning back to the cardinal. 'I'm accustomed to buying the best. Which is why I asked for you in person.' The bang of a dissonant key. 'Whether you can help more than a parish priest remains to be seen. But you are here now, and the money paid, so sit.' The cardinal does so, out of courtesy rather than any willingness, the tiny chair lost under his bulk and robes. Another note, lower. 'Don't mind him, he'll be finished soon. Music may bring my patient to sense. At this juncture, I'll try anything.'

The cardinal's jaw tightens to a smile and he neatens his crucifix over his robes.

'My father had a confessor.' Vilder deepens his voice in imitation: '*Every man must have a confessor, just as they must have a throat to breathe. Or was it to eat?* The old man had more money than the Holy Roman Emperor and the kings of Spain and England put together, and no currency whatsoever with other human beings – except for his confessor. By the time my father died he'd spoken just a handful of sentences to me in my eighteen years, each of them to assure me how worthless I was. But for his confessor: limitless conversation. They'd lock themselves up in his stateroom and talk and talk and talk. I suppose he wanted to guarantee everlasting life. You are a powerful breed. So, to the matter in hand. There was a gentleman I loved. No need to jump, I do not mean in *that* way. We'd known each other forever, worked together, studied side by side.' He points at my master. 'Him. Yes.' He pauses, then something in his tone makes my ears prick up. 'He was dazzling. Valentyne. He – how can I put it into words? – he made everything brighter. *Everything*, I mean: people, rooms, ideas. Lit up. I wanted to be him, not me. He was younger than me, by a few years, but had the maturity of someone my senior. I copied him in everything. You see, *my* character –' He scratches his forehead to find the words. 'I was purposeless. Vain. Uncourageous. Do not mistake me, I had intellect, greater than his, an ocean of it, and charm too – of my own brand – but I knew

261

not how to use these things. Although we were partners in business, and – as I said – he was younger, he was my teacher, and I was in awe. I would have followed him into hell itself. In actual fact, that is what I did.' A harpsichord note, deeper. 'That is not true yet,' Vilder asserts over his shoulder. 'Do it again. What was I saying?'

'That you followed the gentleman.'

'Yes, like you follow *yours*.' He motions at the cardinal's crucifix. 'We made a pact on a particular matter. It was not a small matter. He came out of it well. I – less so. That changed us. We drifted in different directions. Until one day our spheres came together again and he hurt me. Acutely. He broke me. I could not forgive. I'm spoilt you see. I will get my way. I hunted him down. Not easy – but money helped. In the end –' a little laugh directed at his guest – 'we met in a cathedral and I told him I had his dog and he took the bait.' The cardinal looks at me, the harpsichord tuner too. 'Yes, he. It was a lie, though, and I captured Valentyne.'

'Captured?' says the cardinal. A note, deeper still.

'To work for me. Do my bidding. Pay his debt, his debt for making me follow him in the first instance, and his debt for not helping when I was in need. I was mad by the time I'd caught up with him in Venice. I'd been dosing myself for decades. Easing potions. The pointlessness of everything. Do you understand the nature of addiction?' Before the cardinal has the chance to speak, Vilder answers for him. 'Let us just call it the devil within. Such a fiend has always lived in me, held its invisible court. Perhaps every human has one. I'd had addictions before, but after my loss, the betrayal, much worse.'

'And where was his dog all this time?' The cardinal asks, seeming to understand little else of the story.

'I hung all my hate on my loss. If I could not have my Aramis, if I could not be freed, then give me potions. *They* have meaning. Make them for me and atone. For the decades to pass in light. I'd always had tornadoes in my brain, you see, but with Valentyne's potions the world was new. It was a place of warless realms. His dog, you say? Valentyne pleaded to be released, so he could go and find his dog. His dog was all he cared about. How absurd, an animal is an animal. And besides, he had to pay his debt. Even you must understand justice?'

'Where?'

'What?'

'Where was he locked? In prison?

'What did you say?'

'*Where* did they take him?'

Vilder goes silent for a long time. The midday light turns across his face. 'How did you come to find him?' says the cardinal. Minutes pass. He gives an exasperated look at the harpsichord tuner. 'Perhaps you can tell what is it you want me to do, sir?'

'He might die,' says Vilder.

'I see, but my question is the same.'

'Save him.'

'By forgiving you?'

'No. What difference would that make?'

The cardinal is muddled for a moment, then, he says, 'Ah, you wish me to pray for him?'

Vilder jerks his head, taken aback and very slowly his expression changes, as a new thought forms. 'What a fool I am. If you pray for him too, that will save him, is that what you mean to say? Pray for him? It's nonsense. God? Where is he? Where is this god?'

'If you meant that truly as a question, you might begin –'

'Don't riddle me, priest. Don't dare. Get out. Go back to your den. Go back and sell trinkets to the gullible. Go and tamper with other minds. Get out! A curse on you. You desire life everlasting? If you had it, which you never will, you would wish against it in a year. For it is as it was for Prometheus, to be chained to a rock and have an eagle eat your liver day upon day upon day. Humanity has no need of your services, and I even less. Out!' The cardinal, enraged to the colour of his robe, departs, without words, and the terrified harpsichordist attempts to escape in his wake. 'Where are you going?'

'I – I am just a musician, sir.'

'Well, play.'

Shaking, he resumes his seat. 'What do you desire? I – I mean to say, which composer –'

'By God, just play!'

The first few notes tremble, then he finds his tempo. At once my heart quickens, for I know the melody: it's the same lament that the slight, pitted-face prodigy played in the count's palazzo in Venice. Vilder is apparently moved, and when the first piece is over, he motions for more.

'Who is that? Is it Schubert?' he asks, no doubt remembering the conversation he had at the ball in Padua.

'Mozart.'

'That's right, the one they all talk of. Keep playing.'

He plays for some time, and Vilder keeps his eye on the bed for signs of life. Gradually he seems to calm, until suddenly he erupts again. 'Wake up, goddamn you! Foolery enough. Look what I do for you.' He bangs on the harpsichord, seizing a clump of flowers and flicking them about, before shaking his fist at the tapestry. 'I bring you the realms.' My hackles rise as I ready myself to attack at the next act of aggression. 'Do not blame me,' he bellows, clutching a handful of flesh from his chest. 'You did this, not I.' When he's settled, he takes out money and drops it on the keys. 'That will do.'

As the harpsichordist hurries out, the innkeeper stalks in, sizing Vilder up. 'I don't know who you are, or who you think you are, but this is my house and you are not welcome in it. You have until the morning to pack your things and go –' he motions with a flick of his head at my master – 'and take your affliction with you.'

Vilder listens to his steps descend, before seizing the cup of brandy from beside the bed and downing it. He's about to throw the empty glass against the wall, a foolish gesture that can only get us into more trouble, when a thought seems to occur to him. 'Prometheus,' he says, wrinkling his brow. 'Prometheus.' He picks up his purse and rushes out. I go to the window and watch him barge up the street out of sight.

It's almost dark by the time he comes back with a large package. He throws it on the table, unbuttons and rips off his tunic, and lights all the candles along with the fire, even though it's a hot evening. He tears open the bundle and organizes its contents: an iron pan, needles and twine, a round mirror, another bottle of brandy and a number of apothecary phials, the type my master always used. He unwraps the final object, a fearsome-looking dagger and looks at me, unsmiling. 'It is so long since I have practised any chemystry, who knows how this will end.' He mixes a brew in the pot, calibrating pinches of this, drops, scoops, flakes of that, and finally pushing the pan into the centre of the fire. Very quickly the smell becomes noxious and acrid, making him cough and open the windows.

He gathers all the candles together on the table, pulls up a chair next to it and removes his shirt until he's naked from the waist up. His skin has a babyish smoothness – so unlike my master's, which is patterned all over with scars and divots where bullets have struck him – and he has, as I always assumed he would, a crescent-shaped scar at the side of his abdomen, though his curls grandly at either end, like a signature. He sits in the pool of light, holds the knife to his skin, the tip resting against the scar, clenches his teeth and slits it deep. He lets out such a howl of pain that my gut clenches into knots. Even as blood spills out of the fissure, he digs the dagger deeper, widening the incision, cutting a trench through ligament and muscle, before prizing the flesh apart, snatching up the mirror and looking into the wound. Unable to find what he's looking for, he makes a third incision, and a fourth, before putting the knife between his teeth, pivoting the mirror and digging his fingers ever deeper into the cavity. 'Damn you, Valentyne,' he curses, before finally pulling out a stone, a misshapen organ, like a root from the ground. He rips it from its stem and tosses it into the pan on the fire. My ears pop, a silent explosion makes the windows shake. Then comes the grandiose hum, like a choir chanting far away, and everything in the room multiplies into overlapping versions. For a while the stone in the bowl burns like a little sun, before everything returns to normal, and there is just the sound of bubbling.

Vilder douses his wound with alcohol and after he's sewn it up with the needle and thread, he takes the pan from the fire. He waits for it to cool before taking out the stone, now dissolved to a hard black nugget, and pouring the liquid into my master's mouth, lifting his head as he had done with the broth, but holding it there until it's all absorbed. As soon as Vilder lays him back down, Valentyne begins to fit. His fingers twitch, and his legs and arms shake against the frame of the bed. I stay with him, shivering inside with dread, as his convulsions ease only to worsen again. Finally, he twists against the bedhead and comes to a halt.

I stay with him, paws on his chest, dreading the moment when his heart will stop beating. '*Where will life lead us if we hide in corners behind tables?*' he said when I wouldn't go with him down to the shore. '*The world out there is where we will find answers. And joy. And oysters, my champion.*'

Hearing a noise, I look round to find a stranger sitting in the chair with his back to me – and my stomach turns pure liquid. His hair is thin on his skull, but his shoulders are thickset, with a mantle over them like a Roman toga. He sits there motionless as if he belonged in the room. A crazed notion comes to me, that he's a phantom, like one of those pale characters that appeared in the plays I saw with my master in London, an assassinated king or emperor come back from the realm of the dead to avenge his murderers.

When he turns to me, I'm maddened with fear, for I both know him and don't know him. I glimpsed Vilder only once without his wig, and far away. Close to, the transformation is staggering. It is not a toga he wears, just the blanket he's put round himself. I do not calm, the opposite. I cannot shake the notion that this version of Vilder – with thin, sand-coloured hair where his black wig sat – has dwelt secretly in my unconsciousness all my life. My very atoms spin as the notion dawns on me: the shape of his brow, of his nose, the flat facet down the centre of it, the cushiony lips, the pattern of crinkles about his eyes.

Brothers. He and Valentyne are brothers.

I sit, dumbstruck, thoughts coming at me in such a torrent, I cannot keep hold of one before another supplants it. All the events of my past rush at me: the corpse on the beach in Elsinore, Vilder magnificent in London and deranged in Amsterdam. There comes the seismic shock that Valentyne too is a scion of the dynasty that built the doom palace at Opalheim – the very place he was imprisoned. The place that was once his *home*. I recall the mausoleum there, the pair of tombs beneath the fairy-white ceiling of vaults and drops, he lean and steely, she regal and vain. They too are my master's kin.

'Valentyne,' I whine, turning on the spot and digging my paw against his face. 'Valentyne,' I bark.

The heat in the room is insufferable, the fire still burning. I go to the open window, but there too the air is torrid. I exit, run down, barge open the door and stalk across the harbour. They were brothers all this time.

Packs of humans are hustling about the port. All of them are dissemblers, tricksters, keeping secrets from each other, saying one thing and meaning another. There is a gentleman in a top hat and cravat making a young lady laugh, when doubtless he's married to someone else. A well-to-do lady and a fishwife converse, all smiles, when truly they think little of each other. I am happy to be a dog, to be simple at heart. Those of our species may not have skill – we'll never produce music, or instruments to see the stars – but we are constant.

I shoulder through the crowd, not caring who I knock into, and march to the end of a pier. The moon is full and seems to look back at me, and at the humans about. It strikes me how content it is to be alone, on its eternal journey, and how I could learn something from it: to be solitary too. To live only for myself. In Brussels I dreamt the city had magically gone silent and the streets emptied, but now I imagine an entirely virgin world, populated only by animals, no cities, houses, fields, roads, ships or candlelight. I drift the oceans on a raft, wherever the winds take me, in daylight or moonlight from warm-winded tropics to the crisp china blue of the northern seas. There are no ports or harbours or lighthouses, just empty beaches, banks of bull grass and realms of untouched country beyond.

But even as the fantasy puts its wings around me, a nagging feeling draws me back to the room.

Vilder sleeps in a corner, holding a bandage to his wound, whilst my master lies unmoved.

Return to me, I find myself saying. *I have not the strength of the moon. My heart can withstand no more. I have nothing in the world but you. Return, my beloved.*

19. Valentyne

Antwerp, June 1815

A snap of fingers wakes me. It's daylight and I'm in the corner behind the bed and Vilder is standing by the open door motioning at my master. The coverlet rustles and my master's arm lifts shakily from it, palm bending to shield his eyes against the light.

'Where?' he mumbles, twitching back the blanket and sitting up very slowly, facing the windows. Vilder nods at me and withdraws before remembering something. He reaches round to the nightstand, picking up the stone he'd incised from his flesh last night and pocketing it, before retreating to the landing, leaving just his shadow slanting across the door. Valentyne's feet tremble to the floor. He sits, head bobbing, an old man – centuries old. A breeze catches the curls on the top of his head and for a while he doesn't shift, just tilts his head to the occasional call of a gull. I should go to him but I cannot. I cannot move from my hiding place. Nerves pin me there.

Valentyne pushes himself up from the mattress, and drops down again. He drives harder, launching to his feet, steadying himself before limping over to the harpsichord between the windows, his back to me, and resting his weight against it. 'Harpsichord,' he says, and I can just make out the corner of his eyes crinkling in a smile as he smoothes his hand against the veneer. 'How long has it been?' He aims his index finger and pushes firmly on to a key, producing a ringing cloudless note. 'Ah,' he gasps. 'There you are. Music.' He plays a chord and it makes my heart jump. He picks up a stray stem from the top of the harpsichord and smells it. 'And jasmine too. How fortunate.' He turns and shuffles over to where the tapestry hangs, whilst I timidly slip under the bed along the opposite wall to the corner below the window. Vilder remains hidden like a thief behind the doorframe, watching his sibling.

'How sublime,' Valentyne says, lifting his hand to brush the neck of a peacock, before tracing his fingertips along the line of hanging boughs. 'Yew, sycamore, willow. English trees, but orchids grow between them. And, look, there are lotuses in this forest pool. How enchanting.' Valentyne goes to the nightstand by the door and picks up the pan and inspects it with his nose. On the point of putting it back, he suddenly freezes, aware of something behind him, something terrible perhaps. He tries to straighten his crooked back, broaden his shoulders, but he's a shrivelled husk. He turns anyway, to face whatever is lurking. The sunlight blinds him and he shields his face again with his palm. He runs his worried eyes around the room, from the bed, along the wall and finds, in the corner, a dog sitting upright. In his fright he almost falls and has to steady himself against the nightstand.

Go to him, I tell myself, but I'm still unable. I take a single step forward and sit again.

'Tomorrow? Is it you?' A bolt through me. I've waited a hundred and twenty-seven years to hear him speak my name. 'My Tomorrow?' I cannot breathe or see or hear, and the smell of him, dormant when he was sleeping, is almost unendurable now – midnight in a tall forest, stiff parchment paper and a whisper of pine sap.

He shakes his head and when he tries to speak his voice is striped and broken. He marshals himself. 'Pardon me. I – I thought you were my dog. I had one like you. The same –' he fingers his brow – 'light patches here and on his belly too. Like yours. Tomorrow he was called. He was hope itself. I don't know where I am,' he says, eyes muddling. 'Close to the sea . . .' He motions towards the windows, trailing off and becoming lost in thought. 'The battlefield. Where is this place? Which room is this? The harpsichord, the tapestry. Whose bed is that? The battlefield – such a ringing in my head.' For a moment he panics, fidgeting his fingers, but once he leans against the bedstead he calms again.

'I am sorry, you must think I am mad. You look so like my Tomorrow, you see. The same light-coloured brow. He was the finest creature. The wisest. I have lived four centuries, you see,' he says, adding conspiratorially, 'There's no harm in telling you. And the people I have met –' he makes a dismissive gesture with his fingers – 'my champion was nobler than them all. His heart, you see.' He fingers his chest. 'He came with me, you know, uncomplaining, at my side, everywhere, on my crusades. I gave him no home. I took him as a puppy, the size of my hand he was. Four weeks old, or less, I took him from his mother and – she was a fisherman's dog in Elsinore, an honourable giant she was, like her son. And I gave him no home. How it has shamed me for a hundred and thirty years, my selfishness. From city to city to city. And then the wars, for *my* sins. And he uncomplaining at my side. How patiently he came, my champion, how uncomplaining. No home, the poor wretch. You think I am mad. You look at me as my champion did when I was foolish. And I was often foolish.' He freezes, his face going blank for a moment, like a beach before the tide rushes back in. 'That my champion thought I deserted him, that is what torments me most. Desert him? My virtuoso? The cathedral,' he mumbles, 'the battle-field. You find me mad. I talk too much. Well, I have been alone you see. You are so alike, truly. Who is your master? Does this room belong to him?'

I step forward out of the glare of sunlight and look up into his eyes. Now surely he recognizes me. He peers down closer – and sees my scar. The shock is so great, his chin jud-ders, his head jerks back in panic and he loses balance, skidding to one side before collapsing on the floor. I rush to him. 'I dream, I dream, I dream,' he pants, reaching out his fingers. He hesitates before laying his hand on my head. He pulls me across the floor, clamps me to his chest and though he is thin and the bones of his ribs press against me, I can feel a power within him like a chasm opening, a magnificent canyon, a place of profound and exquisite refuge. 'My Tomorrow? I have found you?'

Vilder has come to the doorway. When my master sees him, he lets out a choke of fright and stumbles to his feet, try-ing to shield me behind his legs, but clownishly slip-sliding.

'I come as a friend,' Vilder says, helping him up before standing back again. 'I found you at Waterloo, *we* found you, brought you hither and nursed you.'

My master shakes his head, looking from me to his brother and back again. 'I – I understand nothing.'

'Well –' Vilder takes in a breath and lets it out again – 'I went to Venice in search of you, and found your dog instead. You are reunited. And recovering. That is all that matters.' He clears his throat and straightens his collar. 'I do not expect to be forgiven, Valentyne. Not ever. On that I am set. But I will do your bidding in whichever way you choose. Tell me only where you wish to go and I shall convey you there.' My master listens carefully, his palm resting on my skull. 'No apology will suffice. The devil could reverse every ill in the history of the world, before I could redress my crimes. I love you, brother.'

Vilder's pupils dilate as surprised by the phrase he just uttered as if diamonds had fallen from his mouth. He blushes. 'I will give you time to think, and to enjoy your reunion and I'll return tonight to hear your orders.' He exits, passing the innkeeper, who's watching again from the landing. 'The cardinal has worked a miracle after all.' A moment later, the front door slams shut.

My master sets about inspecting me, as giddy as a child probing a wrapped parcel on Christmas Eve. 'How is it you've survived, my champion? And not a day older.' In answer to his question he gently fingers my scar, touching the stone beneath, on which a drift of guilt passes over his face. 'Let me get my bearings. Come with me to the window. I dare not leave your side.'

We stand together, I with my front paws on the ledge. Vilder is drifting through the quayside crowds to the pier, not swift as he usually is, but in a deadened trance. The ascending sun casts a gilded tulle over the harbour, making it seem like a living painting. I notice our harpsichordist greeting a band of fellow musicians disembarking from a ferry. Some of them take instruments from their cases and launch into an impromptu song that draws a crowd around them. Nearby, as harbourmen are unloading a giant wicker crate from a ship, a brace of peacocks escape from it.

'Look,' my master says. Having just regarded the likeness of the birds in the tapestry, it's surprising to see them in the flesh. At once a pair throw open their tails in a fan of emerald and turquoise and a cheer goes up. Only Vilder stands out: he gazes at the scene blankly, as a murderer might regard a crowd before his own hanging.

He returns before nightfall, but my master does not let him into the room, rather receives him on the threshold.

'Oysters,' Vilder says, setting down a crate. 'The bold ones you like.'

Valentyne replies in a friendless tone. 'I assume you have money. Would you leave me some?'

'Of course.' Vilder hands over his purse. 'Take it all.'

Valentyne removes a brace of notes and gives the wallet back. 'When I am fit again to travel, I shall leave Antwerp. For where I shall not tell you. It hardly needs to be said I have no desire for you to find me. Ever.' Vilder is about to reply, but my master cuts him short. 'I have thought about what you said, and you are right: the devil could reverse every ill in the history of the world before you could redress your crimes. You told me you desired not to be forgiven. Well, I grant your wish.'

Vilder complies with a little nod and I have a vision of what he must have looked like as a child. For a while there's silence between them, until Vilder turns to go. He stops at the top of the stairs. 'He waited. In case you hadn't understood. Tomorrow. He waited for you, at the cathedral in Venice. You need to know that.' Beneath his jacket there's a stain of blood on his shirt at the side of his abdomen. He stares down at me and there's respect in his gaze. How curious, after all this time, that he looks at me the way I first wanted, that I've finally impressed him.

'*Tomorrow we begin again,*' he says. '*That is your phrase, is it not?*' And he goes.

★

275

We find London unrecognizable and I must remind myself that a century and a half has passed since we left it on the day they boned the neck of the king. London Bridge, once an old friend, a frantic, boisterous muddle of buildings strung across nineteen uneven arches, is nude now, its tenements and halls long gone. Decrepit and unloved, whole chunks of stone have come away from the base. But there are *new* bridges, at Blackfriars and Westminster, and more beyond, bold symmetries of stone that could be made of air and light, coaches sweeping across them to the swishing of whips. Indeed, carriages are everywhere, ten times the number there used to be, giving the impression that the very ground of the metropolis is in constant motion.

The old medieval cathedral up on the hill has vanished, replaced by a domed palace of white marble that truly could be twinned with mine in Venice. On either side of it, stretching far to the west and east, a showy battalion of a hundred more churches, halls and banqueting houses. My master was always bewitched by the aliveness of cities, the transformations they would go through, but this panorama has such focused confidence, such self-regarding swagger, as to make him timid. Traipsing up a brand-new boulevard he looks scared and keeps apologizing for getting in the way of people, though they ignore him, no time to spare. The streets that once reeked of gunpowder now smell of oil and science and gin. We get lost and find ourselves marooned on a building site of an immense crescent, being shouted at by labourers and engineers, until eventually we muddle our way to a familiar gatehouse.

'At least St James's still stands. Do you remember, my champion, our time here? Or was it here? I'm disorientated. Is this all there is of Whitehall?' When a guard struts out, chin

276

butted up unsociably, he says, 'May we speak with the lord steward of the household?'

'The lord steward?' the man repeats in a mocking tone, glancing at the ill-fitting suit Valentyne bought in Antwerp.

'I mean to say – whoever might be responsible for employment in this household. If there are situations vacant, I mean to say.'

The official that comes to meet us, more than three hours later, is barely older than an adolescent, and as inhospitable as a viper. He does not invite us in, but interviews my master on the pavement, bemused by his talk of *chemystry* and *medicaments* and actually laughs out loud when Valentyne asks 'for an audience with the king or queen'.

'In Berkeley Square there is a clairvoyant who is now a herbalist,' the viper offers. 'Perhaps try there. Good day to you, sir.'

My master takes the rejection, and all the ones that follow at the back entrances of grand houses all about the city in seemingly good spirits, keen to prove to me, as much as to himself, that all things have solutions. But in truth he's disheartened by the unfriendliness of the new breed of Londoners, by the sheer volume of change, by the flaunting of greed, the belching of chimneys and, as my master puts it, 'the greater than ever gulf between those who have and those who have not'.

In the end we have a little turn of luck. A gentleman cartographer, who takes an interest in my master's knowledge of the far-off regions of the continent, in particular the 'inscrutable Arabic peninsular', offers us a position and lodgings. He lives with his rowdy family in a townhouse in a newly minted square close to St James's. 'A home for my champion at last,' my master declares, breaking open the door of the little mews house tucked behind it, finding a bare room that smells as damp as my den in Venice.

The time we pass there is not unhappy, due in large part to the warmth of our hosts. The cartographer's six children are inquiring and mischievous, and treat our house as a home from home. My master greatly enjoys their visits, but sometimes, when one of them shows an unexpected kindness, or falls into a soft sleep on our settee, a sadness sets in.

We go to visit the new cathedral (going up the steps and entering the bronze doors, both of us stay riveted together) and study the tombs there. ' "*John Donne, 1631*",' my master reads. 'And here Van Dyck. Do you remember how he put you in the forefront of his portrait, whilst I was obscured behind a chestnut tree, and then scrubbed out entirely?' After St Paul's, we drift up river to Westminster, to view the memorial stones there. 'Ben Jonson, John Dryden, Oliver Cromwell. Can you imagine the conversation they're having?' Visiting churchyards to see who has died, and how long ago, and if they were once friends, becomes a compulsion.

After three years, my master having distilled what he could from the ingredients of new London, buying all the usual medical paraphernalia and a new holdall, such as we used to use in our campaigns long ago, and inscribing it with the symbol of the snake and the rod, we pack up and leave. Despite all his protestations, I knew we would.

We arrive in Portsmouth in the rain and slosh through muddy alleys to the naval encampment at the harbour, where my master starts up a conversation with a lieutenant. 'A ship sets sail at dawn,' he calls to me over the gale, careful of avoiding puddles that lay everywhere. 'To Africa, Xhosa. It is not as far as it sounds and they need doctors.' I sit and look at him very directly, to show resolutely my disapproval of the plan he's proposing, to begin his crusades again, and in such an extreme manner. 'It's just the rain,' he says to me. 'So tiresome.' A platoon stamps past, knocking him, and he sinks into the mud. He holds his leg up and lets the water pour out of his boot. 'Just the rain. Tomorrow our affairs will be better.'

I wish, more than ever in my life, for human speech. I would say, '*Enough.*' I would shout, '*No more. I will go no more!*'

He watches a sergeant hustle the platoon on board, looks around at the grim packs of young men that litter the docks, down at the rivulets of red dye that run from new uniforms – and he does not need me to tell him. 'What do we do here with these soldiers?'

And then, he begins to weep.

'*This* is not the place we should be.'

20. The Inheritors

Opalheim, Westphalia, spring 1818

We stand before the gatehouse, my master staring up at the stone escutcheon above the arch. Three towers below a jewel-like moon. It was not an easy journey here: a nauseating sea passage followed by a relay of stagecoach trips, thrice put on the roof with the luggage, nights in lacklustre inns, surly pro-prietresses and bed-bugged mattresses – and then a day and a half's walk from the turnpike. But now at last the tempera-mental spring weather seems to have tired itself out and warmish sunlight has broken through the clouds.

'Half an hour's walk up the drive to the house?' Valentyne says and I notice that all colour, and courage, has deserted his face. He takes a deep breath. 'Do we do the right thing, my champion?' I don't allow him time to think, but push my snout against the gate and it opens with a whine of rust.

Halfway down the drive, there comes a rumble behind and a cart catches up with us. We pause on the verge, expecting it to slow down, but it hurtles by, its rear laden with shrubs: orange, lemon and palm, peculiar exotics for here. No sooner have we set off again, when another one comes. Beside the driver, sits De la Mare, Vilder's retainer, rake-thin and sombre as ever. He sees and recognizes us, but does not tell the driver to stop. In fact, the carriage picks up speed and vanishes into the chasm of pines. My master is more apprehensive than ever, but makes a clownish roll of the eyes.

When we come out into the open, into the valley, the first thing I notice is the lake. What had been a desiccated crater is in the process of coming back to life. There's water in it, and pockets of wetland plants, soft-rushes and lilies. Young trees, willow and bay, have been planted round the borders and a dozen or so labourers are installing more. Indeed, there are workers everywhere, the terrain from here to the palace under renovation. The last of the old formal gardens, the bygone grids of yesteryear, are being eradicated, the ground dug up here, flattened there, irrigation channels incised through it, statues erected, even a columned folly constructed on the crest of a slope.

The palace too, the once anaemic gargantuan felled lion of a place, on whose walls the sun seemed loath to shine, is under reconstruction. There is scaffolding up the entire central tower, which once used to point at a slight angle, and the stonework is being cleaned. My master eyes the scene, more mistrustful than anything else.

De la Mare is waiting on the front steps, standing guard it seems, and regards our arrival with apparent surprise, as if he had not just seen us on the driveway. He was always gaunt, but more so now, and greyer at the temples. *'Monsieur?'*

My master takes a moment to gather his wits. 'Good day, sir. Is –'

'*Non. Il n'est pas la.* He is not here presently.'

'Are you expecting him to return?'

'He told me to say he is riding.'

My master wipes the dust from his hands and glances at me, before answering, 'He told you to say he was riding, or he *is* riding?' De la Mare's insincere smile does not crack. 'He knows we are here then?'

'I cannot say.'

'You cannot say if he knows we are here?' De la Mare shrugs in commiseration. 'Well, *monsieur*, we have come a long way. We would appreciate some refreshment at least and –' he motions towards the entrance – 'to sit down.' He's about to go in, but De la Mare bars his way.

'Not there, *monsieur, non*. They do the ceiling. All over the house. *Suivez moi, suivez moi.*' He leads us through the stables to the rear, checking every second we're still following obediently. In the kitchen we're fussed to a seat in the corner, given a jug and some bread and left. I would rather wait outside, than have to hold my breath against the stench of meat. There's a band of unspeaking cooks, one moodily boning the carcass of a cow, none regarding us with respect. Only one person, an old butler who sits polishing shoes in the corner, seems to recognize my master, as the prisoner who escaped that is, not as scion of this grand estate. My master must be heir to it, at least in part, and should be treated as such. He never practises superiority, always takes humans for what they are and not what they're worth, but he looks a little crestfallen. He doesn't speak a word until De la Mare returns some time later, a little redder in the face than before.

'My master has returned. He would like to see you –'

'Good.' Valentyne stands.

'But tomorrow is better.'

'Tomorrow?'

'*Il est très fatigué.* He is very tired and gone to bed.'

'Bed?'

'*Désolé.* There is a good inn –'

'An inn? You'll put us in an inn?' Some of the kitchen staff turn their heads and the butcher makes sure we see his boning knife, as if my master were some common brawler.

'Or –' De la Mare makes a pacifying gesture – 'you may sleep the night in the east wing. The rest is, *en chantier*, under construction. There is an engineer from Paris, who fits a hot-air system. *Chauffage.*'

He ushers us quickly through the house. When we pass the door that leads along a corridor to the banqueting hall where I was imprisoned, and my master before me, Valentyne stops. From within comes the sound of banging. De la Mare pointedly shuts the door and guides us on, down narrower passageways, eventually showing us into a sparse room with windows looking out on to an obscure courtyard and little in the way of furnishings but a tipsy four-poster bed.

After De la Mare has left, my master says, 'To an inn he would make us go? I suppose I should have guessed –' he blows the dust from a portrait of a flame-haired queen – 'that he would return to his old ways.'

'He is very sorry, sir, truly,' De la Mare explains the next morning. 'He will be back first thing tomorrow, and will see you then. He did not want you to be woken.'

'But I was not sleeping. I challenge anyone to sleep on that mattress. It must be older than this house. Is he *riding* again?'

'*Non, non* –' a colluding laugh – 'he has gone to Stendal to choose silk for the bedrooms. He had an appointment and – well – he had to keep it.'

'Silk.' It takes a good deal for my master's courteousness to curdle, but when it does, his fingers heat up. De la Mare's smile is more embarrassed now than insincere. 'Tell me the moment he returns. Do you hear me? The moment.'

'*Oui, oui, bien sûr, bien sûr.* I shall pay a visit this afternoon and make sure you are comfortable.'

De la Mare does not return in the afternoon, or the evening, though two footmen come to change the mattress, and another to light the fire, which gives off barely any heat, but a good deal of smoke. Extravagant meals are brought – which Valentyne is too agitated to eat – and, bizarrely, a platter of exotic fruits. Valentyne picks up a pineapple by its neck. 'Who on earth does he think he is?'

In bed, he tosses and turns for hours, unable to sleep, turning his ear to any murmur from the stables, until he finally loses patience, springs up and throws on his clothes. 'This is absurd. I will see the house at least.'

I go with him, returning to the main section. There are ladders here and there and tables of paints where frescoes are being restored. We take a candle from a sideboard and go into the chapel. As my master studies the tombs, his breathing changes, growing heavy and slow. The kneeling couple are fenced behind a rail: the man stern and lean, the lady beneath outstretched veils. And Aramis is there too: the soldier who still looks like a boy, standing with one foot out and swagger stick poised in the air.

We ascend the principal staircase to the apartments on the first floor and he halts at the largest of the doors. He passes his hand down the length of a keyhole, which is as wide as his hand, and he hesitates a moment before pushing against it, the gargantuan slab of oak turning into the room. He enters cautiously. Dawn light sifts through three arched windows. On the back wall there's a discoloured rectangle, where the back canopy of a bed must once have hung, a *state bed*. Valentyne stares at the absence of it and is lost in thought.

Going back to the landing, he notices light coming from

under a door. He creeps up, puts his ear to it and there's a faint rustle within. 'Vilder?' There's no reply, just the creaking of the house. 'Vilder, are you there?' At once he snatches the handle, but it's locked. His brother is inside for certain, and close to us: I can smell him. But there's no answer.

'I wish to depart immediately, but I'm told there are no horses. That there is no one even to convey us back to the turnpike.' My master has waited until after lunch the following day, before collaring De la Mare in the hall.

'Regrettably, you cannot leave, *monsieur* –'

'I can and I will! Has he not committed crimes enough? And you too are part of the conspiracy. Does he not consider it gracious of me to come in the first place?' There comes a clamour from the banqueting hall, of something falling. De la Mare flicks his eyes towards it. 'Is he there? Is that where he is?' Valentyne flies off, but De la Mare blocks him.

'*Monsieur*, you cannot –'

My master pushes him aside and races down the corridor into the room just as a shutter closes it to pitch black. There is the sound of discordant pants, of someone beetling away. The air is no longer trapped and mouldy as it was, but clean with the scent of beeswax and lacquer.

'Damn you, Vilder, damn you.'

Just panting in the darkness.

My master throws open the shutters one at a time until light and colour flood the room. I notice the floor first. It had been nothing but cracked tiles when we were imprisoned, but is now a playing field of glossy white marble shining back the colours of the room: lazurite, green earth, yellow lake, light red, vermilion, peach black, cadmium, ultramarine and purple ochre. Looking up, it's as if the air itself has transfigured into living washes of pigment, before I realize it's the paintings that glow, hundreds of them tiered up to the ceiling. They are the pictures Valentyne etched in the years of his captivity, and many more besides, finished and mounted in frames.

'W–what is this?' my master stammers.

'I took some liberties and coloured them in,' Vilder says from the shadows. He's pinned in the alcove of the farthest door. 'And cleaned up my paintings from our younger days.' He reaches out his arm, motioning towards a group of large canvases. '*What is it*, you ask? It's your life, Valentyne, and Tomorrow's too. And a little of mine, for what it is worth. This is your house too, Valentyne. It was left to us both after all.'

My master stares at Vilder in the corner. He makes no reply, but turns and looks at the paintings. In one, he and Vilder are on horseback, facing forward, a sun-bleached vista behind them, a silver river twisting between a mountain of ruins, temples and palazzos. Squinting against the Mediterranean sun, comrades in arms, heads high and brows steady, they're young pioneers. In the adjacent painting, against a backdrop of tundra, they're wide-eyed, red-cheeked, belted into furs, a sleigh and pack of dogs ready to take them to the ice mountains in the distance. There's a canvas of Venice, Valentyne and Vilder on a terrace over the Grand Canal, side by side again, whilst at their rear the Rialto Bridge lays only half constructed. The brothers are painted – sometimes alone, sometimes together – examining maps in palace chambers, at desks with quills in hand, in closets being fitted into clothes, at royal assemblies, pageants and funerals.

'It will not work,' Valentyne says eventually. 'This spectacle you've arranged. It's not enough. I'll not forgive.'

'Nor should you.'

My master peers at him in the shadows. There's something indefinably strange and diminished about Vilder: not just his voice, his mass. 'My mind has not changed. You could fill fifty rooms with paintings and – it wouldn't be enough.'

'No.'

'I came here to see the house, not you. To pay respect to our mother. I have not visited her in two and a half centuries even though I was locked just yards from where she rested. Nor our father either, whatever we thought of him. I came to pay my respects. You always complained that I was a wanderer, that I never took an interest in the place. You found it ridiculous that I'd rather be someone's guest than enjoy a share of my own domain – even though I had every right to make that choice. Well, now I'm here. But I meant what I said, *our* association is finished.'

'Quite. And soon I will depart and leave you here in peace.'

'Don't be absurd. The house is yours. I have no need for it. Heavens above is this a game of hide-and-seek? Come out from there.'

When Vilder steps into the light, trying to keep upright, Valentyne double takes, and I too. He's older, alarmingly so. He picks up the fallen set of ladders and holds on to them with studied dignity. 'What's wrong with you?' my master asks almost accusingly.

'Wrong?'

'Your colour. You look –'

Vilder chuckles. 'Are we not as old as the wind?' His laugh turns to a cough and it takes several rasps to clear his throat. My master stares at him for a long time, and an entire drama seems to play in the spheres of his eyes until Vilder crouches down to stroke my head. 'It is good to see you, sir. You are welcome.' Close up, an uncommon variety of rot emanates from his insides. His salts and minerals are out of kilter, his blood muddied with urea and other waste. The three of us remain there soundlessly.

'It is fine what you've done,' says Valentyne. 'With this room.'

'Thank you.'

'And the gardens too. Very fine. I have not seen water in that lake since —'

'Ancient times. The river had stolen away below the mountain. We had a job to lure it back. Grand notions. But a start has been made at least.'

'Why are you so thin?'

Vilder considers his reply. 'Because I was too fat before?'

Valentyne sizes up his brother. 'You are not forgiven.'

Before sunset we take blankets, a picnic of food and build a fire in a cradle of rocks by the lake. My master continues to be silent, but after some cups of wine the brittleness begins to crack. They talk about nothing in particular. For a long while the sun seems to hover over the horizon, not wanting to set, intrigued it seems by how things will turn out for these two unusual humans by a lake.

'You should paint again,' my master says. 'I'd forgotten your talent. You were better than I at everything.'

'Except dedication. Of that, I had not one iota.'

'What about your admirer at the Castello Roganzuolo? *Sei un dio quando dipingi,* he said. *You are a god when you paint.*'

'Tiziano? He was drunk when he said that. Or in want of a love potion.'

'Not he, not Tiziano. Barbarelli.'

'Giorgione.' Vilder claps his hand to his chest. 'A maestro.

Thirty-three when he died? The waste of it. Masaccio the same. Marvels we'll never know.'

Apart from the fact my master is slightly taller than his sibling, naturally leaner, his hair still thick and he a couple of years younger – whatever that means when you're their age – there are so many subtle similarities between them, I wonder how I never saw them. The cadence of their voices, the quickness of their eyes, the way their hands pause before their mouths as they consider things. They communicate – like brothers do – unmannered, with little need for eye contact, often silent. I study Vilder as he goes on to some other story of long ago, but I block out his voice, concentrating only on the movement of his mouth.

In the hall, on our way back into the house, Vilder starts to cough again, and in his effort to stifle it, it worsens to a fit, his neck reddens and the veins below his eyes turn dark blue. He fumbles to the table and sits, clearing his throat over and over in hacking rasps. Wet dots of blood sprinkle on the wood. The noise draws De la Mare, night-shirted, to the top of the stairs, but he stops when he sees Vilder's not alone. When his convulsion has passed, Vilder takes a handkerchief and dabs his mouth with jokey gentility.

'I'll be patient no longer,' says Valentyne. 'I insist you tell me what ails you?'

'I have told you. Age. Brother, we were born in the same decade as Joan of Arc.'

Valentyne is not amused. He stands over his brother, until the other's smile drops away. Vilder reaches into his pocket and places a shrivelled black stone on the table. I know it immediately, but Valentyne is nonplussed. 'It saved you, I think, and for that I am grateful. Eternally.' He hitches up his shirt to show the scar at the side of his stomach, not the neat curlicue he once had, but a ragged and livid disfigurement. 'Antwerp. Your revival. And my undoing. Do you see now?' And he neatens his shirt down again.

It takes some moments for my master to understand, but when he does he too must sit. In the silence there's just the wheeze of Vilder's breath. 'But –' my master begins and stops. 'Why don't you repair it?'

'Repair?'

'Begin again.'

A guffaw. 'Begin again?'

'Conversion immediately. I have jyhr with me, a small quantity I manufactured in London –'

He's about to rush off, but Vilder holds him fast. 'Sssh,' he says quietly as if talking to a child. 'You do not understand. I said it was my undoing. And my undoing is what I desire. *"A coward dies a thousand times before his death, but the valiant taste of death but once."*'

'What?'

' *"It seems to me most strange that men should fear, seeing that death, a necessary end, will come when it will come."* Julius Caesar says it on the day of his undoing, according to Shakespeare at any rate.'

'I know who says it. What do you mean by it?'

'Come now, don't pretend to be obtuse. You are the valiant Valentyne, that Caesar speaks of, and I the coward. For I have died an infinite number of times, in a litany of ways. I have died every day. And the disgrace of it is unendurable. I would like to have – no, I rephrase – I *shall have*, a more permanent solution.'

'You mean –?'

A shrug, a smile. 'Would it be so bad?'

'To die?'

Vilder tries to lift his brother's mouth into a smile with his thumb and forefinger, but my master shakes him off. He's forlorn for a moment, then resolution returns. 'No. No. I forbid it. It is the insanity of the – I shall fetch my things.' He rushes off.

Vilder and I go together and stand in the bedroom doorway watching as Valentyne tips his things across the floor, snapping up bottles to read the labels, but unable to make out anything in the dark. 'I forgive you, you are forgiven. There. If that's what you want me to say. Why must you continue to taunt me?' A capsule rolls under the bed and he has to crawl under to fetch it.

'My younger brother, always helping me. However cruel I am, he forgives. However conceited. Remember the times I visited you at court and would not allow you to say you were my kin, too vain to be connected with an employee?'

'In the past, yes. But I see you are changed.'

'Let me die.'

'Why?'

'Because I'm a coward.'

'You are not. What is it you did in Antwerp? The black stone. Look.' He pulls up Vilder's shirt to show the scar. 'You cut yourself open. For me. That took nerve. You nursed me too did you not? You said you nursed me.'

'One *single* good act in all my life.'

'No, no, you realized you were wrong and made amends.'

'And two days ago, when you arrived, I was too spineless to face you. *One single good act in my life.* That is the sum of me.'

'No, no, I'll not hear of it.'

Vilder takes my master up by his collar. 'Tomorrow waited for you. *He* sat on cathedral steps and waited. A hundred and twenty-seven years. *He* has courage. I cannot even contain the notion of what he did in my scared little mind. Or what you endured. You are both legend. *I* am a coward.'

'No, no, surely you see – your realizing that is in itself laudable. It takes courage. I've done wrongs too. I have blame in this.'

'Let me die, Valentyne.'

'No.'

'Let me die. It shames me to live.'

I'd only seen my master livid once before, in Whitehall more than two hundred years ago when they argued then. 'No! I forbid it!' He picks up the phials and leaves the room.

21. Valentyne and Vilder

Opalheim, Westphalia, summer 1818

The most surprising thing about Vilder's decline is how sociable and warm he remains throughout it, how dignified in his downfall. It took only a few days for Valentyne to realize he would not win the battle with his brother, that Vilder's course was set and my master could not stop it any more than he could a boulder that had dislodged from its furrow and started its descent down a mountainside.

As summer comes, Vilder's condition worsens. His hands and feet swell, whilst the fat evaporates from the rest of him. His skin darkens, particularly around the eyes and he can't stop scratching himself. As his body deteriorates, his mind ever more reinvigorates. He becomes fascinated by everything. He explores the mansion with an archaeologist's zeal, as if it were new to him, opening up more and more forgotten rooms, uncovering disregarded artwork and scribbling intricate diagrams: 'To help you with the restorers – after I have left.' He spends nights in the library, too busy to sleep, poring over books like a wide-eyed youth, hungry for any and all knowledge, forever shaking his head in amazement at the things he discovers – or remembers – repeating passages to himself out loud, drawing his hands over ancient maps and astronomy charts. He even finds time to set off on excursions into the hills or the forest, sometimes camping overnight and returning full of stories and pocketfuls of fossils. He raids through the wardrobes, dressing up in his old clothes, a pageant of yesteryear, of epochs before even I was born. I note, as I always did, the flair he has for dressing, a poise that is entirely unaffected and that enriches whatever room he inhabits. He plays practical jokes on his brother, or on De la Mare, appearing like a ghost at the top of a stairway, as a medieval knight, or an Italian count. There is such a quantity of noise and he is so endearing that I forget we're living in the time of his decay.

In the middle of the night he totters into our bedroom in his nightshirt. 'Valentyne, are you here?'

'What is it?' says my master, sitting up.

'I need to talk to you. On an important matter.'

'Can it wait until morning?'

'No, no, it is urgent. Let me climb into bed and speak with you.' Before my master can stop him, Vilder gets under the covers and shakes himself warm, giggling. 'The *chauffage* will not come a moment too soon. I've always been a coward for the cold. Remember how we used to make a camp when we were boys? What a miser Father was even with fires.'

There is a spell of silence, before my master says, 'What is the important matter?'

'In fact, there are two matters to discuss. Firstly, when I leave, you will burn me, understand? You'll not agree on that point, I know. All humans differ on it, but do it. As the Romans did. Free my soul to the wind, so it may take its chances elsewhere. In another body it may fare better.' He leans up and looks around. 'Where is Tomorrow?'

'Ssh. He's sleeping in the corner there.'

'Remarkable how he waited. I think I know why you called him that. I think I know.'

There is another pause before my master says, 'And the second matter?'

'I need you to make another promise. Will you?'

'If you'll go to sleep.'

'I want you to find a lady, Valentyne.'

My master had been half dozing, but at once his eyes open completely. 'What?'

'A lady. Find one.'

'Why do you say that all of a sudden?'

'Because I have thought about it continually. How despicable I was in Amsterdam, how rudely I spoke of the women you admired. Of Adriana, from Rome, you remember what I said? It was monstrous. It plagued me, you know, for decades? You were right to have loved her, to have loved them all. You saw a quality of magic that passed most people by.' My master makes no reply, but I can see that his face is beset with emotion, though I cannot tell if it is worry or regret. 'Aramis was generous, you know?' Vilder continues, 'much more than you might believe. And gentle. He was the opposite of aloof. People did not realize. We laughed so, Valentyne. Laughter to tear you in two. He was kind. A gentleman warrior. A rare breed. My boy soldier. I wish you had known him more. Find a lady, Valentyne. It will thrill you so. Will you promise?'

'You go to sleep now.'

'I'll take that answer as a yes.'

'Sleep now. It is gone four.' He pulls the coverlet back over his brother.

'I think I guessed why you called him Tomorrow, but tell me.'

'You sleep.'

★

By degrees Vilder's skin patches with scabrous rounds of puce red. He has trouble breathing and is often seized with muscle cramps. In time he's unable even to eat and must be spoon-fed by my master, ceremonies that lead to many disagreements, some of them bizarrely comic. And he's forever hauling himself up, insisting he can manage without help, shuffling to a commode – which my master has stationed everywhere, just in case – only to stand there for ages, blushing with humiliation, unable to pass any urine at all.

Despite his steady decline, he insists on keeping up a regimen of activities, inside and out, regardless of the physical pain of just putting one foot before the other. Being led around the estate he'll stop suddenly, bend down and stare at plants, gently fingering their flowers and asking his brother a multitude of questions as if these ordinary shrubs were the most rare species on earth. Then, in the very moment of rapture, he might look up, his eye on some distant crease of land and he'll suddenly remember – or so it seems to me – the unknown vale that awaits him. At once he'll grow frightened and confused. At these moments my master might draw in a deep breath on the point of bringing up the forbidden subject again, *of still possible salvation*, only for his older brother to find his nerve once more. 'Do not suggest it, Valentyne. For I shall not listen.'

When a tempest comes barging across the plain, rattling every window and door in the palace, Vilder demands to view it from the best vantage point. Reluctantly, my master shoulders him on to the rooftop. I go behind, tail tucked between my legs, only half coming from the arched doorway at the top of the stairs, the gale flapping my ears back as Vilder throws out his arms to the thrashing rain, cheering at every whip-snap of lightning.

'I wish to end here,' he announces one day, shaking his walking stick at the door to the banqueting hall. 'With our world about me.' When he smiles, I notice how thin he is, skin like thin vellum stuck to his skull. 'Help me, will you, with pillows, that we may camp on the floor like the Moroccan desert.'

Valentyne makes several trips around the house until he has brought a mountain of cushions and laid them out as a giant bed. One evening, he makes a fire, pours wine for them both and they sit in silence, Vilder propped up, flamelight illuminating little pockets of life within the paintings.

'When was it? Which summer?' Vilder says. '1457? Is that when we met at San Marco? I remember that morning with such – such clarity, the hope we had, the sense of the everlasting.'

'Yes, yes.' My master smiles, remembering too.

'The light in the city that morning, the mosaics of the basilica, such blazing gold. You were thirty then? Thirty-one? I a little older, but we were young, weren't we, Valentyne, in our hearts, like children? We'd arranged before we each set off. You recall? Two years previously, before I sailed for Italy and you for Arabia on our quests. We'd arranged then to meet on 21 June in San Marco, in the Piazzetta, beneath the statue of the winged lion. By the sea. Ha, such planners we were, such adventurers back then: 21 June, the apogee of the year.'

My master nods in remembrance, but lets his brother talk on. 'I'd arrived some days earlier, from Florence, so elated I couldn't eat or sleep. The wonders I'd seen in Florence – Masaccio, Brunelleschi, Donatello – genius to electrify the brain, doors opened into other universes, real-size statues with souls, all that guileless medieval chicanery swept away.

The power of art. And science too. Engineering phenomena. Santa Maria del Fiore – I thought of you when I saw that dome the first time in Florence.

'When you arrived, on time – you were always on time, Valentyne, before even time was invented – midday beneath the winged lion of Piazzetta San Marco, the place we'd arranged. The twenty-first day of June 1457. You'd come from Tabriz and were aflame as much as I. The wisdom of the Arabs, the miracles of mathematics. An hour we stood talking over each other, hugging, sharing stories, the sun dazzling on the water, on the cathedral windows, on the orchid pink of the doge's palace.

'It was your first time in Venice. Unbelievable that you were a novice. You were awestruck by the light, the glass, the colour – cinnabar, malachite, lazuli – the music, silk, spice. You were astonished by San Marco. *The greatest rectangle in all civilization*, you said. *All the world is here.* There were tears in your eyes. *Greeks and Turks and Arabs and Germans side by side. Here*, you said, *a man may be true to himself.* You were right, Valentyne. It mattered not where you came from, where you stood in society, your creed, your religion, none of it. Recall the world we'd grown up in? The cold grey north. Catechism, flagellation, austerity, strictness. Life after waves of the Black Death. Remember the bleak decades we'd lived through before our travels? Our father falling first. One of the richest men in the world, who'd always had his way, who'd dominated everyone, who must have thought he'd be eternal – powerless against the plague. Then our mother taken within a year of him. Remember, my brother? How she locked herself into her bedroom to keep us safe? Perhaps you were too young to understand. How it snowed on the day of her internment? How alone we were afterwards? In our palace. Our inheritance. The appalling quietness of it. Noiseless snowfall against the windows of the long drawing room. Emptiness. Just each other and an empty city of a house.

'But on that morning in Venice all was forgotten. The world was ours. We were unchained from our past, weren't we, Valentyne? We went to the workshop together, to meet my new friends Gentile and Giovani, the brothers Bellini, who'd find such fame. You laughed in shock when you laid eyes on their pictures! *They have imagined the unimaginable.* You had to touch Saint Paul to believe his robes were not real: the quality of shot silk. Do you remember all this, my brother?

'We went with them on their boat to Murano, to the glass factory of their friend, where charcoal-faced sorcerers alchemized soda ash into clear crystal. Recall how they made a phial for you and you asked for a special inscription, and you sketched it for them, the family crest. I was surprised. Usually it was I who took pride in our heritage.

'It was the night we returned from Murano that we sneaked on to the roof of the doge's palace and you told me of the stones you'd brought back from Tabriz, the plain dust that might contain, locked within the innermost realms of its atoms, a power to halt time. Recall how I joked at first, asked if it might give me thick hair like yours? You told me it was called jyhr. It was hot that night on the doge's roof; the sky hummed with starlight. It was then, intoxicated by Venice, by beauty and mystery, by the hope that burnt through us, it was then, Valentyne, that we conceived our plan for immortality.' Vilder clenches my master's hand. 'My brother, I am sorry. So sorry that I blamed you for taking me down the road on which we travelled.'

'But I did take you,' says Valentyne. 'It was my fault. It was I who brought the stones.'

'No! Absolutely not. Of course I blamed you when it suited me, because I was not the person you were, because I liked to blame and cause trouble and be a coward always. But it was *I*, brother. That night – good grief, it is three hundred and fifty years ago that night on the roof. I was so charged, so confident in the world, so torchlit. I had such insatiable need for betterment. I could not countenance an earth in which I didn't exist. If beauty was to be produced – and, gracious, the beauty that followed in the century ahead went beyond all imaginings – no, if beauty was to be produced, I wanted to be part of it. I am the older of us and I am to blame for taking us down that road, Valentyne, the road on which you must travel now alone, and I am sorry.'

'Sorry?' Valentyne casts his palm around all the pictures in the room. 'For this? For this abundance? For these sights we've seen? These marvels. These giants we've met? These inventors and builders and lovers and trailblazers. Us three. In all history, only *we* have had this fortune.'

We stay in the banqueting room day and night, I on Vilder's bed and Valentyne in a chair, his fingers always resting against his brother's. Between unsettled bouts of sleep, Vilder grows restless, calling for books to be brought until there are piles of them around the bed. Vilder gropes them up in turn, avidly scanning passages, marvelling over illustrations with hallucinatory intensity, before nudging them aside and requesting others. As the days pass, tea-coloured urine seeps on to the blankets and Valentyne asks again and again if he might change them, but his brother won't allow it. 'No time, no time,' he keeps panting, unfolding the pages of another tome, every minute, every new piece of information vital to him.

Gradually he spends more and more time sleeping, his breathing shallows, his legs blotch purple, the warmth drains from his hands and feet, pooling its minute strength in the lukewarm shallow of his abdomen. His anaemic blood collects on his underside and his front turns as yellow and stiff as waxed paper.

At dawn, he calls out suddenly, rousing my master from his armchair. 'That one,' he demands, shaking a clumped hand towards a tome he's returned to again and again. 'Show me.' My master leans it on his brother's lap and turns the pages slowly. It's a picture book. On each leaf are hand-painted illustrations of faraway lands, realms beyond any I have travelled to, where the trees and palaces are strangely coloured and curiously shaped, realms that perhaps belong to another time altogether.

'This place, w-where is it?' Vilder stutters, voice hushed and reed-thin, wax-paper mouth twitching with a smile.

'It is Japan. Mount Kita, in the south of the country.'

'And this here?'

'The Caspian Sea and the Caucacus.'

'And this?'

'The realm of Brazil. The Amazon.' A deep breath. 'You asked why I called him Tomorrow,' my master says. 'Tomorrow is hope, is it not? If he has that name, he will surely last. I meant him for you, you see. Originally. For you. But how could I part with him?'

Vilder cups his hand beneath his brother's jaw. 'As I always thought. The day I left Amsterdam, with Aramis in a box, I guessed. But so much better you kept him for yourself: for what a poor guide I would have been. My younger brother, always helping me, always honouring me. My guardian.' He reaches out his hand and folds his fingers round Valentyne's. 'Will you keep your promise?'

'What promise?'

301

'Dear Tomorrow, you must make him keep it.'

'I will do it, as you ask,' says my master, 'on a pyre, in the Roman way.'

'Yes, yes, but not just that. Make a family, Valentyne. Find a lady. Find a way to find a lady. An inamorata.' My master blushes and shakes his head. 'I do not jest. You are the greatest discoverer of remarkable people. With every one, you hit the mark. Do it again. Serve yourself for once. How I love you.' He turns back to the illustration and carefully studies it: a verdant jungle valley of palms and firework-blooms that hang over an emerald river. 'Brazil.' His eyes wilt with regret. 'I have not been.' He follows the twists and turns of the waterway and, as it melts into the coral sky, his finger stops.

Although Valentyne realizes Vilder has died, he does not move for a long time. He stares at the corpse, a red smack of irritation on his face, the expression that a moneylender might have as he obstinately waits for a debtor that will never come. At last he stands, shunting back the armchair, removes the book from Vilder's chest, puts it to one side and exits the room. I pivot my ears to the hard clump, clump of his bootsteps along the corridor. For a moment I stare at Vilder's blue-white hand hanging from the side of the cushions. I press my nose against it. There are already traces of rotting sweetness and I quicken with anger. He could be any dead thing. How unjust that Vilder, who lived for centuries, embattled and desperate, but a giant of a human nonetheless, courageous and marvellous even with his flaws, that he should smell the same as ordinary men, who allow themselves to be carried through their small lives unthinking.

On a plateau just west of the palace I sit with my master as he collects wood for the pyre one branch at a time, silent, mirthless, single-minded. The surprise of death is as shocking today as it always is and I wonder if I will ever get used to it. Memories of Blaise spool back – *You've been my life* – before the last rattle. And Sporco too. I can't consolidate the vision of his single glazed eye staring from under clods of soil, with the golden-haired rascal who, at a Paduan ball, barged through quadrilles of dancers, threw his head back and let out a great bellow of delight. '*The realms, the realms!*'

Later, my master comes out with the weighty bundle: Vilder wrapped in a blanket. De la Mare and all the other people of the house pour out to watch. I am at the front, tail high out of respect. My master shoulders the body on to the pyre, straightens it and ignites his torch. I can't help but remember the beginning of my life and the body we found on the shore.

Now, as then, Valentyne sets it alight.

22. Tomorrow

London, 1833

There's a loud cheer behind the double doors of the debating chamber before they're flung open and the lords pour out. My master gets to his feet expectantly, watching from the shadows, as the noisy tide flow past, black jackets, loosened bow ties and rumpled white shirts. 'More happy faces than displeased ones,' he whispers to me, 'a good sign.' He spots someone he knows and waves – a man who has often visited our house.

The man finishes his conversation and comes over. 'Victory,' he says to my master. 'Resounding.'

My master claps his hands together. 'You hear that, my champion? This will be a day to remember: 28 August 1833. A great day.' The gentleman is nearly carried away with the others, but my master holds on to him. 'But wait, the terms?'

'Paid apprenticeship of four years in the case of domestic, and six for field hands. *Full* emancipation for those under six.'

'And compensation?'

'The West Indian planters to receive twenty million.' He raises his voice over the swelling victory chants. 'Well, they may have it, with pleasure; they have sweated for it in their own way, in the heat far from their homes. They may have it if it makes them happy. But for now, in all the British realms, from here to India and beyond, we may curse those men who call their fellow a slave. Come and join the celebration.'

'No, no,' my master says, stepping back to the shadows. 'So much to do. We're closing up the house.'

The man puts a hand on each of my master's shoulders and looks him in the eye. 'Though few may know it, you have helped our cause enormously, sire, and I give you thanks.' He raises his voice over the din. 'The United States next, but they must surely follow.' He goes back to his compatriots, and my master, his entire body a smile, slips away unnoticed.

By the following morning, we've packed up our house and I watch from the front door as our trunks are loaded on to the roof of the cab. 'To Opalheim at last,' my master says, patting my head, rushing to finish the last of his business. It seems an age since we left for London, nine years almost, my master in a permanent state of busyness since the very minute of our arrival. Years of summits and meetings and conclaves, endless cabals of gentlemen talking long into the night: brandy and port, cigars and burnt-out lanterns, wives frustrated in hallways, children listening from landings, as bad tempers flare up in the silk-lined salons below, resolutions sworn, walk-outs threatened, truces made, broken and made again. A decade of diplomacy, of winning over, of clawing up and down the country, of shivering through the ports of the north, timid of their scale and the tough new breed of harbour men, my master interviewing and inspecting and asking and teaching.

And how the world changed in those years. The cloth mills began to purr first, with modern thrums and endlessly repeating taps. The engineers came next, with maps and measuring instruments, and then armies of dirt-faced workers dug in their spades and veined the country with canals. It's been the age of confidence and pushing forward, of coal smoke and blast furnaces, of steam power, machine tools and rolling mills. '*Smells of the future*,' my master calls the new scents that singe the air: acids, potash, bleach and concrete. A million more countrymen have flocked to the city, keen to be part of the untameable adventure, even as they're packed like hauls of fish into slum tenements. There's greed for growth, and in keeping with it the silhouettes of humans have broadened, men with bullyish wide shoulders, women with giant gigot sleeves, all the better for pushing to the front. Most startling of all is the 'travelling engine' we went to visit in a city where long red chimneys broke the skyline in place of church spires: a living machine that speeds along iron tracks, making the fields shake. I was hesitant, but my master was in awe of course. '*I am a fool for invention.*'

On the point of mounting the cab, a lady cries, 'Valentyne.' Anne, alighting from her own carriage of amethyst blue, hurries across the street.

My master is taken by surprise, embarrassed apparently. 'Did you not receive my letter?'

'I did and set off the moment I read it. How shameful of you to disappear without my permission.' Valentyne blushes, to which the lady laughs. 'I am playing with you, dear man. Well, partly.' Anne has brought perpetual sunshine to our stay in London. She's bright and clever, and never stops smiling, except for when she encounters injustice or poverty on the streets. Then she intervenes. Many of the other society ladies look on her and smirk behind her back, mistaking her optimism for foolishness. She notices. 'All is well,' she asides to me, hiding her dismay. 'The kind humans far outnumber the cold-hearted ones.' She's tiny and rare like a forest flower, but her scent has the everlasting vigour of granite.

'So you return to your angel's lair,' she says with a smile, 'wherever that may be. *In the mountains of the Rhineland* is all I wheedled out of you. But you shall come back soon, shan't you? I cannot survive London alone.' Before Valentyne has the chance to answer, an exciting notion takes hold of Anne. 'Or perhaps I could visit you in your domain?'

My master is one of those humans incapable of lying, even in his face. 'Oh,' she says, reading it perfectly. 'I see.' Valentyne fumbles for her hand and she lets him take it, even as her eyes redden. 'Men are thus,' she adds sotto voce.

'What did you say?'

She straightens her hat and puts back her smile. 'Just farewell. Just – that it has been the most uncommon pleasure, Valentyne, to know you.' She runs her warm fingers down my back. 'Look after him, champion.'

We mount the cab, but my master gives no command to leave. He watches from the edge of the window, as Anne exchanges kind words with her chauffeur, before installing herself, her picture-book face making a final quizzical appearance in the window. When her coach sets off, Valentyne quickly reaches for his door handle and half turns it, but stops himself. He keeps his hand clenched on it until she's rounded the corner and vanished.

All the long journey home, he's impossible. He speaks not a word to me, barely offers me a glance, and certainly no pats of commiseration; he may not know it, but leaving Anne has upset me too. He's short-tempered with everyone, fellow travellers, farriers and ferrymen, making me ashamed to be his companion. He complains about food, how he can't sleep, how the suspension's ineffective, even how summer has come too early.

Coming down the drive to Opalheim, from the forest into

the open valley, the lake is in riotous health, fringed with wild flowers and canopied by matrices of darting birds. The gardens have matured to a multicoloured splendour and the house, in spite of its scale, has the sunny, unruffled aspect of an old friend.

It is my home, the place to which we return, the place my master can never deny.

This alone is cause for celebration, but my master barely glances up. As soon as we enter, he tosses his hat and gloves on the table and stalks through the building straight to the chapel. The stained glass has been fixed and cleaned, and the effigies too. The man is as gaunt and unwelcoming as ever, and Aramis is unchanged, but the lady, beneath her veils, has a radiance in her face that could not be gleaned when the statue was dirty. Valentyne glares at them vindictively – his father, mother, the lover of his brother – defying them, it seems, to come back to life. He even throws malicious glances at the air, challenging – I'm sure – Vilder to reassemble from the vapour and return to existence. Gruesomely he repeats Anne's words, *'Men are thus'*. I exit and leave him to his ill temper.

I pad the corridors, only half observing how changed they are from the doomy, decrepit passages I first encountered. The work that Vilder started is complete, as much as it can be in such a place, everything correct and clean. I long to enjoy it, but I'm angry with Valentyne for reneging on his promises, for taking up new crusades. Politicians and generals are all one to me.

I cross the hallway and there's the sound of a door opening high above. I peer up and in the gloom of the top-floor landing stands a man I recognize, though only just. De la Mare, stooped and ancient, hair gone, chest wheezing up and down.

I greet him with a sway of my tail and he proffers a little bow in return, before retreating once more to his attic room.

I'm drawn to the banqueting hall, our once prison. The windows are thrown open and great blocks of light stream through, warming the floor, whilst making it as ethereal as clouds. I could be walking in the air, through the colours of my master's paintings, through the scenes of his life. I go to the window, stand up with my paws on the ledge and watch a gardener carefully wade out into the lake to tend to the water lilies.

I hear my master enter, but make a point of not turning round. Then he's at my side, watching the gardener too. I look up – I can't help it – at his blank face colouring amber against the sunset and at once, nonsensically, I think of the chapel, not as I've just seen it, but my first encounter, when bats slapped their wings in the darkness and the tombs had a dreadful quality. Vilder's demise was proof that my master and I are not guaranteed, that we may not last. At once all my gripes come back in a torrent: the wars, the waiting, the winters, the losses, Sporco and Blaise and all the others.

My master lays his hand on my head and when he talks there's such plainness in his voice I think at first he's saying something mundane. 'My champion, who every day is led into battle with his troubles – and everyday wins the fight. What was it I said that Christmas Eve, when the young chaplain came to hear my admissions? I said you were my soul. No. Much more. You are the soul of *all* men. The most unexpected creature.'

He holds his hand there, as he did each day of the decades we shared together, and a bolt of hot pleasure sprints through me. All my gripes and vexation evaporate and there is a forceful setting-right in my head. I'm reminded he always put me first, that he spent a hundred and twenty-seven years pining for me in a prison, a hieroglyph of Tomorrow for every day I was absent, that as soon as he could, even as madness ravaged him, he limped across Europe to find me.

My master says, 'Do you think I should ask her to visit? Anne.' My tail, which had been sweeping the floor, stops dead. My master smiles uncertainly. 'Tell her our obscure secret?' Some moments pass before he speaks again. 'We will have to think about that. Think very hard.'

I don't know the answer to his question either, but the asking of it reinvigorates me more, and at once I look forward to our return to the world, to our quest – wherever the next may be. For what point does life have if it is not an adventure?

How lucky I have been. What a fortune I have still. I could have perished centuries ago, after a handful of ordinary years – having never seen the realms. I remember Vilder's finger on the picture of the river the moment before he died. '*I have not been*,' he said, the wilt of regret in his eye, a regret that went far back, a regret that he hadn't been as strong as his brother, that he hadn't had the fortitude to embrace the life he'd been given.

There is the great lesson. There is no sense in burning for the past. No reason to fear the troubles that might come. No reason to fear them today.

My master's hand is on me. The lake before us.

And tomorrow – tomorrow we begin again.

Acknowledgements

First and foremost, thank you to Clare Conville for all your inspiration and intelligence. And of course to everyone else at C&W.

To Jess Leeke and Jill Taylor at Michael Joseph for brilliantly powering it along. It's been an absolute pleasure so far. And also to Laura Nicol, Beth Cockeram, Rebecca Hilsdon and Bea McIntyre. Great thanks to Peter Joseph at Hanover Square Press & Harper Collins US for all your support. To Richard Batty at Wilder Films and Peter Morris at Soho Voices for the amazing job.

Closer to home I'd like to thank all the Southalls, for creating paradise, and to my partner in crime in all matters, Ali. My final word is to Daphne, Velvet and most particularly Dudley – and *all* the dogs: our friends, muses and guardian angels.

Reading Group Questions

1. Why do you think the author chose to narrate the book from Tomorrow's perspective?

2. Is immortality a burden or a privilege? Would you choose it over mortality?

3. Discuss the title and its implications.

4. Why do you think the relationship between humans and dogs can be so special?

5. Loyalty and friendship are two of the most important themes in this book. How would you characterize the difference between Tomorrow's relationship with Valentyne and his relationship with Sporco?

6. Is Valentyne against suicide on moral or religious grounds? Or is there another reason?

7. Despite being brothers, Valentyne and Vilder turn out quite differently. Why do you think this is?

8. What is next for Valentyne and Tomorrow? Will they live in peace with Anna? Or will they go back to the battlefield?

9. How do you think the characters in *Tomorrow* view the progress of history?

10. In your opinion, how much should life be 'a mission' and how much 'an adventure'?

A Q and A with Damian Dibben

Tell us about your background – what made you want to become a writer?

I originally studied visual arts before a progression of professions from scenic designer to actor and then screenwriter. I learnt a huge amount from all of them. I felt confident in what a person might say, how they would think and in what way their stories could unravel. Soon, entire worlds were forming in my head and writing novels became the only answer.

As a screenwriter did you think cinematically when writing *Tomorrow*?

Films were perhaps my first love, before I fell in love with books, and I always think cinematically. I like canvasses and themes to be as ambitious as they can be. I love the detail, from what a room should look like, or a valley or a storm, to how a certain piece of clothing feels to its wearer and how it catches the light.

This is your first book for adults. How was the process different from the writing of your children's trilogy?

It shouldn't be different, but somehow it is. As a writer for adults, I have been much more rigorous with detail, more nuanced, more philosophical and, dare I say, darker. The story of a man and his dog who are hundreds of years old may sound fantastical, but I wanted no element of fantasy at all. The trick – and the part that took the most amount of work – was to make the world of the book seem entirely plausible. That said, a book – more than anything – must entertain, must make you want to turn the pages, and the rules for this are the same for adults or children: the story is everything.

What were your inspirations for writing *Tomorrow*? And why did you choose to write a novel from a dog's perspective?

Sometimes when I look into the eyes of a dog, I seem to see something ancient, a 'soul' some might call it. The idea was born when I was travelling around Europe with my own canine and I realized that dogs have stood beside humans for thousands of years. Taking the point of view of a dog, particularly one who has lasted centuries, allowed me to look at humanity in a fresh and novel way, to notice its triumphs and failings from unexpected angles. In my opinion, the steps it has taken forward are ultimately much greater and more numerous than those it has taken back. I wanted to explore the past so it could illuminate our present.

How did you find writing a whole book in the voice of the dog? What were the challenges?

It was tricky at times writing from a canine point of view, but liberating in its own way. To a large extent, a dog 'sees' through odour and this opened up fascinating possibilities, not least because the past was a very pungent place. Otherwise, like any narrator, mine is able to relay human conversations and inter-actions which are vital to the story.

How did you differentiate between the way that dogs communicate with humans as opposed to with each other?

As the narrator, our canine hero is erudite and learned (more than most humans in fact), but otherwise when the dogs are communicating with each other, it is always simpler, less lay-ered and more about the here and now than when the humans talk. The dogs have no subtext, whereas people have more of it than anything.

Did you turn to any previous books that have animals at their centre when you embarked on writing a book from a dog's point of view?

'Adult' children's books such as *Watership Down* and *War Horse* pointed the way as to what was possible and gave me faith that I wasn't mad. I wanted to deal with big themes, loyalty, loss, war – and actually the animal perspective never hin-dered this, only helped.

Tell us a little about the dog who narrates the story. Is he an ordinary dog or special in some way?

He is an ordinary dog – a faithful companion – like any other, but he becomes extraordinary due to the sheer amount of time he lives. His wisdom and compassion grow richer over the centuries, though so does, necessarily, his heartache. Being a dog and an ancient creature gives him a picture of the world that is more complete than any human might have.

What type of research did you do to ensure authenticity for the two-hundred-year span?

I have studied history in one way or another throughout my life, mostly through constant visits to museums and galleries, which I love in all their varieties. I grew up next to the V&A and Science museums and have been returning to them ever since. Having written The History Keepers books (about a boy who loses his parents in history and joins a secret service to track them down), I knew how to go about my research, but yes, there was a huge amount of it for this. From Elizabethan times to the Industrial Revolution, from Denmark to Venice via London. I had to understand every detail of life, above stairs and below, on the road and at home across two and a half centuries. I found the more I knew, the more incisive I could be with the right detail and not overburden the reader. War and battlefields were the hardest to unravel. Just understanding the logistics of Waterloo, an area of conflict that was two miles long, took weeks to get my head around. That said, *all* of it was completely fascinating, the notion of losing myself in past worlds.

If you could go back to any of the time periods Tomorrow visits, which would it be and why?

To me, all periods of history, in every continent of the world, are fascinating in their own way. In the Western world the sheer, unstoppable momentum of change and advancement from the Renaissance onwards is enthralling, a wildfire of learning and creativity that carries on until this day. The second half of the seventeenth century would have been particularly worth experiencing, with the world-changing discoveries of Newton and Galileo, the golden age of Amsterdam and the ambition and splendour of Louis XIV. Though of course there has always been a downside to progress: with it comes wealth and with wealth comes war.

Are you working on a new book?

Yes, and it's exciting! I am currently writing *The Colourist*, a thriller set in Renaissance Venice about how far artists were prepared to go to discover new colours. Think *Perfume*, for pigment. In essence it tells the story of the Renaissance, the great protagonists such as Leonardo and Michelangelo, through the eyes of a lesser-known painter, Giorgione. It's an incredibly rich world at the greatest crossroads in history.

Damian Dibben will return with . . .

THE
COLOURIST

COMING 2020

Read on for the mesmerizing
first chapter . . .

It was the age of fame.

It was the time of the young, of fortunes made and city states. It was the moment of glass, of mapping seas, of emeralds and lapis lazuli. It was the age of dynasties and patron princes, of books and banks, the pen, the compass and the clock. There, in those years, stood wide silhouettes, broad shoulders and hips, puffed sleeves slashed and cuffed, brocades, velvets, and gold, gold, gold.

You've heard talk, I am sure, of Leonardo and Michelangelo, great even in their lifetimes. Perhaps you know Mantegna, the brothers Bellini, Tiziano, Piombo, Lotto. And maybe some of you, once or twice, have caught the name Giorgione. You might recall a painting of his, the colours within it like a vivid dream, for he was a colourist beyond compare. The centuries had been dark before this one had begun, but all at once the age promised a thousand things.

It was the age of colour.

And they thought it would last forever.

I

Winter's Envoy

He'd always imagined the little island of Poveglia was the sort of place from which you'd be able to enter the underworld. That there might be a hidden fissure of rock and a staircase that went deep into the earth. He pictured descending it, as Orpheus did, or Aeneas, in search of their dead lovers, down, down to the fiery realm below.

The island was a clod of sand and mud in the southern reaches of the Venetian lagoon. There'd been a town on it once, but foreign invasions, more than a century ago, had left it almost uninhabited. A cavana, church and leaning bell tower sat deserted with their doors smashed and roofs down; whilst what remained of the town's timber homes had become passing places, or hideaways, for smugglers and vagrants; though even they vanished when the island became an unofficial burial ground during seasons of the plague. If you looked closely enough at the ground, you could see pieces of human bones in the earth. Only birds – great, cawing factions of herons and gulls, indifferent to the dream of Venice – had been constant. For over a hundred years, they had been the true rulers of Poveglia.

Zorzo, as he was known in the city, was approaching the island by gondola. He'd hailed the ride from San Marco. He hadn't been able to find the boatman he usually used, a whiskered merrymaker who was full of Venetian tales, and found instead a gondolier he'd never come across before.

'Let's hope the rain stays away,' he'd said, embarking. 'We've not met before. I'm Zorzo, and you?'

The man had seemed to resent the question. 'Tullo.' He'd turned his back and jabbed down on the oar.

It had been a journey of less than an hour from Venice, but the weather had turned in that time. A chill gust had picked up and the sky darkened to the colour of aged tin before it began to sleet.

'There,' he called to Tullo, pointing towards an old pier that had all but tumbled into the sea. The wind rocked the gondola and kept pushing it back, but once it was close enough, Zorzo slung his satchel across his shoulder and jumped ashore. 'You'll wait here?' he asked the gondolier. 'I don't know how long I shall be. You'll be well in this weather?'

The other man answered by yanking tight the mooring and taking shelter under the awning. 'It's your money.'

Zorzo picked his way through the mud towards a shack set back from the quayside. He paused at the door, turning his ear to the burr of voices within. Before he'd first come here, the tavern on Poveglia had such a doomy, secretive reputation that he'd wondered if it really existed at all. Indeed, sometimes it didn't: he'd make the journey to find it had closed down, or moved from one shack to another. Or later on, had reconfigured itself in its original location.

There was a far-off tolling of bells from the city: midday – though it could have been dusk, the sky was so dank and layered with clouds. He'd arrived an hour ahead of time, hoping that somehow his associate, Caspien, might be early too and their business could be concluded quickly and in daylight so he could get back to Venice in good time. He and his team of apprentices, his *garzoni*, were at a critical point in the commission they'd been working on, a portrait of a young noblewoman. They were ready to add detail to her gown, which required at least five different versions of black, and Zorzo wanted to see the pigments side by side before they began. In addition to this, and more importantly, he'd been invited to a banquet at the Ca' d'Oro that evening. He gathered his wits and entered.

Some faces peered round at him from the gloom. Caspien's was not amongst them, or anywhere to be seen. That was no surprise: he was never on time. Zorzo crossed the room, moving with what he'd judged during his half a dozen trips here to be the right degree of certainty, and sat in the corner where he had a clear view of the shore through one of the glassless windows. A fire spluttered in the blackened chimney place and, amongst the handful of benches and trestle tables, sat the usual assortment of rogues: black-market traders, army-deserters, drifters and gamblers. The scene put Zorzo in mind of the underworld again: the tavern could be its antechamber, where dispossessed souls gathered to await their fate.

Zorzo waited. An hour passed, then two. Customers drained away, others arrived. A fight broke out over a sack of eels, with a fisherman accusing another man of theft. Weapons were brandished and during a tussle the sack fell and its contents spilled out, dead eels for the most part, but some live ones too that flapped across the floor. *Creatures of the night*, as Zorzo's father always called them. The row was patched up, boats came and went from the pier, Zorzo checked on Tullo several times (still waiting, still unsociable), the rain worsened for spells, lashing down in torrents, before lessening again.

Later in the afternoon, Caspien still hadn't come and Zorzo resigned himself to the fact that he would not get back to the workshop in time to see the newly ground black pigments. He'd wait another hour, two at most, then he'd have to return for the banquet. He opened his satchel and took out some charcoal and paper and, angling himself so no one would see, started sketching from his imagination. He let the charcoal guide him, down from Poveglia's tavern, through the crust of the earth. He drew triple-height chambers of jasper and black marble, with chimney places all about, alive with giant bonfires. In the largest of the caves, he envisioned a tourmaline throne sitting empty. Once started, he dashed off image after image, and with every drawing he made, a woman appeared in it. She was in the background to begin with but moved closer into the foreground with every new drawing. She wore a long gown, her hair curled like flames down to her hips, and her face was always turned just out of sight. He wondered who it was. Persephone, perhaps, the goddess of the underworld. But it was not: the stranger in his drawings was entirely lost. She possessed secrets, locked up inside her, that even she didn't know about.

As it was beginning to get dark, Zorzo noticed a boat approaching, rocking from side to side, tiny sails frenetic in the wind, a man balancing on deck, a boy crouched at the rudder. Zorzo could tell, even from a distance, it was Caspien, along with the young helper who always travelled with him. Zorzo went out to meet them.

Some years back, it had been Caspien's idea to convene on Poveglia, and the arrangement had stuck. Caspien was, in his own words, 'wanted' in Venice, though it was never clear by whom or for what crime. Even so, they could have liaised safely enough on the mainland, in Mestre for example, where there were plenty of out-of-the-way places that were beyond the reach of the law. But Caspien, Zorzo fancied, liked the drama of the haunted island; of covertly coming ashore with his travelling trunk, eyes alert, as if spies were on his tail – which, quite possibly, they were; of strutting into the tavern and starting up conversations with people he didn't know. He was unreliable, a liar by habit, but it didn't matter to Zorzo. It wouldn't have mattered if he'd been a lunatic or a murderer, for Caspien was the best in the business. That's why Zorzo was always prepared to wait. It was why everyone who required his services waited.

Getting close to the shore, Caspien shouted over the wind, '*Guten Abend, guter Herr.*'

His boy leapt into the water, disappearing up to his shoulders, before swimming ashore, pulling the boat with him by the tie rope. Caspien always docked halfway along the beach, never at the pier. To make a quick getaway, Zorzo supposed.

'So winter has sent her envoy,' Caspien called. He was lean and angular and had a mercenary's face that was riveted with scars, but his clothes were flamboyant, albeit filthy. He wore a scarlet emperor's cloak, fur-lined and belted at the waist with a Medici collar, a German *Barett* hat with an upturned brim, from under which his mane of thin blond hair flapped in the gale. Caspien was one of those men that people called 'a character'. No one knew if his name was real or invented, or where exactly he came from – Bohemia perhaps, or Odessa – but he talked fast, in a thick Germanic accent and was always full of schemes.

'I thought it was one of the Three Wise Men arriving,' Zorzo said, 'who'd been blown off course.'

'Indeed, I follow my own star.' Caspien nodded, before bellowing at the boy, 'Not to a branch. Tie us to that rock there.' He jumped down from the craft, took hold of his trunk and waded up on to dry land, peering from side to side as usual.

'How are you, Otto?' Zorzo asked the boy.

'I am well, sir,' he replied obediently, fixing the rope to the rock.

'Is he treating you well?'

Zorzo meant this seriously, but received another rote, 'Yes, sir.'

Zorzo was fond of Otto, always struck by how sweet-natured he was despite enduring a thankless life trailing after Caspien. He was permanently on the go, ready at his side, and was never shown affection in return. Where the boy came from had never been explained; if he was Caspien's actual son or just adopted by him. 'He is a shepherd – a prince who never ages,' Caspien had said once. It was a bizarre comment, but in truth Otto didn't seem to grow. He'd looked ten or eleven when Zorzo had first met him, some years back, and still did. But this was surely due to not eating enough rather than immortality. He was slight and fragile, but a workhorse of a child.

'Do you not have a coat?' Zorzo said.

Otto wore just a shirt and thin jerkin, both of which were soaked through.

'No, sir.'

'Don't listen to him,' Caspien said, coming out of the sea. 'Is he complaining? Anyone would think he'd never sailed or seen a storm before.' He put down his trunk and shook the water from his cloak. 'Good evening, Signor Barbarelli. Am I late?'

'Late? Well –' Zorzo knew that chiding his supplier would be unproductive, so he said only, 'We may have some trouble seeing in this light.'

'No matter, no matter. I'll stay for you, *mein Freund*, until morning. Then we shall see. We shall buy some Black Sea brandy and play at cards,' he nodded towards the tavern, 'with whatever flotsam has washed up this night, whatever band of penniless dukes and prosperous beggars there might be in there.'

'I can't wait until morning,' said Zorzo. 'I need to be somewhere.' He didn't mention that neither could he afford to keep the boatman standing by the whole night. 'Best to do it now. It's dry inside.'

He turned back to the tavern, but Caspien said quickly, 'I'll drink in there, but not do business any more. What I carry is too precious. There's shelter up there.' He pointed at the church on a knoll set back from the shore and led the way up to it. They didn't go in, rather stayed on the porch. The chapel door hung open and Zorzo could make out the derelict innards, upturned pews and fallen masonry. The boy came last, heaving the trunk, and set it down on the flat stones in the portico. It was the case Caspien always travelled with, the type that an aged duke or duchess might have carried their jewels and glass in, decades ago: a battered block of black oak, two feet wide and deep, studded with rivets and fortified with iron straps. Biblical vignettes had been painted on the side and front panels, though the only one that was still discernible was an image of Jonah inside the whale.

From under his doublet, Caspien fished out a gold chain with a key on the end, looked around to check that no one was watching, then unlocked the casket and opened it up. Inside was an inner skin of smoother wood. Caspien ran his hand along the grain, undid more clasps and pulled up the secondary lid to reveal a tray of many square compartments. Zorzo's stomach did a little turn, as it always did, with excitement and trepidation. The smell was familiar and intense, particularly from verdigris – a copperish mineral that reeked of urine, but produced a vivid green – and from madder root, with its scent of mulched autumn leaves, which made red. In each stall was a different substance, some half wrapped in paper or pushed into phials: rocks, powders, quantities of pure metal, cubed cakes of dried earth, crushed bone, dried bark. These, Zorzo knew, were pigments in their raw form. Anyone who was not a painter, glassmaker or dyer might see little more than plain stones and portions of dirt, especially in the failing light, but if they looked more closely they'd catch tiny burns of colour, of indigo, ultramarine, vermillion and malachite. 'The destiny of every colour,' Caspien had said once and repeated often, 'is to break free of its ordinary beginnings and dazzle the world.'

Caspien unhooked a lantern from his belt, took out a tinderbox and, shielding it from the wind, lit the flame. Otto went and sat on the steps and wrapped his arms around his chest to keep warm. Zorzo wondered if those were all the clothes he owned or if he had warmer ones on their boat.

'So – what are you looking for?' Caspien asked.

Zorzo shrugged. 'In theory, everything. Supplies are low,' he chanced a smile, 'but so is money. Though I'm owed by the Contessa Lippi.'

Caspien screwed up his face. He was fond enough of Zorzo, but he was a businessman first. 'We are all short, Herr Barbarelli. Why don't you tell me what you're *most* in need of?'

'In particular – blue,' another smile, this one more for himself, 'I'm a fool for the colour.'

'Isn't everyone – in this age? Fools for blue.' Caspien's fingers hovered across the compartments, before stopping over one of the stalls. 'This is a very good smalt. From Constantinople.'

'Smalt?'

'Don't jump to conclusions. It's vibrant, this one, has a bulk on the canvas, and it dries fast. Very vibrant.'

Zorzo looked closely. Other painters – good painters – used smalt without a problem, but he'd always found it second-rate. It had a fake, manufactured quality and he could never get away from the fact it was essentially crushed glass – and just as cheap.

Seeing his client was unenthused, Caspien moved on. 'Azurite,' he said, taking up some stones and spreading them across his palm. 'Triple the price, but nice and pure. A warm, greyish blue.'

'Your boy is freezing,' Zorzo said, seeing Otto's skinny arms had now started to shake. 'He should have a coat.'

'He *had* one,' Caspien bristled. 'Didn't you, you rascal? And he lost it in Rome. Left it in the Piazza Navona. And now he must learn his lesson.'

Being discussed made Otto tremble even more, and Zorzo took his own coat off and handed it to him. 'Wear this for now.'

'No, sir,' said the boy, amazed.

'Give it back to me when you've dried off. I can live a few minutes without it.' Still Otto resisted, so Zorzo put it on his lap. 'Take it, please.' He waited and, eventually, the youth had no choice but to put it on. 'It suits you,' Zorzo smiled. The coat was too large, but it changed the boy; its dark cinnamon brocade with fox trim brought a distinguished quality to his face that made Zorzo want to paint him. He picked a piece of azurite from Caspien's palm and held it to the light. 'None already powdered? That's a week's work just to grind it down, and to get something I don't even know I'll like. Greyish, you say?'

Caspien pulled a face. 'A week to grind it down? You have boys to do that, no? A difficult customer you are.' He put the stones back. 'Indigo?' He uncorked a glass phial and showed Zorzo the dried leaves squashed inside. 'From the Caucasus, *woad* as they used to call it, but it has more in common with Tyrian purple.'

The painter shook his head. 'Plant dyes – they –' he searched for the word, 'they lack mystery.'

'Masaccio never complained about them.' Caspien primly corked the bottle and snapped it back. 'Nor Perugino, nor Uccello, nor Michelangelo for that matter. ' He took a deep breath and began again. 'Other colours then. I have a carmine lake that is the best I've had in years. It would suit you. Very dramatic.' He unwrapped one of the paper parcels to show a wet, crimson chalk. 'Kermes beetles, hundreds scratched from Prussian oaks. Subtler than cochineal. Exceptional tone. Really, it would suit you. Or this cinnabar that produces an uncommon vermillion. Very unexpected. The colour of the sun.'

He was about to show it off, when Zorzo held up his palms. 'Caspien, honestly, I can find all this from the *vendecolori* in San Marco. The reason I come here and wait in the cold for hours, if not days, and take my chances in that godforsaken tavern is –'

'If you don't want my services,' Caspien began packing up his box, offended, 'there are plenty of other buyers, and wealthier ones. '

'The reason I'm happy to wait, the reason I love seeing your face, is because you are *the* colourman of Europe.' This was true. For all his tall tales, Caspien could produce treasure: pigments that were more than just colour, that were a mood, or a war, or a woman. 'You, with your mad king's garb and odd habits of meeting on plague islands, are the maestro. You have no equal.' This was enough for Caspien to release his hand from the trunk's lock. Zorzo smiled mischievously. 'So no more of this dallying.' He tapped the bottom of the trunk. 'What have you got down here?'

Caspien offered up a mischievous smile. '*Expensive* pieces.'

'Can a dreamer at least take a look?'

There came a sharp gust of wind. It knocked the lantern over and nudged the church door open a little more. A second blast made the bell in the tower ring. The men peered inside the building as the bell's chime echoed around the stone walls. There was a pair of desecrated sepulchres, one with a human effigy turned upside down against it.

'I didn't realize they still rang,' Zorzo said, unnerved.

Caspien took another look about, before removing the central section of the tray to reveal a hidden panel below. He fished a new chain from his neck, with another key, then unlocked the panel – which was metal, for extra protection – and opened it. The inside was lined with dark chartreuse velvet, and contained boxes. Caspien retrieved one of them.

'Lazurite,' he whispered devotedly. 'Ultramarine, of the finest pedigree, from the Kokcha mines in Afghanistan.' Zorzo held his breath in anticipation as Caspien carefully prized open the lid and handed over the box.

The hairs on the back of Zorzo's neck lifted at the sight: the unmistakably luxurious blue of ground lapis lazuli. This was no pretend pigment, no plant dye or ground glass. There was nothing like it in the world. But there was barely any left.

'That is all I have,' said Caspien. 'But I can give it to you for fifty soldi.'

'Fifty? That's what I have to spend on everything. Fifty for such a small quantity?'

'For ultramarine it's a good price. The Kokcha is where the ancient Egyptians first dug for the stone so they could honour their pharaohs with it.'

'The last you have – really? What about those other boxes?' He motioned towards them, but Caspien blocked him with the back of his hand.

'Those are all accounted for.' Zorzo tipped the box to the light and the lapis tumbled like liquid treasure. 'If we call it fifty soldi, I'll throw in a packet of chalk too – red chalk, the same that Leonardo uses.'

Zorzo calculated in his head. With fifty soldi, he could buy a whole palette of colours at any of the material shops in the city and still have enough to live on for a month. It would be sensible to turn down Caspien's offer, but sense had nothing to do with it. The ultramarine, scant and expensive as it was, could not be denied. He took out his purse, counted the money and handed it over.

'Someone comes,' said Caspien quickly. 'Put your wallet away.'

Two men were approaching from the dark part of the island, walking towards the church. Caspien pocketed the coins he'd been given, locked up his box and drew a dagger from his belt. The strangers didn't break their stride or change their course, and only stopped when they saw there were people on the porch. Zorzo, now at full height, was a head taller than the others. For a short while they all stood in silence.

'Good evening, sirs,' said Caspien, keeping his dagger out of sight.

They were militiamen, bearded and rough, and carried swords about them, almost certainly army deserters taking refuge on the outer islands, lying low until they'd been forgotten.

'If you've come for evening prayers,' Caspien nodded at the open door of the church, 'you've arrived two centuries late.'

They glanced at Otto, and then down at the trunk, making Caspien clutch tightly at the hilt of his dagger.

'We come for shelter,' said one of the men.

'Well, be our guests.' Caspien motioned towards the sepulchres inside. 'There are some others in there, long gone.'

Still the men lingered. They were interested in the trunk; all at once five sets of eyes seemed to be trained on it.

'It is just painting equipment,' said Otto, stepping into the light, pointing in turn to Zorzo and Caspien. 'This man sells pigments and this one paints with them.' It was a brilliant stroke, Zorzo thought: for how could anyone make trouble in the face of such a boy.

One of the men nodded and they both shuffled into the church. Caspien waited until they were out of earshot before re-sheathing his dagger and saying, 'I take back my words. Let us resume in the hostelry. There is safety in numbers perhaps.' He took hold of Zorzo's collar, looked at him very intently and whispered, 'You see, I have something else to offer you, *mein Freund*, a story to tell you, about a colour that no one has ever seen, one more precious than even ultramarine. A colour that could make you famous.'

Another blast of wind, mightier than ever, sent the bells ringing once more. The chimes drifted out across the island like a fog and Zorzo shivered. He studied his associate carefully, before narrowing his eyes in a smile.

'Lead the way.'

2

Prince Orient

'Go down to the pier,' Caspien said to Otto, 'and keep a lookout.' Other clients, Zorzo knew, his colleague often made arrangements with several people when he visited Poveglia.

Inside, the men installed themselves on a settle close to the fire. There was a friendlier atmosphere than before: the men who'd been arguing had gone, candles had been lit and a party of locals were celebrating the recent birth of a child. Caspien bought half a bottle of sack – the Black Sea brandy he'd mentioned – and poured two cups, drinking his own down in one gulp before filling it again.

'Have you heard of *prince orient?*' he said.

'No. Who is he?' Zorzo took a sip, but feeling his tongue burn against the drink, put it down.

'Not who, but what. "He" is a mineral. And a colour.'

'Which colour?'

'From the Lusatian mountains in Bohemia. Very rare. Very valuable. As I say, more remarkable even than lapis.'

'And what is the colour?'

Caspien studied his palms before saying, 'I hate to ask you when funds are low.'

'Ask me?'

'Well, any information I give you could turn out to have great value.'

Zorzo laughed, understanding. 'No, I cannot. I have no more money. You took it all.'

For some moments Caspien remained silent. 'Really? I saw you count it. It seemed your purse was –'

'For you. I have no more for you. I must live, you know? And besides –'

'Yes, yes, mouths to feed, wife and children, I understand.' He made an offhand gesture.

'What?' Zorzo couldn't tell if Caspien was joking.

'Everyone has a story.'

'I have no wife and children. I am not married.' From the look on Caspien's face, Zorzo saw the man was genuinely surprised.

'Really?' Caspien tilted his head at his client, appraising him in a new light. 'I always assumed –'

'No, no,' Zorzo said quickly, at once keen to change the subject, feeling an uncomfortable prickle, a long-ago guilt being dredged up into the light. There were plenty of things that Zorzo could have said on the subject of family, had they been better friends, but instead he managed only, 'I have not had the pleasure.'

'Not married, huh?' He narrowed his eyes and again tilted his head. 'Now I see that in you.'

'What I meant was I need the money for my staff.' Through the window, Zorzo could see evening settling over Venice, throwing up a faint halo against the city. The banquet would be beginning soon. He could not be late. 'So tell me about the colour.' Caspien didn't take his gaze from the flames of the fire. Zorzo downed his brandy and held his breath against the sting. 'How much?'

'I think – another fifty is fair.'

'Fifty? Are you mad? No.'

'It could earn you a thousand times more.'

'I can't give you what I don't have.'

'Forty then.'

'Twenty is my limit.'

'Thirty and it's yours.'

'What is the colour?'

Caspien kept his lips shut tight and offered a sympathetic shrug.

Zorzo chuckled, resentfully, and emptied what remained in his purse into his palm. 'I should be locked in a madhouse.' He put a few coins back in his purse and handed over the rest. 'Tell me.'

Caspien loosened his belt and angled the seat a little closer to the fire. 'There's a mine – as I said, in the Lusatian mountains – that has a singular history. Few people know its exact whereabouts any more, but it lies roughly a week's journey south-east of Dresden.

'They began digging it at the turn of the fourteenth century, during the time of John I of Bohemia, when the nation was enjoying a period of triumph. Those hills were loaded with copper and silver – they still are, no doubt – and the mine was successful. In time, they discovered a seam of a new mineral, not a metal but a rock, like azurite but harder still: prince orient. I don't know who first realized its property of colour, or how it came by its unusual name, but some weeks after the first haul had been brought up, miners began to be taken ill.'

'Ill?'

'Peculiar maladies, so go the accounts: slurred speech, numbness, seizures, loss of memory. They started to die. A few to begin with, but soon dozens – every man and boy that had been down that mine, which really was all the town had.'

'I beg your pardon, but this is the mineral you are trying to interest me in?'

'No, no, it wasn't the prince orient. Not at all. You see, whilst digging, they'd ruptured a seam of quicksilver – mercury, as some call it. Those who understand the strange properties of metal say that under particular conditions, quicksilver makes a vapour of itself. It is lethal to inhale. But those poor souls in the Lusatian mountains would never have known that. In that age, superstition ruled even more than it does today, and that is saying something.' Out of habit, Caspien looked about to check no one else was listening. 'They believed they'd disturbed the Devil and he was waging war in return. They threw back the haul of precious mineral – except for a small quantity that had been sold on, which I shall tell you more of presently – and closed up the mine, burying its entrance. For nearly two hundred years it lay beneath the ground, winter after bitter winter.'

'So you've been to this mine?'

'I know of men who have. The mine – indeed the whole stretch of mountains – fell into the hands of a wealthy merchant from Augsburg, an entrepreneur. His men discovered the abandoned shaft, opened it up and began quarrying once more. The quicksilver must have evaporated over time, somehow – for no one, according to my source, has grown ill. They dig there now without peril.'

'And who is your source?'

'A most reliable one.'

'It sounds like a fireside yarn of yesteryear.'

'Well, that is what it is. And there is the fire in front of us. But whether it turns out to be a tale of wonder or terror – like every good tale must – is yet to be known.' Caspien's tone was macabre now and Zorzo had to remind himself that his associate enjoyed being theatrical.

'And who is this wealthy merchant?'

Caspien peered about the room from beneath his brow (if he were not a travelling merchant, he would surely be an actor) and answered in a low tone, 'He is called Jakob Fugger. Do you know him?'

Zorzo thought hard: the name had a familiar ring, but he couldn't place it. 'No.'

'Well, he is your man. He and his family have a palace in Venice, which they are due to visit this month. Good luck.'

Zorzo waited to hear the rest, but nothing came. 'So that is the information you mean to give me?'

'Rich information,' said Caspien. 'You have the name of the mineral and of the man who owns the mine – and therefore prince orient – *and* you know where he will presently be.'

Zorzo took a deep breath and exhaled again. His tone was newly combative. 'So why have you not searched him out yourself?'

'I'm wanted in Venice, *mein Freund*, I've told you dozens of times.'

'And in Augsburg? His home? Are you wanted there too?'

Caspien poured himself what remained in the bottle. 'I don't understand you at all, Herr Barbarelli, I hand you a treasure and you bite my hand. Are all Venetians so short-tempered?'

'What about everyone else you've "handed" your treasure to for thirty soldis a piece – did they not bite?'

'I beg your pardon?'

'Do you really mean to say I'm the only one you've told? You said you've just been in Rome. I have no doubt who you were visiting there, with his unlimited funds. Have you told him too?'

Caspien looked down the barrel of his nose at Zorzo. 'You are the only one in Venice. So you are fortunate: you have a start on the rest. And Venice is your city.'

Zorzo laughed. 'Truly I am a fool.'

'If you discover a new colour, *mein Freund*, your name is made across the continent. Maybe across time. Your name will describe the age. Imagine if men and women five centuries from now still spoke it? And you deserve it, *mein Freund*, I heard you have talent. Great promise, they say. Once you are settled, the world will be yours. Great promise.'

Zorzo did a double take and his eyebrows froze in an upward position. He'd forgotten that Caspien had never seen any of his work, little of it as there was – barely a dozen canvases, and those no doubt forgotten in the back rooms of only half-interested collectors. He thought of Caspien's maxim – that the destiny of every colour is to break free of its ordinary beginnings, and dazzle the world. He wanted to say, 'Don't you see how I have already broken free of my beginnings, that I have already dazzled the world'. He wanted to tell him that he had only just begun, and that when he was through, he would never be forgotten.

'Well, put me out of my misery,' Zorzo said instead. 'What is this astonishing colour?'

Caspien did another of his dramatic pauses. 'That's just the thing. I have no idea.'

'Pardon?'

'But I do know the word *colour* does it no justice. By all accounts, it has more in common with light, and with the night,' he made a flourish with his hand, 'with starlight, they say.'

Zorzo understood why fights broke out. He felt like the man whose sack of eels had been stolen and wondered if he should demand his money back: he was taller and stronger than Caspien. Then Otto hurried in.

'Someone's arriving,' the boy said.

'Pardon me a short while.' Caspien bowed at Zorzo and went out with the boy.

'I'm leaving anyway.' Zorzo trailed them down to the shore.

A faint golden light was approaching across the water. In the drizzle it looked like an apparition, a young god or goddess advancing in spectral form. Then he heard the rhythmic cutting of oars and a shape emerged from the darkness: a barge. It was grand, certainly for Poveglia, with a canopied cabin at its centre and a team of oarsmen, two at the prow, two at the aft. There was a figurehead of a sea goddess with her arms outstretched over the water, whilst the lanterns lit about the deck caught the gilded colour of the hull. Caspien smiled: money was arriving.

Zorzo realized he knew the boat too. It belonged to the painter in whose workshop he'd been apprenticed as a boy: Giovanni Bellini. He was eighty by now, Zorzo knew, rich but famously still working and an almost holy institution of Venice. His brother, Gentile, had died just a year ago and had been buried with pomp at the Basilica di San Giovanni e Paolo, where royalty were entombed.

The barge drew up beside the tumbledown quay and a pair of the sailors jumped ashore to secure it. The cabin awning was pulled back, revealing two gentlemen inside. One stood up, leaving the other seated, drew the curtain behind him and came out on to the pier. He busied himself cleaning some dirt that had found its way on to his stockings. He was not dressed for voyaging, and certainly not for Poveglia: he wore a velvet cape that swagged to the ground, velvet slippers with jewelled shoe roses and carried an ivory-tipped cane. Like every painter in Venice, Zorzo knew him, Vittore di Fonti – and braced himself for some acerbic *bon mot* to come his way.

Di Fonti had one of those professions that couldn't easily be explained. He was not an artist, not at all, but worked with them, as an agent of sorts, a facilitator between wealthy patrons and those they employed. He'd recently become an adviser at the ducal palace for 'matters of beauty', as he'd put it. Of course Zorzo did not begrudge the fact that di Fonti had worked his way up from being a bootman to holding one of the most prized roles in the city. He had the ear of the Doge on all matters artistic, including buildings, sculpture, commissions, even music. Zorzo was proud that the republic allowed its talent to rise to the top. But in his opinion, di Fonti had none. His taste was old-fashioned. He liked art to be ornate and decorative, not to show its heart, or reveal anger or mystery. This would be bad enough, but his manner made it worse. He was a snob who never considered the consequences of his insults and would be kind only to people who might better his position – traits that Zorzo could not abide.

'Good evening, sir,' Zorzo chanced in his friendliest voice. 'We have picked fine weather for Poveglia.'

Di Fonti held his hand up to his face, as if a light were shining in it. 'Who is that?'

'Giorgio Barbarelli, sir. Zorzo, as some call me, Giorgione others.'

Di Fonti paused a moment, like some giant self-regarding raven at the end of the pier, before giving the faintest of nods. 'Signor Barbarelli.'

'What cargo do you bring?' Zorzo said jokingly, coming forward. 'Is it who I think it is, the young Bellini?' The question was amiable, but di Fonti treated it with suspicion, so Zorzo added, 'We are old acquaintances. I used to grind his pigments once. I shall bid him hello.'

'Best not to,' said di Fonti quickly, 'the signor is out of

sorts. The rough seas and – the weather, as you say. Added to which we are late.' To make himself doubly clear, he stepped forward to block the way.

Zorzo knew that di Fonti hardly had the power to stop him, but nor was he in the mood for polite war. Di Fonti was one of those who engaged in it continually, and for no apparent reason.

'No matter, we shall see each other soon enough.' He picked up his holdall and threw it over his shoulder.

'Are you working on anything?' di Fonti asked by way of consolation.

'Of course, always working. A portrait for the Contessa Lippi.'

'Lippi?' di Fonti tilted his head in commiseration. 'Is your business now concluded?' he enquired with a nod to Caspien.

'Yes, signor.' He called to his gondolier, 'Tullo, we're leaving at last.' He turned back to di Fonti. You're cleverer than me. I always turn up on time and have to wait.'

'No, no,' di Fonti chuckled, 'Signor Caspien is kind enough to send us word from Mestre when he is due to arrive.'

'That is kind,' Zorzo agreed, deadpan.

Caspien was hovering, looking from one to the other, clearly keen for Zorzo to get on his way. He took Zorzo's arm, cajoled him towards his boat and mumbled in his ear, 'The information I gave you will prove a fine investment – you'll see. And here is your red chalk, don't forget it.' He pushed the packet into Zorzo's hand.

Zorzo stopped and whispered in return, 'The prince orient that wasn't thrown back –'

Caspien was nonplussed.

'You said a quantity from the mine had been sold on, some of the prince orient. What happened to it?'

'Ah. Did I not tell you? That is the best part. It was acquired by a renowned gentleman: none other than Giotto di Bondone.' Zorzo must have pulled a face, because Caspien added, 'The painter. Giotto. Good luck with your search.' He was turning back to di Fonti when Zorzo caught him by the arm.

'Fugger, where is his palace?'

'I don't know –'

Zorzo gripped tighter.

'I'd tell you if I knew.'

Zorzo leaned in close. 'Could you at least not mention it to di Fonti?' Sensing this was not enough for Caspien, he added, 'If something comes of it, I'll pay you back. Please.'

The request was direct and frank, and Caspien could not deny it. 'I'll do my best.'

'I know there is a charitable man in there somewhere trying to get out.' Zorzo put on his cap. 'A pleasure, as always.'

As he was about to embark Otto stepped forward, 'Sir, your doublet.' There was something about the way the boy looked up at him, holding out the coat with both hands, like it was a precious relic, which made Zorzo's heart plunge.

The words came out before he'd thought about them. 'Why don't you keep it until I see you again? I have plenty of others at home.' This was not true: he had two more at most, and one of them so shabby he only used it when he was painting. It had not been expensive, but it appeared so. 'It's for him, do you hear me?' he said to Caspien. 'And the money I gave you. Buy your boy a feast. He deserves it. Let your conscience make you.' He bowed at di Fonti, 'Sir,' before jumping aboard the boat. 'Back to San Marco,' he smiled at the gondolier, 'and quickly if you can.'

As the boat cast off into the lagoon, Zorzo watched Caspien climb down into the golden barge with his trunk of materials. Through a gap in the awning, Zorzo could see him open it and Bellini lean forward to look. How marvellous, Zorzo thought, that at eighty, he still has the spirit to ride out to Poveglia on a stormy afternoon – in the name of colour.

Caspien must have asked him what he was looking for, because Bellini declared, 'Ultramarine.'

He said it like an old general might shout, '*To war!*'

He just wanted a decent book to read ...

Not too much to ask, is it? It was in 1935 when Allen Lane, Managing Director of Bodley Head Publishers, stood on a platform at Exeter railway station looking for something good to read on his journey back to London. His choice was limited to popular magazines and poor-quality paperbacks – the same choice faced every day by the vast majority of readers, few of whom could afford hardbacks. Lane's disappointment and subsequent anger at the range of books generally available led him to found a company – and change the world.

'We believed in the existence in this country of a vast reading public for intelligent books at a low price, and staked everything on it'
Sir Allen Lane, 1902–1970, founder of Penguin Books

The quality paperback had arrived – and not just in bookshops. Lane was adamant that his Penguins should appear in chain stores and tobacconists, and should cost no more than a packet of cigarettes.

Reading habits (and cigarette prices) have changed since 1935, but Penguin still believes in publishing the best books for everybody to enjoy. We still believe that good design costs no more than bad design, and we still believe that quality books published passionately and responsibly make the world a better place.

So wherever you see the little bird – whether it's on a piece of prize-winning literary fiction or a celebrity autobiography, political tour de force or historical masterpiece, a serial-killer thriller, reference book, world classic or a piece of pure escapism – you can bet that it represents the very best that the genre has to offer.

Whatever you like to read – trust Penguin.